RISING SONS

ROBERT LEVINE was born in New York City in 1941 and grew up there and subsequently in Hollywood, where his father was for many years one of show business's most respected lawyers.

After taking a degree in English Literature and then travelling around Europe, he began a successful career as a theatrical agent in Beverly Hills. In the late 1960s he left Hollywood to take a degree at Oxford and for the next six years lectured widely at colleges and universities in the United States. In 1975 he returned to Hollywood and since then has written several screenplays. RISING SONS is his first novel.

ROBERT LEVINE

Rising Sons

FONTANA/Collins

First published in 1982 by Fontana Books

© Robert Levine, 1982

Made and printed in Great Britain by
William Collins Sons & Co Ltd, Glasgow

To the memory of my father,
whose voyage was nothing like.

BOOK 1

Route North

CHAPTER 1

It wasn't just sea sounds leaking into his dreams. Something was burbling out on the deck . . . choking . . . trying to rouse him.

Thin and stately, white-headed and old, Jacob Solomon staggered up from the bed, heart hammering at his chest walls. Unable to open his eyes, he felt his way onto the balcony without waking Carmen.

Jacob kept a telephone there, in a wooden box, one that was well eaten up by salt, shat upon by the gulls and pigeons. But he didn't mind the box's squalor. The dirtier it got the louder the telephone seemed to ring. Which was why he had installed the line. The balcony was the one spot in his beach house from which he would always hear the alarm: the outdoors phone was his hotline.

And Jacob was sure, quite sure, it had been ringing.

He lifted the wooden cover. The phone sat flaccidly while a moth slogged across the corroding red buttons one hard step at a time. He picked up the receiver. Nothing.

Jesus.

Maybe he was starting to feel the debt of his sixty years after all. He had missed an emergency call.

The special line rang only seven or eight times a year, never more. Jacob's patients were all under twelve years old, most of them boys, outpatients. In the normal course of things each of them got through a week without causing mortal injury; then, at the end of the week, Jacob listened to each child explain how he had tried to live by the rules and stay out of trouble during the preceding days. Once in a while, however, Jacob would notice something worrying, a slight rupture in the child's glance, a speech broken off and hidden, and he knew that some Fury was sure soon to fly out. So Jacob kept a separate phone number to connect him that much more closely with the wild boys in his life.

1

There were times when even the telephone was too slow. The year before he had been called after two homicides: one boy of eight had opened his baby sister's fontanel with a hammer and awl in the interest of his rudimentary science. And then an eleven-year-old had slaughtered his father. The reason? The child wouldn't say. More often, though, the red telephone did warn Jacob in time. For those of his charges who were chronic alcoholics, pillpoppers, bullies, self-flagellators, runaways, and depressives, Jacob ordinarily caught the interim between thought and deed, and deflected any mischief. But there were always those who could not be stopped, not for anything, who were determined for havoc and self-destruction. Who strode across the civilized world like infant colossi and made men weep and wring their hands. It had been something like that, Jacob remembered, with his own sons before they fled.

Jacob watched the shore birds below his balcony. They walked unmolested on the sand, their Sunday peace unbroken. It was just possible a wrong number had shaken him from his sleep. A misdial? Somebody drinking at sunrise? Maybe. Unconvinced, Jacob decided to call his clinic for any messages. But his hand froze on the phone before he ever had a chance to dial.

His hotline was ringing again, shaking in its case.

'How's the weather in Malibu?'

It was Joseph, sixth and last of Jacob's sons, the only one with whom he'd staked a friendship, the one son he knew for certain still to be alive.

'Overcast burned off yet?'

Jacob flexed the cord of the telephone to its full length. The balcony rails looked over twenty-six miles of albacore-crammed sea all the way to Santa Catalina Island whose skinny isthmus Jacob could make out easily. There were pelicans offshore. Cormorants. Sandpipers.

'About five miles out there's a ketch and I can read his numbers from here. It's clear.' Most Sundays Joseph brought his young family out to his father's beach house. The visits were always easy, unbuttoned good times, chatty, cold drinks, smorgasbord, unspectacular days

2

maybe but everybody got along well. 'You planning on coming out?'

'Not today . . . next Sunday, maybe . . . .'

Jacob wasn't disappointed. He and Carmen could profit from a Sunday alone, neither working. They'd waste a day together. It occurred to him, though, that his son had called at an awfully early hour. And on his hotline. 'What's up, Joe?'

There was no answer.

'I didn't even know you had this number.'

Again his son paused without speaking. And in that truncation of time Jacob Solomon sensed that some kind of grief was coming his way. He gently slid the balcony door closed, sealing him from Carmen's hearing if she were awake inside.

'What's going on, Joe?'

'Some guy just called. An Indian. Says he's a Chilcotin. They're a British Columbia tribe.'

'His business?'

'He wouldn't talk over the phone. He's on his way over.'

The pinch of old injuries ran up and down Jacob's nerves. *An unexpected visitor?* He had feared one for years. Jacob turned to make sure once more the door behind him was shut tight. 'Go on.'

'His name is "Sam", and he's the one who adopted them up there, I think, got them all their Indian gadgetry. He might even live with them. If I remember right, Mark described him as some kind of crazy man. That's all I know.'

Jacob drew the telephone away from his lips. Rage's engine, long since cold in him, was suddenly driving again. He had managed to forget so much. He had even thought they were all dead by now: Eric and Bobby and Mark and brain-sick Douglas . . . even Thomas, who had once been the gentlest of sons. All dead . . . corrupted by anger.

Maybe he had only hoped they were dead.

'What do I care if some Indian has stories to tell . . .?' Jacob waited for his one constant son, kind and conversable, who didn't flee from his father, waited for him to reply. 'Give me one goddamned reason to disturb my Sunday rest worrying about it!'

3

'Dad, he's looking for you, not me.'

Jacob understood. One way or another the Indian would find him out and deliver his message. Jacob's sons weren't about to leave their father alone. It was silly to ever have thought they would.

'When did he say he was coming?'

'Right away.'

'I'll be there before him.'

Jacob showered in silence. The bathroom, at the end of his beach house, jutted right over a set of pilings and rocks, a barely adequate breakwater during flood tides.

He was a great lion of a man, fair-minded but forceful, and he liked the vulnerability of living on top of the sea's back. Winter storms could drag the entire beach away in a matter of hours, or one good temblor in the geological fault immediately off Malibu's shore could throw the tide high over his house and against the palisades on the highway side. But he just scoffed at nature's rages.

During a series of tempests last March Jacob had nested happily while other people evacuated to higher ground. The fishing was great with the water so perturbed, all kinds of food kicked up. From his spot on their balcony, with the rain streaking down and a fresh gale against his cast, Jacob had caught a fifteen-pound halibut. He had lifted the fish out of the surf, filleted it, poached it in Alsatian wine and tarragon, ate it with his young wife, he and Carmen, a banquet for her thirtieth birthday on their balcony after the rain, the wind still puffing a bit though it was clear and the moon cast shadows on the deep.

It had been the two of them alone, isolated and at war with the elements . . . and having a damned good time of it.

'Sorry I woke you.' Carmen was up, sitting against the brass tubes of their bed. 'Old men's bones make noise. The grease gets dry.'

'You didn't wake me. I heard the phone.'

His woman for four years, Carmen was only recently Jacob's wife. She hadn't lost a minim of her beauty since they met. One of her breasts was hidden, the other rose above the flounce of the sheet's embroidery. Light gathered like

4

treasure in Carmen's hair, hair as long as Rapunzel's and of the same colour and fineness, something once seen would never be forgot.

Jacob's own first sight of her had been at Joseph and Rosalie's wedding, Carmen walking around like a vision of grace, smiling and drifting on the air, summer itself . . . a gossamer, gauzy yellow dress wound around her, brightening the native honey of her skin. She was bonneted in white with her hair a jewelled filigree tucked all around at the edge, a tiny white purse, the fringe of her dress white, too, like all her trim. Her grey eyes had caught Jacob and, though he was a big man, levitated him. Put him down gently after. She had a perfection he had never seen in flesh before, not in his entire life.

'What did Joe want? They coming out?'

'Not today.' Jacob, who never lied to Carmen, nevertheless said only that Joseph had wanted a hand with something. He rubbed again the white curls at the back of his hair which never seemed to dry. His palms were wet, too . . . an unaccustomed nervousness.

'You want me to come with you?'

'No, no.'

'Try to get back for breakfast. I bought us some smoked fish.'

Recently Carmen had made her first sale as a screenwriter after years of doing all kinds of street jobs, record promotion, dancing in bars. Having survived on next to nothing she now wanted to spend some of her first fat paycheque frivolously, and on her husband, who had seen her through a long time tapping at her typewriter keys without any pay at all. 'It's the real item . . . mild-smoked Nova. Better than your ordinary lox. At least that's the line all the countermen gave me.'

'Very fancy.'

'Very expensive is all.'

Jacob was in the shadows by the door, his capable shoulders towards the carport below. 'I won't be long.'

'We were supposed to have a marathon walk today,' she reminded him. 'Low tide is around ten.'

'We'll walk.' His conscience thrashed around for the

right way to tell her how much he loved her. But when he looked at her, his mouth full of stones, he saw she had touched the hard truth without his speaking. 'Hold back the tide a little, would you?'

'If you're going to be a while, Jake, just call.'

Then Jacob left, thinking all the while that it didn't matter if his sons up north had sent someone to try to shake him from his peace. Things were different with him now from the last time he had seen them. He was not the man he had once been. Did they really think they'd frighten him and Carmen with some lunatic Indian? Frighten the lion?

Let them just try.

In Los Angeles midsummer Joseph looked strangely sallow as he stood in front of his house.

'Don't you sleep nights?' Jacob asked.

'Saturdays, sometimes.'

Jacob didn't like these signals, but then late nights in the law library came with Joseph's first job. His son, he knew, had his own ambitions.

'Sam beat you here. And he's an Indian, all right . . . or else he's got a great touch for disguise.'

Jacob shook his head. He expected little truth from the Indian and would doubt all, split every hair. 'What the hell does he want with us?'

'I can't tell yet. All he does is laugh.'

Father and son turned up the path, arm in arm. Joseph's house, a low and hard-angled bungalow hidden from the street by banana plants and bougainvillea, lay in the flight-path of a local airfield – private planes, nearly all small ones. Though a little noisy the house had rooms and rooms, a whacking great garden for their child. It was a house of little pretence, about right for a young lawyer and his family who wanted to live inconspicuously.

'Had any breakfast, Dad?' Joseph asked his father as they stepped over hedges towards the front door. 'There's eggs.'

'Just take me to the Indian.'

'He's out in back.'

Sam sat on a bench in the garden talking to himself. Laughing. Pleased to be in the world, it seemed. Not a young man, it was nevertheless difficult to tell his age exactly, for his hair was sable as the night sky without a strand of grey. He had the look of a man who had seen whole eras pass away. Rags were the mark of his passage, second-hand clothing, none of it fitting him. His threadbare trousers were of blue serge, his square-shouldered wool jacket of another blue – not a suit, just another scrap that hung down past his wrists, half-obscuring his beaten, crusted brown hands . . . hand. One was covered with a leather mitt, had been lost in a fight with a bear, or so went the story he had told Joseph while they waited for old man Solomon to come. He had a shirt on, too, white man's shirt, a scruffy, short-sleeved cotton that had little of its collar left and what there was of it was too big. Closed tight around Sam's scarred throat it bunched over his tie, a thick and hand-painted thing that he had tied with a hangman's knot.

And he had on boots, mean, blood-stained, boots worn right down to fibres and strings, and wrapped around Sam's curiously small feet like clods of earth.

Jacob could see several of the man's toenails and, embarrassed by the sight, turned away. The Indian noticed and laughed very loud.

'What's that around your neck?' Joseph had wanted to ask earlier, asked now.

'That's m'sack.' But Sam didn't look at Joseph when he spoke, only at the father.

'What's in it?'

'*Ha ha!*'

'Money?' Joseph guessed the obvious just to keep the Indian on line and talking.

'No money, but don't need money. I get around with m'hand . . . gets me rides, food, women, too.'

'So what you got in your sack, Sam?'

He pulled the pouch loose of its straps and shook it empty onto the bricks of the patio. 'That's what.'

There were several carved sticks, dry and white, bone-like. One of the smaller ones had the shape of a primitive fishing lure and had been notched on the top. But when

7

Joseph, intrigued, went to touch it, the Indian scooped everything away, tapping his collection into a neat pile and then back into the bag.

Jacob watched the Indian's eyes grow wild and bitter as he held the pouch and rattled it in front of Jacob's glare. 'Bones, you bet . . . cut from m'daddy's fire . . . been carried for thirty-seven years. I been to war with his bones . . . *your* war. What you think your boys gonna do for *you* in the end, eh? Eh, old man?'

Wearying of Sam's antics, Joseph stepped in front of his father's rising ire and asked the Indian directly what he wanted with them.

'Nothing much.'

'But something. So tell us.'

'Gonna do that.' Sam raised his hand, windworn hand shaped in funeral fires out of which he'd plucked ancestors' char and ashes, and tapped Jacob on the chest. 'I'm gonna tell you about y'boys.' He had no words for Joseph. 'You interested, old man? You wanna hear? Eh?'

He wanted an answer and would take it only from Jacob. So Jacob, who hadn't yet spoken a word to the Indian, was forced to nod.

'*Ha ha!*'

As he spoke Sam's hair swung jubilantly from side to side. It was his chance at last to sing the tales of the five boys and how he'd strapped them to the mountain's harsh ways. He spoke so fast that neither Jacob nor Joseph caught a fair fraction of the narrative. Sam was caught in the whirlwind and there was no slowing him.

The way Sam told it, the deeds of the Solomon sons were as much those of his tribe as their own. The old Indian had a claim on the five: Those boys were like his sons, and he the father spirit, they his heirs and issue.

Jacob and Joseph didn't get it all, but they got this much: *The brothers had gone north and met Sam in a little township on the edge of the world called 'Chezacut' (and the Indian repeated the town name a score of times, angrily often, sometimes philosophically). They had taken odd jobs and wintered it out, making trouble for themselves with all the locals,*

*White and Indian alike. When the thaw came Sam took
them back through the forests and upland marshes to the
tundra above treeline, right up to the mountain's crown
with the gods, taught them the ancient ways to live . . .
'saved their necks, saved their asses', he did, had stolen half
a museum's Chilcotin hardware, things just sitting around
in glass cases with labels around their necks like con-
demned men, tools and bark baskets and juniper bows
and clothes, rabbit and lynx twined together into robes,
leggings . . . had given them their real names of Wolf,
Raven, Little Bear, Elk Man, Pretty Marten, the five of
them the real Chilcotins now, not like Sam's tribal brothers
gone to Vancouver and Prince George and gin-ridden dark
towns along the highway where there was nothing except
death at an early age and a bath every two weeks to please
the social worker . . . no more Chilcotins sweeping crazy
down the mountain onto those Bella Coolas stinking from
fish oil . . . ha ha . . . just the Solomon boys and they'd made
plenty of good trouble, there'd been fights and knifings and
Sam thought somebody was dead in one of them, didn't
know for certain but sure hoped so . . . lots of stories going
around but everything said those boys were terrors and he
thanked the Great Spirit for that because it was time for a
little terror in the mountains again, those five mountain
boys the only Chilcotin sons now, his own sons, the only
Stonies left, the true inheritors –'*

The Indian suddenly stopped.

My sons? Jacob staggered away from them, even in
thought.

'Ha ha!' It was as if the Indian had heard Jacob's unvoiced
meditation.

'That's all?' Joseph had looked for some personal communication from his brothers. 'Nothing else?' Joseph was
sure there was more.

But Sam was distracted by something more important
than fathers and sons.

'C'mon.' Sam's voice turned as gentle as a fawn's wonder.
'You come here.' Sitting on the bricks with his legs crossed
in the immemorial posture of his fathers, the Indian
waved his one living hand at a child crawling towards him

9

from the rumpus room doorway left open. 'You come here.'

Theresa, three-year-old daughter of Joseph and Rosalie, grew legs, stood on them, reached one after another step towards the yellow-brown man on the garden floor . . . child without fear, fat little child with a smile for the Indian and an interest in every God-given thing.

He pointed her to the ground and she sat just like him. '*Eske tseke.*'

Her lips tripped uncertainly. '. . . sssski.'

'Ha ha.' He touched his own head. 'Serts-*Ee* . . . serts *Ee.*' Then he said it again even slower. The Solomon men could see that Sam had catechized children before, blown his pipe and they had followed. 'Serts-*Ee.*'

'Sirs . . . zee.'

'Ha ha!' Now Sam hit his chest over his heart. 'Setsi-*Ee.*' And followed with ear and eye and arm and more as the child tried in desperation to tune the magical words through her own weak pipe the same way he had, touching each organ in turn to connect the word to the thing.

In the end, when Theresa had mastered her small lexicon, he chanted a song for her, talked and sang in alternation, christening her in Chilcotin as he laid his hand on her head and held her small face as if in holding her he had the world. '*Shaiky*', he said. 'You, "little eagle".'

'L'tuh eeguh.'

'Ha ha.'

'*Theresa* . . . ?' Rosalie, in a housecoat and looking vexed, leaned through the open doorway. 'What's she doing?'

'She's all right.'

'Get her in here, Joseph.' Rosalie spoke without compromise.

But the little girl had ears for only the Indian. She waited for him to direct her. 'Fly, Little Eagle,' he told her, smiling through all his broken teeth, 'follow the wind.'

She went.

Indian Sam had his powers, and, Jacob guessed, a persuasion with his own sons as well. Sam was cunning. In the Solomon brothers he'd certainly found the right boys to bewitch.

10

Before he left Sam begged a meal, explaining that food would do as well as money, fee for his embassy.

So Rosalie fed him. Theresa napped. And the Solomon men watched Sam eat a week's worth of food, much of it sticking to his face and hair and blue coat. He had done his speech and if he heard Joseph's repeated questions about the brothers' health there was no way to know that. Sam slopped away at his food until he finished everything they had given him, ripped off his jacket and rubbed the crumbs from his face.

He stood up and laughed his idiot's laugh one more time. 'I suppose if you got m'money I could use it.'

Jacob Solomon and his son gave all they could scratch out of their pockets, not even seventy dollars. The Indian held it in his hand, waiting for guilt to thicken their offering. But that was all. He looked at Jacob with malice. 'Heard y'were a fairy, got no fire in the peep . . . ha! Stinking dead salmon.' Sam stuffed the bills into a torn pocket.

'How about you, Sam?' Joseph was vexed by the Indian's attack on his father. 'How many children have *you* made on the mountaintop?'

'*Ha ha!*' The Indian knew what he knew.

Finally the two fathers, the real one and the brothers' parent spirit, white man and Indian, exchanged a look of absolute understanding. That done, Sam hobbled out of the house on his broken boots to wander where he would . . . anywhere at all, but certainly never back to see Jacob Solomon again.

A stunned Jacob shook his head back and forth hoping to fracture his memory and let spill out everything the Indian had told him of his sons.

'I wanted to hear a lot more,' Joseph said.

'I heard enough.'

'You think they sent him or was he just scamming a meal and some few bucks?'

Jacob could feel the shanks of his fugitive sons' sharp boots prodding him forwards. 'They sent him, all right.'

'I wonder, Dad. Sam might know them, probably does, but those stories were plain old invention . . . the stuff of a

11

frontier novel. Nobody could last out the life he says they're leading.'

This time, however, Jacob knew better than his son. 'He had a message . . . very clear, very simple.'

Son looked at father blankly. 'It wasn't clear to me.'

'That's because it wasn't meant for you, Joe.'

'What was the message?'

'*I said it wasn't for you!*'

Then, without having made the promised call to Carmen, Jacob left his son and Rosalie and grandchild as swiftly as he could.

The lion was on the move.

CHAPTER 2

By the time Jacob got back to Malibu, Carmen had already eaten. The instant he returned, Carmen scanned his face like an operatic score. For a while they hardly talked. Unable to disguise his mood, and too restive to eat anything, Jacob put on his deck shoes. 'I promised you a walk.'

'I'm willing.'

They needed to get out.

It was afternoon and the slack tide long past, so they had to climb around the rocks while the rising water pushed steadily in. Although neither Jacob nor Carmen was at all clumsy, nevertheless he managed to step into a field of sea anemones and she gashed herself in a fall trying to avoid the spray of the tide's first large wave.

'Wrong time to be in the pools,' she told him.

'You want to go back?'

'We're going to have to swim in if we wait much longer.' Carmen saw a flash of panic in Jacob's sea-green eyes. 'What's the matter?'

'I can't swim well in the ocean.'

Carmen had some trouble believing that. She knew

Jacob as the most vigorous of men who defied every one of his sixty years. She thought it was something else bothering him. 'I take it you don't want to tell me what happened at Joseph's?'

'Let's get back on to the beach and I'll tell you everything.'

He began by describing Indian Sam, ornamenting his own memory of the man with some few facts Joseph had given him. The important thing was that Sam, a British Columbia Indian, a Chilcotin, might know his sons and how they were living. Sam had rumoured the Solomon sons fought with local people, ranchers, and sportsmen. Perhaps they had more serious troubles, were ill or barely surviving.

'Surviving doing what?'

Carmen knew the five older sons only from their single meeting years before at Joseph and Rosalie's wedding, when they had humiliated Jacob savagely, and for no reason. That experience had been so harrowing that Jacob had never told her about the tense years leading up to it. And she, for her part, had never asked. As for what happened after the wedding, Jacob knew no more than Carmen. Nor did anyone else. The five brothers had fled immediately to a mountaintop somewhere in British Columbia.

The idea for their flight had been a scheme hatched in a lonely moment by Mark, Jacob's second son. A hare-brained scheme, it had seemed to Jacob, conceived like a punishment. None of the older boys had made a life for himself that counted for much, none of them had married, all were down at Prosperity's heels. So, unable to cope with the world in which they'd grown up, the brothers had sworn with Mark to observe a Stone Age life in the wilderness, in pursuit of adversity, an uncorrupted world, self-mortification – God-only-knew-what, but something *in extremis*, that was for sure.

'They eat thistles, tree bark, roots, and stones. They wear branches for clothes. They pull bones from the burning joints of dead men and wear them around their necks in little bags. And it might be they hunt bear with their hands.'

13

Carmen jumped from the last rock back to the sand. Her jeans were wet to the thighs by now. 'Did the Indian say that?'

'He did.' Jacob wanted to tell her that he more than half-believed Sam. 'And in winter they sleep underground.'

'And that's how they survive?'

'Sam thinks they've got a pretty good life.'

'Oh Jake . . . .' There was nothing she could say to him. His life with the older sons had been a lost cause long before she and Jacob had met. She lived with quite a different man from the one they had known as their father. 'But what was the point of the Indian's trip? Just to upset you and Joe with some country fables?'

Jacob stared dumbly into the breakers.

'Did he say, Jake?'

A wave crashed, the whitewater rushing up the beach dragging kelp it had torn from the ocean floor. Jacob read the seaweed's configurations like a fortune. *He was a fairy, was he?* Is that what his sons thought? The redskin was no fool. He had intended to provoke Jacob, probably improvised most everything he had said, would have used his claws and teeth if he had to. The wish to attack, though, could only have come from his sons. They had always wanted to scratch the lion's back. 'They sent him to pack me down with guilt. Get me to stoop. The idea is to see me enfeebled, then stick the teeth in deep. It always goes something like that. Except that I never holler from pain. I don't die'. He looked up at Carmen. 'I wonder what they would say if they knew I don't think about them at all?'

What he said was almost true.

'Sam must know where they are up there, I suppose.'

Jacob's feet sunk deeply into the sand.

'. . . what part of British Columbia? Where are the Chilcotins from?'

'Chezacut.'

'What's that?'

'Chezacut. A village.' His speech was wooden, his mouth a marionette's. 'But they're not there anymore. Now they're constantly moving in the middle of nowhere, fifty or a hundred miles from towns, farms, a post office, from any life at all . . . I don't know . . . .'

He was immobile. His legs didn't work. All of a sudden nothing in him was working.

'*Jake . . . ?*'

He looked towards the horizon and the purple-flecked sea. There, just beyond the vanishing point, he thought he could see five phantoms rising from the shoals, sea-grass and foam stuck to their beards, their bodies covered with the scales of loneliness and hard life.

Maybe he had only hoped his sons were dead because they were dead to him.

'I don't know what you're thinking, Jake, but you'd be crazy to try going up there to see them.'

Carmen's hair was blowing back into her eyes and mouth, sand on her lips. He reached to her and brushed everything gently away until she shined gold again.

'Of course I would be.'

'But you're thinking about it.'

'Am I?'

'Yes.'

Jacob paused. Thought about it. Understood.

She was right as rain. She always was with him.

Since Joseph's halting and stuttering over the hotline that morning the idea had been there, flickering on the rim of his mind. He hadn't realized it was there until Carmen gave it voice. She had seen it first, he only by her reflection.

Pure, golden reflection.

Carmen pulled him out of his hole in the sand. 'There's a bottle or two of bubbly wine on ice, if you want it.'

My Christ he loved her, this golden girl. 'Splurged on that, too, did you?'

'You'd shit if I told you just how much I spent.'

Pure. Twenty-four carats. She had the golden touch on him, she did.

'I'm cold and I'm thirsty and I want to go in.' And the way she spoke Jacob would have sworn it wasn't even caprice.

'C'mon, sister. I'll drink your wine.'

For the rest of the afternoon Jacob and Carmen lay on lounge chairs outside, sunning, nibbling at cheeses, drinking both bottles of her champagne, just pissing away the day with pleasure . . . all the while reaffirming the splendid thing between them.

Not that they talked about anything in particular. The hundred sundry ways they had for succouring each other were hid in small gestures, indirect questions, touches, or found crouching in the shadows of words. If friends had been sitting with them, buzzing at the same table over a meal, they would have heard all that Carmen and Jacob said without ever suspecting that the words were a kind of love poetry, the ensemble playing of hearts.

By eight o'clock, though, the sun had pinwheeled all the way across the sky and in its final orange flashes Carmen, stupid with drink and snacks, went in to take a bath. Before going she propped some cushions under Jacob's legs to take the strain off his back, then wrapped a travelling rug around his waist.

'You planning on staying out all night this time?'

There were times when Jacob felt the need to keep a vigil for those several lifetimes he'd already lived through.

'Might be.'

'If you get hungry wake me and I'll make you some eggs.'

'I don't eat eggs at night.'

They had gorged on a thousand thousand midnight omelettes.

'Good night, Leo.'

On her way inside Carmen shut off the balcony lights so the lion could be alone and see the stars.

'Good night.'

Jacob looked up. The stars were all there. They had guided him across Poland forty years before and he knew them all.

Events from the past began filtering back.

The rug around him now had kept him warm as he fled across farms towards the Baltic. It was a blanket of many colours, soft Angora when he had started, soon stiff with horse urine. Jacob's mother had stripped it off a daybed in their Jihlava house during the last, fat-mouthed goodbyes. Both his parents, perhaps not so innocent of their own future, had stayed behind hoping there would be no war. The war came anyway and ground

16

them into oblivion somewhere after their debouchment from Terezin . . . probably in the death camps.

At the time of his flight, Jacob hadn't been entirely unhappy to leave Czechoslovakia. Born in Moravia in 1918, he followed a medical course for a while (Jacob's father had been a doctor himself, a neurologist, who studied with Freud for several years and trifled with psychoanalysis). It happened Jacob took up with a company of actors before taking his degree, however, preferring cafés to consulting rooms and afternoon assignations with lace and cordials, and a certain Fräulein Flehmig, to a general practice. All that ended, in any case, in March of 1939. Slovakia declared itself an independent state and Hitler's stormtroopers moved – unresisted – into Prague.

Survival meant flight and so Jacob got to the Baltic, and then by boat almost all the way to the sweeter waters of the Thames, where he disembarked at Tower Docks. For Jacob, England was grey and unhappy, and the Soho gaslights, however charming, couldn't dispel the gloom after Poland was attacked and all of Europe at war.

So Jacob moved farther west, following the Irish bishop's admonishment to travel the imperial road to America. He found no deliverance in New York, though, only a cash job hawking hotdogs in Coney Island. He went farther into the continent.

In Montana several Czechs were forming an air squadron to fight alongside the Allies. Jacob took the aviation training but a slight colourblindness kept him out of the action in Europe. He stayed to help train the new pilots.

And also, Jacob met a woman just home from college in Pennsylvania, a gentle girl descended from great-great-grandparents who had settled early in Montana. The family still lived in a gabled, dormered, three-storey house their originals had built. Swedes. Once poor farmers, they ranched sheep richly now. Her name was Eva Bjornson and neither she nor her family quite knew what to make of the huge, ginger-bearded lion of Judah who swaggered daily into their front parlour with his pungent humour and his cosmopolitanism and his somehow unflawed speaking of a language that had graced his tongue not yet three years.

17

They resisted, but Jacob got his woman.

Eric, the first child of this Solomon-Bjornson union, followed hard upon the marriage. A breech birth who came into the world blue with strain, he was a big and sulky child who had, however, a quite wondrous, if infrequent, smile. Mark arrived next, just at the end of the War. And soon Eva was cooking another. Her easy proliferation worried Jacob, for hardly had the marriage sheets lost their lavendered freshness when he could already feel the contraction of life, the cutting off of possibilities, confinement. His urge to move on renewed itself and so, with his swelling family Jacob went farther west, to California and the realms of gold where he did well. Very well. Alone he found a job in a film processing laboratory (anything to do with the movies seemed romantic beyond his wildest fancy), and soon he had his own lab and the beginnings of a small, a modest, a very European-scaled fortune. Despite considerable precautions taken Eva made two more children, and they had five now, all sons. A larger place was a necessity, and he and Eva bought a ranch: thirty-seven acres of avocados and lemons with a rambling house that in their years there the Solomons never did finish adding rooms to.

For a year or two this country life Jacob had arranged brought him satisfaction: his sons were outdoors nearly all the time, building a world of play in the loose-pack black topsoil, the irrigation ditches, the spiky higher reaches of the lemon trees, their companions possum, stray dogs, snakes. But they weren't happy children. Oh no. As the sons grew shoulder to shoulder – enormous children, a brood of Hercules close in ages – they became querulous, short-tempered. Alone they ranged in the groves, a small and angry horde, their play ever rougher, brutal, secret.

Or perhaps it just seemed so to Jacob. His sons were a mystery to him and he wasn't being let in on the secret. (At least they were growing up independent . . . were building interior lives. And that was where life was lived, wasn't it?)

When a sixth was added to his already unmanageable bunch, Jacob went into revolt. He wasn't convinced any longer that mere fertility had made a child between him and

Eva every time they clapped together under the orchards' cold shadows. She had, he believed, some darker purpose in mind. So he cleft their conjugal life in two. They crawled into separate beds at night, in separate rooms. He had intended this as a gesture, a temporary arrangement. But the estrangement stuck. He and Eva fell into the habit of being apart. A bad habit. Like the bad habit of remoteness he was also getting into with his sons.

From the moment the room division was made, Jacob began to feel a stranger in his own house . . . that there was no place for him at home no matter how many acres he owned or sought to buy. He was constrained to change his life, to set its centres elsewhere.

Turning his business over to younger associates, Jacob buried himself in the university and went right through to a doctorate in psychology five years after, choosing to work with difficult children – but not those who were seriously ill. It wasn't exactly medicine but it gave him status very much like a doctor, and the children and parents who relied upon him called him 'Doctor Solomon'.

The actor-refugee-wanderer-pilot-capitalist became a kind of doctor, after all.

A wise lion, he was, who hoped to salvage all his young charges by cozening them into believing that men could be better than they seemed to be, better than their acts. He roared that men were reasonable. Curious advice for small children.

Very curious advice from a man who had hid from murderous peasants while flying the Nazis, one who had seen photographs of his cousin Neiman's kidneys, heart, liver, intestines, all being cluckingly displayed to the cameras by the Iron Cross (as 'Kosher meat') during the Bucharest pogroms . . . a hymn to sweet reason from a man whose hours made sure he was almost never home with his own children, who found it a relief to be away from them, who to the unaccomplished eye seemed to have let go of the wheel and left his sons to steer for themselves through the isolation of those avocado and citrus trees surrounding their ranch house home . . . groves as dense as the night of childhood, or the primal forest itself.

19

And yet it would have been hard to say that Jacob's absence from his home was all his fault. His sons had formed a group so packed in feelings for each other that everybody else was excluded while they, friendless, parentless (not exactly parentless as they were continuously in the garden with Eva, doing God only knew what, some sort of cabal they were making with her), raised themselves according to some primitive call . . . lonely, wild and cruel.

They were a strange, strange, strange bunch.

Something else was going on, too. Jacob Solomon, great and tawny man that he was, had no habit of fear with other men. But he was actually frightened of his own sons. *Physically* frightened. They grew every day, it seemed, to staggering sizes. Whenever Jacob came back to the ranch there were always skirmishes, nothing grave on the face of it – arm-wrestling, shoving and the like – but something more than routine adolescent rebellion in the older boys. Soon enough the younger boys joined in as well, Jacob having to square off against several of them at a time . . . never any serious harm done but the rounds of rough tumbling were never just play and Jacob had no illusions, his sons' arms were smoking with malice and it was only a question of time before things got out of hand.

Eva ignored it all, of course, Eva and her garden, her fruit trees and berry bushes and row upon row of legumes and herbs. Any time the heat turned up between Jacob and his sons she minced away on her wooden shoes to prune and pluck and seed and spade . . . would kneel in her smock so low that tendrils held her, leaves threw up a camouflage, and soon she was well lost to sight, the artist invisible, unreproachable in her art. *But she knew*.

The sum of all this was that Jacob became isolated from those he wanted most to love, wife and children. He never took Eva out. Never the boys, either. Their contact was as immaterial as ghosts at supper. His remoteness had, like a lasso, drawn its frosty collar around everything. The lovers, he and Eva, who had started their conjugal life with such haste and vigour, were growing cold in all things, passionless when together, until there wasn't a single temptation left. She went to various doctors to explain her weakness; and he, for his part, smoked cigars, drank the fieriest of brandies, played Wagner, read books those infrequent evenings he was home; together they would look out over the long, grey esplanade of old age that was rapidly (and prematurely) opening up before them . . . just sit there and look.

Things couldn't go on like that forever.

In 1959, not forty years old yet, Eva Solomon died.

She had wasted away quickly. The little food she ate, the vegetables she cropped and steamed for herself after her sons had eaten – she alone in the kitchen and ever thinner – all that food converted into a black-headed beast that grew in her womb until its spores spindled into her blood, spreading to every patch of her body and laying roots down into her weak spring of life.

The cancer hadn't been the sufficient cause of her death. One night, when the ranch was dark and only Jacob awake – in a room even farther away from hers by then – Eva stole away for a night ride along Ventura Boulevard. And right into a beer truck. Whether faintness got her to cross over the centre divider or whether she aimed for the truck was a question to be deposed for the rest of Jacob's life.

What was sure was that Eva Solomon lay clear of her car, dead amongst a thousand broken bottles of Olympia beer – dead long before her time.

Two days later the hearse bearing her, and a limousine, drove up the gravel path to the ranch. It was a rain-swollen day and Jacob, unable to find any signs of his sons inside the house, went into the groves to gather them for the funeral.

They weren't there. They weren't anywhere he could see. No Eric, Mark, Bobby, Thomas, or Douglas. Only little Joseph, asleep in his father's arms, exhausted and confused.

He needed his sons, very much, but as he had not been there for them they were absent now for him. Neglect, hardening between father and sons over so many years, had finally sealed up every chink in the wall between them. Jacob was in a prison house and couldn't breathe.

He panicked.

It was a crazy thing to do but he told the hearse driver to sound the horn. Reluctant to blaspheme Eva's corpse, the man refused.

'Honk, goddammit!' Jacob, shivering in the rain, bareheaded, roared at the wind until blood ran down his throat. The driver still hesitated. Jacob shook him. *'Go ahead and do it!!!'*

And the man, completely undone, started to honk distractedly, so hard that the horn stuck for a full five minutes before, desperate, the sorely put upon driver just pulled all the wires he could find until it stopped.

The two men, strangers, wept together for some time.

During the funeral Jacob continued to hear the sound of that horn, as if it were trying to wake the dead. His sons, who had made their own way to the gravesite, stood a few feet apart from him. Several times Jacob tried to close the distance but they kept him away. There was no question but that the six Solomon brothers knew in their own green understanding that their mother's hands hadn't really driven the suicide car, that Jacob's had. Those hands that had lost the familiar touch of husband and father had guided the wheel.

So went the story that all of Jacob's sons (except the baby, Joseph, who was too young to moralize) would have oathed on their souls to be true.

But was it true?

That hardly mattered. There were those who would live their lives, and pull down the temple, believing it was so.

The consequences of Jacob's loins stood across from him hovering over the coffin. An army of sons, each with a cord, holding their mother's casket. Jacob gripped a cord in his hand as well yet he couldn't help feeling that his children carried the whole weight, were refusing to let Jacob bear his wife to her grave or lower her into eternity.

Douglas, the next to youngest, about whom Jacob had developed considerable guilt, was the one son openly crying. For a long time Douglas had been exhibiting signs of some imbalance of mind. Jacob suspected brain damage.

The two, father and young son, caught each other's glance. Seeing his father's look as provocation, Douglas jumped across the open grave and pulled at the cord tying Jacob to his wife's casket. The case lurched out of everyone's grip and tumbled to the bottom of the grave, hitting flat the hardpan beneath so that the seal broke and the coffin opened part way . . . while Douglas – eight years old – dragged his father after it into the hole, wrestling furiously . . . father and son slugging it out in the grave.

Jacob embraced his son, restraining the boy's anger with his arms, and lay atop the broken casket while his cheeks cooled against the wood's smooth veneer. Jacob's eyes pried inside the box. The jolt had discomfitted all the mortician's art, had shattered even his dead wife's final calm, her once wondrously soft hair brittle as straw.

Lionlike Jacob Solomon crouched in horror, smelling fire somewhere, the very stink of Hell.

Then his five other sons roughly pulled Douglas and him out of the ground. There was murder in every hand placed upon him and the acrid, flintlock smell of fury about them all. He would never forget it.

About what happened afterwards that day, Jacob couldn't remember a single other thing. Much the same was true of the following weeks . . . and months. In fact from the time of the funeral until he sold the ranch some six years later, Jacob Solomon stayed in a locked room at the extreme end of the house and had only the most perfunctory of contact with his sons. Practically raising themselves, they rejected his every attempt at communication, even the housekeeping money he stuffed in jars by the kitchen door. The older boys worked odd jobs. They didn't need Jacob at all. They were doing the marketing, cooking, tutoring each other, driving to school, disciplining the little ones, making house, managing . . . managing without him until one by one they left to find their way in the world. A few went to college, some to war. None married, nor found jobs for a lifetime. They dispersed, declined, fell by the wayside like unsprouted seeds until Douglas took permanently to the streets at the age of thirteen and Jacob was at long last able to secure his own release. Together with Joseph, the one child who never spurned his love, Jacob began to reconstruct the home life that had been trampled by the long file of children who had marched inexorably out of his wife.

The lion grew older, white, whiskered. He exulted in the knowledge that perhaps his line would not be ending with his issue, for Joseph was taking a wife. Jacob would have some measure of peace in his old age.

But first Jacob would have to witness the savagery at Joseph's wedding, when the five recusant brothers (Joseph trying to hold the mould from cracking) had got criminally drunk and then overrun Rosalie's parents' Bel-Air house, had terrorized the guests, knocked over sconces and torches. And there would have been more violence paid out, not so randomly either, had not the wedding pavilion itself caught fire and the whole congregation made to scatter into the hillsides, the lawn and garden shrubs aflame, flowers squealing in the heat, the sky and sun and day smoked over, the feast blotted from everybody's memory, people just happy to have lived through it.

Direct from the ruins the older brothers had sped northwards to Canada, somehow to make a society of their own there though with few enough skills to survive at all. Being alone in the world had proved far too tough for his sons, for every single one. They needed each other, and the violent authority of the primitive horde that during the years past they had become.

And that was the last anyone had heard of the Solomon boys until Indian Sam came down from the ice fields with a message for their father, pricking Jacob to remember all the troubles of his earlier years and to realize that they weren't entirely vanquished, whatever he wished, not extirped quite . . . .

CHAPTER 3

The morning after the Indian's visit, Jacob found himself on the balcony still, where Carmen had left him to ruminate all night long.

As Carmen was off xeroxing her script, Jacob went to the local library, a mile or so beyond the Pier, where he read maps and looked through several books about Canada, Indian life, vacations in British Columbia. It was the most casual kind of research, alarming nobody.

He had a problem locating Chezacut. It was missing from some of the atlases, marked in others, though never twice in the same latitude. There just wasn't enough information to get a fix on the town.

Jacob rocked backwards on the large, civic-scaled chair. He wanted to know more.

'Hire a plane . . . jeep, maybe . . . I don't know.'

'Stumped, eh?'

The agent admitted it. He was a mere cipher for the great carriers, could book you from metropolis to metropolis was about all. Jacob had found him in the shopping plaza across the street from the library, about to go to lunch. Instead, Jacob proposed to buy sandwiches and bring them back, if the man would open his routing bibles to inspection. But despite pickles and corned beef and beer they could find no trains, buses, boats or planes to Chezacut, not even a gravel road as far as the two of them could discover.

'I can get you to Williams Lake,' the agent told him, 'but I don't have a clue what you've got to do after that.'

'What's the best way there?'

'You in a rush?'

'Nope.'

'Then take the train. Change at Seattle . . . change at Vancouver . . . .' The agent's fingers, full of mustard, ran across the timetables. 'Change once more at Lillooet. You get an overnight there, it looks like.' The man smiled at Jacob out of his Hawaiian shirt.

'What's to do in Lillooet?'

'I've never been to Canada.'

Jacob, who had lived for six years in Montana, an arm's reach from the Canadian border, had never been either.

'In fact, I've never been north of Stinson Beach. I always seem to wind up in the tropics. Girls and beaches.'

'Where's Stinson Beach?' Jacob asked.

'Just north of San Francisco.'

Jacob liked this man, his breezy unprofessionalism, his pineapple shirt and yellow fingers tracking the routes and byways to the cold country, to Williams Lake where his sons might somehow be found.

It was all as if Jacob were going to go.

But he didn't buy any tickets. Not even for the first leg of the journey, which he thought he might just buy as a charm to keep him from wasting any more time thinking about such foolishness. All Jacob got was the timetable, ripped straight out of the book by the agent himself.

'It won't be missed . . . nobody I know is gonna be going anywhere that way.'

'Thanks,' Jacob offered.

'Sorry I couldn't be more help.'

Jacob left the rest of the beer and went back to the beach house. The agent had helped, all right. He had driven '*The Coast Starlight*' into Jacob's head – Los Angeles to Seattle. And though Jacob had every intention of staying put at home, the train ran right through all his nocturnal imaginings.

For weeks.

Even if Jacob awoke every morning swearing to himself that his business in life now was to love Carmen, still during his sleep mice were nibbling at the lion's paws . . . northern mice. By September they had fed and engrossed on the harvest of Jacob's night-time thoughts, rats more than mice by then, teeth ever sharper across the lion's paws, blunting them . . . drawing a little blood.

It was getting to be a bit obsessive. He returned twice to the library to find out more about Chezacut, the lakes nearby, the mean temperature and snowfall. He could taste the pitch of the pine trees.

At the tail of summer, a season entirely without rain like one of Pharaoh's plagues, Jacob learned that there was to be a conference on children's speech disorders in San Francisco. The scheduled dates were September 21st and 22nd, a straddle over the equinox.

Carmen dug around in his portfolio and found the circulars, the schedule of seminar topics, a reservation form for the conference gala that would end the two days of talks. He hoped she could see what an excruciating bore the whole thing would have to be.

'Are you interested?' she wondered.

'Might be . . . if the papers are any good.'

'What do the titles sound like?'

Jacob shook his head.

'You can always jog up and down the hills up there if you get bored.'

For weeks Jacob had been exercising furiously, dashing up the crack-runnelled roads that fingered into the palisades across the street from their beach house. The canyons were short there but well sloped, the switchbacks steep.

'Sounds like you ought to go, Jake.'

'I have a feeling it's a move in the wrong direction.' Jacob meant 'northwards'.

And Carmen understood him exactly. 'I told you already what I think about that . . . . I had the impression you'd forgotten about the Indian?'

'Oh he was eminently forgettable.'

'Go to the conference, Jake.'

He looked at her, brooding over his inability to decide.

'Just come home afterwards, that's all.'

Unlike Jacob, Carmen could say simple things simply.

Her grey eyes hammered him hard for an instant, but he was sure it was the look of love not doubt. A quick kiss. Then Carmen was gone, off to an appointment with a writer's agent.

There hadn't been a wrinkle of suspicion in her face. She had been wholly convincing. But had he been? He could feel the train timetables burning right through the flap-pockets of his jeans, where they had been mouldering for more than a month. She had absolute trust in him, that was clear, golden trust.

San Francisco was clear, mild, windless, smelling of welcome and expensive pleasures . . . its essential character unregenerate since the Gold Rush days, stamped in the streets forever. Houses were painted very particularly. As were window-boxes. The veils and damask of summer mischief. Women. Hills. Wharves. A sea shining below on several sides. Bridges. A city to look at before being ravished and consumed. For the first time in many years Jacob remembered that he was a European.

Dutifully Jacob registered at the conference, wore his name badge, listened to three general papers and then, after lunch, sat in on a seminar. The subject of the talk touched him a little too closely, though. It was about the oddball speech patterns of juvenile schizophrenics – the falsettos and manic chanting Douglas had uttered as a child. There had been every reason to test Douglas at the time. And Jacob would have done it if his child hadn't been so unruly, biting and kicking at the least sign of a parent's love. Jacob had hoped Douglas would just exhaust himself, and that being with so many brothers would bring the furious little boy to rule in a more natural way than therapy of any kind might.

Of course Jacob should have gone ahead with some medical supervision, despite the boy's fists. What, after all, was the whelp's fury next to the lion's? He might have saved his son from the streets . . . and the mountaintop after.

The seminar ended, mercifully soon. Jacob ducked out before the question and answer period. Went back to his rented car for a cigar he thought he'd taken from the humidor at home. No cigar.

There were more papers to follow but Jacob stayed in the car, strapped himself in, drove right off campus, pointing the car's wheels straight down the peninsula and towards the airport, and Los Angeles after that.

But it didn't work.

He wound up driving in circles, then stopping at a rum little bar near Golden Gate Park, with fish nets and glass floats and blowfish hanging. In the darkness he ate some hot slop and drank beer out of squat-bellied bottles with wide, obscene, threatening mouths. A map of Manila harbour had been laminated onto the tabletop.

He drank until he was rosy and it was a quarter to four. Planes flew to Los Angeles several times an hour.

He went outside and staggered to the Granada, unable to see in so much sunlight. Traffic was sitting in clumps on the larger streets, rush hour already. His blood beat anxiously.

It ought to have been such a simple thing, getting back to his home. (It had seemed so simple to forget five savage and graceless sons.)

For the moment he had no choice about going back. The traffic couldn't be managed.

Instead of fighting his way to the airport Jacob distracted himself in the Canadian National Tourist Board office. None of the staff knew anything about the little town of Chezacut, nor of the mountain plateau surrounding it.

'Cattle and Indians and not much else.'

Jacob turned round.

A young woman was looking sourly at him. She had short hair, short fingernails, frankness, an obvious health. Nothing to get in the way of a rugged life. The backpack resting against her leg had a Maple Leaf stitched to its flap.

The office was in the process of closing. Jacob and the girl were forced into the hall.

'I've been to Bella Coola a few times.'

That was over the coastal range from where his sons were supposed to be, but it was the same region of the world. 'Tell me about it.'

'I don't know about hunting or fishing . . . anything like that.'

'Just tell me what you know. Whatever you can.' She was regarding him with real suspicion, irritation bridged over her nose, she sure that he must be a hunter or a fisherman when all was said and done.

He pulled her to the marble floor with him, sat her against the wall. *'Please.'*

The girl broke into her backpack and found some old issues of *Beautiful British Columbia* and *Wildlife Review*. There were also photographs she had taken of the fiords, chilling escarpments that dropped down to the waterwhittled coast. Somewhere lost in all that splendour lived his five refractory sons, hidden in the sprawl of beauty, troubled, an irritant to the locals but unrootable.

The girl showed Jacob where she had been. Piecing together several sections of survey maps done by the Department of Mines, leaving nothing out, she traced her path at four miles to the inch, remarked what salmon-choked river she had ascended, through which cedar, balsam, spruce, and hemlock forest, what flowering alpine meadows she had slept in, what nubbing, axillary mountain crests, what high terrain she had then crossed. It was bleak as tundra up at the ridges, mere mosses and lichens and dwarfed shrubs. There were glaciers and ice flows, the thick-ribbed mountain chewing itself up, then on the other side spare and arid woods that she had followed down to the dusty badlands of the interior, brown and rolling rivers, open vistas, pasture lands, the last frontier before roads were paved again and the buildings made of machined lumber and metal siding and the great painted beasts of trucks hunkered along the highway with equipment to clip more of the frontier away.

She talked of the birds, too, of the bald-headed eagles and the osprey, and the rust-belted kingfisher that stole fingerling trout from the streams, of the intelligent jays, grey and edgy on the borders of her camp, of the emerald-tailed race of magpies she saw only at the rise of light for an hour, never longer, of the solitary raven, the gregarious waxwing in the pastures, and the foolhead grouse of the farms running around cattle and underleg, of mountain chickadee and goldfinch and nuthatch and tit.

And of the flowers and bushes and ferns and vines and shrubs and trees. Of snow berries, soap berries, salmon berries, thistle berries, mountain blueberry, huckleberry, wild strawberry, brambles thick with fruit, contagious with black juice.

And of the sounds of the forest, the animals and the compacted vegetation underfoot, and wind and the many sounds of water in all its different forms and all its motions, from the pattering of the rain to the gruff burial dirge of the ice slipping in low and rumbling tones.

And the lighting.

And the rock and soil.

And snow. Permanent and perfect.

And the quiet, sufficient unto her thoughts . . . like the sound of her own death.

Holy holy holy.

Jacob was struck dumb by what she had said, the sanctity of her description.

It might well explain just why his sons were up there, all five together, if his wits would lay open to what the girl was trying to tell him.

She, for her part, seemed embarrassed when she had finished, packed up her maps and pamphlets, catalogue of a saint's life, and stuffed them haphazardly back into her pack, cramming them in hard. Jacob had intruded. He hadn't meant to. He hadn't thought of these things as private.

Then he wondered how it would be if he were to intrude into the wilderness itself? To go up there.

For what? *To see those bastard sons after everything that had happened between them?*

It was possible, just possible, that they really weren't well, that the wilderness threatened them and they needed succouring.

But from him? He was better off leaving the Indian to rescue them.

To go . . . ? actually *go?*

And he had been so close to forgetting them . . . all five. Go?

Yes.

No more screwing around . . . ? Getting on that train for real and going?

Yes yes yes. Whatever the costs. There was just no staying behind if his sons were up there. Everything that had gone before between them was nothing.

Indian Sam was busy trying to steal the paternity of his children – and certainly would if Jacob didn't go up the mountain in order to claim them for himself. That had been the Indian's message:

CLAIM YOUR SONS OR LOSE THEM

Nothing would ever be right again until he did this. However much he loved Carmen, she was beyond the rainbow's end right now, a dream that would vanish into air as all bright spirits do. She could never prove a more substantial thing until he had sorted out the truth of things with his sons first.

The risks in going were no greater than breath. He had lived on the knife-edge of mortality for some time, so what danger could turn him away? But the risks of *not* going could be mortal.

All his life Jacob had been on riddling voyages. As he looked back on things it all seemed to fit. His life wasn't so formless as he had thought. Only this last piece, large and jagged at every corner but unmistakeably the right piece, was needed to give his life shape, solidity, truth, significance.

HE MUST GO AFTER HIS SONS.

'I'm keeping people,' the girl told him, anxious to get away, her own mind laden with the imagery she herself had concocted.

'Thanks, young woman.' He tried to pump her hand. 'I might just go up there myself now, if my bones are still young and supple enough to take the pounding.'

'You'll need more than that to survive.'

Oh he believed it. And he liked this woman. She was brave and sensible. There was nothing left that hadn't been said. Jacob thanked her one more time, then watched her find the stairs and clatter quickly down to wherever she was going, bound for her own glory.

It was evening as he pulled out of the subterranean parking, the sky turning a soft red, a fogless night coming on, as calm and free a time as he had ever seen in San Francisco.

The roads were jammed but he got onto the downtown skyway anyhow, hugging the right lane just over the level of the rooftops and docks, traffic moving much slower than the wilder thoughts in his head. He squeezed onto the feeder lane to the Bay Bridge, horns hooting savagely behind him, but he wasn't about to be frightened from his resolve.

In a few moments Jacob was headed east, quite a different way from the airport, towards Oakland. Then onto the bridge itself. The lower deck. His car's tyres screamed on the roadway grating as the car rocked back and forth as if it would fly over the railing and into the driving currents of the bay below. Jacob held the track steady.

Above the bridge's four great spans Jacob recognized Venus: The love planet blazed over Alcatraz. He thought he could see the goddess herself climbing the sky, moving eastwards, too, in pursuit of Jacob. She looked just like Carmen. Only a few hours away from Carmen and, Christ, how he already missed her. It was a hard question to know why he was running from her so fast. He remembered how her goodness had screened him from the hurly-burly of his sons' anger at the wedding years before, how she had kept him from falling into the dolours about his sons during the years since. And yet, knowing all this, why had he spent a summer dreaming of his sons' refuge in the high country and wanting to be there with them shoulder to shoulder, thigh against thigh?

What mattered to him, her or them? Rubbering in corrections in the book of his past, or his one and only chance for an old age of some considerable love with Carmen?

Jacob had the exact change for the bridge toll, paid, drove straight on looking for a way to turn off and think this whole thing through. Venus was still above him, hanging amorous and pendant in the sky.

Even if he wanted to he couldn't get out of the flow. He went straight south towards the Oakland rail terminal. Jacob had never been there before but he drove straight there now.

A train was waiting in the station. (*Forgive me, Carmen.*) The timetable gave him half an hour.

In telephoning the car rental company he found, not unexpectedly, there was a complication. They didn't want him leaving the car at the station – nobody took trains these days and they would have a bother picking it up.

'I'm leaving it here,' he told the word-stuck operator.

'You can't, sir, we'll never get it back.'

'It's here nevertheless. The keys are under the right-side

visor. Charge me a drop-off fee . . . by all means, do that.'

'But it can't be picked up!'

'Then it will rot, my dear, right down to its sturdy little Detroit chassis. It's here, I repeat, and right now running fine except for a little pull to the right when I brake. I'm going now. Thank you.' There was not enough time to continue fussing. 'Goodbye.'

Inside the station. More activity than Jacob had anticipated. This was a more humbling view of the real American landscape than that seen from an airport lounge. And in fairness to the operator he'd just turned off, there were few in the crowd who looked likely to be renting cars.

It took ten minutes more to get to the head of the ticket line. The station clock was rushing towards eight o'clock.

'I have no reservation. But I want on this train.'

'Where to?' The clerk strapped himself in front of his ticket puncher.

'Seattle . . . then Vancouver.'

'No lounge seats left.'

'I have to stand the whole way?'

'You can have a roomette, if you want . . . or a bedroom. Damned expensive, though.'

'A room with a view.'

The clerk looked up at the clock and started punching his console, ten, twenty, thirty keys. He cleared an error and went through the whole sequence a second time. The machine reiterated musically.

Jacob watched the platform emptying rapidly. He snatched the ticket, scribbled his signature on the charge slip and flew out of doors, no baggage in his hand but his overnight grip, ran through the steam hissing from the train brakes and jumped aboard in the middle of the train, nowhere near his berth, then pushed through the crowded hallways all the way to the last car, his Pullman, which he got to just as the train jerked forwards out of the station.

He found his bedroom. The porter unlocked it.

Hurriedly Jacob unpacked his few clothes, washed his hands and face, fiddled with every convenience and gadget in the cabin. Then sat down and dropped his face into

34

supplicant hands for a single cry of relief. And thanks-giving.

One of the dining car attendants rang his bell up and down the train for dinner's final sitting. There was a knock at Jacob's door.

'Last call!'

'Thanks.'

But the knocking continued.

'I'll be there. THANK YOU!'

A third unsatisfied knock and Jacob opened the door.

Someone stood in the shadows, her face natural fire.

Jacob sucked in his breath, moved aside so the woman could come past him and into the room, out of the hallway. She didn't want to do that, though.

'I had an instinct you'd try something like this.'

His head shook, and shook . . . couldn't stop shaking This simply was not happening.

'When were you planning on calling? Two days down the line?'

'How could you know . . . ? I didn't myself until five minutes ago.'

'I know about you, Jake.'

Carmen had found him, even at the beginning of his flight.

'Now what do we do?'

But she wasn't about to tell him. The train was going north, all the way, and they were on it together, which is how it should have been from the beginning.

He, for his part, wanted her with him . . . yet she'd have to return home once they got to Seattle. Even if she had other ideas. Jacob could see the flush of revolt already incandescent in her eyes. Well, he'd soon extinguish those hopes. Seattle would be the northern limit of her reach.

CHAPTER 4

Seattle.

Jacob had not been there before, though he'd heard much about the place over the years, the islands, the waterways, dollar-sized and luscious local oysters, the perfect imploded cone of Mt Rainier south of the city, the white-browed Olympics across the sound. But there wasn't time for all that now, his stopover only one full business day, ten till five, before he caught the connection to Vancouver.

Seattle, as scheduled – except that Carmen was still around. Having once sniffed the day and place of his secret jump north, having bounded after him and caught him, she wasn't about to unlock her jaws' grip. All last night he had vowed to ship her back to Los Angeles in the morning, whether she wanted to go or not, would bind her and crate her and send her live-freight but however she went she was going back.

It was already way past noon, however, and she was at his heels, dogging him, refusing to go anywhere except where he went.

With this one day in Seattle Jacob had improvised the idea of a trip to Eddie Bauer's in order to outfit himself, a store said to be even better than Abercrombie and Fitch, nearly as expensive, too. The lions stalking in the display windows and the bears standing wide-paunched and angry, made it all too clear this was a store that could provide for a king's leisure and sport.

'You're going to be way over-equipped, Jake.'

'The boys can use the gear. I'll leave it behind.'

'But you've got to carry it *in* first.'

'Please, Carmen . . . .'

'You haven't done this kind of thing before. It's not like an hour's workout in the gym.'

'I *said* I'll manage.'

For nearly four years, the time they'd been together, Jacob had followed a fitness class – not every single day, but often. During the last year he'd been running hard on the beach, too. And since Sam's visit he had worked furiously to bring his body into final flower, a late harvest and maybe even a last one, but one thing was sure: up there it would not be his body that would fail.

Just then the salesman returned with the backpack Jacob had selected, this one in a muted gold colour.

'May I try it on?'

'It's the same as the floor model, sir, exactly the same.'

'I'd still like to try it on now. If something isn't right it's better to find out here than at the trail head, don't you think?'

'No problem.' The salesman patronized the two of them with the store smile. Quality-control at Bauer's was too good for problems like that. 'Would you like to try the other things on, sir?' Jacob had looked at more equipment than a young and experienced mountaineer half his age would dare to tote. Was the old man expecting to climb K-2?

'O.K., let's see it all.'

The boxes came out of the storeroom: expedition two-man rip-stop nylon tent and rainfly in the same colour as the backpack, stuff bags, parka, wind shell, anorak, rain poncho and pants, gaiters, silk undergloves and lined ones to slip over them, wool trousers and shirts, the mummy sleeping bag filled with three pounds of prime grey goose-down and sewn in overlapping stitches that would keep the down evenly distributed at seven inches of loft, wool socks and wicksocks and a nylon undersock, balaclava and sun glasses, the special Norwegian lightweight underwear, camp moccasins, portable stove and canisters of fuel, fire ribbon, windproof/waterproof matches in a sealed container, plastic water jars and a Sierra mess kit, ground cloth, and endless incidentals including a small pre-packaged safety box of the 'ten essentials', repair tape, first-aid kit, countless more things . . . and at the end a suggestion from the salesman to throw in a couple of fifty-foot strands of nylon rope – a tool there was always some use for, normally unexpected and almost always life-saving. So two packages of electric blue nylon cord got tossed in as well.

'You can always hang yourself with it, Jake.'

Jacob looked at her. It was no accident that he and she

were together. That was exactly what he had thought about the rope.

'Your feet, Jake . . . your feet.'

Nothing was wrong with his feet except that he had on only socks, no shoes.

'What about the boots?'

The salesman had left them in the shoe department, now went to get them.

'Jake . . . ?' Carmen was amused.

'What?'

'You can't carry all this.'

'Would you stop going on about it?'

She said nothing more but handed him trousers, parka, socks. The boots arrived. 'Put these on while we load the pack for you.'

Together Carmen and the salesman shoved everything in, laced up the pack flaps. Their eyes caught each other's for a moment. The salesman had less disdain in his eyes now. He had begun to sense there was more here than a man taking up a new sport, something infinitely more serious was going on.

Then Jacob emerged from the dressing room and he made the others forget any idle, bleak speculations.

It was Jacob Solomon covered from cap to toes. The Mountaineer: from the brilliant gold and orange balaclava to the triple-welted tips of his steel-shanked, vibram-soled expeditionary boots. Jacob had disappeared completely, other than for a few odd spots of skin at the edges of his sunglasses and on his cheeks . . . was like Man new-made, his hoary head all hidden.

'The pack, please.' Jacob knew to kneel putting it on.

It wasn't halfway on and his breath was strained already.

'Wait a minute.' Carmen stopped the salesman, then dropped fifteen pounds of sandbags into the top compartment of the backpack. 'Now try it.'

'What's that for?'

'Food, Jacob.'

'I expect to find some of what I'll eat along the way.' Now he was really struggling to get his arms through the straps and the pack hoisted flat with his back. 'I've survived in the wild before without canned goods.'

'It isn't rural Poland you're going to.'

Helped by the salesman Jacob finally got the pack to sit right, though it wasn't tight yet. Carmen reached to a nearby bin and pulled out an ice-axe, rubbed its long white ash handle. She watched the salesman put out both his hands to Jacob, who was unable to move.

'Rise, Jacob.'

And somehow the old lion did.

But the thick plaid pattern of the trousers couldn't hide the trembling in his knees as he rose. There were some seventy-five or eighty pounds on his back.

'How does it feel?'

'Like I suppose it's supposed to.'

'Put your arms forward.' Jacob did and the salesman pulled the arm straps. 'Suck in air.' Now he cinched the padded hip belt. 'Better? The more weight you take on your hips the lighter the pack will feel.'

But it was the weight of Sisyphus' stone nevertheless.

'Walk around. You can't tell anything if you just stand there.' Carmen fingered the adze end of the axe while Jacob made short turns around the mountaineering department. Then his circles grew wider.

'Think you can do that for eight hours a day, maybe longer?'

'I think I probably can.'

'Up mountain gulleys, across fast streams?'

'Carefully and certainly.'

'Keep on walking. I want to hear you say you can't carry the load.'

'My Christ, you're tedious.'

'Keep walking and we'll see.'

He did. He walked right around the shop, maintaining his smile the whole way . . . but his spirits were sagging, right down through his collapsing back and hips and plummeting through his legs, knees, ankles. His feet, even in those worthy boots, felt flattened by the pressure. There wasn't room for self-deception here: Jacob had no idea how he could support this burden for any length of time.

Despite a Herculean effort to hide his strain, he trudged back to them and rested the pack heavily on a counter-top.

39

Carmen, he noticed, had a smaller version of the same pack strapped to her back.

'Take that off, Carmen.'

'I need a pack anyhow.'

'You've never hiked in your life.'

'I've got my own money on me, you know.'

'Take it off!'

'Don't you fucking roar at me, Jake.'

His temples had grown red and damp, for he had unthinkingly zipped up his parka and the goosedown was greedily paying him back all his body heat for his efforts in carrying the pack. 'Pull this damned thing off my back, would you?' Jacob dropped to his knees, retracted his arms through the straps, tore the jacket away from his superheated chest. The salesman caught jacket and pack, took them away, went for a moment out of earshot.

'This business is between me and my sons. How often do I have to repeat that?'

'I understand.'

'Why do you insist on interfering then?'

'You won't ever get to them, Jake.'

'I'll get to them just fine.'

'They don't want you up there.'

'Would you just take care of your own business! Leave me to go into whatever wilderness I want, while you wander back to Los Angeles . . . or wherever the hell you want to go. Now, *enough*!'

He went to pay.

Carmen fumed without moving from where she had been standing, the pack still on her back. She had put an additional fifteen pounds of sand into his carrier before he lugged the dead-weight around the store, hoping this might tumble his self-reliance. He just didn't understand the nature of this game he was playing with his sons. For Jacob it was all a quest of the highest spiritual order. Perhaps his sons would understand that, too, when he ascended the last switchback and marched into their camp. Maybe so. But Carmen didn't believe it. For there were memories that should make for bloodier, grislier expectations than Jacob had in mind. And she sure wasn't about to let Jacob Solomon deliver himself up to the primal wrath of his five renegade sons unprotected and in the middle of nowhere.

Her hands itched. She went to the cash register and, just as the final tally was being punched onto his Master-charge, Carmen made him buy the ice-axe she had been handling for some time. It pleased her, this axe. There was something demure but lethal in its balance. And it seemed when she gripped it almost instinctive to make the motion of the mountaineer's self-arrest.

The argument about her going farther north came up again several times during the afternoon, but it got no further than a lot of bellicose staring, a few curses, tight lips.

The two of them consigned his luggage at the train station then walked and trammed towards the pierside, to Pike Street and its multi-tiered market overlooking Puget Sound and the ferries all over the water world up there pulling in and out of the slips below, its thousand merchants in full cry, its thousands of people with fists of money jingling like a musical responsory through the long halls.

It was autumn's first day, warm enough, but fresh gusts stirred the sky. The locals all seemed to be wearing mountain clothing, hearty boots, wholesome leather coats or lumber-jackets, babies in papoose.

'Log cabin folks,' Carmen said with some sharpness. 'Hearty' was just another style to her.

'We're farther north. That makes for a moral dimension to life. It comes with the bad weather.'

Carmen, still unimpressed, said it looked like summer despite the clothes.

'Summer is only an idea,' he promised her, 'a reverie.'

They were standing at the fish stalls, watching a man slice fresh sturgeon into steaks, right through the beast's primordial armour. Jacob, intrigued, searched patched pockets for his Churchills, bit the end off one with his incisors, lit the cigar until it was blue with fire.

'None of the other hearty folk are smoking, Jake.'

'All us moralists get one great dirty pleasure.'

She wondered aloud if Jacob might be the only man in

41

the Northwest seeking the righteous path. 'Or maybe you're just the man with the longest way to go?'

'Maybe so, little Blondie, maybe so.'

And for that he bought her lunch of a packet of little freshwater crustaceans with pink bodies and beads for eyes and long beards, sold by the pound, and hard work to eat by the piece, lots of shelling, but they were sweet and tender.

They sat down to eat on wooden cases full of fish, were made to move so the dripping crates could be opened, sold. Jacob asked and was told the fish were a sort of greenling, called 'kelp trout' by the locals, rarely found commercially, small fish cased royally in wine-coloured skins speckled gold near the fins, golden mouths . . . a fish oriental in its beauty, come straight from Scheherazade's cave.

Jacob noticed that he and Carmen had been for a while touching arms, hips, as they watched the fishmongers lay out the catch. It was getting harder and harder to tell Carmen she ought to get back to Los Angeles . . . he wasn't even so sure by now that he absolutely wanted her to. Anyhow, she wouldn't go home.

What could he say?

They crossed the international border shuffling his gear from one train to the next, this time the British Columbia Provincial Railway, took the train up the Fraser River valley past the canyon and beyond. There was the lie-over in Lillooet before the last bit up to Williams Lake. The greater flood of people was coming the other way, holiday people on the way home, rafting parties, sportsmen, men with fingers scarred from trout teeth and under their arms packages wrapped in a paper that couldn't staunch the smell of smoked fish.

At Williams Lake they left the train for good, and with it the press of vacationers. Jacob made one last feckless attempt to turn Carmen around, pleading only weakly as the two of them sat in the coffee shop of the Cariboo Lodge waiting for the feeder bus service to take them west into the remoter parts of the province.

'C'mon, Jake, eat up.' She wasn't having the conversation again.

42

'Can't eat.'

She wasn't surprised. They sat surrounded by a hundred or more ranchers all come to Williams Lake for the calf auctions, all with the same cut-up hands gnarled around coffee mugs, all eating morning steaks. Jacob and Carmen had eaten nothing but prime tenderloin since entering Canada. His palate was in revolt.

'The road's dirt all the way from here, you know.'

'We're gonna miss the bus.'

'I don't understand why you're so bloody hot to see this Chezacut burg?'

Carmen sighed. 'Because it's there.' Then she lifted him with the not inconsiderable grip of her hands. 'Let's go.'

Some eighty miles later, about midday, the gravel highway joined the Chilcotin River coming up from the south. Off to their left they saw the last of the Chilcotin badlands, wide-spread cliffs and hard angles of sandstone, hardly any vegetation near the river, the earth and banks crusted like burnt bread, Carmen and Jacob both getting more and more the sense of a poisoned land, the waters flowing brown, turbid, fast, silting in a long, arrogant curl back to the Fraser.

This wasn't the land that Jacob had imagined . . . at least not yet.

He could see that Carmen was disappointed, too. The country looked smaller than he knew it to be, much uglier than his expectations, unprepossessing, lacking the magnificence he would have liked as the backdrop for his sons' wild flight from society, certainly not the land once described to him by the woman outside the tourist board office in San Francisco.

'Cheer up, Jake.'

The bus stopped in the middle of the road, let them off with their bags to just stand there for the transfer to Chezacut, coming God only knew when, nobody having bothered to tell them.

More problems. Rain clouds were making their desultory way in from the coast, having squeezed through the glaciers of the coastal range on the back of a rough and rising wind. They both could see lightning fork down only a few miles ahead, the jagged light cutting a thousand ways as it fell. Jacob had all his outdoors gear but they had bought only a few things for Carmen in Vancouver, and in the mild sky then nobody had thought about rain. He gave her his poncho just as the first rain dropped.

'Happy you came along?' he asked her, not too meanly.

'I never saw this as a pleasure trip, Jake.' Carmen stopped to watch two small Indian boys riding the same horse cross over the road, take a good look at her and Jacob before walking slowly on towards Redstone. 'Anyhow, it's not me who's getting wet.'

But she had spoken a little too quickly. Minutes later they were on the minibus to Chezacut, these final forty miles through the woods and over a prehistoric road, the ground very stony, full of gapes and water-gouged cuts, runnels of mud and black water sloshing under the wheels. It got so bad at one point the bus's speed dwindled to a few knots per hour, they rose and fell as if at sea in a gale. Carmen, who had suffered years ago from car sickness, was the colour of a lime and soaked in sweat.

Jacob felt for her hand, found it hot and wet. 'We can't be far from Chezacut.'

'If we're a half a mile we're far.' She could hardly pipe out the sounds.

The driver had already glanced in the rearview mirror and seen that Carmen wasn't doing well at all. He looked again now and grew worried. 'You want me to stop?'

'No.'

'It's not a problem, you know.'

'Just keep going.'

'Road smooths out soon.'

He was right. Only moments later they drove onto a better patch, reasonably graded, the bus suddenly picking up speed. Rain had made a bad drive much worse.

'And people think we're having a drought up here . . . Christ!'

When the bus finally stopped Jacob made Carmen rest in her seat without moving for several minutes, just the two of them, the driver and his only other passenger, an Indian woman whose eyes hadn't once crossed anyone else's on

44

the bus, already gone. The rain had slowed but was steady. Jacob listened to it, he not as tired as Carmen perhaps but dismally depressed. Dark afternoon. Drizzle. He looked outside.

Chezacut. Not a town at all. A collection of mis-shapen houses, cold and groaning, and jumbled in no particular way on either side of a dirt street so rutted and worn that anything but a truck would snag. In between the houses some of the greater world's flotsam had shored up – old car fenders and saw blades and hand washers, rags and more rags, the only colour striking his eye the carcass of a dead dog, red. One large structure, obviously the store, and no lights on anywhere. Not a picturesque western town. Just a grotty native village, colourless, grey in the grey afternoon light. The road simply ended at the front door of the store, then turned back on itself for the return journey to Chilanko Forks.

They had wanted to get to Chezacut, Jacob for his reasons, Carmen for hers. Well, they were there.

CHAPTER 5

They got no help in the store.

The proprietor was unhappy about talking to them at all. He was a thick and ugly man, square and powerful, a man whose humour had been formed by his bad skin and bulbous, pore-crudded nose which stuck out in front of him like the devil's lantern lighting his way. When Jacob and Carmen came in he was making coffee for the bus driver and a man recessed in the shelves' shadows. Carmen looked hungrily at the pot but wasn't invited to share a cup.

The best the man would do was to direct them to a house where they might – he said only that they 'might' – get lodgings, maybe meals, too. About the Solomon brothers the storekeeper had nothing to say, nor did the driver nor the man in shadows.

'There's a town drunk somewhere who might wag his tongue with you – if he's awake or you can find him.' He didn't explain more.

Jacob asked about mail that had been sent to his sons at the Chezacut postal address (Joseph had written them during their first year in the mountain). He was told that the post office had been closed for some time, all mail going now to Alexis Creek, some seventy-five miles back towards Williams Lake.

'You remember nothing at all?' Carmen pressed, 'not even hearing about them?'

People who encountered them didn't forget the Solomon boys.

She might as well not have asked. Reluctant to talk to Jacob, they certainly weren't talking to a woman they didn't know.

Jacob led her back out into the rain, his spirits bowed. He felt as far away as ever from his sons.

By the time they found the inn the day was brightening. A stream ran in front of the door, out of the alder and bright aspen woods. At one end of the house was a shed where several logs had recently been worked, alder chips splintered everywhere, the brilliant orange flesh of the larger pieces stacked against the wall and stained in parts by the cloudburst.

Carmen stopped Jacob at the bridge and pointed to a small garden that made up the side yard. Ringed with flowers and trellises, there were hundreds upon hundreds of row feet mature, ready for harvest. This was altogether different, something like the hospitality they had hoped to find. Babbling drainpipes, newly painted, channelled the last of the flood away. The rain had otherwise done no more harm than shining the lintels and glossy shutters. A brass-nobbled door. Open wide. A hall light burning.

There was nothing hidden here.

They went into the saloon, also open. In the centre a fire was going, the swollen bark whistling as it pulled back and

46

opened the wood's hard flesh to the heat of the fire, sap snapping and turning shades of green and crimson. And the smell of cedar. Incense cedar.

A bench ran the perimeter of the two windowed walls. Otherwise the long timbers of the bar dominated a counter-top of some tapped metal, hard to believe it was copper but as they came up to it there was no doubt that copper it was. Some ten or dozen stools were evenly spaced along the bar's length. On the last, slumped over, his coat covering his head, was a man asleep, his head on the counter and his body stiff.

There was something more.

The room was a treasure house. Not of stuffed trophies bagged in the area, as Jacob and Carmen had expected they might find, but instead there were artifacts of men, of Chilcotin art in coiled basketry and rugs, ceremonial cloth-ing, bark armour, a stone battle mace, effigies and talismans and masks.

Jacob looked around. 'I have this feeling that the frontier is just over the hill.'

Carmen's nose was in the air.

'What do you smell?'

'Somebody's cooking apples.'

They hadn't taken along a lunch, unsure how rough the ride would be. A wise precaution, as it turned out, but now both of them were ravenous.

'What time is it?'

'Four-thirty.' Jacob had bought a steel-cased watch for the trip, waterproofed to one hundred metres.

'I wonder if we can get a meal right away?'

'We can ask.'

He had taken but one step towards the door when it opened and a woman, very obviously the owner of the establishment, came in.

Eleanor Lytle was a woman of some personal force, a long-lived but long-regretting spinster who had no dreams left. For a number of years she had run the once-lively lodge that her parents had built. With the fishing and hunt-ing trade moved away a hundred or more miles, and only infrequent custom now, she nevertheless kept the house in perfect order. Her idea was to pass it on exactly as it had been given to her, nevermind that she had no heirs. Her accounts would be cleared.

A plain woman, small, she had on a coarse cotton dress that had been well-boiled and starched. 'What can I do for you?' This was business, her manner brisk.

'Is there a room we might rent?'

'Two rooms or one?'

'We can get by with one.'

'You married?'

Jacob smiled politely, his head deferentially low.

'What you do is your business, of course, but you take two rooms here if you're not married. Those are the laws of life as I read them. You take care of the appearances. You know them and you take care they're kept.' She nodded back at Jacob, seeing he understood her. 'A room for how long?'

'We're not sure.'

'Then you'll have to pay the day rate.'

'Meals?' In the presence of a woman whose mind was so clear, Jacob trimmed his speech to its barest forms, not a stray article.

She told them in which rooms food would be served, and at what times . . . promptly. 'That's three meals, you understand. They're all big and you're expected to eat them.'

'We'll eat . . . as required.'

There was a pause. The starch in Ellie Lytle's collar seemed to soften, her posture deflate, though she didn't smile. 'You look hungry to me.' She spoke to Carmen, wondering aloud what kind of snack could be found. 'I imagine one or both of you might like a bath with some of our local salts . . . unplugs the nerves.' In her own way the frontier lady was confirming that they were welcome enough.

Then she surprised them both by asking what was their business in the Chilcotin? Jacob told her he was looking for his runaway sons, told her their name, described them as best he could. She had something to say about them.

The five men had stayed with her once or twice a few winters before. One had done some work on the lodge, painted a few things, had a stutter as she remembered. She had no notion of their current whereabouts. And that was all.

As the woman turned to run Carmen's bath and prepare some sweetmeal biscuits for them, Jacob stepped after her. He wanted to know if there was something he ought to know about his sons, some reason why people were reluctant to talk about them. 'Have they *done* something?' He was fairly well pleading.

'Not anything I know about.'

Their eyes met, hers of such a gravity that he knew she could be as easily moved to speak more about his sons as the mountain where they lay hid.

'Hot as possible on that bath, if you could,' Carmen asked.

'Oh it'll be hot enough.'

Then Jacob and the hostess left Carmen alone by the fire as they went to draw enough water to heat up for her bath.

'She could've said more, you know.'

Carmen started.

At the end of the bar, as if from the dead, a penumbral figure rose slowly into the flickering light. Whatever he was he looked ghastly, unshaven, dressed in tatters of buckskin and denim, most likely ridden with mites and scabies. He might have been a miner just emerged . . . if he did any honest work at all.

Undaunted, Carmen approached until she could see the exact red of his eyes, red as a whiskey label. 'Drinking a little, it looks like.'

'Oh I do drink a little from time to time.'

A man who could bear honest mockery. She liked him right away, what she could see of him. It was enough that he shined so.

Hiding a mouth with only several teeth he told her he was Colin, indeed the town drunk. 'Every town's got one.'

Carmen had already guessed as much. She sat down on the stool next to him, refused to be put off by his smell. The man was full of life's best juices. She could get closer if she had to. 'So why is Miss Lytle a liar?'

49

'I didn't quite say that, did I?'

Nor was the man a fool. Carmen waited for him to go on.

'She probably told you as much as she's interested in knowing herself. But there are rumours anyone could pass on to you. What did Harry say?'

'Who's Harry?'

The drunk smiled hugely. 'Harry owns the store. He used to be a postal clerk until they took his job away. Now he likes to tell people he's our mayor.'

'He told us nothing.'

'Not surprising.'

'What do *you* know, Colin?'

'About what the next man does. Those boys don't plant crops, don't come here to buy supplies. They seem happy just to stay up there playing at being Indians – oil their hair, berries and bark juice on their faces. Something Sam put them up to, I'd guess.' He stopped himself. 'But you wouldn't know about Sam.'

'He's been to Los Angeles . . . visited us.'

That surprised Colin.

Carmen explained how the Indian's visit had led to Jacob's and her trip into the Chilcotin.

'Bad man, Sam. I've seen him drive iron into a sheep's skull. He'd probably be shot if he showed up around here these days. He's got light fingers, among other things.' The drunk pointed to the case of Indian artifacts. 'He's had his hands in there.'

'What about the brothers now?'

'Not much to report about them for the last year or two. They've stayed much to themselves . . . hardly come down at all.'

'Down from where?' There were gold streaks of expectation in Carmen's eyes.

And the old drunk, with an eye for gold, saw her very well. 'I take it this is the hard American dollar talking?' It had begun to occur to him there might be something more than cadging a few drinks in this line of conversation.

'Brand new banknotes.'

He thought he'd ask for a hundred.

'You can shuffle them they're so stiff.'

50

Lifting himself off the stool, shaking out one gangly leg at a time until he felt he could walk without tumbling, Colin went over to the north-facing window, a hand on Carmen's shoulder as he went. He put her nose right up to the glass.

'You see a heavy rise of timber about a mile ahead?'

Carmen peered through the sky, considerably higher now, still some distended grey balls but now deep patches of blue were pushing away the rain clouds, open sky spreading its hand.

'I can see.'

'That's a black butte marking the end of the road going out from town. You take yourselves straight upriver from there towards a cluster of three mountains some thirty, thirty-five miles in front of you. *The Itchas, so called.*'

'Mount Downton.' Carmen had read the atlas so carefully she knew the topography around Chezacut as well as the scrubbed-down hills of Hollywood.

'Downton is right. Getting there isn't any big deal. You follow the water, always taking the left fork whenever the stream divides. You'll come up to the southwest face, which is a huge rockfield – a fan of stones spreading away from a stream coming down the wash. That's Downton Creek. It comes right off the glacier.'

'Glacier?' She doubted it, was beginning to wonder about the rest of what Colin had told her. 'No glaciers until the Coastal Range, Colin. Don't bullshit me!' And she meant it. Her eyes were firing.

'There's a very deep gully there, always got snow in it even though it faces south. Snow field, ice patches – awfully odd colour.' He seemed offended. 'It's a glacier all right. You call it what you like.'

'Go on.'

'Cross over the creek, keep on until you come to a lake. Weather's bitter up there, it's just at the crest of the divide, everything the other side runs towards the sea.'

'And that's where they are?'

He smiled at her innocence. 'I've only just told you the beginning.' Then, for ten minutes, he described the demons of the mountain. There were a hundred false gulleys that seemed to lead into the mountain but only one

51

did, a defile nearly all the way to the far western reaches of the range. That was the road to the mountain's heart. 'If you get lost don't try getting home through the forest south of the lake, thinking it's the short way back here. You'll just trip over the bones of those who believed it was.'

There was one other thing she had better ask him.

'What's that?'

'Do you think we'll find them? Or is the mountain too big?'

He thought and thought, then began to smile. 'It's *their* mountain. You'll find them . . . or they'll find you.'

She nodded. And sighed. She had put it to the old drunk and believed what he said.

Something like an amity had sprung up between this oddly sorted pair. Colin took a good look at her.

'I'll bet you can drink, can't you? A talk-with-the-boys and drink-with-the-boys kind of girl.'

'How long to hike in and out? Eight or nine days?'

That got Colin roaring. He patted her like a mate. 'I don't know of anyone who's tried walking into that mountain since Mackenzie, and that was two hundred years ago.'

'How do we get in?'

'You take horses. Which also gives you a fair chance of getting away from those brothers of yours if you have to.'

'They're not my brothers.'

'Aye, but you look a bit like them all the same.'

Then she pulled out two new fifties and laid them flat on the bartop. 'Is that fair?'

All his life Colin had spun out wild stories about the mountain and gone bust. Now, for telling a few of its simple truths, he was getting more than was just. 'I'd settle for half.'

'Keep it,' she told him, just as Jacob came in with news of her bath. 'You can buy the first round.'

'What you got, Jake?'

In his hand was an old iron passkey. 'Miss Lytle's grandfather was a brewer in England. She remembers playing in the oast house as a child. Now she makes her own.'

Having waited until Colin was gone to collect their bags from the store before showing Carmen the key, Jacob unlocked the bar. Inside were cases filled with formidable brown bottles.

'Split one of these beasts with me, Blondie.' The flagon looked far too big for one person, even if he had an entire afternoon to tipple. 'You've got a minute. The water is still too hot.' He had helped Ellie Lytle carry the hot water from the stove, five boiling gallons at a time. The tub itself was a relic. 'Drink.'

'After my bath.'

Despite what she said Jacob lined up two glasses on the counter, filled them, slid one down the bar towards her. 'What did you and Colin find to talk about?'

'Things.'

'Miss Lytle said he might badger you about the mountains. Apparently he's spent thirty or forty years chasing gold in the Itcha Range.'

'He wasn't badgering me.' Carmen, sitting on the stool where Colin had been, didn't like the way the conversation had started. 'There's probably plenty of gold left in the Cariboo. Lillooet was the biggest city west of Chicago in the 1860s.'

'Maybe so but there has never been a nugget found anywhere around here.'

'So?'

'Colin swears he's seen gold wedged into Mount Downton in veins as broad as a bear's back.'

'Just possibly he has.'

Jacob sipped through the beer's weak head. 'It is late in the year, Carmen, and the first snow could come at any time now. I'm far too vulnerable to waste my time giving credence to the dreams and stories of some old drunk, however charming he is.'

Carmen didn't like that at all. She stiffened. 'He's the only person around here so far who's prepared to talk about your sons.'

'Not necessarily truthfully, though.'

'He talked at some length.'

'Fine.'

'. . . gave me very clear directions how to get in *and* out of the mountain.'

'I have maps.'

'You patronizing asshole . . . he knows more than the maps!'

'Well what the hell would you expect him to say, eh?' He was trying hard not to rise to her anger. 'Those mountains have ruined his life.'

'I have a bad habit of believing in old men.'

Silence. Both drank sulkily.

A few moments later Carmen reached into her shoulder bag and pulled out a brochure that she had been toting around since Eddie Bauer's in Seattle. It was about bears. Grizzlies. She flipped it at Jacob. 'Did you see this?'

He didn't look at the booklet.

She read aloud how a Mayo trapper was killed and eaten by a grizzly as he ran a winter pipeline. 'Not just mauled and killed but eaten, Jake . . . *eaten*. Seems that some bears are getting a taste for manflesh these days, maybe even yours.'

Jacob wondered what she was hoping to do. Frighten him with marauding bears? And then, no doubt, she'd start in on werewolves and 'Big Foot', the Pacific Coast *'yeti'*. Now that he remembered it Carmen had mentioned the voraciousness of grizzlies several times on their way up from Vancouver. Had he missed all her clues?

'There's not much savour left in my flesh.'

'Oh I don't know. It says here that grizzlies prefer old meat, bury their prey for a while until it's nice and rancid before eating it.'

'Any good butcher ages his meat.' Jacob tried to drink from his glass but it was empty. He poured fitfully from the bottle. 'Going to keep me from the bear's mouth, are you? Is that the plan?'

'That's the plan.'

His irony wasn't pricking her very deeply. In fact, gripping his glass with all five fingers, just able to resist slinging it across the room, Jacob realized he was the one getting riled. She was in control of herself . . . and manipulating him.

Mocking the lion.

'That's part of the plan, old man.' She rolled her glass

back down the bar to him. 'Didn't much like the way I surprised you on the train, did you? Or that I wouldn't go home from Seattle . . . or Vancouver.' She watched as he worked himself up to his full, proud height.

It wasn't enough, though. She thought she'd just pitch him higher.

'There's more, Jake.'

His eyes grew to bursting.

'I'm not stopping here, either.'

Hands white on the bar.

'That's right. I'm going up the mountain, too.'

Jacob's fist came down. He nearly split the copper.

'Rage all you want, roar and spit, but I'm coming . . . .'

So many words crowded in his mouth that they cancelled each other out. He tried to speak but it only came out as a laugh. She had humiliated him, she had, outwitted him completely. Had planned it from the beginning.

Finally he was able to whisper that he wasn't afraid of bears.

His saying so didn't convince Carmen. And keeping out of the bear's mouth wasn't just a question of courage.

Jacob imagined the scene, him running from the bear while Carmen, like that Lady Knight in an English poem he'd once read, a great big blonde beast of a military lady, visor up and lance down, Carmen, the Britomart of up here, of the Chilcotin, slaying the bear. He looked at her. Looked again. It was clear Carmen must have been thinking something like the same. They imagined alike.

Suppose he did take her along? Came up to his sons' camp with her in tow? The five of them were up there without any women. Difficult to know how they would react to one penetrating the consecrated borders of their domain, especially one like Carmen. That crazy Indian had made it sound as if his sons had lost most of the restraints that had confined them years before in the world below. What would they do to her, even if she could slay bears and keep them from the hoary head of an old lion?

Of course she couldn't go.

'My sons won't want women up there.' She wasn't listening. 'They don't *like* women.'

'Or fathers.'

'You're not going, goddam you—!'

'And you're not going without me!'

It was all pointless, this hollering.

'You've got some other business to settle first, Jake.' Carmen wasn't going to stop . . . not quite. 'I want to know what you feel about me? You've had four years to think about it.'

'What are you talking about?'

'Do you love me, Jake?'

Did he love her?

'Answer me.'

Did he love this young woman?

It was all well and good to talk about loving her but what was the real story? Nobody could fail to lust after her – he had and he hadn't tired of his lust. And then there was the flattery of it, she picking him out as she did . . . the vanity of all that, especially for an old man grasping with his hands for nothing but a final walking stick . . . .

But *love* her?

'Before I put my life on the line going up into those hills with you I really want to know, Jake.'

Well???

There was something monstrous hiding behind that word 'love'. Something that chilled his blood, always had, for sixty years now. There was no walking around this monster, circumambulating Love's bigness, its grandness, passion, the *utterness* it demanded. Love was certainly a dangerous, a desperate state to be in. He thought of what people had done for a misguided love: poisonings, treasons, Hitler's uniformed millions, even his sons' flight to the mountain-top. One had to give all and never know if it were in a good cause, all judgement gone. In a lifetime he had not done that, never, not for his parents, not for his dead wife, nor his sons. And for Carmen?

One last time he imagined meeting his sons in a mountain pass where he was unable to escape from them. They would ask him if he loved them, as Carmen was now asking about herself. He would have to answer. He would have to say that it was like the old proverb with him: the currents of

56

love ran deep in him, and powerfully, but they did run at their own pace and that was slowly, oh slowly. Could they forgive him that it had taken him so long to tell them . . . ?

And Carmen?

Jacob's hand opened all the way. 'Come with me.' A beginning. 'I love you very much.'

It had the ring of truth.

Jacob's chest was sore with feeling. 'Even at sixty years on.'

'Don't plead old age with me.'

He tasted his own tears.

Jacob Solomon hadn't any real idea anymore if it would prove for good or ill that she had followed him but now it was no matter. They were in this together. All right, then, no looking back . . . the worst was undoubtedly behind them. Those great and ineluctable patterns of human life through which every man must move had thrust the two of them onto the same hard path and he finally accepted that. It appeared that she had accepted it from the beginning. The woman had much courage and much, much faith . . . well.

Carmen had certainly come at the right time. It was the beginning of the last period in Jacob's life. He would never again be young enough for an encounter so prodigious, in the mountains or anywhere else. Once this journey were done, life must be a descending thing, however graceful, towards his summation.

The sunlight, furtive in the Chilcotin skies all day long, was right in the room with them, reflecting off Carmen's eyes. A guiding light.

There was a little beer left in the bottle. She shared it with him. Both glasses clicked. Their hearts brimful, they drank. All the way to the bottom of their inexhaustible cups.

'To the north country,' she offered, while he prayed, his face and spirit as ruddy as a lion's, as sanguine; prayed and prayed for a graceful fall . . . down easy . . . and a faith something like Carmen's, his song of songs.

'To the north country.'

The Mare

CHAPTER 6

On a cloudy Monday morning Jacob and Carmen quit Cheza-cut on horseback, following the river's lead-coloured track into the mountains where they would, God willing, find Jacob's five wild sons and settle his lifelong quarrel with them.

The horses and packs had been hired from Harry Blyde, much to Colin's displeasure, at vastly inflated prices. But there hadn't been anybody else in town to deal with, so terms were agreed. They could have bought a horse elsewhere for less.

The two of them made up a small train. Each rode a horse with saddlebags, while a third horse, an appaloosa mare, packed the heavier gear and followed their traces. The sky sat low and hard over them, not much more than a befuddling mist that completely hid the plateau they were travelling across, the mountain somewhere ahead, unseen but believed in on the strength of an old drunk's exhortations. For the first mile or two they sat towards the front of their saddles, an exalted sense of adventure rushing them along. But that soon changed. It was a long trip ahead. They found their tempo under the grey skies and kept it, horses plodding on by reflex, everyone – man and beast – dreaming.

At one point the appaloosa stopped. When she refused to start again Carmen called to her gently, cajoling her with the loose rein. But the rump-spotted mare had her mind set. Carmen, knowing the whimsy of horses, snapped and tugged at the traces to show the mare which way authority was going to go. Suddenly the horse shied, almost pulling the rest of them off the path and into the bankside rocks.

'What the hell is it?' Jacob had two hands on his saddle horn. 'Snake?'

Carmen jumped off her horse and caught the mare's bit. 'You see anything?'

She looked into the gravel and boulders. 'The horse is just too high-strung. There aren't any snakes this far north.'

'Who told you that?'

'I read it.'

He knew, though, that Colin had told her. 'Whatever it was must be gone . . . the horse looks fairly composed to me.' Carmen was set to remount when Jacob stopped her. It might be time for a rest.

She knew Jacob better than that. 'Sounds like an excuse for lunch.'

It was.

The two of them walked around for a few minutes to loosen muscles. They had stopped at the edge of an open meadow, a lawn littered with wildflowers even this late in the year, some few that Jacob knew the names for, blue and orange and white-petalled blossoms sticking up from the green, many shrubs – Jacob did not recognize juniper – heavy-headed grasses and ferns as they neared the forest side of this nearly perfect bib of field.

'I wish it would get sunny,' Carmen complained. 'Colin said it can go for months here with hardly a cloud in the sky.'

'This may burn off yet.' Jacob was hopeful. It had burned off each of the two days before.

'Now what's she doing?' Carmen had noticed the appaloosa wading into the river, their pack with all the store-bought down wear, sleeping bags, everything that had to be kept dry about to be immersed and slopped through.

They got to the water just in time, the mare almost thigh deep in the flood. Pulled her out and this time triple-knotted her to the trunk of a large tree.

'She's going to be trouble the whole trip, Jake. I felt it back at the stables.'

'We don't have the knack with her yet.' His two ladies, he reckoned, were just brawling a little. 'She'll settle down.'

'You don't know horses.'

Their hands red from dragging the mare free of the stream, they spread out a cloth as close to the water as they dared, started emptying the basket Miss Lytle had insisted they take.

'We wouldn't be eating like this if we had hiked in, Jake.'

He shrugged. 'I think Ellie Lytle likes to overdo things.'

She certainly had for this first meal. To indulge themselves they had cheese and homemade liver sausage, tripe and meat pies, tomatoes and radishes and carrots and slaw, a round loaf of bread. There was plenty of fruit, oranges as well as local apples and plums. Miss Lytle had even baked them a pecan pie, which neither wanted but couldn't refuse to carry along.

'Tomorrow it's the freeze-dried stuff.'

'We don't need to feel too guilty about stuffing ourselves. In a few days we just might be starving.' Jacob tilted his head upstream, towards the fog-bound mountain. 'It worries me they're supposed never to plant things up there.'

'What could grow anyhow?'

'They might come down to the lower valleys and plant potatoes, if nothing else . . . something to depend on.'

'Well, they eat something.'

A frown broke from his pensiveness. 'My warrior sons hunt.'

'They need things other than meat.'

'I expect they gather wild roots and seeds and green leaves . . . but who really knows?'

'Colin says they steal a lot.'

This he didn't believe. 'They can't plunder for a livelihood . There's nobody up there to steal from.'

'They can swoop down from the hills. It fits the renegade image.'

'You might be right.' Trying to cut sandwiches from the loaf, Jacob caught his knuckles with the serrations of his pocket-knife's blade. 'People do strange things when they feel they've come up against the end of their history.' He smiled, sucked away the crevice of blood from his finger. 'We'll see soon enough.'

There was a terrific splash just upriver. By the time they turned a ring had already widened on the water in one of its smoother stretches. 'Must have been a real lunker.' Jacob knew about this kind of fishing. In his dusky memories of Moravia he could hear a wise grandfather (his mother's father) teaching him how to trap the shy, bank-hugging brown trout that swam in those purling, light-twirling, chalk-bottomed streams, streams that used to sing Schubert lieder, he'd swear, and all in the right keys as they rolled through vineyards and fruit farms to the romantic rivers north.

A stuffed Carmen lay down now on the ground cloth, on her back. There was a few minutes when they both said nothing while the air seemed to grow warmer, thicker.

'I've been thinking about Mississippi . . . about growing up. We were in the South until I was twelve, before we came to L.A.' She knew he didn't know that because she had never told him. 'I grew up on a dirt farm.'

'What happened to your accent?'

'The city stole it . . . that and fast living.' She brushed her hair back. 'I suppose Dixie is still there, buried deep, like the dirt in my skin.'

Jacob hadn't heard her talk this way before.

'Just look at the soles of my feet, Jake . . . look carefully. Look at my hands. At the bottom of those lines there's a tiny seam of dirt that I can't get out . . . that isn't ever going to come out.'

'I can't see it.'

'Oh it's there.' Her eyes closed, infinitely fine violet veins tremored in her lids. She was logy from Miss Lytle's beer and food. 'Whatever you want to believe, Jake, I'm just a hayseed. And some day I'll return to type.'

He told her he thought she had some wrong ideas about him, as well. 'I doubt if you realize my mother's family were farmers.'

'Dirt farmers?' There were farms and farms.

'They had orchards and vines in the south of Moravia. I expect you don't know where that is, geography of a different time. Anyway, my grandfather made wine, rather crude stuff as I remember. He had loads of plums, too.' He saw her eyes were staying closed. 'Do you know what *slivovitz* is? Hmmmmm?'

'No.' A sinking voice.

'Plum brandy.'

'Mmmmmmmmmmm . . . .'

Carmen's breathing had completely changed. His lips crept towards hers, touched them. The sweet smell of hops and barley on her breath. She was dozing in the light . . . this golden girl of his.

Something slapped the water again, paddling twice, flat and hard. Three times. Carmen pulled herself into his arms, her eyes wide, the redoubled fears of a light sleep playing themselves out in her hands and feet. He raised her to a sitting position, pushed the ooze of sleep from her eyes.

'Company.' He pointed to a pool at the back of the heavy riffle forming a series of steps. A silver tube rose from the flume trying to jump through to the next step on the ladder, then fell backwards into the soft water.

'Salmon?'

'Nearly home, too.'

She held him very tight. Two more of the gleaming bodies twisted upwards, one of them clearing the step.

'Not long ago they were probably off the Aleutians or somewhere farther out to sea. But they're here now, still jumping, almost spent but on their way to Judgement upstream.' Leaning over her, Jacob took ahold of the topographical map and traced the river's path. 'Lots of creeks on the way up. They'll spawn in these, maybe in the lake, too. I don't know a lot about this kind of salmon.' A pair of kingfishers flew straight up the middle of the pool, chattering as they went, continuing on right over the water steps and upstream. 'Looks like everybody's headed the same way.'

'When I left L.A. I was seventeen. I spent six months with a rock band who played music about as bad as any I ever heard. I was pregnant the whole time. They threw me out before the baby.' She hadn't told Jacob this, either.

'What happened?'

'I had the baby. A rock baby. A girl.'

Jacob shook his head. His woman was a rare creature. He must never forget that. 'And?'

'I went back to some relatives in Mississippi. Back to the dirt farm. She's down there somewhere . . . happy, I hope.' Carmen rolled up the maps. 'Look at what those fish are ready to suffer in order to get to the top of the river . . . and

62

what you're going through to find your sons. Let me tell you, all I could think of was making them take her away from me.'

'You had the courage to have her, and at seventeen.'

'Only because I couldn't find someone to rip her out of me.' Carmen knew the truth. 'She's not thinking about me, that's for sure.'

The lion pulled her up and made certain she had a good stretch. 'We're getting a little behind.'

'If I cut your legs off you'd walk upstream on your hands, wouldn't you . . . ? Nothing's going to hold Jake Solomon back now.'

'That's right.'

She picked up her half of the ground cloth, helped him to fold it, then tucked it into her pack underneath the ice axe. Carmen was herself again, spirited and fire-eating. And ready for all things. 'You'll find your boys.'

Into the forest. The path, only infrequently travelled, wasn't maintained at all. From time to time they found a cairn or other sign that somebody had put up to keep straying strangers on line. The river itself, wilder and more sinuous as the terrain changed, was no longer a sure guide as it sneaked away from the trail, sometimes as much as a quarter of a mile, but they were never too far away to hear its deep-bellied roar.

They went in and out of the trees, though most of the time they were canopied. Around five o'clock, passing across a large meadow, it began to rain heavily enough for them to get out the raingear. Carmen's storm coat was a loan from Colin, was clean enough, had no holes, strong seams. Colin had made up her pack with the equipment she lacked. Jacob, who had never before worn a rain poncho, was surprised at how clammy he got despite the ventilation at the sides.

'I'm cold,' he told Carmen. 'Not cold but damp.'

'It's the plastic. Makes you soak from the inside out.'

The day grew longer. Their discomfort greater. His many years out of the saddle meant that his thighs and calves and backside, unused to the constant pounding, grew resentful and sore that much faster. Carmen teased him about it, reminding him of all that jogging and straining with barbells. But Jacob absolutely refused to think about the physical pains.

'You're not going to snuff my spirits, you know.'

'Don't want to, Leo.'

He whistled in the darker parts of the forest, listened to the beats and echoes of their small train. The horses stepped in small rivulets of rain water that ran along the root systems of trees, hooves clumping on the pine needles, the forest floor, crushed pine cones, breaking dead twigs and the tendons of ferns that bowed over the path.

Most of all, though, he heard her behind him, knew that she was listening to the same sounds.

Later they came upon a pair of hikers sitting on a log, boiling tea. A man and a woman, both in their mid-twenties, looking for all the world like pioneers. They wore the clothes of a century ago.

'Howdy,' said the man. He raised an open hand as they approached.

'Howdy.' Jacob had little enough of the rube in him but it seemed to be the way everybody in the country talked to each other, natural or not. The woman hardly looked up. When she finally did she smiled reluctantly, with a crowd of spade-shaped teeth. But Jacob could see it was the horses she resented. The way to traverse these mountains was by foot, the feet God gave.

He reined his horse to a stop. 'You on your way up?'

'On our way out.'

'How long have you been in the mountains?'

'Ten days or so . . . by the lake.'

Jacob nodded as if familiar with the country. 'Did you happen to see anybody on your travels?'

The young man's eyes twirled. 'It's unlikely there's been anybody up there all summer, or maybe even for years. This isn't prime hiking land. All the action's over in the coastal range.'

'I hope we didn't startle you with these horses.'

'It's a nice surprise.'

Everybody nodded.

'Would you like to join us for some tea?'

'No thanks. Camp is still a long ways in front of us.'

Then the convoy of horses moved wide of the log, splashing mud on the teapot but not upsetting the hikers at all. 'Have a good trip!' he called after them.

Both Carmen and Jacob waved without turning around.

They had not gone much farther along the trail, less than a mile, when Jacob suddenly became aware of a pain in his gut.

'I think we'd better stop.'

'What's the matter?' She didn't like the way he had put that. 'Maybe we should have had that tea.'

But Jacob didn't hear what she said, was already off the roan and running across puddles, wildly looking for a tree to hide behind.

'Jake!'

He grasped a tree trunk, moss and slime all over one side, and fairly ripped his jeans off, thrashing at the poncho to get it out of the way. Leaning forwards Jacob shoved his buttocks out behind as far as he could and hoped against hope that he wouldn't be shitting right into his underwear.

During the flight from Czechoslovakia he hadn't relieved himself in a toilet for months on end. He had begged old newspaper and always wore it around his chest, not just for warmth, either. Shit-stained undergarments had chafed him all the way to the Baltic. There had been no skin around his anus the whole time.

Now he had diarrhoea, badly, too. The loose-running, watery faeces spit and hissed out of him burning as it came, steaming onto the ground around the roots of the tree. There was nothing to do but wait for the next spasm. Patience . . . patience . . . Carmen calling him to see if he was all right. And that had been true in Poland, too – he had never been private in this ridiculous animal business of body expense.

It was such a small thing . . . a shit . . . so little to endure. *Think of the salmon*, he told himself, found himself laughing rather loud, thoroughly unable to move from his position, miserable and wet, yet somehow his good temper held fast.

'Thought you might want this.' Carmen lobbed a small roll of toilet paper in front of him, then walked discreetly away. She had even torn off the plastic, notoriously tough to do with this camper's requisition paper he later discovered. He wiped himself frantically, never minding the pain. Several times. No way to get completely dry. The rain had soaked the treetops and the leaves were dropping condensation on his bare buttocks.

(*Poland . . . Poland*. He had been hungry for days on end, dizzyingly hungry. He had been chased and bit by dogs, never knowing if they were enraged. He had been blistered, splintered, ulcered, scorched, and fevered to delirium. He had gone without shoes. But the only thing he remembered with horror was the chafing in his bottom hole.)

Now, though, it was only the rain on his bareness. It would wash away. All things did.

Carmen had made tea while he was having his ordeal. It refreshed him. It was sufficient.

They broke from the trees. Here was the fork in the river about which they'd been warned. Except that it wasn't exactly as they had been told it would be. There was a middle fork, as well. Had Colin told them straight? It was hard to think him mistaken. But maybe that was so.

'Or just forgetful,' Jacob added. 'So what do we do?'

The rain, weakening for some time, had by now stopped completely. Without getting out of their saddles they opened the map and tried to decipher the landscape, to pinpoint the spot on the compacting topo lines, while listening to the fearful noise of waters colliding past the forks.

Carmen's finger moved over where they had been. Then continued on. 'We should go left – almost straight west . . . must be what Colin said. The worst that happens is we come up some miles short and approach the lake from the south, instead.'

'If the drunk wasn't lying, the forest is impenetrable there. Didn't you tell me he said that?'

She pointed ahead. 'We can see for ourselves in a while.'

The sky was relenting. That grey bowl that had covered them all day was finally cracking apart. The highlands were coming clear, the trembling aspens jaundicing the hillsides as light began to flow.

Following the left fork they rose more rapidly now, their hearts growing lighter all the time, the spaces that they could see more vast, though not the mountain itself yet. Soon the river dropped below them through a gorge, black and spitting, its spray a thick cloud penetrated by these first beams of sunlight, a rainbow over the water constantly re-forming itself, the golden edge leading them to the mountain.

Patches of snow now appeared in crevices, although so blown and browned with dirt that neither Jacob nor Carmen knew right away what it was. Dark rocks everywhere, volcanic, in long files where ages ago they had dried. The soil nearly black here, with much less growth, no more bunch grass, hardier shrubs, small rubbery ones, lichens and moss on the rocks.

The sky drew further back. All of a sudden they began to see depth, grandeur. They came over the top of a rise and into a small, high-shouldered valley, had their first broken look at the mountains in cold majesty before them, the vault of heaven opening especially for them, the mountains resplendent in the dying afternoon light, icy, disdainful, mortally beautiful, white and black, barren as they both could see from here no more than a few hundred feet below timberline, the moraines and cirques of dead glaciers falling in long flights of scree that rolled endlessly downwards in a grey welcoming train. Snow whiter now, increasingly larger fields of snow in their view, some miles away still, deeply pocking the south and easterly faces of the three mountains that made up the range, various peaks, too many to distinguish which of the juttings and spires were spurs and which the great peaks themselves.

'That's the pass to the divide.' Carmen pointed to a slender passage in between the rock cliffs, water chutes coming down each side in long, beribboned falls not more than a foot or so across but three hundred high, wearing away the grey and black stone to unexpected layers of colour underneath.

'How much farther to camp?' Jacob wanted to know.

'Maybe two miles.'

'O.K.'

'Maybe a bit more, Jake.'

He turned around in the saddle and looked at her. 'That's all right, too.'

As they passed through the notch Carmen made him turn around to see where they had come from. The land rolled down for dozens of miles into the green, blue and black of forests, night beyond that, the river lost in the trees, hiding its convolutions under larch, spruce, Douglas fir, and several kinds of pine.

'It looks very different from up here,' he said.

'Now we're sure what all this is going to look like on the way back.'

'You know all the old tricks, I see.'

Carmen shook her head, gave away her secret. 'I've been reading a survival book with some care.'

'What would happen to your theory if it snowed, so that this whole panorama were uniformly white? What then?'

'I'd know where we were . . . . Real snow's not due for weeks, Jake, maybe a month. You don't have to start worrying.'

He wasn't worried. Nor did he believe Carmen knew anything about the bitters of snow and true cold. 'There was a trace of frost this morning in Chezacut, I think.'

'If it snows it snows. C'mon, Jake, ride. Just from sitting here for a minute or two you already look stiff and blue.'

'I don't know if I can take all this enthusiasm of yours.'

'You can.'

They descended into the orderly sprawl of the next valley, an emerald saucer suffused now in the honey-smeared last light, some ten miles long and half again as wide, the river a serpentine gold running calmly, coldly, alpine meadows marshalling it along on both sides in summer's final yellow made even brighter by the sunlight.

'Holy God, Jake!'

'What is it?'

'That's their mountain . . . that's *your sons*' mountain! No wonder they don't ever want to come down.'

In the very last (and nearly violent) throes of amber light, they saw the mountain itself come into view on their right, the white and black hand grasping upwards in the deepening blue sky, its three fingers massive and hoary with rillets of ice, plains of snow, angles of it etched in the brilliant alpenglow, reigning over this calm pastoral of high river, forest, meadows, its beautifully barren crown of dead rock poised in absolute stillness, its snowy locks as pure . . . absolute . . . absoluteness.

My sons . . . up there.

Both he and Carmen lowered their heads as the horses walked into the valley. The mountain demanded obedience . . . even reverence. For perhaps a mile they went straight on, to a fallen tree, where they reined to a stop in the moonlight.

The whole sky indigo. The moon risen. Bright darkness.

'Camp here? What do you think?' It seemed to him the perfect place.

Carmen hesitated for a moment, reached into her saddlebag to find a flashlight, pulled a dead branch from a tree to use as a probe.

'What's the matter?'

She rapped a few times on the log. 'Something's in there.'

He watched. Again she hit the log, harder now. Then prodded in the rotting heartwood with the stick's sharp end.

'Sssssssssss . . . .' It was a serious warning. The horses' feet were digging nervously at the turf.

'Leave it, Carmen, we'll find another spot.'

She poked again. The growl strained higher.

'*Stop it*, Carmen.'

'Let me just see what—'

It came at them, four short legs throwing the dirt and wood dust, two larger animals behind the first, brown fur sleek in the silver light, mouths open white, hissing, spitting, wheeling right towards Carmen's horse and then, as suddenly, away, high over the log and into the forest silence . . . while Carmen, thoroughly stunned, had fallen off her horse.

Jacob jumped down, fussed over her, checking her for scratches or any signs of a bite on her legs.

'Didn't touch me.'

He looked carefully at her horse's grey leg, too.

'Nor the horse, either, I don't think.'

'You're crazy. *Really you are.* You don't drive animals into a corner, especially in their own home.'

'What was it?'

He hadn't thought about that until now. 'Weasel, probably.'

Jacob helped her up. She was all right. And still wanted to make camp here.

'If you take the bags and tent out, I'll forage for wood.'

'Can you build a fire, Jake?'

It was getting colder rapidly and Jacob zipped up his parka, fluffed out the down. 'You're going to teach your grandmother how to suck eggs, are you?'

'Fire away, Jake.'

By the time he had collected enough dry wood she had already pitched the tent and spread their sleeping bags inside on the heavily coated plastic floor. 'We won't need any mats. The ground here is unbelievably soft, not wet, just soft – old wood and needles.' Carmen stuck her nose to the valley floor. 'It smells almost smoky.' She saw that he had gathered stones, too, stripped kindling, was now shaving some splints and paper-like strips with considerable mastery, and quickly, too.

'Why don't you just use some fire ribbon? You paid enough for it.'

'You know, young Carmen, I've kept a fire's spark going at peril of freezing to death – and without matches in my pocket.' He sprinkled dried grass and mosses over the first sputters, built his pyramid over the shavings quickly after, soon had a good fire going. Roaring high.

'Maybe you better get some water, Jake . . . for cooking with.' She gave him a collapsible bucket. 'The water's all right to drink, isn't it? We don't have to boil everything first?' Now she was asking the questions.

'No grazing stock up here that I can see. It's probably the cleanest water either of us has had for years.'

A few yards from the stream Jacob dropped to one knee, looked upcurrent. Frosted moonlight traced the river, gently flowing, bubbling low. He could make out the shape of some horned animal drinking. Reason told him the animal shouldn't be there, for there was little wind and the animal *must* have heard them or smelled them, or surely could see the firelight? Yet it was there, refusing to move.

There was another aspect to this presence, a distinctly human part: These meads and woods and mountains were filled with his sons. In some irreducible way these were *their* mountains and streams and animals . . . their spirits were here and he could feel them as certainly as he felt the cooling currents of air flowing over his cheeks. It was as if that creature drinking were one of his sons.

'Jake?'

Startled that her voice was right at his ear, Jacob slapped a boot into the stream. Now the animal raised its head very high, its silhouette across the night sky. Waited. Waited. Then it crept to cover amongst the trees. 'Move and speak softly . . . please, baby.'

She had discovered in her field guide that the animals they had routed were almost certainly a family of mink.

'Sounds likely.'

'If not mink then possibly marten . . . one or the other. It's not easy to see the differences in the book. The marten look a little larger.' She rubbed Jacob's neck. 'What were you staring at?'

'An animal came down to the stream to drink.'

Carmen looked up the river's twistings. 'There's something there now.'

They both watched in fascination as several creatures came out of the blackness, passed into the silver light. Caribou, they thought. And an elk, as well. Several mule deer. The animals drank and soon slid away, but Carmen and Jacob continued to watch till they found themselves staring into folds of dark and inanimate green. *The spirits of his sons indeed*.

'I'm ready for a belt of whiskey.'

'Drink while you cook,' she told him. 'You're chef tonight.'

'I'm always chef.'

He made her a camp version of beef stroganoff, melding

the dried cream into the still bright-sided pot, both of them thinking how unlikely it was to be eating something with that name up here, ten million miles from the Old World. Afterwards, still not full, they cooked an apple cobbler, also from the freeze-dried recipes. And they drank the last of the home-made beer.

For a short while after dinner the two of them sat around the fire, neither with the energy to get up and rinse out the pots, eating kits, forks and spoons. It had to be done, even though they had reached a point of exhaustion from which neither could return without sleep. Holding onto each other to keep each other up, they cleaned their supper plates in the bucket, hung the food out of reach in a tree sling, checked their appaloosa's tether.

Then they got into their bed, the two compatible bags zipped into a single, smooth bed, clasped each other's nakedness, he kissing her breasts under the raiment of countless stars and the moon's passage, both of them falling asleep right away while the last imploding crackles of the fire and the river's swift glide and the breathing of some creatures distant in the trees gave motion and rhythm to their dreams of peace without end.

Sleep, Father . . . deeply sleep.

CHAPTER 7

A soft pastel light began to refill the sky. Jacob Solomon, seeing roses, awoke. Then he slipped out of bed and passed silently from their tent into the roseate dawn of this gentlest morning he had ever known.

Thieves. In the bodies of magpies. Half a dozen of them were walking to and fro over the light frost, their emerald tails irradiated by the first lines of light spreading from the ridge of hills guarding the east end of the valley. They picked at the final scraps of last night's meal. One bird had

72

its beak all the way inside the large pot and, like Narcissus, kissed its shining image at the bottom.

The birds paid Jacob no mind as he pulled on his trousers, which the dying fire had dried the night before. His socks were dry now, too. Then there were his boots.

His boots.

Proper mountaineering boots. They had told him he would regret buying anything else. These weighed over six pounds and had no flexibility at all. Getting on and off his horse was treacherous with these bloody great boots. But they did transform a man. At Chezacut, over the saloon fire, on their last night there, he and Carmen had rubbed mink oil into the roughed-out leather. Yesterday evening, while watching those animals out to feed and drink, Jacob had fallen into the river. Some parts of him got wet, but his feet, his boots, stayed dry. He could almost *float* in these boots, he reckoned. What a piece of work was a modern boot.

Still unshirted, Jacob couched himself on the ground cloth protecting their tent, and slipped into his boots. He had to wrap the long red laces twice around each hand to have any chance of pulling the boots tight. It was a fight tying them. He'd ripped the base of his index fingers each time so far, and would continue to until calluses formed. His boots' stiffness made sure of that. Men had written odes to boots, great men; some had painted pictures of them, much humbler boots, too: Jacob celebrated his, they were his morning's hymn. He would wear them out if it took another lifetime, so proud was he of his boots. With his boots laced up he felt as if he were walking the path of the world, connected to other men, to all the shodden billions from whom he had spent a lifetime running away . . . he now in the ranks of men instead of amongst the deserters, Jacob standing upright in his boots and doing the most important work of the world, which was pulling weak, faint Love from the pit where she was constantly falling, snatching Love from the ten thousand hungry mouths of furious Death . . . .

Following his path of last night, Jacob went to the stream for his morning's wash. However sublime had been his

73

feeling last night under the rising moon and all the constellations, he preferred the way things were right now, a trace of ground fog overhanging the water, the colours softly focused, everything tending to the straw of the sun-soaked autumn grasses that tufted over the bank. A holy, blessed morning.

Unconsciously he began rubbing his wrist, looked down to see a mosquito sucking jocundly at his flesh. He brushed it away and the insect flew to the water's surface to digest what blood it had sucked. A trout rose and took the insect, eating the mosquito that had gorged on his blood. Nature's own Eucharist, just a long pipe of blood. At some point in his mountain voyage Jacob knew he would eat that trout and keep the blood of life flowing.

Only three magpies left now. At no point could Jacob recall seeing or hearing the others leave. But then he hadn't been watching them that carefully. Strange, cunning birds. The dark beak of one of them hit sharply at something in the grass. A cracking sound.

Jacob walked over to it. The bird had found a button of bright plastic, had rived it in half. Perhaps he or Carmen had lost it last night, but there wasn't an item in their gear that had such a button.

'Morning.' Carmen pushed away the insect netting and climbed out of the tent, fell right into a fit of yawning. '. . . just can't surface.' She yawned again, stretched towards the light. 'What time is it?'

'Almost six.'

'I watched my dreams all night . . . dreamt I was dreaming and just watched.' She was coming awake now, enough to see the white patina of frozen dew on the leaves. 'A frost for real, Jake. Except I don't feel it at all.'

'You're just hot from the eiderdown.'

'We say goosedown in America.'

'Goosedown.'

Carmen pointed at a magpie walking on their sealed provisions. It was the only bird left. 'I didn't know they have those green tails.'

'This race of them apparently does.'

The bird continued its business, indifferent to both of them. 'Very bold, aren't they?'

'Crafty. They're said to be thieves.' Jacob had been sorting amongst their breakfast pack for some coffee. The water on the butane stove was close to boiling. 'Go wash up before you do get cold. We should start riding soon.'

'It's too nice out . . . and too early.' She always had trouble getting started with Jacob, who never slept more than a few hours, but now she managed to straighten her body and begin her morning stretches while Jacob watched. There had been almost no time in his life for the simple pleasure of just watching someone he loved. It made him wonder if he hadn't been a little bit of a narcissist in his life, just a little too much of one.

During Jacob's meditation the last bird had taken position not more than a foot from the appaloosa, which was lying down and still asleep. Strange horse, strange bird.

An old farmer's story came back to Jacob about magpies and lambs, how farmers had to keep the birds away because of their fascination with anything shining, like buttons or coins . . . or eyes . . . .

The hot pan dropped right from his hand, turning over into the flame.

Banging. Sputtering. Startling the mare so she rose from her sleep, or tried to. It was enough. The bird had flown. And Jacob Solomon had saved the mare's eyes.

'What the hell happened?' Carmen came hobbling, half-dressed.

'Nothing.'

'Our breakfast is in the fire.'

'I slipped, Carmen.'

'You did *not* . You jumped. *Why?*'

'Because I thought I saw the evil eye.'

Carmen frowned. 'Don't kid around.'

'I am not kidding around.' He pointed to the horse, explaining what had gone on.

'Do we have to eat breakfast, Jake? Can't we just start?'

'It's probably a good idea to eat something.'

'Let's not. Let's just go.'

He looked at her. Thought. 'All right.' And within minutes they were astride the horses, heading west, both of them trying to recapture the small perfection which had flown away with the last bird.

75

They had begun the day's ride in their windbreakers, were soon down to work shirts, sleeves rolled all the way up. And it was going to get hotter still. 'How far is the lake?'

She had memorized their route by now. 'Ten miles or so.'

'That's not too bad.'

'Not if the country stays like this.'

Here the valley floor was nearly flat, the stream running cold and unperturbed in long, gracious undulations, skirted by meadow and game trails that followed the wide sweeps of river. They kept to the bankside path, content that the only change for some hour or two was the bird calls, songs and warnings, a dipper on the surface of the water, the booming of a large piliated woodpecker, which Carmen's field guide easily identified.

Still the heat held. Carmen let go her reins for a moment and pulled out her shirt-tail, undid the buttons to the bottom. Finally she took the shirt all the way off. Jacob made a bad joke about Lady Godiva but she waved it away without turning around.

She was riding lead today and he watched her from behind. She had real shoulders. A smooth, soft back. Then her sides just wasted away into the delicate circle of her hips. Carmen's skin was as it always was, rose and gold tones whether she took the sun or not, the same all year round, like a painting.

Once or twice, in very long runs along the bank, Carmen cantered her grey gelding, got several hundred yards away from him, the sun on her back, her yellow hair high in the breeze . . . painfully beautiful to watch.

'Don't go too far, eh!'

He called but she was already around a bend, wouldn't have heard anyhow. Jacob really wished she hadn't taken off her shirt. They had run into those campers yesterday; they might stumble on somebody today. Being shirtless might not embarrass her but it certainly would him.

Tied to the pack horse, Jacob plodded on behind. Very hot now himself, he, too, took off his shirt, though not without a shiver of anxiety. Other feelings, silly feelings. Shame. Vulnerability. It was not, after all, entirely out of the realm of possibility that they would encounter his sons here. What if they met her like that, Carmen just riding into the middle of their land as if she were alone . . .? they thinking she were alone?

'Carmen! *CARMEN!!!*' But calling was useless.

A little faster the pack horse behind would go. They trotted to a turning in the river, the trees sweeping away in a wide apron so that he could, for the first time all day, see right up into the massif. A much more chilling view today. This was a serious mountain. Its beauties very cold indeed, and dead . . . the endless business of rocks and snow in constant transaction, vertiginous chimneys of basalt and granite crumbling and re-forming, giving and taking . . . nothing more. And the first wind of the day flowing frostily down the mountainside, splitting his shoulders.

Some quarter-mile in front was Carmen's grey horse. Riderless. Jacob's heart beat twice out of tune. He trotted up quickly.

'I had to have something.' Carmen had dismounted, was sitting in the shade and munching on nuts and raisins and date chips, 'squirrel food' she called it.

'You'd better put your shirt back on. The wind's up.'

Although the sky still had its intense blue, the clouds were marching along more regularly now, and all had silver ribbing.

Jacob reached an arm down and she grasped it, let him pull her up. 'What's the matter?'

'You're soaked,' he said. 'Don't you feel it?'

The seat of her jeans was a ring of water. Carmen rubbed her bottom, looked at the ground. The turf was oozing. 'It's a goddam swamp here. I can't believe I didn't even notice.'

'Get on your horse and we'll find a dry spot.'

She showed some irritation. 'I'm not moving until I change my jeans.'

'Go on.'

There was another pair in the pack. Jacob stayed on his horse while she slipped them on. 'This is nothing more than a little overflow from the river.'

But it wasn't just that. For the next twenty minutes they tromped through the spongy grass, the horses throwing mud all over, up their own legs, onto their riders. Carmen frowned. Jacob, riding next to her now in order to keep out of her horse's slinging heels, asked what was troubling her.

'There was a marsh on the map.'

'So there was a marsh. There are such things.'

'It goes from here all the way to the lake.'

To which Jacob said nothing for a while. Nor were there the voices of birds any longer to distract, relax, amuse them. For some reason, whether it was the boggy ground or the time of day he didn't know, no birds would sing to them. Things had begun to turn around, despite the day's transcendent start – exactly the opposite of their first day out when, starting slow, it had grown to perfection. They must be, he thought, that much closer to his sons.

'Maybe we'd better try higher ground,' he suggested, 'get away from the river.'

'Can't be worse.'

So they followed a rivulet through the trees, going slowly, pushing branches away from each other's eyes. A Douglas fir, broken from the weight of winter ice, dragged its limp arms across the appaloosa's back, ruffling the mare. She screamed eerily and her voice echoed back at them from somewhere indistinct, through the growth straight ahead of them.

The trees fell away all of a sudden and they found themselves standing in snow and rock at the base of a long run of scree. Every way in front of them was up . . . white with snow in the shaded patches, boulders strewn, an endless field of rock – the rockfield Colin had warned them about. Dry ground, all right.

They were touching the toe of the mountain.

For a little while they rested in their saddles and ate the leftovers of lunch from the day before. The food had little savour now. Both of them ate slowly, grudgingly, chewing everything to a tasteless paste. In the end Carmen spit hers out.

'Not very good the second time around, is it?'

'No.'

The scraps in his hand Jacob, too, flung into the rocks, as far up the mountain as he could throw.

It had grown colder, the sky tarnished with grey spots, the sun often behind a cloud.

From nowhere, from out of the rocky field, a black bird appeared above them, circling slowly, eyeing them with a special care.

'Raven,' he said. He needed no book for that bird.

Neither of them moved while the bird was in view. They watched it maintain its near-flawless flight over the fan of the moraine. 'What'll he find in these rocks to eat?' Carmen asked.

'I suppose there will be mice, other rodents.'

'Rats?'

'Rats are everywhere.'

The raven's circles grew smaller and it seemed to fly slower, lower, finally breaking out of its pattern and descending cautiously into the rubble just about the point where Jacob had thrown his food. 'They're scavengers more than hunters.' Moments later the bird rose up, something in its beak, and flew straight up one of the long glissades of snow gullied in the mountain. Into the brightness, shaded brightness. And simply disappeared.

'My eyes are hurting a bit,' he said. 'Where are our sunglasses?'

Carmen took out both pairs, handed him a tube of sun cream as well. 'Maybe you ought to put on some of this.' She twisted the cap off for him.

'You, too.' He handed the tube back to her.

'The sun never does anything to me.'

'*You, too*. The sun is remorseless up here.'

All three horses were labouring very obviously, the footing more difficult with each step as they pushed farther into the fan of rocks. They were at six thousand feet, not so high that the horses should be seriously affected, but the boulder-pocked landscape was shelved so awkwardly that they found themselves going up and down as much as they were travelling forwards, trying to get across the immense field of snow and stones at the bottom of the mountain's great wash, the treeline well below them now.

There was water from time to time, all part of the mountain's plumbing that drained the fields of snow above. By the middle of the afternoon they came to a large stream, perhaps twenty feet across though shallow everywhere, just water over stone. It was Downton Creek, the central artery of the whole mountain aqueduct and the beginning of the river they had followed for two days.

Carmen paused, took a sight-line straight up the river of stone. 'What's that blue shadow?'

'Looks glacial,' he said.

'I told you Colin knows what he's talking about. And better than any goddamn map.'

A pebble fell in between them. Just a pebble. They turned to each other, both with the same thought, the same picture in their minds of falling rocks . . . rocks larger than houses avalanching down the wash.

But nothing more fell other than the light in the sky, and so they carried on as best they could, boulders looming over them on all sides and swallowing both them and the horses.

'How much farther, Carmen?'

'I can't tell anymore.' Her voice was tired. She had some kind of headache coming on.

'The altitude?'

'I don't know.'

'We'll make an early camp and you'll get some rest.'

'I just want to get to that lake.'

Jacob was reaching over to slap some encouragement on her flank when more stones fell, larger than pebbles. The mare shied. A little dust and grains of black, igneous rock poured down from an outcropping above them, as if rolled down by someone.

'Don't move.'

'It's nothing, Jake—'

'—*Don't move!*'

Jacob Solomon looked up into the afternoon sky, his eyes tracking all the hard angles. The wind whistled down, far sharper than anything up till now, shrieking through the piles.

'What is it?' No answer. 'Jake?'

Completely absorbed he prodded his roan through the maze again.

'What did you see?'

'Nothing.'

He was making her headache worse with all his circling and recircling. 'What was that all about?'

But Jacob wouldn't answer. And Carmen, for her part, didn't care anymore.

A few minutes later he awoke from his self-communion to find himself muttering, practising any speech that could explain at the first moment of contact with his sons just why he had come and why he was violating their sacred killing grounds and especially why in the company of a woman – he knowing they had all forsworn contact with women.

A bead of sweat gathered under Jacob's nose. For the first time on this trip he was a little frightened . . . his temples beat . . . he tasted metal on the back of his tongue. Perhaps he would have to mollify his sons, remind them of his newly won strength of mind, of body – if it came to that – and of his readiness to love the five of them. Did they understand? Did they hear? Were they even listening? *Are you listening, goddamn you????*

And anger drove out fear which had driven out Love. The same old game, even up here. Patience . . . patience for old men was his prayer, as his fearful meditation went begging to the rocks and stones and hard places enshrouding him in the mountain.

Come back, Love . . . .

'Tree-tops.'

They had both seen them at the same time. The boulders lowered and within minutes the two of them passed out of the grey, closed-in world that had entrapped them for half a day . . . following the creek, now on the dirt and sedge that ran along its side, frigid creek of turbidly bluewhite water ground by the glacier.

The lake lay several hundred yards in front of them, completely surrounded by very heavy tree growth, decidedly gloomier greens, no trembling aspen here, almost all broad trunks, tall trees, menacing, dense forest without light, more like the forests of the coast. Strange noises – the wind no doubt – followed them to the shoreline, a wind as salt-toothed as Colin had foretold. A ground of bitterness.

'Let's make our way farther west. Didn't Colin say there was a defile at the western end of this valley?'

'What's wrong with right here?' She was beat.

'The whole thing's a marsh. Can't you see that?' He contended with the impatience in his voice. Relented. 'Show me where you think we can camp?'

She led him through the trees a short way, to a brief opening some ten feet square. 'It's large enough to pitch a tent. What else do we need? We're off the boggy ground.'

'What's under those ferns?'

Carmen dismounted, clumped across the miniature meadow tracking several different ways. 'Just the forest floor.'

'Walk it a bit more.'

She did. There was a crack against her shoes. She and Jacob looked at each other. It was a short, small, dead but sharp tree stump that hadn't yet rotted away like the rest of the plant.

'We can dig it out.'

'That's a *tree*, Carmen, not a weed.'

'So we'll put the tent at the edge of the trees instead. What's so terrible about that?' Her eyes had no fire. 'Jake . . . I'm really whacked.'

Under his left eye that tic of his went twice. 'No birds, no game . . . the water is a funny colour . . . can't you see?' She shook her head. 'You won't find any fish in there. I'll bet my life on that. Utterly dead up here. The place stinks of sulphur.' He watched as Carmen sighed, slumped. 'If you want, we can walk around and see if there's a better site on the far side of the lake.'

'It's probably an hour around, Jake, maybe more.'

'There's more than an hour of light left.'

'I'm fucking exhausted!'

'Fine. Rest.' He got off his horse, would walk by himself.

She was beaten. Dirty from the marsh earlier on, dust from the rocks in her nose, mouth, eyelids, hair. Tired and dirty . . . Jesus Christ, dirty again. 'Hold on,' she called to him, he already high-stepping through the trees. 'Give me a minute to take a sip of whiskey and I'll go with you.'

'Why don't you just stay here.'

'*I'm coming.*'

They did things together. That's the way it was with them.

'Give me a swallow,' he demanded, reaching for the bottle.

'A sip.'

'A swallow.'

She stopped him with her hand. 'Hear that?'

A clicking sound, something like an insect, came from the shroud of trees.

'What is it?'

'Squirrels make a noise like that.'

'Only when they're mating.'

She hated when he was too precise. 'Who cares?'

But he did. Where there was squirrel there ought to be bigger game. Predators. And there were none here he was sure.

The lake proved faster to get around than she had thought. When they were nearly at a point opposite where they had left the horses, Carmen pushed her way towards the water until she could see the mountain framed expertly through the branches. It was unholy beautiful, the whole scene.

She was excited. 'This is our spot.'

'Don't sound so proud. You didn't want us to take this walk.'

They had emerged from the tree cover onto a platform of thickly matted grass, a place to sit and take in a perfect vista of the mountain and the treacherous wash they had earlier spent hours straddling. Even the trees at the far end of the lake were less baleful, more slender and spread farther apart: balsam and cedar and mountain hemlock for the first time, and much red alder. There was also a set of rocks at the water's edge, tiny waves lapping at their grey and smooth feet . . . and, if Jacob and Carmen had eyes to see, maybe water gods resting on them.

'We don't have to move camp here,' he told her, the two of them grasping hands and leaning against the rocks. 'It's good enough just knowing about this little crèche.'

'What was bothering you earlier, Jake? You saw something.'

'I saw my own fears, that's all.'

Her body pressed on his. 'We act like shits sometimes.'

Jacob wouldn't disagree. 'There's no wind at all this side of the lake. Curious, no?'

'Not so cold, either.'

The day hadn't lost all its brightness, even with a lattice of clouds woven across the western sky where the sun had just started its descent. The whole scene was yellowing, the mountains and snows, the lake and the trees, even the rocks where they sat were being gilt, alchemized into something golden and precious. She uncaked some of the mud from her shoes, dipping them up to the soles in the lake. 'I'm always so filthy.'

He sniffed cautiously. 'Hell may stink like this.'

'Have I ever told you about me and dirt?'

'Yesterday.' He smiled but well understood that for her it wasn't just a question of a few slivers of sod in the palms of her hands. It was a sense of some extraordinary sin she felt and which he only dimly understood, something to do with her lost child.

The lake seemed to be on fire. Just burning. Flames on the surface . . . Hell's top furnace.

Carmen was looking strangely at the water.

'I want to clean off.'

'You're exhausted.'

'But I feel better.'

'There's snow everywhere around the banks, so imagine how cold the water is.'

'With the wind down the day feels warm again.'

She could answer anything, but he found himself holding her back nevertheless. 'You can't go in.'

'How cold can it be, Jake?'

'Damned cold.'

'Not if I jump in and jump right back out again.'

'You're *not* going in.'

Carmen had freed herself from his grasp, was unzipping her windbreaker. 'Hold my shirt for a towel, would you?'

'This is ridiculous.'

She was already down to her shoes, though, and fast untying them. Naked right after. The Mississippi farm girl gone skinnydipping. Then she ran into the water up to her knees, higher, fell forwards and began to swim out towards the middle of the lake.

'In and out,' he called fecklessly. '*In* and *out!*'

Carmen kept right on going. A good, vigorous swimmer, she did at least have the sense to keep her hair out of the water, had pinned it up before slipping into the lake.

Jacob watched through secret eyes. For there was some shame here that he had hid from her, from everybody: He didn't believe there was another person in the world who knew he couldn't swim. Not a soul. He had sailed across the Baltic, through the North Sea, up the Thames, watching water the whole way. Terrified. He had just never learned how. And on the boat to America he had made it a point never, not once, to go anywhere on ship where he didn't know the direct route to his safety davit should the alarm be sounded.

He cupped his hands. '*CARMEN . . . PLEASE COME IN!!!*'

Hearing him, she turned away from the glowing mountainscape and waved. He returned the wave thinking that the lake, however shallow, was fathoms, full five fathoms or more, deep. She had been in for ten minutes already. She had made her point, over and over. She should come out. Right now.

Carmen's return was slower. As she entered the shallows, her breasts dazzling in the dark water, he could see there was a problem of some kind. He called nervously. She called back.

'The bottom's all muddy. I keep sinking.'

So she stopped trying to walk in and swam until the bottom scraped her back. Then came out, brushing the grey mud off her calves and ankles.

Jacob rushed to her and draped the shirt around her shoulders. 'You're blue . . . the proverbial blue. Just like a child.' He rubbed her arms, neck, lustrous shoulders. 'And frozen . . . my God!' The shirt too wet now to do more than brush water away, nevermind, he had already taken his own off and was rubbing down her thighs, rubbing, rubbing, drying . . . .

Carmen laughed mischievously. 'I can't feel a thing from my neck down.'

'Very smart, very smart.'

But he wasn't mad at her, of course, just as she wasn't quite so indifferent and impervious to the cold as she pretended to be.

'Enough, Jake. I'm warm . . . you're tickling. *Enough*.'

'Not until your skin has colour again.' He wouldn't let her go until she was entirely rid of her chill and dry as a sea-wanderer's biscuit. And when he had conviced himself she was he rose from his crouch, a world of smiles, and made ready to put his woman inside the red rainshell that fit over his parka. But she stood stiffly.

'Jake?' That voice was on the downside.

'What?' He thought for a moment she might have a chill somewhere inside, in her kidneys or liver, somewhere he couldn't get to her pain. 'What?'

'*Jake . . . !*'

From her eyes the gold had entirely fled, leaving them as cold, grey, inert, and cheerless as the frozen stones they had struggled across hours before, her skin still white despite all his ministrations, pale as the mountain's crown. Tension coiled its spring within him. He reached her up to her collarbone, clasped hard. 'What is it? What is it?' Fast and jittery. '*What?*'

No words issued. She pointed merely.

He turned back towards the lake, to where she was pointing. The sight stood his hair, all over his body, quite straight, and the thrill of absolute panic ran wild along every nerve.

Fire.

FIRE.

A thin column of smoke, blue in the bluing light, smoke trailing up and drifting easily eastwards in the prevailing winds. A fire across the lake where their camp was.

And at that moment Jacob Solomon knew that he, and she, should never have come into this world of fire, mountain, water, rock, and wind.

'Oh my God . . . .'

In silence, as taut as he, Carmen grew suddenly nervous of her nakedness and tore the bundle of clothes from his arms, jumbled herself into them, snapping them on as fast as her hands would move. Socks ripped in the pulling on, skin tore as she jammed her feet into her shoes.

Still no words went between them. One look, both pairs of eyes narrowed. He reached for her hand and held it.

'We're going back to the horses.'

'Let's wait . . . .'

'We've got no choice. Let's go.'

Jacob had to pull her for only the first step. She fell into his pace, quick as it was, right after. They made their way around the lake as they had come, breaking the same path again and just as noisily. The trees seemed to have grown much closer together, even more branches holding them back, shrubs, stripling hemlock and cedar grabbed at them maddeningly, maliciously catching the plastic of their anoraks and pulling loose the weave, some of the thicker growth scraping their unprotected hands and necks and even her cheeks no matter how hard they tried to hack the rapacious limbs away.

Some hundred yards or so from the camp they came to an opening in the trees. There were their horses, nibbling at the sedge grasses. Untroubled. Jacob and Carmen squeezed hands, locked them now and wouldn't sunder them as they pushed forwards into the forest.

They came to the last trees. The campsite was alive with colour through the branches, Jacob's eyes swirling after the bright movement, he sure he saw the movement. Sure. For one instant all his past rolled before him. Then he plunged through the final boughs and burst into the clearing.

Fire.

A fire. A camp fire, simple, burning brightly but well enough damped. Their tent up. Their bags unrolled and laid out for bed. A tripod set up for holding a pot. Every bit of their gear taken out and arranged as carefully as Leviticus. All waiting for them.

And nothing, nor no one, else.

Good night.

87

CHAPTER 8

Day 3.

A long and quiet night, unnaturally quiet. Neither Jacob nor Carmen slept well, each trying to hide his restlessness from the other but not succeeding. At least twice did that clicking sound recur, very close to their camp. So sure earlier it was squirrels, now Carmen didn't know what sound it was. A night bird, maybe.

'Jake?'

'Mmmmmm . . .?'

'My mind's racing.'

He could smell her anxiety amongst the bedclothes. 'Do your breathing exercises.'

Carmen sat up on her elbows, pulled back the netting, looked into the blankness. 'I can't see a thing.' The moon had gone down long ago and there was barely enough light to see the trees silhouetted against the gauzy night sky. From the ground looking up, the tree trunks appeared to be collapsing together, and ten times the size as during the day. 'The trees are falling.'

He sighed.

'I swear to God . . . *take a look!*' She half-believed her own fear.

Jacob leaned over, turned his head up and did look. 'Night and your imagination – that's all.' Perspective and proportion went all askew in darkness. That was another thing he had learned in Poland. Just hold on for the clear, sweet, reasonable light of day. The woods would be quite shrunk by then. But these *were* big trees in fact and not only in fancy, and they certainly did fall from time to time in the forest, sometimes right on philosophical heads.

'Try to sleep, Carmen.'

'Sleep yourself.'

They lay next to each other and stared upwards into nothing.

'What do we do in the morning?' she asked.

'Just exactly what we would have done in the natural course of things if there hadn't been a fire lit and waiting for us nor any of the other things they did . . . if *they* did them.'

'What was it we had planned to do?'

'To find them.'

'They've found us.'

'So they have found us . . . if it *is* them.'

They would only argue, so they stopped talking altogether. Neither got back to sleep, though.

After breakfast they spoke again. The sun hadn't risen for them. The lake fell under a fog and all that happened was that the sky got progressively lighter until it was grey. She watched him practise his orienteering with a liquid-filled compass.

'Suppose they don't come.'

'Oh they'll come, all right.'

'Maybe they've made sure we have a camp far away from theirs so they won't have to see you at all, Jake.' Agitated by all this waiting around, Carmen wanted to take a walk. 'If it's what they really want to do, they won't have any trouble finding us anywhere around here. They have already.'

'I don't want to go wandering around. I want to stay here.'

'Stop kidding yourself, Jake. Chances are they're watching us right now, could reach out and poke us if they were inclined.'

He just shook his head and waved his hand.

'Well I'm not standing around any more, I'll tell you that.'

She turned to go, and would have, but at the edge of their confine she tripped walking under the hemlock, fell head-long to the grass, knocking something over. Jacob rushed over, sure she had got caught in some kind of trap or snare. Next to her in the deep-swollen grass was a basket. And a dozen or more eggs, all different sizes and colours, against the green.

Jacob ran his hand, both hands, through his sage white hair, longer hair now, unshorn since he first had news of his wayward sons from Indian Sam. Was it possible? At least *five* times this morning Jacob had walked right by the spot where the eggs lay now, on his way to fetch water at the lakeside. No basket had been there and it would have been impossible not to have seen it. *Five times*. In learning to hunt highly-strung game animals, what stealth had his sons acquired? What diabolical cunning?

'A conundrum?' Jacob wondered aloud with her. 'Is that the idea?'

'Cat and mouse.'

Too frightened to face him, his sons must have supposed they would drive him and Carmen away like this. The lion snorted.

'Damned stupid kind of game.'

'Too late to use for our breakfast, too.'

Jacob leaned down and picked up the largest of the eggs. It was about the size of a goose egg, a cream colour with streaks of dirty brown, very likely Canada goose. Very heavy in his hands, he weighed it up and down. A dead gosling inside maybe, this late in the year it would be an old egg indeed. As would they all. 'Meaty egg, this one, must be over a pound of pure protein.' Four-hundred-fifty-four grammes of rotting, stinking protein.

Then his touch grew alert. He rubbed the egg in his fingers and found it remarkably smooth. Carmen watched him, curious now.

'What, Jake?'

He tapped the egg with his index finger. Lightly at first and then harder. Then sounded it with his knuckles. Squeezed it between his palms. Hard egg . . . and not from cooking. With all his might Jacob flung the goose egg against a large stone and the egg, sparking off it, flew at a low angle right into the lake. Egg? No eggs.

'Eggs, my ass!' Jacob knelt down and scooped the remaining stones in his hands, felt their depressing weight, crashed them down into the basalt rock at his feet, one jumping back right at Carmen and catching her flush on the kneecap.

'Culled stones, ornaments, tricks!' And all egg-shaped.

For a few moments he stood there fuming, unaware that he had hit Carmen. Nor noticing her limp.

'Where's that survival book of yours?' His voice had only grimness.

'What for?'

'I want to know more about the local flora.' That's what he said but he meant very specifically mushrooms and berries and edible roots and leafy greens and anything else that might sustain them. There had been a message in that false food. 'Would you just *bring* me the book, Carmen?'

Still uncomplaining of her knee, she fetched the book and left him sitting on the basaltic stool to read. But she could see he was hardly reading at all. A short time later he slammed the book. 'I want to get out of here.'

'Back to Chezacut?'

Jacob thought and thought. Distressed sorely. 'Let's just explore a little . . . *west* . . . see where we are, gather some berries, take our time. Not break camp . . . just spend a nice day, eh? Eh?'

She nodded and they fled from the lake as if fleeing the fall of a sparrow.

Once away from the lake they found the terrain was easier, the forest thinner; flat and striated rocks broke up the black trees, shrubs grew openly, unpropped, bracken and gorse, no meadows but at least, thank God, some open space to unclutter the mind, free the breath. And for the most part they had got rid of the fog, which seemed to be hanging only over the lake. Good news.

But bad followed close upon. At the edge of a shrubbed field, brilliant with yellow and purple flowers, the land fell over a ridge and plummeted away. They had come to the far western reach of the valley. Below them, some two thousand feet down, was a river coiling its way to the sea between the set of mountains they were in and the coastal range just across, the heights over there much taller than their promontory, peaks of eleven and twelve thousand feet that were snowbound all year, decked with glaciers like prize ribbons, icy romping grounds for climbers, dream-worlds, unutterably perfect cones, swansdown. Colin had been right again. No way out of the valley going west.

'We might scramble down with a rope and hardware but I don't think we'd stand much of a chance with just our feet and hands . . . do you?'

Jacob shook his head, reined his horse away from the cliff.

'We're trapped, Jake . . . we are.'

'Don't talk nonsense.'

'If we go south it's the forest. Colin told me we'd never find our way out, said he didn't think he could himself.'

But Jacob had nothing to say about that. They could always go home exactly the way they came into the mountain. He couldn't imagine what Carmen was imagining. Earlier he had overreacted; now she was doing the same. They needed to let go of this greasy pole of fear. 'We must have passed that elusive western defile . . . if there actually is one. I want to find it.'

'It's there, Jake.'

'All right then, let's find it.' A good distraction, and practical.

'Why would Colin lie about that and be right about everything else?'

The old drunk hadn't been right about everything, but he did not remind Carmen of that. 'Then we'll find it, won't we?'

And then what? he wondered. Steal up into their mountain when they weren't looking? If they *ever* weren't looking. Go up into their mountain? Madness. His sons would follow Carmen and him, ridicule them, try to make them lose their way. There was no running this time, not away from them nor towards them. *Stand ground*. That was the way. Screw his courage to the sticking place. But not run. The exits were closing anyway.

Blueberries. Mountain blueberries.

'Christ they're good.' Her mouth was fast running with the juice after Jacob had told her he was absolutely sure, book or no book, these were safe to eat. 'How could we have missed them on the way?'

'We have yet to find your defile, you'll remember.'

They had found about everything else, though. The blueberries grew shyly at the edge of the forest even when subdued in shade . . . retiring plants, never found in profusion. There were fewer salmon berries, always difficult to find, a larger fruit and less luxurious to eat, something like raspberries but on a rounder button, a duller red, nearly pink. The survival book had been clear about these, as well. The other sorts described, service-berries and soap berries and half-a-dozen more, they'd seen patches of. And, in the case of bear berries, Jacob was just as happy not to have discovered any. Emphatic warnings jumped out at him on the subject of accidentally happening upon a bear gobbling up berries late in the season.

There were mushrooms. Lots. What attracted him was a flat, ochre fungus growing on tree trunks, looking for all the world like French *cèpes*. Of these he was ninety-nine per cent sure the book had granted licence to pick, eat, enjoy. But until he and Carmen were desperate – if that time did come – he would pass them by.

Comfortless, ill-omened plans. Premature ones, too. He and Carmen had both been assuming the worst, perhaps wrongly, and the berries couldn't colour over their unspoken thoughts. Fear begat fear begat fear. The two of them had better find a way to calm down. They might even be welcome yet, to stay and speak with his sons just as he wished . . . and love them after.

'Slow down,' he cautioned. 'Eat too many of those and you're going to spend a full day on the pot.'

'As it happens, I haven't been able to go since we left Miss Lytle's.'

'That means nothing. It'll come sometime. You can go weeks without if you have to.'

'I'd rather have the shits.'

He remembered Poland, though. 'You may prefer the shits but diarrhoea will drain you . . . maybe even dangerously.'

Fairly warned, Carmen picked the choicest fruit, all the blueberries she could find, and a second bandana she filled with the blackberries growing tyrannically along the southern exposure of this small clearing.

Jacob was already mounted, sitting rigid in the saddle. 'Are you ready?'

'I can always throw berries at them.'

He waited until she was firmly on her horse and looked up at him. Her eyes had grown brighter, her colour much better for the mountain fruit, mountain treat. 'How would you feel if I went along by myself first . . . ? Talked to them, told them about you being with me, that we're married and happy—'

'—Let's go, Jake. They already know I'm here . . . and they won't care who I am.'

Jacob nodded. Then he turned his roan towards the hard trail that led back to the lake, and to the meeting these many years in the making . . . hoping the hide and seek was finally over.

Over the trees he could see the smoke again, lazy and blue. They had relit the fire. That was no surprise. Just what Jacob had told himself they would do. They were not such unknown quantities, his sons. This time they would be there, waiting.

The fire upset Carmen, however. He could feel her tense up. 'Just speak very little, Carmen . . . that's important.'

'There's nothing I'd want to say.'

'I've got a feeling nobody's going to talk much.'

Scampering. It was she and Jacob who had surprised this time. The two of them trotted quickly ahead and could see, for certain, several figures spreading away from their camp in different directions, caught out by Jacob and Carmen's return. Good. Maybe he'd put a scare into them. The sky, still foggy over the lake, was already darkening towards night. One distinct flash in the trees across the lake, much too quick to tell which son . . . pebbles were falling amongst the moraine rocks where others of them had leaped. Sons. Spirits. Vanishing from him and her.

From where they stopped to dismount the camp seemed unchanged. Just the fire lit, burning much smaller this time. Some hidden felicitation there, no doubt . . . like that breakfast of mountain rock in a country eggbasket.

They went on.

Carmen stopped dead. Tried to stop him.

The mare. Of course. The mare.

Oh.

The appaloosa was on the ground a few yards beyond the fire, an arrow in its head . . . the appaloosa, its stomach cut open from the neck to the rear legs, its guts everywhere all over the camp, every pack opened and the blood of the animal poured into everything, their gear out of the packs, bags, parkas, rainsuits, food, ponchos, fuel, toiletries, rope, water jars, shovel, everything, ice-axe, everything, everything, extra clothing, first-aid kit, everything, everything, everything covered in blood, thick and stinking, blood and intestines and faeces, everything, like the leavings of a massacre wherein the goods themselves were the enemy, all horrible and putrid and left to stink in the black Canadian autumnal wretched mountain air.

And on the fire roasting, the heart of the beast, still pumping . . . oh God in Heaven pure . . . still beating with life.

He tried to walk, tried, struggling forward, his arms raised above his head while he sank deeper and deeper into the bloody turf with each step, into a fit of fainting, a sickness, his stomach already taut and retching once the smell of that blood and offal hit his nose, spewing his vomit towards the cursed mountain, still walking as if trying to reach those who had fled, his fists flailing and beating the air, weak as he was ready to beat them once and for all, to do it, to do it . . . Jacob hearing laughter and mewing and deep groans of hatred as he went out, and not sure if it was his own gloating or that of his sons . . . .

He had turned red-faced, had actually fainted from anger. It took Carmen several minutes to bring him around. With a bandana wet in the lake water she wiped him as free of his vomit as she could manage. Pressed the cold cloth against his forehead and cheeks and old neck, pressed until he made a few sounds, then rocked him back and forth, back and forth.

'Let me up.'

Pushing her away and himself to a crouch, Jacob looked around, took in everything through hardened eyes, saw the carnage by the dying firelight and the few granules of daylight remaining.

'I do not believe what I see. I do not believe this.' He wouldn't let her touch him. 'I wasn't born to see this.'

Jacob began to curse them then, in low, currish growls and snaps, in a language she couldn't understand, though she could make out the rancour without knowing the words, the rage and implacable bitterness, primitive, primal, execrations repeated by fathers and sons over generations out of mind.

Like lamentations and abominations.

The oaths wound themselves down to foul breathing, then silence for a long space. Finally Jacob forced himself to stand up, shakily, like a man unwilling to walk again.

'I want to clean this foulness up . . . .'

The sky was a uniform, lightless blank. 'In the morning, Jake, when we can see what we're doing.'

'I'm doing it *now*.'

'We can't see.'

'*We can see*.' He wiped his chin. '*I can see in this dark.*'

She looked into the last of the fire, thinking that was what he meant. It would need more wood. But he hadn't meant that at all. He would see by the light of the fire within him.

Together they toiled, managing to scrub everything clean of the blood and the rest of it, to lay everything out to dry except for those things, food mostly, that had been ruined beyond salvage. Now, in the night's fall, the insidious fog settling itself once again over the lake like vaporous ice, its thousand frigid fingers touching everything, obscuring all, anaesthetizing all, Jacob and Carmen faced a long and cold night without any extra clothes, without sleeping bags; even the tent was of no use in that, wet as it was, it would now convect moist currents around them for hours, or even all night long . . . still they erected it and hoped the nylon would somehow ventilate, though in the thickening mountain mist there was little chance of that. Cold night coming. Cold . . . hungry . . . night.

Neither of them talked about the food.

Neither knew what to do, what to think about that, no, for they now had nothing to eat as all their provisions had been opened to let the mare's blood in, every package fouled, every can, even the sugar and salt and condiments, even the *empty* jars had been filled with ritual blood.

Exhausted, stupefied, desolate in spirit, Carmen and he sat down by the basalt rock and watched the fire crackle and sputter out.

96

'What about tonight?' She had to clear her throat, the damp air had congested her voice box. 'What the hell are we going to do tonight to keep ourselves from freezing to death?'

His head shook, twitched in reflex. He put his hands to his nose and pressed the nostrils together. 'I can still smell the blood.' He snorted the air again. 'It's still there.'

'You keep talking as if you're the only one suffering.'

'They're doing this to me, not to you.'

'I happen to be here in the middle of this goddamn mountain with you.' She ground her hands into the mountain soil, covering over the telltale tracery of dirt-creviced red in her palms. *Is it going to freeze tonight?*'

'No . . . I don't think so, not with this kind of fog cover.' Jacob reached out and touched her hair. 'I know you're here with me. I haven't forgotten.'

'All I want you to do is to settle up with those stupid fucking sons of yours, one way or another, and then we can climb down off this mountain.'

'That's all done, Carmen . . . settled. My account rendered . . . right down to the last hair.'

'What does that mean?'

'Come the first light of dawn, we're leaving. I don't think it was wrong that I came. If I hadn't . . . well, anyway, I have. It's done. For good. *Done*.'

'So you think, do you, they're just going to let us leave, *just like that*?'

Jacob smouldered for a while. '. . . done.'

Carmen got up. 'O.K.' Brushed needles, leaves, moss off her wool shirt. 'Let's throw some kind of bed together for tonight. I'm tired of talking. And it's getting cold.' She saw his lids grow heavy. 'Don't sleep yet. Your eyes are rolling.'

Using their ponchos and the rainfly and whatever else they could improvise, they managed to build a rough bed over the ferns with branches gathered of spruce and yellow pine. Then, for the rest of the night they locked themselves in each other's arms and tried to sleep, dreaming of heated rooms. And by their bed, within easy grasp of Carmen's free arm, was the ice-axe.

Unlike Jacob, Carmen had other ideas about the five

wild men out in the woods, about what they might be capable of doing to this hoary old man, innocent but caught in their design of blood.

He slept. She, as tired, did sleep some, too.

In the middle of the night Carmen awoke from her light sleep to the sounds of slurping, grunting, the smell of unclean animals. Her hand tightened on the axe. She awoke Jacob.

'Something's eating the mare.'

Jacob pushed the boughs away.

'Jake, what are you *doing*?'

He was up to a crouch.

'Stay here. They're scavengers. Even if you chase them away they'll just come right back.'

'I'm not going to let anything eat that horse.'

Now she sat up, too. 'Take this.' It was the axe. 'Who knows? They might be rabid or something.'

'Give it to me.'

Hardly had Jacob got to the edge of the campsite when the furious eating all of a sudden stopped. The beasts, whatever they were, had heard him mincing over twigs and pine cones and dry grass. The wind out of the north was slight and carrying his scent away from where he knew the mare's carcass to be, but it wouldn't be long before the animals picked up his smell. In the interim he stood perfectly quiet. They began eating again, ripped much harder at the horse's flesh now, glutting themselves, snorting at smaller beasts who had gathered around for a share, the forest he had once thought dead now stuffed with carnivores of every kind, carrion eaters, vermin.

It grew so uproarious around the mare that Jacob hesitated to jump in, thought it might be dangerous to break up that kind of food frenzy. In the night sky the very faintest tissue of moonlight behind the mist made it possible for him to see the treetops, and about where the mare must lie, the swirl of eating animals. And one set of green eyes . . . looking at him. He could sense a long body stretching out behind those eyes, eyes luminous in the near-total darkness, but he could actually see nothing of it. The snapping and ripping stopped. More eyes turned on Jacob.

'Dogs, Jake.' Carmen was breathing into his right ear. She whispered as low as she could but in the forest night all the creatures heard.

'Coyotes, maybe . . . wolves.'

'I've got the flashlight.'

'Don't, for God's sake, *don't* turn it on.'

'They'll freeze if I point the light at them. It confuses them.'

'*Don't.*' Fear gathered in cold sweat under his moustache.

'Why not?'

'*I don't want to see.*'

She sighed, rested her chin on his back and waited for him to decide what to do.

Suddenly he screamed, bellowed, and stood high in the air twirling the axe menacingly over his head as if he, Bellona's bridegroom, could scare them off by this kind of pretence. The eyes were still there. He cried again, louder, this time a cry to curdle the blood. And took two crunching steps, lunges really, straight towards the many sets of eyes and dim, hulking shapes.

It was enough. The animals, all of them, fled in panic right into the night, some few so terrified that they landed in the water before splashing away up the creek, others to the rocks, more to the trees, the forest, the safety of blackness.

'The light *now*!' he screamed at her.

She turned it on and there was the mare.

And a lone wolf. Calm he was. Eyes green and cold as the eyes of a saint. At the edge of the trees, at the edge of the light beam, in a moment gone, slipping effortlessly into the oblivion around them, still close by but unseen and unheard.

Jacob approached the carcass. His lungs were flat from his yell and charge, his breathing unable to hold the air, sounds of beasts still bounding away, some going farther than safety . . . going and going to the vanishing point.

He saw the bloody, membraneous hulk. Carmen came up behind him, held him around, their stomachs tight, gullets stuck.

'We're going to bury this horse.' He barely whispered.

'They'll only dig her up and eat her anyhow.'

'Let them dig her up. We'll bury her deeper . . . and deeper.' His voice rose, stone grating on stone. 'And deeper and deeper and *deeper*, but *nothing* is going to devour this poor stupid beast while we are here . . . you understand . . .? not even after we leave,' he added. 'Not even then. Not over my dead body.'

Oh she understood. Here they were in the middle of the mountain, surrounded by a madness which she could comprehend only in the merest part, and Jacob Solomon was still struggling to pull the world into form and shape, to teach, to remind everyone, every beast and every flower and every stone, of God's intended order – those rules for living which all the dumb victims of Creation seemed not to know, only he knew, only Jacob Solomon. She loved him but thought he was a fool.

'Yes, Jake.'

Carmen spoke this with resignation, then stuck her golden hands into the earth near the downed and partly-eaten mare. And for the better part of the night she dug away with those small, precious spades, he with the ice-axe, making a grave amongst the complicated roots of the hemlock where the mare had fallen, in this forest where Carmen knew very well – whatever else he wished to believe – she and Jacob were dismally, mortally trapped . . . .

CHAPTER 9

The fourth day broke unnaturally silent over the lake. Dawn already far gone, Jacob and Carmen slept on, arms entangled. Sunny and clear. Insects. The horses' grunting woke them both.

Jacob bolted up. He could see nothing moving, nor could hear anything but the horses pawing the ground. His watch had stopped. Carmen, too exhausted to get up, blinked her reddened eyes at his broken watch and nodded, no words needed: The time was whatever it was . . . the time was now.

After lighting a fire he filled a pot with water from the lake, set it over the stones. Then took a rag and did his best to clean her hands, bleeding and raw from digging half the night. Her fingers wouldn't uncurl, the hands cramped. When the water was hot enough Jacob propped her against the hemlock tree and set her ruined hands into the bowl to melt the spasm while he got to work elsewhere trying to reconstruct their camp.

With indefatigable industry Jacob dried all the gear that they had bathed clean of the mare's blood in the descending darkness the night before. He worked like a man possessed. Everything had been tossed along the shore after rinsing and left haphazardly while they slept. Now, having made rows and stacks of everything, all of it folded and creased fastidiously, Jacob walked up and down amongst the lines, a general marshalling his troops, bringing them to parade. What they had packed into the mountain would go out exactly as it had been, clean, fresh, functioning, perfect.

The nylon emergency cord had disappeared, so he improvised a hanging line out of the guys for the tent and drooped their sleeping bags over, distributing the down fill evenly. The parkas he dried in the same way. A little wind had come up earlier, now it turned southerly so he retied the line in order to catch the freshets directly, like tacking a ship, and the wind sweetened their gear that much more quickly.

Jacob Solomon was getting it done so they could get gone. And more. Cleaning this way helped him to keep his self-control, his mind orderly. He was an old man who feared madness after what he had seen last night, and felt himself just holding on by his ten fingers, no more sure than that.

Carmen wouldn't say so but she was hungry. He knew that. Jacob had salvaged a little bit of food – some beef jerky and a parcel of dried fruit – but even with the slaughter washed away in the stream he still felt everything was tainted. The smell of horse flesh, blood and flesh, was in the food and in his head and there was no way to extract it from either.

101

It was two days back to Chezacut, going down the way they had come up. If necessary they could make that without any food at all. Water was plentiful, free-running everywhere, and it alone would sustain them. In fact they could go five or six or even more days like that, as long as they could keep warm and not spend too much energy moving around.

Two days by horse. By foot it might be another matter.

Suppose they tried to steal the horses, those sons of his? They might do that. It was definitely *not* out of the question. *His* sons? Jacob smiled bitterly at the idea. They were somebody's sons, but not his. That Viking, his dead wife, had wanted them. Let them be hers, those bastards . . . the cruel, marauding, barbarous horde of them. Or maybe the Indian's claim on them was the right one.

But if he and Carmen really were forced to walk out? How long would it take them? Even without straining at all he could feel the calories burning off rapidly at this altitude. They would need some *real* sustenance then. And suppose they had no choice but to return by the forest Colin had warned them of . . .? or to scramble down the cliff face at the western end of the valley?

Could he expect to walk out, anyway? In the two short hikes they had taken, around the lake and then yesterday near the valley's edge, Jacob had done badly in his boots . . . his special boots. Now he wished he had worn them a little more before venturing into the mountains. What had happened to the moleskin? Without that to patch his blisters and the rest of the hot spots breaking out all over his tired feet he had no idea how he could make the – *how many?* – thirty or forty or God knows sixty miles out of the mountains if they were forced to take a detour. Anxiously Jacob broke into the neat piles he'd made, desperate to find the foot dressings. Not here, not in the first-aid kit or repair kit, not in the plastic bag of miscellanies. It had to be there but, like the nylon cord he had missed earlier, it wasn't. Nor could he remember seeing the bandages . . . not since – good God – not since Eddie Bauer's in Seattle. He needed protection from these boots of his – *from his own boots*. They were attacking him at a thousand little points. He'd

102

wind up doing something serious to his feet, permanent damage . . . and here he was careless about the goddamn moleskin!

Jacob did what he could to rally himself. It was summer still, thank God, warm enough. They'd walk slowly. They might get hungry past hope but they could make Chezacut. Carmen was not going to be done in by anybody and he certainly wasn't about to let anything happen to her.

Just as long as the weather held. Or if there were a snowfall that it didn't blanket the land or stay more than a day . . . or two days . . . or freeze so they couldn't walk at all.

And what would happen to Carmen if something grave happened to him, if he broke an ankle or leg in the snow? Who would rescue them? Nobody even knew what direction they had taken out of Chezacut except for that miserable, black-faced drunk who would be way too deep in his stews ever to worry about alerting a search party.

His mind was running now, tripping helplessly on things unknown. And running into grizzly bear. They couldn't be more than twenty miles from the borders of Tweedsmuir Park where, Jacob remembered, hunting parties went after grizzly because bear were so thick on the ground up there. *Trophy grizzly.*

Fear was curling around his legs. His arms. The insects swarmed in front of his eyes, sedge flies of some kind, smelling him, licking him as if getting a first taste.

And then Jacob Solomon finally began to realize it was not just a question of surviving this mountain trip comfortably. It was altogether different. It was a question of surviving it at all.

'How are your hands?'

Carmen shrugged. Her hands were not well. And she was limping from the bang on her knee.

'I have a little food,' he said, 'and you ought to eat.'

She shook her head. Pride shook it for her.

'You have to eat something.'

But there wasn't any way he would be getting her to eat now. Her royal neck was stretched towards the mountain, her eyes fixed stonily on the moraine, up the stream bed

103

towards the endless juts and frets and spires hiding the glacier. 'They're coming.' Carmen sat propped against the tree, spoke without feeling. She pointed at the distant rock pile. 'They're crawling this way . . . over the rocks.'

He couldn't see. Didn't believe she was seeing anything more than her own fears.

'Just keep looking.'

Yes. Five distinct shapes discernible, far away, coming closer. And on foot. Jacob made a quick calculation. 'They'll get to the lake in twenty minutes, maybe half an hour.'

'Well then we've got the time, don't we?'

Too stunned to think his sons were finally going to confront him, Jacob at first didn't mind her. But then he glanced suspiciously. 'Time to do what?' No answer. '*Time to do what?*'

'To leave, Jake. We've got horses and they're on foot.' She watched his mouth turn down meanly. 'Let's just go.'

He had been leaning over her but now stood up to his full height, brushing the pine needles and grass off his pants. His white hair and beard glittered in the strong, unfiltered mountain light. Ripped off his sunglasses. He wanted to make sure she could see exactly what was in his eyes.

'I am not running away from those bastards . . . never again . . . *never.*'

'That's the way you told me they talk, Jake.'

'Maybe but that's exactly the way it is. I won't budge.'

'Then why have you been telling me for the last four years that I matter to you? What's it going to be, Jake? Are you going to get me and you out of here or play their goddamn macho games instead?'

Their eyes grappled. The world's weary body was weighing down on this single square of turf, the point beneath their feet a crossroads.

'You know *you* said last night we were going . . . *you said it*, goddamnit!'

But he just moved his head back and forth.

One tear swelled in her right eye, refracting the sun like a jewel. She wasn't a woman often giving to crying and fought it now. But it made her whisper. 'They're going to kill us, Jake.' He didn't hear. '. . . kill both of us.' He hadn't heard and she knew then there wasn't any way that he could have. She, after all, had once abandoned her own child. There was no mortal way in the world she could now make him do the same thing.

So Carmen got up and stood next to him, put an arm around his waist, laid her soft hair on his shoulder. Kissed his neck, wishing to God she could just seep into his skin. She was crying.

'You have it all wrong, Carmen . . . lovely Carmen . . . I'm not worried at all about the manliness, me against them and all that. Maybe I was at the start of this trip, but not now.' He grasped her feverishly with both hands, strangling her wrists. 'I just won't believe they hate me. I try to imagine their hatred and can't *bear* it. I made them. My loins shuddered for them. They grew right out of my flank . . . do you understand what I'm saying . . . *I can't bear it!!*'

'Ssssshhhhhh.'

'BUT DO YOU UNDERSTAND ME???'

'Tell *them*, Jake . . . just tell them.'

Then he placed Carmen sitting down against the hemlock again, seeing she was faint and pained, told her not to get up when they came into camp, not to move at all nor say anything. The two of them waited without speaking, the horses growing more and more uneasy . . . waited under the black shade of the forest until the trees trembled and the boulders of the wash seemed to loosen.

'Where did they go?' They had disappeared below the level of the stones and for an instant Jacob wished they might never come.

'Behind you, Jake. They're behind you.'

He spun around and there they were, all five, in a ring.

Pity drove out the anger he had been feeling, whipped it away into the hills. Jacob groaned to see his sons so.

They had clothes, of a sort. Most likely what they had originally gone into the mountains with. Wool jackets, tartaned MacGregor, jeans, hiking boots. Of a sort. Tattered and ripped and frayed and begrimed and bloodied and scorched . . . not by use, oh no, but ritualistically rent . . . hated garments.

105

All his sons, their lustrous hair he remembered as ginger and brown and nutmeg and black, now hardly hair at all, uncropped year after year, straggling and pulled at . . . beards wild and stuck with food or just dirt and bits of trees they must have gathered as they walked, and sand and God knows something that looked like it might be flecks of their own shit picked up some way and just left there to rot. Their skin aged and calloused and badly scraped and cut in places, still bleeding, wasted under the skin, fatless, sinewy and strong perhaps but so wasted, bodies mortifying right on the bone, the five of them hardy enough to have survived at all but ill, battered, diseased, abused, ruined of their beauties and their youth utterly blasted away.

They had certainly, and swiftly, and completely lost every precious square of sense. His sons were crazy. They had made a Holocaust of their own.

No greetings.

Father looked at sons again. And again. Nobody would speak first. He wondered if anybody would ever speak. He searched for a single, apt question, something that might pry open their darkness and let him at least see what was in there – not disturb the darkness, God knows not that – just get a glimpse of the worst.

'Why did you kill my horse?'

The question passed slowly before his sons like a moving target in a shooting arcade. But none of them seemed to register it. He pressed on. 'You slaughtered that horse for no reason.'

'We killed only one.' Eric's voice had no tone, no middle to it, as it drummed over the stones. He was the oldest, had once long ago been the best of sons. 'We could have killed all three.'

The hatred was palpable. Jacob didn't understand it, never had. They were possessed of a hatred towards him way out of line with anything he had ever done. 'I want to know *why* you killed the horse. Was it because it was *my* horse? Was it something only to do with the horse? or something else? *What*?'

'We left you two horses to get off this mountain.'

Eric again. Or somebody impersonating Eric. It was like trying to have a conversation through a periscope or trick mirrors. He was talking to people who seemed to be there but who really weren't. These were the effigies of his sons.

'Why did you light the fire?' He waited for any one of the five to speak, to make any gesture at all. 'Why do that and lay out all our things?' Again he waited in vain. But he would not stop trying. 'Why kill the horse? and then ruin our gear with the blood of it? Why?' Still won't answer? 'Why aren't you talking to me right now? Because we go nowhere until the bunch of you says something about all this. So speak . . . .'

It was useless, as Carmen had promised it would be. She had known.

But he couldn't leave it at that. They were going to have contact, touch at some point, he and his sons. He would not go home without it. 'If you don't want to talk what are you doing here? You came to us . . . down off your mountain to see us . . . to see me. You've followed me for days now. You want something of me. What?'

'You had two days to get out of here.'

It was Mark who spoke. Black Mark. In his son's hair Jacob saw something like a comb or clasp holding the broken black strands. And those mockery eyes, raven-like. Jacob sensed that their transformations weren't quite complete, not yet, there were things here he could recognize and remember, the obscure malice, unexpressed anger, ancient grudge. Maybe if he irritated them enough he could tease out the old patterns, make them talk to him, however bitterly. Even though their unnerving silence had settled over them like dust on the eyelids of the dead, there were smiles behind their beards and Jacob was sure he could hear them. So he harangued them again and again on the theme, chipped, poked, pried, picked at the rind until he touched the sweet and nervy flesh inside—

'—*Shut up!*'

Eric nodded at his brothers, uttered something to them in Indian babble, more grunt than speech. What he said got Thomas to go towards their father with a basket, of a kind with the woven one that had held the stone eggs. An animal

107

skin covered the top. One more grunt from Eric and Thomas pulled the skin away, heaved the basket at Jacob's feet. A chine of beef oozing blood hit Jacob's boots. A rough cut of meat, slivers of spine in the marbling. And a thick stink that Jacob smelled right away.

'Fr-fr-freshly killed.'

The one farthest away from Jacob laughed. As big as the trees, still sprawling, Bobby had managed to keep his bulk unshrunk. His curls ran down below his shoulder blades from a crown now entirely bald. His eyes mere wrinkles under puffing brows. 'Haven't had fresh horse for fucking years, old man.'

'You *bastards*.' The disdain flew from Jacob uncontrollably.

Now more laughter, not just Mark and Bobby, all the rest were sniggering. Ridicule. This was what they had wanted him for.

'Eat . . . *eat*. You gotta be hungry.'

'*Eat!*' All of them echoed their fat brother, all as giddy as he. '*EAT!*'

Jacob grabbed the meat and slung it into the lake, not in anger but as a way to stop his anger . . . difficult to find the words for what feelings were strapping him . . . wanting to blow apart the whole infernal world of guilt rotting inside him that was bursting to come out . . . yet his patience held things in.

Let them laugh at him. *Let the stones howl*. Let it be so. He had climbed their black mountain as Love's own missionary and could endure the flouting and hissing. Love could help him do that . . . could . . . patient, never-faulting Love that suffered long and was not easily provoked nor puffed up, nor lost its grip ever. He would speak with the tongues of angels, even if they didn't want to hear he was sworn to speak. And would.

'This self-hatred – because that's what it is that got you up here – is killing you, you know. I've come to see all of you . . . maybe help you to break out of here.'

They jeered and crowed but he was going to have his say.

'. . . however pathetically meagre my care for you was when you were little, however much you resented it, never-

108

theless that's the way things were. Nature made a crazy choice of me as your father, maybe, but you were *my* seed, my sons, and whether you like it or not you'll always be my sons. You can't disinherit a father. Nor I, you.'

He was warming to his speech. They had turned silent, sullen. Jacob thought they were finally listening, though he was dead wrong.

'And you can't run away from me by coming up here and playing Indian. I won't disappear with the air . . . not even at twenty thousand feet up.' He was prophet at last in the country of his sons. His speech grew hotter. 'Do you know what you look like? Eh? Do you have *any* idea?? You look at each other, don't you? Each of you must have aged a dozen, fifteen years since I saw you . . . *more*. How long do you think you can keep this charade up before you kill yourselves for real? Jumping off a cliff or starving or gangrene or God-knows-what? That *is* what you're going to do if I or somebody else doesn't get you to climb off this fucking hilltop! I'm your father! Can you hear? *I'm your father still!* And I'll be *goddamned* if I'm going to let you five die up here! *Do you hear . . .? I WILL NOT LET THAT HAPPEN—!*'

The lion of Judah stopped. He had been roaring.

And the five of them? Jacob looked.

'Can you hear me?'

No answer.

'Do I make any sense to you?' Gently. 'Tell me.' Gentler.

No answer and no likelihood of one ever.

They stood in a circle, eyes as blank as the white sky. This was all there would be. All by himself Jacob had been speaking and speaking, feeling and feeling, but nothing came back at him save a distant, hollow, humiliating silence.

He might as well never have come.

These weren't his sons any longer. He had pulled the cords that he thought bound them together and found only slack. They were not his but the mountain's.

And he was sorry.

Requiescat. He would leave them and love them after in silence.

Carmen stood up. She walked some yards forwards to where Jacob was, came next to him and put her shoulder against his. He had almost forgotten her. Now he kissed her on the forehead.

'Cheep . . . cheep . . . cheep.'

That was the insect sound they had heard around the lake their first day here, which Carmen had told him was a crowd of squirrels. His sons made the sound. It would have been them before, as well.

'Cheep . . . cheep . . . cheep . . . cheep . . . cheep . . . .'

The sound of a kiss. They had, his sons, heard Jacob and Carmen kiss. This was their imitation. And it got louder.

More vulgar, too. Obscene. Seeing Jacob kiss Carmen had stirred a primitive sexual envy.

'*Cheep . . . cheep . . . cheep . . . .*'

Carmen pulled at his arm, as if he should turn around and go with her, just go away, give his back to his sons and leave the camp. Jacob's eyes, though, were transfixed on one of his sons. All of them were squealing the same note, all his sons, even Thomas without the trace of a slur or stutter. One was drooling, though, his eyes bankrupt of sense, his whole face contorted. He led the others in making that sound. Jacob had heard it once before. It was the scream of a double child, an infant split in two by pain. They had sung it at that speech convention. It was his poor, poor, demented son, his Douglas.

Jacob Solomon's heart fell away.

He stumbled forwards, out of Carmen's grasp, went up to Douglas, Douglas like a lost bird unable to stop its nervous call. He moved to within inches of that spitting mouth. 'Speak to me, Douglas . . . *please speak.*'

And to Jacob's surprise Douglas's mouth circled like an imbecile's, lips cracked and fleshy, and a single word dribbled out over his ginger-coloured beard.

'*Daltsha'n.*'

'What?' Jacob was nearly kissing his son.

'Tell him again.'

'*Daltsha'n . . . daltsha'n . . . daltsha'n . . . daltsha'n . . .*'

Indian dialect. Sam's language.

'W-what does it mean?'

110

'. . . daltsha'n . . . daltsha'n . . . daltsha'n . . . daltsha'n . . . .'

It meant something true. It was the Chilcotin word for *'dead'*. And Douglas, no matter how his father begged him to explain, would not stop saying it. '. . . daltsha'n . . . daltsha'n . . . daltsha'n . . . daltsha'n . . . daltsha'n . . . daltsha'n . . . daltsha'n . . . .'

'Douglas . . .' Jacob's hands were shaking, flat against the pulls and tears of his son's jacket. 'Speak to me.'

'Cheep . . . cheep . . . cheep . . . cheep . . . cheep—'

'—Speak! Stop whipping me for things I never did!' And louder still. 'STOP IT!! *SPEAK TO ME, YOU BLOODY IDIOT!! SPEAK TO ME!!!!'*

Jacob's patience had gone and only the dust of it blew in the rising wind. There wasn't another sound but that in all of creation.

The chirping stopped.

A horrible scream. Some kind of vibrato, back on the uvula. Eric looked at the sun overhead and cried again. All the sons stiffened.

And Jacob jumped away, touched Carmen with his still-trembling hand and moved with her step by step backwards into the darkness of the trees, his eyes never leaving Eric's, they the same envious, predatory colour of the wolf's he had seen in the middle of the night. He moved farther back, into the protecting net of trees, keeping the woman behind him, always behind. They must not touch her. No.

To the hemlock. His fingers on the runnelled bark. Grip on the handle of the axe. 'Get out of here . . . *now.'*

But they weren't going away. The group of them spread out wider, moved across the stream towards the campsite. Jacob could see their teeth bared now, all of them with several teeth missing and great gaping yellow holes in those few that were left, gums and tongue diseased. Eric put a hand in one of his jacket pockets, pulled out a large piece of cloth. He held it high like a pennant, caught the other end with his mouth and ripped the cloth into strips. Four long strips. Bindings.

Jacob kept the ice-axe in front of him, moving it spasmically from hand to hand. He was a big man. He had trained hard to come here. He would . . . yes . . . he would use his axe. 'Go away,' he breathed. 'Just go . . . and then we'll go.'

One of them farted. The others laughed. A special coarseness . . . the human pack. Men in hordes who knew ancient ways of murder. Sure of their way. Devoted to each other. Feeling a kind of saintliness . . . especially on the hunt, doing the great act, the royal sport of father-murder.

Like the hordes descending.

Like the sons rising.

They were dancing. Their feet moved in a controlled ecstasy, like boxers but slower, all five advancing on their father and his woman, legs feinting, hips lying, no weapons in any of their hands except the skill of well-practised movement, knack for aggression and attack . . . backing Jacob and Carmen tightly against the tree trunk.

Jacob swiped at them as they fleeted by, once, twice. There was a smell each time they came close, not sweat but something nose-clogging, dizzying. They were nimble. They were baiting him as had been done with bears for sport since before counted time.

His eyes followed as many of them as he could, aching eyes, strained from looking so many ways at once and through the smoke rising from his sons' hands. One of them came in close enough to touch his calf and Jacob threw the axe towards that side but the quick-footed son was gone, back in the dancing circle around him and Carmen.

The smell much more intense now, making him gag . . . the smoke thicker. Carmen coughed. His hands were growing less sure on the axe handle. All five of them – were there still five? – were lunging in now, poking him and sometimes Carmen. Fingers drifted by his nose. Vials open. Tiny bark bottles . . . smoking . . . smelling. A numbness rising up his nose right for the brain.

The axe started to go . . . floated to the ground, which wriggled underneath his feet. There was no control left in his legs to bend down and pick the axe handle up from the—

—sky . . .

. . . pick it up . . . pick axe . . . pick . . .

slick . . . world turning . . . a host of hands around his old, poor, help me Heaven . . . head . . . around . . . all falling . . . smells of something like old . . .

old old old old old old wood . . . wooooooooooddddddddd . . .

ooooollllllldddddddd . . .

. . . Love . . .

forrrgggoottttttttttttttttttteennnnnnnnnnnn . . . .

The Rising of the Sons

CHAPTER 10

Confusion juggled him.

It was quite impossible to move. Just his eyes at first. Then his whole head.

He could see his cell but everything was in double. It felt like morning. Light from above filtered down through a hole in the rocks.

They had drugged him. They had taken him somewhere. They had left him in a stony enclosure. But they hadn't killed him. Not yet, anyway.

He was surprised they hadn't.

Movement returned to his other parts slowly, from the neck down one section at a time. He was still seeing everything in twos, no coordination between his eyes, each taking in its own scene.

As the numbness of the drug went, the pain came on stronger. And the cold. Under him the ground burned frigidly into his flanks. He was lying on stone, the cell stones all the colour of sand in this subdued light. It seemed to be dry around him but as he reached to grasp the wall his hand slipped into a crevice. Inside was the residue of last year's snow, wet and grainy, nearly black from the rock dust that had blown into the cave.

When he finally forced himself to rise, fingernails scraping on the flaking rock, he found he was sore on his right side, his sleeping side, from lying all night long against one of the sharper stones. For some minutes he paced back and forth the few feet of his cell until his body began to straighten out. He was standing up, his mind reasonably clear, when he first realized Carmen wasn't with him but still with his sons somewhere.

Jacob searched the cave for some sign of her. Nothing. The dust on the cave floor showed the tracery of his own footprints. He put his foot on top of the naked prints. Some few of them were smaller. Smaller? Thinner and more delicate, as well. He heard hope's wings fluttering above his head.

The lip of the cave some four or five feet above him, he pulled at the rocks, searched vainly for a foothold, a toehold. Each time he wedged his toes into a seam and tried to pull upwards, his feet slipped. He hugged the rocks. It wasn't that he didn't have the strength to pull himself up. Jacob sat on his haunches, eyes heavy. Stiff with cold. He didn't want to go anywhere if she were gone.

Oh my Carmen . . . carmina. He remembered her voice.

'Jacob?'

The drowsy world was calling him back, he thought, the drug not gone yet.

'Jacob?'

Her shadow passed over the roof of the cave. She looked down, the sunlight behind her a coronet around her head. Jacob saw her through spongy eyes. Could say nothing, shook his head, sure it wasn't her but only a chimera . . . the Devil coming to cudgel him for bringing her into the mountains.

'They've left us here.'

'I'm cold,' he said, still talking to a phantom.

'You're naked.'

Then Jacob, on his haunches, looked at his hands, his arms, his long and still-slim legs, heavily veined near the knees, all the hair of his body white as the driven snow. Naked. The only things he wore were the strap marks on his wrists and ankles where they had bound him.

Naked and insensible with cold, maybe, but he would not cry for that. Carmen was with him.

Though she had earlier hoisted herself out of the cave, Carmen was too weak to be much help to him. It took him only two tries to jack up to the top and over. He found her engirdled in a blanket of several animal skins pierced and sewn together, rabbit and lynx. There was a second robe lying on the ground nearby. It had a terrible, musk-like smell that made him dizzy again, but he needed to wear something, put the coat on, fur side against his nakedness.

115

They were somewhere very high, banished, very obviously being left to die . . . or survive against the worst of odds. This was the middle of a mountain, an immense basin of large rocks, far-distant ridges circling all the way around them. The inside of a volcano, not a deep crater but endlessly wide.

'They left us these, too.'

Carmen showed what she had found outside the lair. An hour before he awoke she had climbed out to see where they were. Under the blankets had been a stone knife, crudely cut and sharpened with flints, and a small object carved of bone, almost elliptical, though flattened and notched on top.

Jacob's breath steamed in the air as he examined the bone. It seemed to him a talisman of some kind. 'For bad luck?' he wondered. It also looked like a fish, a fingerling . . . perhaps a primitive fishing lure. 'We'll keep it, whatever it is.'

In the meantime she had sat down.

He could see now that she, too, couldn't stop shivering, even under the protection of the robe. Thin, diaphanous clouds covered the sky from rim to rim, gauze over the sunlight filtering all its heat and most of its washed-out light. Summer was gone. Amongst the rubble, in every cavity's shade, lay snow that had not melted all year long. His sons had left them in the most desolate spot he had ever seen, frozen and crumbling rock, not a single living thing. Jacob's lips flapped in disbelief as the wind beat against him in short, hard fits.

'Where do we go?' It was a lustreless question. He had no strength nor will to go anywhere. And, he could see, she had even less. 'Where?'

'I don't know.'

In the short while they had been sitting there the sun had already declined some small ways, enough for Jacob to guess which way was true north. He pointed and asked if she agreed. She didn't answer. 'Carmen?' Still nothing. 'You memorized that map. What's the best way to get off this mountain? North?' He looked at her. However dispirited he was, Carmen was worse, her strain much greater than his. Some inner dejection more than the effects of the drug or the cold were keeping her motionless, forcing her eyes to the ground. He had seen this coming ever since they found the appaloosa drenched in its own blood. 'Carmen? Sweet Carmen . . .?' Dreaming. Not even listening to him. He kneeled down to her. 'I am not going to let you die because of me.' Her eyes blinked mechanically. 'Listen, try to visualize the map. It's in your head. You can do it. Now what if we go north? I'm sure they wouldn't expect us to try getting out that way, but can we . . .? What do you remember? What about the north face?'

'Colin said always go north . . . north, north.'

'Did he say that for certain?'

She could barely nod but she did. The wind blistered the backs of his legs beneath the robe, his ears, fingers, but he listened only to her needs. 'Do you have the strength to walk?' Jacob knew it wasn't a question of physical vigour. She had climbed unassisted from the cave. What mattered was getting her to remember who she was, the spunky woman who had survived life on the streets and braved the adult world with a child in her belly when only seventeen.

They had to get out of the crater and start a descent of the mountain, but first they had to believe – both of them had to – that they *could* survive.

'Walk behind me,' he said. 'We'll find an easy pace and we'll stick to it.'

'My knee is swelling.'

'We'll go easily enough . . . just follow my pace.' He lifted her up, got her walking over the stones.

So halting forth, the two of them shoeless and bitter with cold, hungry, on the margins of panic, Jacob and Carmen trudged away from the sun and towards an imaginary point they believed to be true north and a way out of the mountain.

Barefoot. Walking over rocks.

Every step a greater agony. The soft pads of his feet hadn't been hardened in the city by all his running. Now infinite stones cut deeply into his flesh no matter how he stepped. There was always some jagged corner or covered pebble he couldn't see. Even the few round stones always managed to strike his heel right under the bone, bruising it worse each time, shooting pain straight up his spine so bad that his feet hesitated to touch the ground. The pace slowed even more.

'Don't turn around anymore.' She had been swivelling continuously since the beginning of their march. 'Just look ahead,' he warned her, knowing that though they'd been going for some time, that the ridge behind them looked as close as ever, it seemed they had hardly begun to cross the saucer of stones. Yet she kept glancing over her shoulder, as if sure they were being pursued.

Jacob pushed her on, encouraged her, or browbeat her, did whatever he thought would make her take the next step. She complained of a fever and he didn't doubt she had one. The hunger could do that, the exhaustion, the altitude, even the malaise or sense of sin or guilt or whatever it was that was costing her the greatest part of her strength. When her knee buckled and she fell forwards, Jacob wondered if she wasn't still feeling the drug. Water might help to flush the rest out. Hard by was a wedge of ice and snow still white and un-molested by grime. After scraping away the surface he chopped into the heart of it with the knife and grasped a handful of the purest snow. Then made her suck it.

'Cold . . . .' She pushed it away.

'Keep sucking.'

'It hurts my teeth.'

'Doesn't matter. You need the water.'

Nor would he continue until she had taken some real amount of water, more than the few drops she told him had filled her up. His concern deepened. Carmen might be more feverish than he had thought and she was letting it infect her will to carry on, a will already badly distempered. The water would cool her. Maybe.

He was about to force her to drink again when he saw the spoor. It looked fresh enough. And large. Black. There was no doubt in his mind it was bear droppings. He wondered if she had seen it, because if not he would say nothing.

But she was staring at him. 'I already saw it.'

118

Jacob's heart sank.

'There was more near the cave.'

'It's days old.'

She wouldn't be fooled. Her listless grey eyes didn't blink away the truth. 'It's still warm.'

That seemed to Jacob more likely to be her fear talking. He bent down and poked the leavings with his toes. It was fresh, certainly, but not warm. Whether it were a matter of several hours old or a day or even two he couldn't be sure.

The frozen waste around them, hardly a lichen marking any of the rocks, not a tree or shrub, not a weed crooking its body up from the poisonous rubble, made it hard to believe there was anything to attract or keep a bear around. The spoor must be the sign of a bear in transit who wanted to get out of the stony wilderness as much as they did. A single bear. Perhaps even one going in the opposite direction, away from them.

Perhaps.

Unless his sons knew a bear was tenanted in the volcano and therefore bound to stumble across the two of them, or them him . . . or was the plan for the bear to *stalk* them?

The day had turned bitter. Winds whipped relentlessly as they went towards the ridge, plodding heavily. When he saw she had turned around again he knew now it was the bear she was looking for. But her fear made her walk no faster.

At one point Carmen pointed furiously behind them.

He wheeled around. There was something out there, all right, but not the rushing hulk of a grizzly. From their rocky cage in the middle of the crater they had risen over several hours high enough to see above the volcano's south-facing ridge. Some miles in the distance were the tips of the coastal range etched against the sky, enough light yet to see their white spurs.

'Mount Waddington . . . right where it should be.' She was remembering the map.

The sight had cheered him, proof they were heading about north, and had given Carmen a minute wedge of energy. He took her hand and together they pressed their ascent towards the topmost rocks of the opposing ridge. Twice they thought they had reached the summit only to discover there was another outcropping above. The snow grew much more dense, the ridgeline corniced and for certain right ahead, drifts pushed up against the final boulders.

The very last steps. Blood rushing. Damning the pain, feet frozen anyway, glissading backwards nearly every stride, she fell into the snow while he scrambled up through the ice and stones by himself, desperate to see the soft valleys of the great interior plateau beyond, endless gentle valleys wrinkling away from the mountain back towards the Fraser River where all the waters would drain. A long descent they would have but a peaceable one, through humane lands, verdant, luscious with late-summer fruits, small game, fish in the salmon-clogged streams. That was the dream that would carry them down – food, warmth, rest, escape . . . escape. Jacob rose over the cornice and looked.

Looked again.

No valley. No plateau. Not even what he had most feared – no sheer wall of basalt or granite plummeting down. It was worse.

It was the same thing they had been seeing all day. More rocks. Colder. Greyer in the day's fast-diminishing light. An identical crater to the one that had trapped them since they awoke from their drugged sleep, the same heartless moonscape. And the snow, its ghastly dust colour, was if anything more insidious on the far side than on the one they had already crossed.

The volcano had a double cone. They had lugged all afternoon right into the mountain's false heart where a thin ridge separated the two halves of the crater. They had only got in deeper.

Carmen came up next to him. He pulled her back from the snowdrifts, held her in his frost-pinched arms. And let her cry . . . .

For a little while he left her to her own thoughts, just as he wished to be left to his. Day was nearly gone. Frigid, blue-grey grasps of night penetrated at every point in the eastern sky. And try as he might to think otherwise, Jacob Solomon was certain they sat under a snow sky. His hands reflexively crushed two rocks together. He and Carmen might not live through this. They might not be alive tomorrow to watch the day die. Neither he nor she.

Carmen's shoulders were pulled in, her knees as well. She had folded herself onto the snow bank and sat there, spiritless and unmoving, looking nowhere in particular, nowhere at all.

But Jacob was hearing Sirenlike voices with very different advice. From the darker crevices of his mind one voice growled that their escape was hopeless and he should deal with that fact, the only practical thing to do was to find the right hole, make himself comfortable and let death enter unresisted. Another voice, in less fretful tones, told him to walk straight across the second crater, too. It was the voice of Love, a voice he had been getting used to and learning to depend upon. And Jacob knew that against all tribulations of his body so long as he kept alert to this other voice he would live . . . she would live.

Die of hunger they might, or die of cold, hypothermia bleed all their bodies' warmth, but he would not die because his sons wanted him to or because he despaired of escaping from them. Absolutely not.

'We have to get off this mountain, Carmen, tonight if at all possible. At the very least to the other side of the crater.'

'We won't get there.'

'We will try.'

She just sat there, though, doll-like, refusing to get up. Jacob put his arms underneath hers from behind, lifted her. Then he led her down the slope, nearly carrying her as all she could manage was to drag her feet along, helpless in his arms, white and rigid with cold.

As they went the daylight went, too. Into a greyness. Jacob kept his eyes fixed on a spot at the other end of the crater for as long as he could see. He thought about the Jews in their march to annihilation. Something like this it must have been, the few left with strength carrying the others along. All the photographs he had seen, in their compellingly grim black and white and grey, all were barren . . . it was the *barrenness* of the Holocaust he found wrenching. Not the arithmetic of it, not even its ghastly geometry of bones and skulls and mass graves. It was the utter desolation of spirit. Nobody talking. A race of gregarious people sullen and quiet and alone. Everyone too stunned even to *dream* of a different world. Families splintered a thousand ways. And all these years Jacob Solomon hadn't cried for the memory of his mother, father, countless uncles and aunts and cousins, friends, rivals in young love . . . *not once* for father or mother.

A terrific soreness pressed in against him, countless times stronger than the stones sharpening themselves on his feet or the flesh-searing cold. There were tears to come before he died, plenty of them, tears of filial piety . . . .

Carmen tugged at his hand. The day had gone completely. Jacob was struggling in the dark without the use of his eyes. And they were still in the middle of this second crater. She had a dozen contusions from where he had swung her against the rocks; he had a hundred of his own. They could not go on, not that night.

He took out his knife and cut more snow, sucked, drank, forced her to do likewise. Then, finding a hollow amongst the higher rocks, they crept into their shelter, he advancing with his meagre knife in front of him against the bear that must be inside, jaws wide, standing on its rear legs with arms spread massively and its claws dry for want of blood.

All they found was a smell. Something living had been in the cave and had left behind only the smell of decay.

This was their portion: the smell of the end.

His nerves jangling, heart unsure of itself, Jacob smoothed a bed on the softer crush of rock and lay down in the darkness with Carmen, one shawl underneath and one, woefully small, over them. She passed into sleep right away, hugging him for warmth.

He held onto her and listened to the wind's rising and falling, waiting for whenever sleep would take him. In short lapses he did sleep, not deeply though, always part-conscious of Carmen's rhythms, how cold or hot she was becoming, her heart's racing. It was like holding an infant, its precious store of life and heat kept alive by another's

122

love. He didn't really know just how tenuous was her grip on life at this point. He thought the string connecting her was fragile indeed.

Once during the night Jacob opened his eyes expecting to see stars above him but instead saw snowflakes drifting down upon the two of them through the skylight over their makeshift bed. The snow had come.

Again Jacob closed his eyes and tried to listen for Love's golden voice, dropping into a light sleep wondering if Carmen might really die in his arms, freeze to death . . . lose sensation first . . . then sleep as he froze . . . if it would go like that?

None of this frightened him. For the first time in his entire life Jacob Solomon feared nothing. In the middle of his being he was still.

And an instant later when he awoke to find the earliest traces of light reluming the eastern sky this peace was everywhere around him. Even in the woman dead-asleep in his arms. Even in the sky from which all the snow flurries had been swept away.

CHAPTER 11

By morning Carmen's toes had turned blue and completely numb. They stuck out of the blanket that had been wrapped around her. She stared at them. There was little or no feeling in her ears and cheeks, either, but that she found less worrying. There were miles and miles to walk on dead feet.

Despite the numbness in her extremities, inside she was little else but fire. Her fever had climbed very high, scaling the ramparts of her last defences.

Light poured through the aperture in their rock enclosure, dazzling her eyes painfully. She wished Jacob would close off the light. Carmen paused. Forced her eyes open. Sat up.

123

'Jacob?'

A thin patina of snow had fallen on the floor of the shelter and there were footprints on the snow, just a single pair leading away in the direction they had been marching the night before. No other signs, no paw prints or marks of a scuffle. So the bear hadn't stolen him in the middle of the night, nor had Jacob's sons been following. Jacob had already started nevertheless.

She went outside to find him. Her eyes shaded with insensible fingers, Carmen scanned the saucer every way, expecting to see him walking somewhere along the ridge. But there was no Jacob in view anywhere. A shadow in her mind lengthened, seemed to steal away. Had he just gone on alone?

Gone?

His path was clear. She started over the steps, fear whirling inside her, her frostbitten feet shuffling forward out of control. She snapped questions at the mountain air, called out his name over and over until the rocks echoed her disbelief. '*Jacob!*'

'Don't run!' And again. 'There's ice . . . *DON'T RUN!!*'

Jacob was waving at her from the ridge they had been unable to reach last evening. The falling darkness then had misled them. They were not so far away from the edge of the crater and he was retreating from it towards her.

When she slipped he was there to catch her, rubbed her frigid skin to start her blood moving. Then he saw her feet, the blue lobes sticking stiffly from them. With great care he touched her fingers, nose, ears, her cheeks. And then he bent down.

'These three toes only?'

'They were blue when I got up.'

He couldn't lie. 'They're frostbitten.' He shook his head slowly, medically. She might lose these toes. 'Try to walk as much as you can on your heel.'

'What's the difference . . . my toes are numb?'

'Stay off them anyway.'

Carmen pointed towards the ridge. He nodded but would say nothing. She could see for herself. They went up together.

It was there, all right. Just as they had hoped for and expected to see the day before when they climbed up the false ridge in the centre of the volcano. What they saw now was both good and bad.

The sun, with Providence finally showing an even hand, was shining. A haze hugged the mountainside as it spilled down towards the plateau many miles below, at the bottom of which lay safety. The haze wouldn't let them see all the way, though, only eight or ten miles. Somewhere the other side of that gassy curtain were the forests, the trembling aspens, the cottonwoods, the mixed pines, the willows they had passed when coming up to the lake. And beyond that, warmth. Food. Even hospitality.

'But a long, *long* ways away, Carmen. We have a big mountain to climb down first.' There was no joy in his voice, nor desolation. Something more precise. 'We have a fair chance.' Jacob lifted his face to the warming rays of the sun. '*That* is our ally. We need to come in from the cold. We have to move while we have the sun.' They had a fair chance.

He could see she didn't believe him. Partly because she couldn't feel the warmth of the day, thinking it was all her body's making. 'Your fever's gone way up.' She was having trouble standing. There was the frostbite, too. She might not have the strength for the descent. Well then he would carry her on his back. If her shawl didn't keep her warm enough, well then he would give her his and go naked across the barrens. Why not? He could.

'It's my body, Jake, it's just giving up.'

'I have body enough for both of us. But I do need your help. This isn't just a pep talk. I *need* you.' She nodded but it was reflex, not what she thought to be true. 'There's at least eight good hours before the sun disappears completely. It's crucial we find our way to the bottom of this slope by then, find some real shelter at a much lower altitude. We *can't* bivouac on these rocks again.' He couldn't bear to see her so flaccid, dreary – not Carmen, not his woman . . . his wife. '*I will get us down!*'

He wouldn't talk anymore. He took her to the ridge's last rocks and pointed her down the cliff, then started climbing.

It took them three hours to descend only several hundred feet. They could see a little farther to the east of them the cliff was vastly more precipitous, but where they were it was bad enough. Boulder sat upon boulder's back, sometimes forcing them to jump as much as five or six feet, Jacob catching her before she slammed down on those blue toes of hers. The sun had thawed their frozen cheeks and noses. It had done more, though, had parched and reddened them, signs of a bad burn clear to both Jacob and Carmen.

Soon the angle of descent changed. Eased. He made her stop and rest but she wanted to get farther down, to a pool below, she driven by her impulse only, he sure it would cause her to fall.

'Sit down and rest your legs and feet.'

'We're hardly moving, Jake.'

'It's as fast as we need to go.'

Carmen, unable to sit or stand, kept pointing downwards. '. . . must drink, Jake.' She tried to continue by herself but he caught her arm, sat her down hard on a rock.

'We will rest for five minutes and not move.' Still Carmen struggled to get up. And then, for the first time in the years he had known her, Jacob hit his woman. A quick, stunning slap on her cheek. For a few minutes she lay against the stone shelf where they had stopped, but when he did finally rise to continue she stood up right away and followed him down the slope.

At the pool she wept. They had passed tiny puddles already, but at the edge of the small tarn was a border of bright green, blessedly Irish green. Grass. Colour. Some few hundred game blades, life beginning to shudder forth from out of the stony aridity.

As Carmen bent down to drink a chipmunk moved over the rocks and came to the edge of the melt opposite her. Sunlight spangled the water. She and the creature drank together, watching each other.

'Drink more,' he warned her after the animal had gone, 'as much as you can.' She did what she could. Then he. It was as if he were opening the doors to a true perception. That was Plato's own water he had drunk, the Ideal 'water' itself.

When he raised his lips from the pool he saw Carmen

trying to smile, showing her teeth's translucent, exquisite masonry. Her first smile.

But they weren't down yet. Jacob set his jaw hard. Accidents in the great expeditions nearly always happened on the way down, when tired men thought they were home free. He had to help Carmen stand up. They had fifteen hundred or two thousand feet yet to descend, several horizontal miles, and Carmen could barely hold up her head. Her fever was getting dangerously high, near to parboiling. *Home free?*

And yet, and yet there was something working for them now that hadn't been yesterday . . . not even ten minutes before. She had found the way to smile. He was sorry he had hit her but it had changed things, certainly for a while.

They had a chance, a better one all the time . . . if they got down out of the rocks they had a chance.

More and more running water. Streams gathering head.

The pitch altered unpredictably now: sometimes they had open stretches that were almost walks, sparsely-grassed and covered with a few shrubs, sliding gravel; then more steep grades of rock. At one point they found themselves at the top of a falls, which they had to loop around. Right over the lip of the spilling water they had found a small tree gripping its countless fingers into the granite, leaning out over the precipice without fear of falling. The hardiness of living things. A tree standing up and surviving even without ground of its own. An example for them. Nature's lessons were abounding.

The pounding spray cooled their faces and arms and very tired shoulders. Well in decline, the sun would set in three hours or so. And the fall of rock, though stippled more densely with robust pines, seemed to carry on down endlessly below where they were standing. Mild as the day had been the night would prove otherwise. He thought about that bivouac while his eyes searched hard over the terrain for something . . . anything.

His eyes stopped moving.

To his right, though the pitch was somewhat steeper, Jacob noticed an enigmatic perspective of rock. Instinctively he lurched towards it, scrambling over the twists of high boulders. Carmen called after him but he yelled back for her not to follow, not yet. In a moment he dropped out of sight.

She knew he had found something and she went after him.

It was a stream. A thin, nervous gorge, difficult to follow down. Steep. But soon the stream grew a little broader, the gorge as well, making a reedlike valley that continued to fatten. Grew wider.

And wider.

And less steep. He waited for her at a bend in the water. His face was red with pleasure. He picked up her hands and kissed each of her fingers. Up above he had seen the first cut of a ravine. He had gambled it would be transformed into something very different. 'Come see,' he said.

Jacob led her around the turn and there was a path, a game trail along the streamside. A clump of trees growing in a tiny meadow. Several spots of flat, open ground. And below?

The two of them plunged down the mountain.

They ran with hands locked together as the water coursed wider and wider in between the steep canyon walls constantly feeding the flow. Their path, at first a bed of hard grass and pebbles, soon gave way to a carpet of immaculate emerald, trimmed smooth by the action of countless running animals, predators and prey. Down they went, down and down quickly, together.

A mile along. Several smaller creeks joining, the water true black, smooth and fast-moving, foam-flecked for a while over small stones but soon losing its wildness as it slackened into flatlands, meadows bordering the stream on both sides, heavy copses bunched around the canyon sides and trees cluttered up the slopes, weeds and tall-stemmed grasses by the tree trunks, a balminess in the air, bees mingling among the wildflowers, paintbrush, thistle, Queen Anne's lace, periwinkle, valerian pink, songbirds in the mixed growth, canyon cedar and vine maple, the trees shadowing a wading bird that stood in the eddies dreaming over its hunched blue-grey shoulders . . . water bugs skipping over the backwater, reeds growing, cat's-tails, and water lilies . . . *lilies on the stream*.

At a widening in the watercourse, a deep pool, the two of them paused. Fronds and fiddleheads waved across the brook, the water was transparent but all of jade, the grass almost purple. Not far down a beaver dam. Ladybugs. A sweetness everywhere . . . a perfumerie . . . the music of the water. Paradise.

PARADISE.

Carmen dropped to her knees, right into the soft turf by the stream, sank deeply into the grass, lay down and bathed in its richness, scooped up the soil underneath with her beaten, blunted, welted, frosted hands, showered herself with the soft black earth, bugs crawling down her, worms, roots of dandelion, plunged her fingers down again and again, planted her feet and pushed down as deeply as her strength would let her, digging a small hole and putting those raw and swollen feet entirely into the earth . . . screaming almost maniacally with pleasure, difficult to catch her breath, her voice whistling in pitch with the water's sacred flow . . . rolled back and forth on her hips, threw off the shawl and turned over onto her stomach to wash her body in the blackness of the land.

Feeling had returned. And it was all of joy.

Now Jacob, too, he who had for so long held off, fell to his knees, pulled her into his arms and wept . . . he and she weeping uncontrollably as the whole dismal nightmare of their past days shuffled off them like dead skin. Shuddering together, then more tears until both of them were so limp that they swayed to the ground and lay there, clasped together, utterly vulnerable, two passengers pulled from the flaming hulk of his sons' murder mission. Saved. Survivors . . . saved.

Warmth. Food. Shelter. These three things. In the tea-coloured late afternoon sunlight Jacob reckoned he had only two hours to make ready for the night.

And it would be he alone. Because as Jacob looked at her now he could see more clearly what the expenditure of energy yesterday had meant to Carmen, followed by this

129

day's descent with her right foot hardly more than a stick she could use for balance. The three middle toes of her foot were still blue, quite cold to his touch though the temperature in the air was in the sixties. He took off his blanket and wrapped her foot in it not knowing what else to do, he sure only that under no circumstances must he try to put the injured digits in direct contact with heat.

With exceedingly filmy eyes Carmen watched him in his ministrations. Now that the excitement of having found some refuge was wearing off, a deep tiredness clutched her and started to drag her away.

'Don't sleep yet.'

'. . . unnnnnnnnnnnn . . . .'

'A little water first, then you can sleep.'

Only remotely could she hear him, as if he were talking at the end of a long tunnel. The fever was roaring. Reflexively she was making sounds as she breathed, something like hiccups.

Jacob brought her hands full of water from the stream, rubbed her simmering forehead, her neck, the throbbing at her temples . . . cooling her . . . stroking her. He positioned her over the water.

'Try as hard as you can to lean over and drink.'

She cranked out the directions to her muscles but nothing happened. And again. A few inches she rose, struggling to get up like an infant fawn. More of the wheezing hiccups. Jacob was forced to nurse her from his hands. She sucked. Sipped. Most of the water cupped in his hands dribbled away but she did get some down. Swallowing was difficult for her, as well, the fever and hunger having made most of her control involuntary, a slight disorientation he had noticed earlier now much worse.

It was useless trying to keep her awake. He had to trust her to the nursery of sleep. So Jacob laid her down on the very softest tufts, made a pillow for her head, covered her with his shawl, and watched her go down. And when she was finally asleep he kissed her burning ears with lips parched and cracked as much from worry over her as from the mountain's abuse.

Then he got up to take a careful look around the garden

130

they had somehow (God's grace providing) found when in the sorest need of their lives. There was work to do and not enough time nor light to do it right. The sundown would just have to hold.

He began with the fire. Naked, unmindful of the bites and scratches on his arms, Jacob plucked dried grasses from the tree bases, gathered every dead branch and spar, ripped the twigs free of their sockets, stripped bark off an ancient cedar. That would get it started. Then he planted stones. Arranged a windbreak from the air currents he knew would be blowing stronger down the river when night came on. Found two sticks naturally forked to improvise a hanging grill should they succeed in finding something to cook.

Tricks. His mother, the peasant, had taught him these things fifty years earlier. *Fifty years ago.* He had rehearsed these skills as a child, setting up an outdoor kitchen for his farmer grandfather. It had all been a kind of show for his mother's parents to let them know the young Jacob wasn't spending all day in the gymnasium learning fractions and declining Latin nouns. Jacob's mother, far-sighted woman, teacher . . . .

Other tricks. There were berry bushes copious with fruit but he passed them by for the moment as he roved downstream, his eyes searching the ground under every tree, every shrub, flower, weed, shy reed. They needed to eat something hot. If they had a pot he could cook her a broth of nettles. He had eaten that as a child, too, had made the soup himself. No time to imagine how he would weave a pot or dish, maybe tomorrow. There were things enough to nourish right at hand.

He plucked the best looking cat's-tails. There was pigweed and something that looked like cow parsnip, but at the latter his fingers just stuck on the leaves of this knee-high plant with its purple-streaked, toothy leaves. Something smelled foul about it so he kept to what he knew for certain. Dandelions he dug with his primitive knife, cleaning the adventitious roots, plucking the leaves and stuffing them with his booty, too. He still needed more substantial food, something she would savour, for Carmen would have trouble eating . . . something that would tease her distant, capricious appetite.

And then there it was. In abundance. Jacob fell on a patch of them and stabbed at the soil, loosened the bulbs and pulled them up. *Wild onion*. He was ecstatic. He knew just what they were. His mother had shown him.

'We're winning . . . .' He thought to himself about the bloody ordeal his sons had laid down for him to try to survive. Clenching the long sprouts Jacob raised his hands heavenward, shook his ecstasy at the sky. '. . . going to win this one fight . . . not about to die . . . nor be killed by anybody . . . both going to live.'

Insects dancing on the cold running stream caught his eye. For a moment or two Jacob stopped to watch a few up-winged creatures sitting on the surface and drying their wings as the current rushed them along. Hatching aquatic insects. Delicious food for trout. Superbly vulnerable just at this moment. From behind one rock came the telltale splash, fish lips smacking against the insect. The trout disappeared back to his hole.

Protein. More than anything else they needed that fish. In his mind's eye Jacob scrutinized the small talisman his sons had left for them at the cave. He thought and thought. It just *might* be a lure of some kind, after all. The trout took another insect. Same trout. Same spot. He had got a good look at the fish this time, some sixteen or seventeen inches. Jacob would make a line somehow. And tomorrow they would eat trout.

His grandfather would have expected Jacob to be able to capture wild trout. The man had owned the clearest eyes Jacob ever saw, not a trace of yellow next to the irises. Why such clear eyes looking at him when he was a child? Had the old man needed them to look into young Jacob's future? The fishing lessons had included the names of the most important artificial flies, those the great Halford in England had written about. His grandfather, farmer though he was, read diligently, widely, in several tongues. The Latin name for that family of up-winged flies was '*Ephemeroptera*'. Oh Jacob had learned his lessons well. In Latin, no less . . . on a Moravian farm!

Arms full, Jacob made his way quickly back towards their camp. The sun had passed below the trough of the canyon long ago, just as he and Carmen were entering the valley, but only now was the heat of the day fast disappearing. They needed a fire as soon as possible. His eyes stuck on the ground looking for flints. Shadows confused him. There were stones and stones, not exactly what he needed. If there were no flints he would be forced to strike a spark in another, far more difficult way, one which he knew only in theory, again from years ago. But now he knew how long and taut was the reach of learning, of civilization's chain, and that he could do everything necessary for Carmen and himself to survive.

He returned to images of his earliest times, to mother and to father, too. A lifetime crowded in his memory.

The great strength of his mother had been her ability to be hurt. She had endured endless abuse. It was not a very modern virtue, this endurance, but none the less laudable for that. She had been a woman keeping up her spirits in a family where her share of affection wasn't enough to fill a Sabbath winecup. Nobody had treated her well in that family of egotists, not husband not children. It was the Jewish virtue to accept persecution because God was on the side of those who suffered. And Jacob's mother had not argued with her destiny. She was kind and long-suffering as much by nature as by precept, hurt by even the *thought* of unkindness, a woman who rescued dogs from drunken owners, who succoured the Nazi postman, her long and capacious arms always open.

And what was wrong with that? Why had everything these days been stood on its head so that suffering the injustices of the world was shameful, while those who clacked and tooted and cursed and strongarmed and bombed indiscriminately for every imagined wrong were the only virtuous? *Were clenched fists really more godly than hands clasped in supplication for a better world?*

Of his parents, which had faced the end better? His mother, after all, had been better prepared and no doubt in trying to imagine her executioners' pain she had lessened her own. But his father in the death camps, what good there

133

were all his jibes and gambols? And his pitiless wit? How had a man of opinions thrived on a diet of thorns and pebbles and ashes and tears? How?

And which one of them would have been able to keep the darkness away right now, like Jacob, bending over the cuts and shavings of a diseased alder and rubbing stones on the touchwood? The wisdom of parents was that they had endured long enough and well enough to teach us how to do the same, that they found ways to make us hear the voices of the dead. For the dead always had something worth the listening and, curiously, they spoke only to the living. Just as Jacob's mother, and his mother's father, were speaking to him now. They would keep him alive, him and Carmen . . . if Jacob had the ears to hear.

Carmen awoke to the sound of a fire crackling. She was sure it was in her head. No smoke came from her ears or nostrils, though her face was hot. She reached up to touch her hair. Hot, too. When she felt her toes she screamed.

Jacob came running, pushed off the spruce boughs he had rigged to make a windbreak and pinced her arms so she wouldn't batter her still-frozen foot.

'. . . foot's on fire . . . .'

Once or twice she tried to swallow, no saliva in her mouth and she couldn't unstick her throat muscles. Then she gagged, mercifully, and coughed the passage open. Tears drained steadily from both her eyes. '. . . my foot is burning off . . . .'

And how was he going to tell her that the pain was probably a good sign? Though not delirious she was in such a heightened frenzy that she only half-comprehended where they were and what they had been through.

Jacob tried again to get her to drink. Every swallow an affliction. He went back to the stream twice more and she took down what he brought. No doctor he, nevertheless Jacob hadn't any doubt that she ought to eat something soon. The enclosure of stones he had constructed next to the fire held the baking roots and wild onions. Carmen might resist but hunger had its persuasions.

'Jacob . . . .' She was whining, very afraid. 'Jacob!'

134

'Hold on, hold on . . . I'm right here.' She cried in his arms, shivering hard. When he felt her less tense Jacob held her against his knees, freeing his arms while he scraped onto his finger the cambium layer of sweet, highly nutritious pulp he had taken from the bark of a cedar. Her mouth was slightly open and as gently as possible he laid the food onto her gums. 'Chew this slowly, or suck it if you can't.' For a few moments her tongue worked over the thimbleful of food, then the pulp started to trickle out of her mouth. 'You can't eat any of it?'

'Don't make me . . . .' She gagged again.

'Try once more.'

'. . . please . . . .' She was moaning at him. 'Please . . . *no*.'

He sighed, pushed the other food away as well, the camras root, the onions. She wouldn't want any of it now and he would just have to let her decide when to take nourishment . . . trust her own body . . . and he stop forcing her.

At the edge of the shelter a pebble fell. A moment later another hit nearby, then several, all sliding down the cliff, hitting sharply by the base of the trees and rolling to the stream.

'Wh-wh—!'

Carmen clutched him as fiercely as her meagre strength could tense her fingers. She was stiffened like a dry brush. Waiting. A few more rocks. She nearly bolted upright.

And screamed.

She was worse than he had thought. Now she was trembling and very nearly delirious. Jacob rocked her in his arms, explained as simply and softly as he could that stones had been falling all day, and most likely every day for some millions of years. That was why he had built the shelter so close to the stream and away from the cliffs even though they would be better protected from the cold and wind under the trees. Rocks tumbled and tumbled. 'But it's just the mountain talking, my sweet . . . *sweet* Carmen.'

When the next fall of rocks broke the night's silence, though, she clung to him just as tightly. If she had heard him she had not understood at all.

It would be a long night, one of little sleep for either of

135

them, for he would nurse her through this night. She had surprised him in how little will she could muster to help herself survive. Jacob had certainly expected something else from her. But he would cast no stones. There had been no need for her to come into these mountains yet she had, and he had no doubts he would be dead if she hadn't chosen to come. She had fortified him in other times, when he had given a less good account of himself. But she seemed so crushed, her faith at its farthest ebb. And that he didn't understand at all.

Well . . . tired as he was, Jacob knew he could go without sleep for another dozen nights if necessary, but whatever happened he would not die in the mountains, of that he was absolutely sure, and he would keep his promise to her that she should not die for having made the voyage with him. A green and golden valley had saved them . . . that and the instruction of the dead.

CHAPTER 12

It was their seventh day in the mountains. The Sabbath peace hovered above him drowsily in the air. Not a breath of wind . . . not one. Warm. God's own garden. A natural place crowded with every living thing that crawls, creeps, flies, swims.

In the grass beside Jacob two silver objects glittered with lively specks of red and black pebbling along their sides, dots of the same colour as carefully printed on their tails though more muted. One considerable rainbow trout, and a smaller one. He had found a fishing line easily enough, for his sons had inadvertently provided one. Jacob had removed the long string of caribou gut from one of the skin blankets. The bone talisman, a lure after all, had turned out to be good luck.

Jacob lay naked in the grass, chewing on a twig. The

brandy-coloured pelts of his blanket were separated and scattered nearby. How he would restitch the skins was not a worry. There would be needles enough, of one kind or another. He improvised well.

During the early part of the day, having held Carmen's sweat-wrapped body all through the night and finding her cooler near dawn, quieter, too, Jacob had left her and gone off for a Sunday morning by himself in order to take the trout. Both of their bodies were in dire need of protein now, of some animal or fish fat, too. The bone lure had seemed primitive in design but their luck was on, this past day or two. And the trout not at all suspicious. The little one he had caught right away. The big trout, the fish he had seen gorging on flies the evening before, had taken much longer to inveigle onto his line. Knowing how skittish trout could be in a small stream, Jacob had lain by the bankside above the fish's window for over fifteen minutes in case his approach had spooked it. Only after the fish had risen once or twice to take something at the surface did he begin to float the lure past the trout's hole in short, smooth retrieves, hand-winding the line. And the big trout, true to his cannibal instincts, had slapped his jaws around the lure certain it was some wayward infant fish struggling in the current. Jacob had banked him with a single sharp pull, clubbed the fish before he could flop back in, gutted both fish and lay back to take his ease.

The mountain talked to Jacob. A tiny slide across the water plunged into the deciduous growth on the other side, right at the cliff's base. Somebody angry over there . . . a thousand hornets rushed out of their nest, looking for any intruder. Jacob had been watching them for a while now, considering ways to steal their honey. He had no fear of being stung; however, they might swarm and a honey pot wasn't worth the risk.

So no honey. Anyhow, honey brought bears. Berries would serve for sugar and energy.

He had ideas about simple snares for small game, game birds, too. Nor was he averse to the idea of eating squirrel or muskrat or snake or whatever they could find. The only thing was that bonds between himself and this green world had formed quickly. In a matter of hours he had stuck roots into the earth here, had sucked up nutriments. Nothing native to the valley was their enemy. The savagery necessary in trapping animal life – even for his meat – seemed all wrong. An old sentiment, as old as Eden, but he felt it strongly now, for the garden all around him was as gentle as the original one. Idleness and luxury and ease. And a sense of the holy. He had done his task on the mountaintop well, had got the two of them safely down. This was his earned rest. He and Carmen would eat the trout and then, for the rest of the trip home, eat animal flesh only when they absolutely must. No more killing.

Now all he need do was bring Carmen to full health again . . . make her gold, true coin, the way he'd always known her.

The garden eased him into thought.

Last night Jacob had begun to understand something about Carmen . . . and about her baby, fathered by a gang of rockers and delivered up to the dirt farm, where the child could be hidden and Carmen's shame obscured. Well, in her mumblings Carmen had spoke too much. And strangely. Squalid, sordid, disgusting clips of her memory, the jism-spattered conception bed, the ferocious, blinding jabs of drugs, a rocker girl's cheek and eye scraped away by a mean mad drunk sideman, meals eaten from motel bathroom floors where they had lain cold two days running and were already bubbling with bacteria, the fevers, the humiliation, the cold. That was like the horror she and Jacob had endured together in the mountains. Her mind had gone back to those times and the memory was enfeebling her. Carmen must have had a sense of Fortune returning to the same point on the wheel, her past miseries starting over.

But there was much, much more. What Carmen had done to her child by abandoning her had not been forgot – not by Carmen. The very first day on the trail she had told Jacob about her teenage pregnancy. All this while Jacob had thought Carmen's voyage into the mountains was to protect him. Protection played a part, but surely the real reason she

138

had come with him was to make a peace of her own with her lost child, just as Jacob had been hoping to do with his sons. It was as if Carmen's child – unnamed and dismissed at birth – were high in the mountains running in the pack with Jacob's sons. And when it became clear that there would be no peace between Jacob and his children she had begun to fail. That bitter little child – born in the streets – had sucked her mother's strength vampirishly, had fevered Carmen, depressed all her vitality. It was only justice, after all. Retribution. And as children are remorseless so this child in Carmen's mind wanted justice first, forgiveness after, if at all, should Carmen survive the penance due.

The lesson was hard, for both Jacob and Carmen: *Parents Kill.* Oh yes, kill. That was what children thought. Kill in a thousand, sundry ways. It was impossible to count them all, or know the worst. Jacob's way had been neglect, again like Carmen. It had been the theme of his fatherhood.

He remembered one night in particular, when his children were still young. He had inadvertently stumbled on Eric, his eldest, being masturbated by a woman twice his age in the front seat of a Pontiac. Seeing his father, Eric had panicked, had run huggermugger for the fruit trees, his pants trailing after him, and hid there for several hours. A gross humiliation. Typically, Jacob had let his son make sense out of the humiliation all by himself. Not because Jacob was hard of heart, though. No. It was the old reality principle. Jacob really did believe in it. And, he had himself been deeply embarrassed to see his son exposed so and helpless in sexual clutches.

Eric's maiden sexual encounter had been interrupted by a peeping father. *My God.*

Over the following several days Eric had been stricken with anxiety. Jacob knew this only because Eva had told him. The groping in the car had brought on a genuine existential terror for the boy, Eric's first experience of death's terrible magnificence. The truth about life, about its certain end, had burst into Eric's thinking with full force. He was overwhelmed. And, of course, he blamed his father. To his son, Jacob had been for some time already an absent God. Now he was a malicious one who brought shame and death into the world – into Eric's world. In a simple physical sense Eric was right: Death came with life and, undeniably, Jacob had given him life. Eric, precisian that he was, saw things with an absolute clarity: *Fathers kill.* His father certainly did. He hated his father ever after. Except for Joseph, all Jacob's sons did.

But what, after all, could Jacob have done? Had he been less neglectful, had he not constantly found ways to slink off to his clinic, had he faced a desperately bad home situation head on and not let bad habits congeal over the years, his children might have survived those difficult years (difficult for *all* children) and grown up. *Might* have. There were limits to what a father could do. Even so, when only a few years later Eva died it was a reconfirmation of what his sons all felt: Their father was a killer. They hated him worse. They would raise themselves. No longer would they feel themselves obscure and unimportant. They had each other. What did they need their father for? He hadn't turned away death from knocking on their mother's head.

There was something else, of course. *Repression.* A very insidious beast that did its mischief understairs. The human mind was the very perfect place for plots, with its lighted and its darkened rooms and closed doors in between. Jacob's sons hated him, all right, but far beyond his deserving . . . far beyond.

Why Jacob had been neglectful was harder to speak about. There were obvious reasons from his sour relationship with his own father. But that wouldn't answer all. Jacob's sons had arrived, had marched out of Eva with a terrible cadence, six in just over eleven years, and had reminded Jacob of his own end. Couldn't they understand that just as parents kill so do children? Nothing confirmed one's personal finish more certainly than the birth of a child.

In generation was mortality.

What was the answer to all this death business, then, that seemed to cluster around children? Perhaps his sons had once suggested an answer, Jacob being too caught up in himself to realize it.

He remembered Mark coming home from Columbia

University some years before, having been tossed off the basketball team. Mark had been full of talk about how a man had to find a way to make a space between himself and everything he had ever known – parents, culture, even his former selves, everything . . . to say *goddamn* to everything. It was a journey that had to be taken by everyone once. It was the one Jacob himself had always tried to take but never knew how to get started. Were his sons doing his business for him?

Jacob wondered. In some way were they not *wise* to have come into the mountains, driven by a madness, yes, but an inspired kind of madness, a wisdom that deranged but still wisdom? *Saying goddamn to everything,* that was just how Mark had put it in one of his fulminations. This insolence, this rejection of the world one was born into had a kind of survival value – it became the basis of each succeeding generation. In fact, it might even be the very prop of civilization itself. The world changed, men had to adapt.

All creatures save Man, after all, were suited to live only in the world their parents had known. When Nature shifted the terms of life it was mere chance if a species adapted. Their survival was regulated by the probability tables, numbers only. The trout in Mt Downton's streams, so fussy, so selective in their diet and worse than the worst health food faddist, these trout were always and forever unadventurously trout. Trout. Middle-class to the middle of their beings.

But there was a time when men must cease to be men and must become something else. The shape and texture of things human were changed thereby. Men like animals . . . men like gods. The evolutionary odds were dramatically altered – maybe for good, maybe for the worse – but at least one species of creation wasn't sitting around waiting to get sucked into oblivion.

Men would rather go kicking.

Some men had a kind of daring. Everybody felt a dose of it in adolescence, but the burden of civilization was carried by the few who didn't quite give it up. Even if they were only characters in a book. It didn't make for easy lives. That was no matter. Defiance stormed out of their blood. Heroes might have died young, not always, yet in their few years they lived more than the rest of us crawling out our time.

For he who dared was he who lived . . . *really* lived.

Like Odysseus, the blinded Cyclops on the shore still chewing the remains of Odysseus's crew in his filthy great mouth, like Odysseus recklessly screaming out his own name so that the eyeless giant would know down all his dark days exactly who had outwitted him, put out the giant's only eye and escaped from him . . . who had *dared* do it.

Since waking from his drugged sleep on the mountaintop Jacob had been asking himself why his sons had done this to him? *To die?* or *to survive?* Left for what? Here he was in this peaceful valley, escaped from his bloody ordeal, still ulcered from the cold, his feet skinless, bruised to his bones, chafed by wind, and yet he felt little anger towards his sons for subjecting him to an ordeal. *They had done worse to themselves.* Malicious as their attack on him at the wedding four years before, they had right away retreated to the mountains. And had endured so much more than Jacob was ever like to know. If they had abandoned him on a mountaintop, well, many years ago so had he left them. They had asked their father to be as good as they, to survive if he could. They had themselves.

It was just.

Instead of the bitterness he might have found in his heart he felt only pity. God how they had looked! And not only their much-tormented bodies. Jacob had seen deeply in their eyes a thousand ghastly *incubi* dancing . . . all his sons in Hell's clasp.

So he would pray for them. And hoped that they might realize the whole point of surviving in these mountains was to be able to find a way back, though they, his poor sons, didn't yet seem to know that. In the meantime he wished they were high on the cliffs above, right now watching him, their father, at sixty-years-on struggling to be born again, come at last to the great event he had been waiting a lifetime for . . . swimming the Hellespont and stealing fire from off Mt Olympus . . . .

142

It was about midday. Jacob strung his catch through the gills, gathered the rest of his gear and walked upstream to feed Carmen and himself, him and his four thousand appetites . . . feed the four thousand. Today was a holiday, the Lord's easy day in Paradise.

A strange sight he returned to. Carmen, the sun glowing aureate on her skin, knelt by the water with her hands gently laving in the water.

He said nothing as he came up, nor interfered with her wash, but it made his heart light to see strength tremoring in her limbs. Her eyes looked wonderfully clear of the fever.

'Clean, Jake.' She raised her hands towards him.

He nodded.

'*Clean* . . . once and for all.'

There was nothing uncertain in her voice.

Jacob laid the fish near some green stakes he had earlier cut for cooking their food. He kneeled down beside his woman, took her hands and opened them to his lips. Unable to speak, stuffed with the unexpected joy of seeing colour and health returning to her so quickly, Jacob kissed her palms, her fingers all the way to the tips. She was leaning on him, still very weak, but the fever had broken for certain and she was mending.

'Clean,' she repeated, as if disbelieving. It was a hymn of thanksgiving. 'The water just washed everything away.'

Jacob believed her. But then he had always believed her. The mote was not in his eye but in her own. Carmen must finally have made her peace with the child in Mississippi. Her long silence, the guilt she felt, had broken open with her febrile utterances the night before.

'Do you think you can eat something?' She looked at him as if to say she didn't know. 'We'll do it slowly . . . a little more every few minutes . . . push the stomach out bit by bit.'

'I'll try to, Jake.'

'We have to do it. And right now.'

She managed to help him make the meal.

They ate. Just as Jacob had described. They stopped for a while. They ate. They stopped. The several roots, the leaves he had picked made a salad, the sweet wild onions,

143

the larger of the trout. Today she tried the tree pulp again and found it edible, even pleasant, aromatic, reminding her of ginger for some reason.

In the late afternoon, both of them having slowly nodded off where they were lying drowsy from the meal, just then the sun slid towards the top of the canyon and its beams struck directly on the water, dazzling them both and waking them up.

'Don't move.'

Carmen froze. A yellow-whorled insect looking something like the hornets Jacob had seen downstream was walking on her breast. He leaned over and gently blew on the bug padding along. Sensing wind, the creature sailed away over the turf and across the stream.

'It looked like a wood wasp,' he said, 'and they don't have a sting.' Though a half-truth, it was also only half a lie he had told her, for as a child Jacob had seen such insects around the ramshackle picnic tables in his grandfather's vineyard trying to suck juice from open cider bottles and the broken fruit always lying around. Then he explained about the honey they could have had and why he hadn't gone after it. She said he shouldn't hold back from doing whatever was necessary to keep them alive.

'Anything, Jake.' Even though she was sensitive to stings.

He nodded. Everything was falling into place. All Carmen's quality was in evidence again. She was, he reckoned, the most beautiful woman in the world, all in all.

All in all.

Jacob kissed her shoulders. Her nipple, already teased by the insect's soft shoes, stood partly erect. This, too, he caressed with a dry mouth.

'Kiss my breasts all over.'

'Rest, Carmen.' It wasn't sex compelling him to touch her, not even love. Something yet more powerful, some kind of identity of being, as if she were an extension of him, he of her. 'Rest.'

'Kiss.' She reached around and clasped his hair, the white waves all crudded with the mountain's discards and days of sweat, pulled the longer strands down towards her, *pulling* his head. 'Your mouth is hard,' she told him, not complaining though.

'Dry is all.'

'Kiss.' His lips enclasped as much of her breast as he could stuff in his mouth . . . eating her. 'Kiss . . . kiss.' Carmen's fingers squeezed his skull. 'I'm feeling strange.' He paused, thinking she might be relapsing into the fever, but she told him it was just the opposite, not sickness but health . . . and more a feeling of fertility. She could actually sense the egg dropping, ovulation's mighty engine pressing towards life. He wondered about that but she was sure. '*Kiss*.' With real force Carmen shoved his head further down her torso, he resisting but his mouth staggered over her taut stomach, her skin alive again, rose and silver and gold . . . further down. No matter how Jacob tried to raise himself from her body she kept him pressed tightly against her, his own clock starting now and he less certain making love would spend strength they needed to get out of the mountain. His mouth grew softer, rounder, wetter, he overwhelmed by the first real stirrings of desire since they entered the wilderness and astonished that sexual energy could have such power in his weakened body, unless he were as fertile as she right now, the alchemical mix of life's fluids perfectly balanced in him, too . . . he smelling her, feeling her whole vagina pulsing against his lips as he lathered her with his tongue, he growing stiff in the stalk as her magical hands did their art down there.

She told him to come into her, her voice shaking. Caught wholly in her web now he slid all the way into her in a single, uninterrupted motion, all the way to the top, she lifting her legs around him, the two bodies fused at endless points, contact like one body. The rhythm of their pumping was slow, not violent at all, coordinated in the same direction, frictionless, the symmetry of a simple cycle turning perpetually over and over and over and over and over again.

At the instant he flooded her with sperm she had a sudden rush of elation different from any orgasm before, an agitation in her nerves all the way up and down her body so jolting that her eyes sprung open to the canyon lines and watched the shimmering sun, nearly disappeared now, she seeing in its disk something like a face. She blinked but the face remained.

On this day their resistless will to bring some love into the world would make a child. She could almost hear the infant voice crying in her womb, just as she could see its face in the last rays of sunlight . . . .

They rested in a deep heat, sweating diamonds.

For some time neither could move much, then later Jacob rolled off her, entirely enervated. He lay face-down in the turf, hands above his head clutching the long grass, an ominous chill in his blood as if he had just lost some vital part of himself – even the heat of the living man.

Then he fell asleep reminding himself that if she did conceive there would be no killing with this child, it would be a child of the light.

Seeing him asleep, Carmen got up and went to the edge of the stream. The frostbit toes on her right foot were still faintly bluish, but she could move them normally. So she put her foot in the water, felt only a gentle prickliness. Certain her fever had completely gone, she slipped all the way in and moved towards the centre of the pool, a slow breaststroke so effortless there was hardly any movement on the water's surface, the coloured tracery of clouds above her still perfectly reflected.

The deepest point was under her now, seven or eight feet deep, slick stones on the bottom and some sand, all of which she could see. She put her head under. Washed her hair. For several minutes she glided back and forth, the cold of the stream bearable and nothing like the dead lake where she had taken a swim before they had been stolen by Jacob's sons.

Jacob was up and watching her. Like a water sprite she was, the long tresses of her hair flowing back behind her as she moved soundlessly through the water. These were graces that he had never seen in real life but knew only from literature, paintings, the music of the great dreamers. The stream was the Rhine and she one of the maidens guarding Wagner's gold. All rainbows ended right in their pool. It rendered him weak watching this distressingly beautiful woman whom destiny had put in his arms. But she had always taken his breath away.

He came to the water's edge. Carmen was swimming away from him, one slow stroke and then a long, easy glide. She made her turn, saw him. Smiled. She had noticed Jacob's consternation every time she approached the stream. 'Want to try it?'

He shook his head.

'You can't get into any trouble here. Come out to the middle of the pool.'

He took the deepest breath of his life. 'You know I can't swim . . . not a stroke . . . not even tread water.'

'I'll teach you.'

'What do I do?'

'Walk towards me.'

After a few steps Jacob stopped, put his toes all over the bottom, felt the moss on the stones. His eyes tightened.

'If you slip the worst that can happen is you'll go under and come right back up.'

But his muscles wouldn't coordinate. There were years of fear in every step, their pull tenacious. She kept waving him on and got him to take another few steps. 'All the way out, Jake.'

'How deep is it . . . *really*?'

'Just a little over your head.' He was waist-deep now but stuck. 'You won't drown.' Still he stood motionless. 'I'll catch you if you tumble. Come on.'

As he moved cautiously ahead he stepped off a ledge and the water went from his stomach to above his chest. He panicked, thrashing his arms and spitting water, then finally righted himself as his feet found purchase on a sand flat.

'Keep walking.'

Jacob's head kept shaking but his feet pressed steadily forwards. The finger of sand continued to the deeper water, the footing easy, gradual . . . until the water was at Jacob's neck.

'Don't stop. Just continue all the way to me.'

'One more step, Carmen, and it'll be over my head.'

'That's right.'

147

Jacob looked strangely at her. 'What's the point?'

'Come on.'

'What are you testing in me?'

'Everything, Jake, *every damned thing*.'

And then something unexpected happened. Jacob remembered that since they were at the top of the mountain he hadn't had a single moment of fear. About anything. Fear, like the anger it often led to, had been learned and could be unlearned. It wasn't natural, fear, just a habit within every man that *seemed* natural because of so long use. He had had enough of it. He would swim this small sea and then oceans beyond. He put his foot out, stepped forward refusing to close his eyes as he plunged in over his head. She was on top of him just as he fell and buoyed him up, held him as he spit out water, kept him afloat and then laid him carefully on his back and swam along with him, telling him how to use his legs in order to propel himself through the water, he not fighting her or the slight current, just moving with her, letting himself be led, feeling the extraordinary world of mobility for the first time . . . floating on a green sea . . . floating on a sea of faith . . . just floating . . . floating . . . floating in Paradise . . . .

It was a long way down. Down from the canyon walls. From near the top.

A long way.

The stone flew slowly out from the cliff and accelerated hard into its trajectory only when it reached the midpoint between the facing cliff walls, right over the middle of the stream. The stone, the size of an eye, fell past the dwarfed shrubs grappling to the canyon sides, past the conifers on the lower slopes, right down to the valley floor.

It struck at one end of the pool not ten feet from where Carmen and Jacob were swimming in tandem. Entering like a dagger, so straight it hardly made a sound. Jacob heard it nonetheless.

She felt him jerk in her arms. 'Just a fish . . . relax.'

Fish? 'Not with us in the pool like this, it isn't.'

'Then a stone falling.' She had got used to the earth slides.

'I'm feeling the cold. Perhaps we ought to get out. It's been long enough for the first time.'

Carmen kissed the round point of his shoulder. Steering Jacob to a point where he could stand, she let go of him to see if he could paddle in to shore by himself. He splashed trying, went under, righted himself quickly. 'I'll walk in.'

Just then another stone fell, this one by the downstream riffle at the bottom of the pool. Carmen and Jacob looked at each other and then, instinctively, up the cliff sides. They could see nothing but the canyon.

In the sky, though, a trail of geese, snow geese, were passing south towards their wintering grounds in the Salton Sea and farther down the Pacific flyway to the deserts of northern Mexico. Birds of passage flying in a wedge and making a terrible din with their honking. It took several minutes for the entire cloud of birds to pass over, waxen and yellow in the dying light.

'When can we start going home, Jake?'

'Whenever you feel strong enough.'

'Tomorrow?'

'We'll see.'

The next stone didn't land in the water at all. Rather it clanged off a streamside boulder, raising a little wisp of powder, atomizing as it hit. And another fell into the grass, very near the spot where they had been making love.

And another.

He didn't like this loosening of the earth . . . so much rock falling, so spread out. Something else was going to tumble down the mountain, things so far only the prelude to a greater song.

'What is it?'

Jacob scanned the entire cliff opposite their shelter. 'I can't tell where they're falling from.'

'Maybe we should move camp, Jake?'

'I don't understand how the stones are falling so far from the cliffs.'

'Well, they are.'

His eyes burned from the strain. 'We *will* move downstream. The valley's wider there, just not so idyllic.'

A shadow rushing. Both glimpsed its fall at the same moment, ducked together. The largest rock so far banged into the bank, spitting dust and grit on impact—

—*Whack!*

Still larger . . . closer . . . a deadly rock, one that could mince skulls and brains.

'Get out of the water,' he told her. *'Get out!'*

Carmen stood still in the shallows. Looked into the hillsides. A cry stuck in her throat . . . and died there.

The mountain was coming alive.

A man stood amongst the trees a quarter of the way up the canyon walls. Watching. Waiting. An Indian man. A Chilcotin.

Stones were landing everywhere around them, coming from several directions at once. In the trees on both sides of the stream there were noises, calls and guttural howls, the barking and yapping of dogs echoing from one cliff to the other, men storming in the mountain and the gorge shaking with the sounds.

When they looked up again the Indian was gone. The calls, all the other movement as well, stopped as suddenly as they had begun. Carmen took a few steps away from the bank, held onto Jacob, the two of them in the pool naked and cold and defenceless.

One at a time, from behind boulders, out of the trees, the lost tribe of his sons reassembled. Five men at war with everything in the world, with rock and sky and ice and wind. They had brought dogs as well, bred of wolves and strays.

Jacob had no idea which son was which. He looked but saw only the pack of them, converted from the sons he'd fathered into creatures of the mountain. All wore moccasins and long leggings, breechcloths. No shirts but robes of sewn skins, the same rabbit and lynx blankets they had given Carmen and him, much better sewn. Their bodies were painted, their whole bodies, in red and black that split right at the nose, red below, black all above. Jewellery, ornaments, dentalia shells and teeth. Their hair oiled. Nothing at all like what they had been only three days ago. And caps that covered all their heads but their faces, caps of animals, almost masks, with the ears and tails of each beast's fur dressed in their hair, which for each was knotted behind his ear and laced through the cap.

Five animals: *a wolf, a raven, a bear, an elk, a marten* . . . where once had been Eric and Mark and Bobby and Thomas and Douglas. All his sons risen from themselves into something terrible and wondrous and sad. Stooping slightly. Shaven clean.

And each carried a large bag made from the pelt of his animal familiar. And in each bag were stones.

The raven threw the first stone.

It landed in the stream, far short of Jacob and Carmen. Each of the others in turn picked a stone from his bag, threw it wide of the mark.

The circle of sons tightened. The stones landed closer, slapped hard on the water, but still they were thrown carefully not to hit, not to wound.

Jacob Solomon raised his hands. He spoke softly, had the idea in his head that his sons had come to share an understanding with him. 'We have to talk.' They threw stones. 'There are things we've *got* to talk about . . . things you *must* hear from me.' They yipped. 'We're cold. And naked. Stand back for a minute and let us out so we can put on our shawls . . . and you'll talk to me . . . yes . . .? in your own voices?' A plea sent on the wings of the dove.

They cast stones.

Carmen broke from his arms and before he could grab her she was gliding quickly to the bank, hoisted herself up onto the grass.

'Leave them alone, Carmen!' He held his balance in the stream.

She stood ten yards from the marten, pointed a long finger at Douglas as if she knew him. But there was nothing in his eyes – no understanding, only meanness and the bright circles of animal hunger.

'Get back,' she warned him. He stood closest to her robe.

The marten threw a stone at her, though only half-heartedly.

151

Her fury was beginning to uncoil. *'Get back!'* She herself reached for pebbles in the stream.

He whistled a stone past her ear. That completely unsprung her and she lunged towards him—

—another stone . . . from right behind her.

And this one did hit her. Right at the base of her spine. *'CARMEN!!'*

She never heard. She spun on her heels to see which of the others had thrown the stone that hit her. The bear and raven drew in closer, undismayed. *'You dirty fucking insane bastards!!!'*

The raven had a stone in his hand, too. He weighed it up and down while she stared into his black and cunning eyes. Then he wound up his arm, with her still looking squarely at him, and threw the stone hard. And true. It struck her in the head just above her left eye. A momentary squint of disbelief passed across her face before her eyes clouded and she fell onto the grass unconscious . . . to Jacob's sight, dead.

It changed everything.

Jacob Solomon finally understood.

His great and grizzled jaw flapped in the breeze coming off the stream. Unable to cry out he lurched uncertainly, actually feeling her pain right over his own eye as everything went white in front of him. Only horror in his mind.

Only horror.

He stepped backwards into the deeper water, away from the sight.

He had thought they wanted him to survive. He had thought they came to say this. He had wanted to tell them he was Love's pilgrim. He had hoped to have his peace with them made.

And it was. But theirs with him was yet to come. To his sons he was now, had always been and would forever world-without-end be one thing only: *the ambassador of death*. That was how they understood his voyage into their mountains. And if the mountain wouldn't kill him, they would . . . *kill the dirty fucking Deathmaker*.

With stones . . . .

The wolf moved forward, pushing his cap down tightly so that the wolf ears entirely hid his own. His envious eyes, green as the water they now reflected, watched his father in the middle of the stream desperately trying to tread water and regain his footing. The others circled closer in.

Stones from each of the sons struck all around Jacob, though none hit him at first. He surfaced, his face bright from struggling with the water, looked frantically from one of them to the next, hoping one last glance from him would get them to rush into the water and save him, which to the end he continued to believe they would do.

But he would not ask for that. Oh no.

Nor fear them. Nor death.

They had hoped to see him drown but Jacob got his toes stuck into the sandy patch and steadied. Just watched them. And they him. For this was the right death. He had not been there for their cries those many years before; now when he got caught up in the deeper waters and the under-currents they would do nothing, too.

'Die, old man.' The words slithered off the wolf's brown and rotting teeth. 'Hurry up and fucking die.'

Dagold-Hin . . . Deneita . . . Daltsha'n.

'You can't kill me.' He spit the words through the water choking him.

'We can kill you.'

'Oh no you can't . . . have done already, years ago.' Jacob fought his way forward several steps, trying to rise out of the pool, got up to his chest . . . his hips . . . his waist came free of the water as he strove with his sons one hard step after the next, but he was coming after them. '. . . thirty years ago you did . . . more.'

The wolf watched. 'I can kill you.'

'Too late . . . the worst is done. You can't do another thing to me. You understand . . .? *There's nothing left to do!!*'

Daltsha'n. A chorus of death from the others.

They were all trembling. Jacob could see the ignorance, the malaise, the fear. The wolf's eyes were bulging with fury.

'*I* can kill you, old man, in the stream or out!'

He didn't understand. Neither he nor his brothers ever would. 'Not the love in me, you can't.' The tears in Jacob's eyes were half of joy. 'You get my body, nothing else. *Not one other thing!*' Jacob was chanting. It was a hymn of praise, its melody the great affairs of men, the tall men . . . all the heroes. It was his song now. And he, he was the singer.

'*Daltsha'n,*' as the wolf drove a jagged stone right into the old man's chest below the heart. Jacob Solomon felt the hot blood scrambling all over his belly, dripping into the water. He stared down at the wound, touched its truth, raised his red fingers and tasted his own blood—'

'—J-j-j-j-j-j—!'

He looked up. Carmen had struggled to her hands and knees, her eyes spinning, as a ribbon of scarlet flowed copiously down, masking her cheeks, lips, chin. *Carmen bleeding . . . hidden by blood?* His Carmen?

But she was what mattered! It was Carmen who had given him a renewed life separate from his sons. All the good he had made flowed from her. He had tapped out a love with her like an ancient jeweller and his filigree. Veiled by *her own* blood?

That did it.

Riot was slipping loose. Jacob saw more than five sons, wild laughter in twenty, half a hundred, a thousand . . . hordes of them, ranks assembling, a mob swelling for the common rite of murder, their faces bright in celebration of the killing way . . . all the primitive children snarling in a pack, the countless millions of them rising for revenge.

Let it be bloody.

He flung himself towards the bank with his fists flaming in the air, driving into the midst of the millions, they pelting him with stones to try to keep him from the shore, but his feet just couldn't keep a grip on the mossy bottom as he tried to move too quickly and fell backwards into the pool completely out of control . . . the flurry of rocks thicker around him though he transformed the stones they threw into golden missiles of his own, picking them off his body and throwing them right back until the final instant when too many rocks struck his old, white head and cracked his skull into many fragments of shattered bone and ripped out his eyes and drove through his lips to the pink gums and roots of teeth below and pressed him down into the current at the bottom of the pool, dragging him along the riffle and on down that stream that led out of the paradisiacal valley and into the world below while all his children unmoved watched him take his last breath, all water, watched him drown, the last flight of his life . . . into oblivion . . . .

Risen all my sons . . . have murdered me.

BOOK II

The Winter Bear

CHAPTER 13

Carmen awoke into a world of grunts and groans.

A nightmare by daylight.

Five men, more animals than men, were scattered along the riverbank on their elbows, on their sides, backs, knees, feet convoluted, one brother lying exhausted on the next, enervated by what they had done, while in the lengthening gloom streams of sedge flies danced over the waters . . . five motionless bodies stripped of their robes, the entire Chilcotin nation in recline, muscles still jiggling from the strain of murder.

One of them shifted to scratch his legs, followed the itch up the great sinews of his shoulder. His eyes stayed closed and he fell back into the whorl of skin and tendon, bone and hair, spit in his sleep, snored.

The murder was done. The rape still to come. And Carmen waited for it without fear, without feeling of any kind, her mind white, dizzy, abstract, empty as the nautilus. They had killed an old man defenceless in the stream . . . who was also their father . . . and what was more, the last of the lions. In killing Jacob they had killed more than they knew. There was nothing left to be frightened of.

But she started when the raven rose.

He stood up and straightened his bird legs, blacked over with charcoal. At the pool side he took off his leggings, his moccasins as well, found a rock sharp enough to lance one of his big toes where the nail had grown into his skin and made a weeping sore, yellow with infection. His legs were bowed across the stream like a bird's. The fast water ran over his bad foot anaesthetizing it and rinsing away pus and grit that had gathered in the wound.

His head swivelled around quickly, eyes passing right by

158

Carmen without stopping. He had turned to look at something else: The others were getting up.

A wolf, an elk, a bear, a marten. And the raven. Each stood, moved, postured, walked like his animal familiar. They were smiling now, lips and eyes glazed red in the twilight . . . mouths licking, smacking. Hunger gave them motion, not remorse.

Pretty Marten and the bear turned over all of Jacob's handiwork, examined it like priests reading the guts of animals. The oven was still warm, roots continuing to bake all this while. Together the two brothers kicked it open, rolled out the roots, snorting in ridicule at their father's attempts to survive.

They didn't scorn, though, to eat what they mocked. Not minding the hot skins they slavered over the pulp, stuffing more and more into their mouths, throwing half-eaten bits into the river. The other three fell into the frenzy soon after, pulling at the tendrils, tearing the bulbs open until every last one was shredded and sucked of its meat however hard it was to chew.

Little Bear took the cleaned, uneaten trout, put it whole and raw – tail first – into his cavernous mouth, then bit it in two. He looked at the head before eating that, as well. A little while later he sniffed out the berries and had rolled half of them tartly in between his molars before his brothers saw and came to take the rest away for themselves.

They seemed to swell on the food, grow almost drunken.

There was a pause. Carmen was sure they were about to turn on her. But that didn't happen.

Having eaten they went into the pool where they had stoned their father to death. Their bodies caked and chafing from the berry juice, they washed everything off, the mud, slivers of bush, sap, scouring their skin with goose grass until the charcoal and face paint came away, too. In the last strands of the sunset all five brothers rose from the water fresh-skinned, far healthier-looking than when they had first clambered over the rocks to capture Carmen and their father, as if grown to health in father murder.

It only took a little water to wash away their crime . . . and a few blades of grass to scratch through the strongest cords in nature. Their unnatural laughter boomed in the canyon. They played in the pool. They slapped each other in riot.

Carmen was still too numb to weep.

Or listen to the wildness of their cries. She had thought they would replay the murder in jest, strut and fret the scene again while in the water, choose one of themselves to represent their father and bloody him a little, drive him under and downstream choking. It didn't surprise her, though, when they made no imitation. They had already forgot what they'd done.

Evening. Carmen had fallen asleep again.

'*Huy huy!*'

Wolf, the eldest, once a boy whose beauty and luminance had stung his father to tears, answered the call of the two returning from downstream.

Carmen raised herself enough to watch Elk Man and another dragging the body along by the feet, Jacob's blood by no means yet fully staunched so that a thick trail of it congealed along the streamside, over rock and thorn and bush as the brothers pulled their father along indifferently.

From where she lay Jacob looked alive. His face seemed to be still set for combat, still screaming curses, though much of his jaw had been torn away and he was eyeless, she could see now as they brought the corpse closer, and every part of his trunk was serrated by the stones they had thrown, pouches and swellings, bones shattered underneath, the body's shape and articulation gone.

She drew back.

Not far from her, by the edge of the small shelter Jacob had built, the brothers dumped the carcass in order to build a carrier. Jacob's naked back, scratched and gritted from the haul upstream, reflected the moonlight. Very few of the rocks had struck him there. Despite the fresh abrasions this one part of him was nearly pristine, something like what Carmen remembered. It was a piece of the man she had loved, white and old and marblelike. The lion's back. He who had carried her halfway down the mountainside in his old age and not slipped once.

She looked up and down his body. Her eyes fastened onto the top of his head. Most of the white hairs had been torn away, the scalp as well . . . the skull case itself broken into.

Carmen stared inside his head. At his brains.

One of the dogs was looking, too. There were five or six wandering among the camp shadows, all reasonably large animals, the size of wolves but with smaller faces, snouts like coyotes and much of their colouring, too, dark patches over the back legs in the tan and grey mottled coats. They didn't seem wild, nor tamed . . . not pets and not just scavengers following the band of brothers.

The animal took a long sniff of the body, licked the feet for salt. And then it thrust its nose right into Jacob's head.

Struggling to her feet, Carmen swung at the dog, missing it. Lunged again, fiercely enough to frighten the dog, which pulled its nose out of Jacob's brains and trotted away into the shadows.

She would kill it if it came close to Jacob again.

The effort had brought back her light-headedness. She looked up. A fat moon hovered overhead. She had trouble keeping it in focus. Then she lay back on the spruce boughs and dropped right into a sleep where Jacob's sons were waiting for her, pursuing her even in her dreams . . . while entombing their father inside a bay tree and lighting the tree on fire until it cooked him as a dish for the gods . . . a fit sacrifice to the spirits of wolves, ravens, bears, elk, and marten . . . .

When Carmen opened her eyes again the five brothers were standing in a line. A kind of funeral train. The carrier they had built was loaded with Jacob's body.

It didn't take her long to realize they were waiting for her to fall in behind them. For an instant she thought she would refuse to go along. But she knew that one way or another they would drag her back into the mountain.

They started. She got up and trudged along behind.

Up the canyon. Towards the rockfall but not all the way. Well below treeline they left the stream and slipped into a small cut in the canyon walls, a tiny spur trail that went up a series of switchbacks. Near the top of the highest trees they emerged onto flatter ground, then passed through a set of huge boulders which turned out to be a ridge ringing a crater not entirely unlike the volcano where the brothers had abandoned Jacob and her three days before.

But once over the ridge she could see in the unobstructed brilliance of the moon and starful night that this was a different place altogether. Though it was hidden it was not a lunar valley struck clean of all life.

It was their home.

While the five of them slept in a lodge open at the sides, a gabled structure loosely covered with mats, Carmen found a place by herself in the rock ledges above the campsite. Although early in the night, a frost was already speckling the stones, and she a long ways from the fire. By propping herself against a boulder Carmen managed to cover nearly her whole body with the animal skin that had been keeping her alive for the last several days. She took special care to shield her frostbitten toes completely under the wrap, two of them still puffy. She knew that she would lose them if they froze again.

It was too cold to sleep. The dogs, still up as well, were baying and barking, though she thought that might have something to do with the shooting stars falling continuously across the sky.

Something jabbed into her flank. Not the twists of the blanket, something hard. Carmen rolled off the pelt, reached around and found a bone. A long bone. No leg of a man, nothing in the human anatomy could have made that. The thing was as tall as her waist. In between the rocks she could see other sticks glistening in the starlight . . . a littering of bones around her, a charnel house. Looking harder she saw skulls, much larger and flatter than a man's head, deer or caribou or moose. Smaller heads, too, that once were lynx, coyote.

The brothers had eaten strange flesh.

There was one more bone, too. Part of the jaw had crumbled away, but Carmen knew what she was looking at.

Chapfallen. Grinning. The memento of a man they might have eaten.

Carmen rolled away from the sight of it and pressed up against another stone. She cried for a time, the emptiness in her mind beginning slowly to suck up images of Jacob from her memory, how he looked right before the murder, the old man floating peacefully in the pool . . . green pool . . . then the first stones . . . then all that she had been made to witness . . . the look on his face when his fingers gathered blood from his wounds . . . the bloody currents stealing away from him as his life spilled into the river.

The tears made Carmen drowsy, perhaps even drowsy enough to sleep, certainly insensible to the shadows crawling around her amongst the boulders.

Out of the night something – the size of a leaping dog – flew right for her head. She gasped and sprang sideways just as it struck the spot where she had been resting. No splintering of the rocks. No ear-cracking noise. A dull thumping sound.

A bundle. Her fingers plied the soft cloth all the way around. Clothing. Old clothes smelling of age and blood, the musk of dying foxes, the urine of dogs.

It wasn't her own clothes which they had probably left by the lake or burned or buried. She unwrapped the package all the way. Everything was frayed. Sweaters and wool pants. Shoes, too, and socks rent with holes. Leather shoes, not matching ones, a kind of half-boot paired with an everyday lace-up old brogue in blond, cracked leather . . . too big for her but never mind, not so very big it couldn't be worn. A pea jacket as well, also badly torn. And a rag which she wound around her neck into a scarf. A heavy toque for a hat. She could improvise mittens out of something that remained.

She coiled the clothes around herself, layer after layer, as quickly as she could, until the sharpening frost no longer chewed her nerves.

The lynx and rabbit robe lay discarded part-way down the slope. For a while she stared at it, wondering if she should leave it there or use it as an overblanket. Which, she asked herself, was their intended mockery? That she had to wear the shreds of unsanctified city garments or that she would have to bend low and keep the Indian gown as well, share part of their barbaric world?

Below she heard some song overlaying the dogs' howling. It was the brothers deep in chant. The real mockery was that they weren't even bothering to listen to her anger.

Carmen moved a few feet down the hill and pulled back the Indian blanket she had thrown away. Draped it over her feet. She would do whatever she had to in order to live, until there was a chance to run . . . until the balance turned and the sword put in her hand.

Dreaming of justice she prayed for a two-handed sword, and a dull blade, and five lingering deaths to set in the scales. She'd know just how to chop the join of their necks and shoulders.

The thought alone warmed her all the way through.

For the next day, and the next after that, they continued to ignore her, the five brothers busy making sanctuary against the coming winter. Carmen, from her perch in the boneyard, watched it all.

There was the winter house to refit. A round pit – what had been their last year's shelter – they redug to a depth of four feet, enlarged it so that it was nearly forty feet in diameter. They made a tentlike roof, laying poles and saplings next to each other before adding a dirt pack. A ladder came down from the hole at the apex of the roof, an opening which would also serve as a vent for their fire.

They had collected the harvest, for some weeks already Carmen guessed, and from fields that would have had to be at lower elevations. The food they had got they put into simple caches raised on standing logs. During the first day Carmen had watched them build three other caches from timber freshly cut, but these were left to stand empty and she didn't understand right away what they were for.

The whole afternoon they worked excitedly on what seemed to her to be a weir of some kind. It was made of willow branches and lashed with rope they had twisted of spruce roots. From their mutterings Carmen understood this to be a snare for salmon. She recognized a sluice trap, as well, with baskets to catch the fish. And long, two-pronged bone-toothed harpoons for spearing any fish that evaded either of the blinds. They would dry the salmon and then eat them throughout the winter as their principal source of protein. The three empty caches could hold a thousand pounds of fish, maybe much more.

Killing salmon right in the act of generation. It was exactly their kind of murder.

And stolen salmon, poached from Indian waters.

Carmen could take only so much pleasure from these bitter recognitions. Every hour she sat there she grew more and more hungry, wild-headed. And colder. The last warmth of the Indian summer had finally gone, despite the constant sunshine. Her clothes were feeble proof against the kind of cold coming on. She had to eat, if only to stay warm.

Not that she wanted to. If she might starve every last gramme of fat off her body so that her waist floated and her flesh consumed itself like a candle, she would then be dry as a toad when they finally turned their attentions to her, as she knew sometime soon they were going to do. And, in drinking nothing, she was passing almost no water; nor had she fluxed her bowels since entering the mountains. She'd be dry as a toad, all right . . . and with a little bit of luck just as poisonous.

But she wasn't ready to die just yet, not with the five of them alive and Jacob unavenged.

In the afternoon of her second day in their camp, the brothers gone to some remote part of the valley, Carmen went in search of water and any crumbs she could steal from their table.

Not large, the valley was nearly a mile across, a shallow saucer of rock rubble and arctic bell-heather, sedge. Deeper in the valley some few tall trees stuck in the rock like a weak beard. Towards the centre the woods thickened, a mix of conifers and aspen formed a mantle around an inner ring of willows. And in the very centre a lake. There was no outlet to be seen but an underground stream drained the valley and kept the sweetwater from growing stagnant. All the runoff from the ridges fed the lake; its one constant source, though, was a tiny falls that flowed right down the eastern face of the mountain and ran across the valley into the trees as a fastwater brook.

Not knowing exactly where the brothers had gone, only that they were somewhere near the lake, Carmen kept to the ridge and sucked water from the falls where it struck the valley sides. The current chilled her as she drank, lips and teeth and tongue, throat, chest. She had to push herself away, rest on the sedge grasses, then drink more slowly.

The brothers' voices rang out over the lake. She thought it might be some kind of hunting cry. Making her way deeper into the valley, to the valley floor and into the trees, Carmen followed a latticework of dry channels that spread into a marsh, game trails traced by continuous use. Several spots looked like sinking sands and so she kept carefully to the signs of where larger animals had walked.

At one point, through a break in the trees, she could see several of the brothers in unstable canoes, dugouts, running a flock of ducks towards the far shore. The birds moved quickly over the water. But they were moulting and unable to fly. A net had been drawn at the bank and when the ducks tried to take land cover under the willows they simply fell into the net. Easy pickings. The brothers on the boats were driving them hard, whooping and singing.

She suddenly stopped. There was another sound, much closer, the breaking of twigs just feet away. A double-trunked spruce stood closeby and she quickly crouched behind it.

It was the bear. Little Bear. Largest of the Solomons. An unsteady mansion of folded flesh, some freckles, bald pate and long ginger curls that fell down his back. His eyes were hidden by his cheeks. Too gross for the canoes, he was gathering another kind of catch. In one hand he carried pole snares with several rabbits still wriggling in the leather wires shackling them. He staked the poles and, looking bored, lay down by a fallen tree next to the sack he was carrying in his other hand.

Carmen watched as he pulled a grouse out of the bag, fondled the frightened bird until it grew quiet under his thumb's stroking. Then he twisted its head until the neck gave. He plucked the bird warm. The others he killed like-wise, except for the last, which he paused over, fixing on the grouse through the eye of his mountain science. He would experiment. He plucked it clean while it was still alive and unmolested, then let it die slowly in the bag.

A bracelet of feathers had formed around his feet. He took one of the longest and while calculating his findings he picked his teeth with the quill end.

One of the rabbits was squirming free. Very gently Little Bear reached down, tied the noose around it again. But the rabbit had a way and within moments was again almost free of the snare. The big man held the rabbit's shoulders while with his other hand he pressed its rib cage between thumb and fingers, locating the hard thump of its heart and squeezing until, in a few seconds, the beast went limp. Then he probed the animal's head to find the breakpoints, crushed it like a nut and took out the brains . . . brains swirling in the rabbit's blood . . . and ate them, raw brains, ate them just like that.

Carmen's breath rushed from her throat.

He heard her and turned quickly around. Her face colourless, bloodless, Carmen rose. Their eyes were fixed on each other. She looked nervously at his huge, punch-bowl hands.

He smiled, and kept smiling as Carmen tripped back-wards into the stream, staggering through the trees to the rocks, then mounting rapidly up towards the base of the falls and her perch farther on, her perch a home of just two days but the only familiar thing in the valley. She thrashed at the mountain, tried to climb, couldn't, slid back down scraping skin along both forearms and wrists and hands, slivering dirt too deep to wash out.

Carmen gasped for the mountain air, sat on rocks and bones, her clothing wet from the thighs down. It took her several minutes to capture her breath. And all the while she stared at a mound of stones next to the stream.

Stared like an idiot.

It was a newly-piled cairn of rocks culled for their smoothness and roundness, set ceremonially one on top of the other. And sticking from the top stones a blade, what was left of her ice-axe. It would have to be Jacob's grave. She hadn't seen the body since they had marched up from the spot where Jacob was killed.

Jacob had been buried within the prospect of his murdering sons.

The thought had a quieting effect on Carmen. She touched the memorial. Jacob was only a few feet from her hand.

So she stayed by the gravesite, consecrating it as her spot, a place where she could begin making plans to flee . . . and maybe to avenge a death. All it would take would be her staying alive long enough, enduring the brothers' own hardships better than they.

And the patience of the holies . . . which she would somehow find.

CHAPTER 14

Several more days passed with the brothers continuing to ignore her.

The rape she had anticipated didn't come. There was no contact at all. Carmen sat on her perch and watched them . . . thinking more and more about the things around her, what directions the wind blew, the lichens growing on the rocks, an animal moving, the men in the willows. Jacob's murder seemed more remote than it should. Even the image of his soft face was hard to recompose in her mind . . . only his voice and good instruction staying with her, all the rest thin, tenuous, disappearing with the year and the shorter days.

Then one morning the five of them were gone.

They had left while she was asleep.

Carmen leaned over the cairn, looked into the camp. The fishing weir, their bone spears, baskets, sluice traps – all the fishing gear gone, along with the horses they had stolen from Jacob and her. The salmon cull was on.

Left her alone?

She couldn't believe it.

Suspicious still, Carmen hurried down the hillside, slipping dangerously. The sun, coming up lower in the horizon every morning, took longer to brush the frost away. Lying over the white skirt of frost this morning was a heavy powdering of snow. It wasn't melting, either. She approached the campsite slowly, poised to run back into the hillside.

Gone?

She stood by the lodge without moving. Listened. Nothing. Walked a few steps into the campfire ring. The stones were dead cold. It was impossible they had just gone, giving her a chance to run. Not yet convinced, Carmen scuttled amongst their things, looking for a sign, looking for everything and nothing.

She found detritus of every kind: tears and shreds of their old clothing, pieces of dried gut, twisted can openers, machined tools falling into disrepair, torn sheet plastic, book pages, broken axe handles, endless scraps of pine and spruce and hemlock and chewed pitch from the same trees, a partly decomposed alto recorder, wild tobacco, the bit-off discards of roots and tubers, burned feathers, a pair of eyeglasses cracked down both lenses, frazzled coils of rope and nylon cords covered with grime so thick the snow hardly discoloured it, shitholes spread over the entire camp without regard for what got contaminated, a pervading stench, most things useless, everything rotting.

And a whole order of things very different mixed indiscriminately with the garbage: quivers of fawn, coiled baskets not elegant but serviceable and strong, root-diggers, bark cups, bark kettles, knives and spearpoints and adzes and arrowheads of obsidian, some of bone, twisted caribou hide that they used for rope, various skins being soaked in water and birch leaves, scraping posts and frames for stretching the skins, for dressing them and smoking them, as well, dyes of crushed alder bark and berry juices and wolf-moss, hammered copper ornaments, dentalia shells, and games of all kinds, gambling sticks and dice of beaver's teeth and bones carved as toys.

Games for their play. She had watched them. Games would just begin. Serious games where they gambled for stakes she didn't understand, guessing the number of quills held in one hand. Running contests. Chasing wooden rings with a long stick. Shouting matches. Insults and fights, some of them seeming bitter to her but never turning out that way. Games with food, throwing it and gobbling it and drinking games and games of manners mocking the world at the bottom of the mountain that they had left forever . . . games with what she thought must be local drugs, swimming in the cold lake and jumping on the horses and wrestling and throwing and shooting different kinds of arrows.

And the game of kick the dog.

Carmen looked carefully around the camp. The dogs had disappeared, too. There were at least half a dozen of them that lived near the camp, came and went in no kind of order. Sometimes the brothers gave one food or even, once in a while, affection; but more than likely the dog was kicked, or a stick thrown at it, or a stone. The dogs would run back to somewhere in the rocks, though she could never see where.

That was their favourite game – 'kick the dog'. Of the several brutal acts she had witnessed amongst the brothers that was the one she least minded. Because she knew the day they stopped delighting in 'kick the dog' would be the day they turned their sport on her . . . .

Having seen all that she wanted of their hard and ugly life, Carmen walked back to the burial mound. Sat down. She listened for the voice of the dead man below her, if he could tell her what to do. *Run?* Run now while they were gone? Or stay until she found some way to scratch the eyes out of each one and hang their bowels out for vermin to eat and their hearts for the mountain ravens? If Jacob's spirit, perhaps hovering right over her, could rattle the spruce boughs and polished stones, plead one way or the other, she would hear. She was sure the right way was revenge, first or last; but with ice on her eyelids, the thump of nothing except faeces in her gut, and a dry and parchment anger in her head that had, after nearly a week with little water and no real food at all, left her bereft of her senses, so weakened as she was how could she find a way to kill the five of them? The truth was, she didn't have much left . . . a day, two, three, no more. She was at the last of her strength.

There was no answer from the gravestones. But she did keep hearing something in the distance. Leaning forward Carmen looked to the forest around the lake. There was the flash of an axe on the larger trees, its mean and dull stroke hardly damped at all by the newly fallen snow.

Not all the brothers had gone. One had been left behind to drudge away in the woods, while keeping a careful eye on her. One brother only.

It depressed her for only a moment. The sound had resolved her doubts. Perhaps Jacob's spirit was speaking after all. If someone had stayed behind then they believed she might run . . . and if that were true there must be somewhere to run . . . a way out of the mountain.

All day long Raven did the back-splitting toil and business of chopping trees for winter firewood, using the axes and hammers of stone, sometimes felling the biggest trees by setting controlled fires. Utterly exhausting work.

It might have been made easier had he used the steel axe, double-bitted, lying under the rust and discards of all the modern tools which the brothers had left to rot. But he wouldn't. The raven – more than any of the others – was the apostle of their purity. He was the one who had read the books and planned the rigours of their lives to follow Chilcotin ways. The tallest of the brothers, well-beaked, black-faced, sour and splenetic, Raven was the most fastidious of men, careful in everything. He and his brothers would cut wood exactly as the Chilcotins had, living or dying that way. He used only stone axes, and fires if needed.

His brothers had left Raven behind because he would be the last one to let Carmen get away. Having set up their refuge, he had the cunning to make sure it wouldn't be jeopardized.

He'd sooner kill her.

As she watched him from a distance, Carmen began to compose a plan for escape. She had heard the brothers talk about the salmon trip taking at least three days. That gave her enough time to find the passage out of their valley. There did seem to be a track down the mountain by the east, but she had an instinct that something there – a rock face or waters gathering into a river – made escape impossible. Colin had exhorted them over and over to nose out the western defile. She would find it. She had to.

In the meantime Raven's wood gathering would leave him so tired he was vulnerable. And Carmen knew how to make it worse. She'd keep him from sleeping . . . and find out if the raven was a nocturnal bird after all.

The first night, waiting until he had just nodded off, Carmen began to sleepwalk. Hardly had she risen from her perch and stolen a hundred yards towards the ridge when, in the rich nightlight, she saw his long legs springing towards her.

She returned to her spot right away, before he got there. And Raven limped back to the lodge angrily.

Later, towards morning, certain he was up and checking to see if she had tried to escape again, Carmen shifted her bed behind a boulder. He was forced to walk some ways up the slope to make sure she was there.

All in all he slept little. The rhythm of his axe the following morning told Carmen how weary he was. While the raven toiled, Carmen rested, gathered strength, and took pleasure in his pain.

During the next night he didn't soar after her so quickly as he had. She knew he was watching her silhouette prance against the moon, along the ridge towards the east. Since she'd discovered by now there was no exit to the valley that way, Carmen wasn't surprised that he permitted her to go farther and farther, Raven letting the valley do the work for him.

In the morning he smiled maliciously at her.

And she kept up the ruse by sulking, making sure he saw her. He went off to his woodchopping buoyant, a smile cracking all the way to his eyes. She liked that.

With Raven paying less attention during the daytime, too, as she had planned, it meant there was no restraint on where she could go in the camp. He didn't give a damn. *Good.* Carmen made a survival pack, walked one piece at a time back to her perch, an extra blanket, a pouch of berries and some pemmican, a knife she'd pulled from the garbage dump. Steel knife. *Machine made.* Carmen didn't intend to play by any rules but her own.

The third day went on forever it seemed to her; but to him it was even longer. When evening finally fell the raven came back to camp, wings drooping, work-wearied, bathed his hands in one of the balms out of his herbal, a compound of aspen root, and went right to sleep without even making a meal of the hot and greasy duckling that burned and dripped on the fire as he dropped off.

Near starvation, cold, a heart still gored by her vision of the murder seven or eight days before, Carmen found a smile. She had played her wits against them, against the raven amongst them, and had put down his cunning completely. First she'd get down the mountain and then, with vengeance at the head, she'd storm right back up.

The moon had fallen long ago. Carmen feinted her way towards the eastern ridge. She would be careful to the end. If for any reason Raven weren't fast asleep, he would still believe her to be going the wrong way. The hard part was for her to slink down from the rocks and across the sedge and arctic bell-heather, descend into the valley and pass right across it under protection of the trees. Her last trick.

He coughed. Twice before she'd heard him do that. But it could make no difference. The bones were rolling. She was in the trees and if he caught her now her dodge would be easy to read. So Carmen just continued over the patina of snow that had fallen in between the willows. No way to walk but slowly. She could hardly step without crunching down heavily over thousands of ice pockets crusting the surface of the marsh, solid after six or seven hours of continuous freeze.

It took her a long time to cross the entire valley. As she approached the last clump of trees Carmen sensed a lightening in the sky. She couldn't believe she had left so late, but she had. An owl called across the lake, still night for him . . . still witching time.

One last dangerous stretch lay before her. Once emerging from the trees, she would have to pass through the open tundra until she gained the first round of boulders on the slope. After that she'd be lost to sight. The light was quickening for sure.

She came silently out of the trees.

Carmen's hands scraped on the rock and heather. Bent nearly double she picked a passage through the tundra without turning around to see if he were up and following, filed into the cirque of broken boulders leading to the southwestern ridge.

She was breaking out.

Not missing a single stride, Carmen circled higher and higher out of the valley. As she went the first heralds of sunlight were returning to the eastern sky. Now it was her ally, helping her over the change in terrain, flatter, striations of rock that formed a puzzle she must break open.

The otherwise solid rock shelf was cut by a number of cleavings, most of them false. One, she knew, would be a passage that continued right through the face of the mountain and came out near the lake where she and Jacob had been captured. She had to pick the right one.

Carmen stopped. The sun had broken cleanly over the ridge, spindling all the false gorges in light. There was only one that seemed to shine by itself, fluttering in her eyes as if it were numinous and pointing her the way. With the morning arched all around her she ran into the cut of rock and followed its nervous turns straight into the mountain. The walls of the gorge rose quickly . . . sixty . . . eighty . . . well over a hundred feet over her head, the passage not five feet wide, so black with shadow that if the canyon's floor hadn't been near-perfect she couldn't have moved at all. As it was she could run.

Just run. Carmen running . . .

. . . running home . . .

. . . her pace overmatched by the joy of getting away from them . . . still running . . .

. . . and falling, violently, her leg nearly wrenched off . . . falling down into the teeth of some mountain demon, frigid metal teeth, great jaws swallowing her foot at the ankle, digging deep, nearly to the bone . . . blood.

Blood. More of her own blood than she had ever seen was spilling out, flowing faster than she had seen it do in her whole life. It covered her leg . . . and a steel trap abandoned years and years before. A trap for bear that was nearly black with rust, and all it had caught in these many, many years lying open was her.

Hours later an ingenious jay flew over the passage. Saw her. It came down and walked within reach of her hand, wondering if she were dead.

'Not yet.' The grey bird jumped back a few steps as her eyes opened wider. '. . . but you'll eat in time.'

Pain incalculable.

Nothing but pain where once there had been a foot.

Managing finally to sit up, Carmen tried touching the teeth of the trap without moving her foot at all. She felt an ugly coarseness against her skin. Then she delicately pulled at the jaws clamped around her, should the trap have weakened over time, or perhaps the locking mechanism rusted completely away. But in testing the trap's strength she used too much of her own, twisted her leg and screamed, her vision gone white with pain.

The trap was whole, and before she could ever pry open the spring her foot would be ripped right off.

The bird, which had skittered away, came back a little bolder. Not long she knew before the real scavengers would be flocking around. She wondered if they would start devouring her while she was still alive . . . and, if they did, would she just let them do it.

Other birds did come, several more jays and the ubiquitous ravens. They waited, though, standing off to the side and watching her bleed to death in her open grave.

Blue light far above. The colour of eternity. The walls of the gorge rose nearly straight up. There were worse graves. She had never decided if she wanted to be buried or cremated. Now it would be consecration to the open air.

A few minutes of sunlight would touch her bones every day. That would be enough to sanctify things, to burn away all the last bits of sin. She would die after Jacob, which was in the order of things, but before her own child . . . .

The sun was just cutting into the canyon. Something on the stone floor had turned bright. It was the knife.

Both her food and the knife had jumped from her arms. Both were lying close, the steel blade not a foot beyond the last reach of her grasp. The birds, hammering away at the bag of tubers and berries, would eat those quickly; but if she could get ahold of the knife, there were a thousand things to be done. Giddy for over a week, and the loss of blood compounding her body's woes, Carmen found herself surprisingly clear-headed: If she had that knife she could as easily try to save herself as kill herself. Animals were known to bite off their legs when caught in traps. She, too, might carve her leg free . . . try to staunch the wound . . . tie up the artery somehow.

And then what? With one foot it wouldn't be possible to climb off the mountain. Then why get free? Only to hobble back to the hidden valley? To *them*? Ask *them* to save her?

There was no choice, though. Jacob had showed her that. One tried to live.

So she pulled towards the knife in staggers, asking herself 'what pain?' . . . creeping towards the knife, carrying the trap along with her foot in it.

What pain? What pain?

A few inches closer to the knife each time, talking to herself in low and dulcet tones in order to chant the pain away. Twice more she pumped her body along . . . effort not able to be borne . . . defeating her . . . pain horrible and humiliating in front of a chorus of birds watching her sink closer and closer to death's jagged grip and—

—pump and pump and pump and pump . . . and pump . . .
. . . touch . . .

touching it. *Oh Jesus Christ I am touching the knife.*

And?

The sun was bisecting the defile, its radiance blasting everything, the steel of the knife, her blood laced over her leg and the ground . . . her bright bone. She could see the

176

bone. For a moment everything was refulgent, golden . . .
blood, bone. All she had to do was cut, carve herself like a
capon, slice the tendons glowing at the joint. Carmen
remembered how Jacob had said he would not let her die.
His voice spoke as if through water, swearing to protect her
again.

She put the knife firmly over the ankle, at its weakest
point, waited . . . waited . . . breathed deep—

—Looked up.

Right up the colourless walls of the gorge. Something
was moving, something, a grey patch against the sun which
had formed a corona around its head . . . wolflike head. A
person? Rescue?

She screamed for help.

The birds battered their wings against the sides of the
canyon, against each other, trying to get away all at the
same time. Quick feet padded along the top of the gorge
towards the entry some few hundred yards back, changing
soon into the same feet clattering into the canyon . . .
sprinting towards her . . . lithe in its jumps, huge strides,
claws out . . . .

His furious hands moved more quickly than she could
see, took hold of the rotting steel and pulled the jaws back
until her leg and foot dropped completely free. He slammed backwards against the stone, thrown by his own
strength.

'*The fish failed!*'

Those were the wolf's first words.

He picked her up in his arms, held her against his matted,
grizzled beard, breath and teeth hot against her neck as he
ran through the gorge, Carmen cradled in his arms, he
snarling and spitting in her ear as he rumbled out of the
ravine and back along the same tracks Carmen had made
hours before.

Back towards their camp.

'The goddamned fucking fish *failed*!!'

Over the flats and striations of rock, right up the lip of
their valley.

'We're going to starve, we are . . . all of us . . . *you, too* . . .
fucking starve!'

177

Wolf carried her right over the ridge and towards the open lodge, hollering at Raven to put away the goddamn logbook he was forever keeping and get together a compress and some of his herbal art – if he truly had any – that would keep the woman from dying.

'. . . going to starve, lady . . . jumping into winter without a single fish, not one, the goddamned shitholing trap cut up like mowed grass by a sonofabitch bear . . . going to have to dig for roots right through the snow and we'll *still* starve!!!'

Those were their first words to her since she had been with them. She was too weak to answer back.

Nor did she speak later when, after Raven had bathed and cleaned her wound and wrapped her foot in a plantain of some kind, the wolf made it clear in his talk to his brothers that this was no joke, that this time they might not survive until spring.

She understood Wolf, the eldest, their chief, his voice full of hard colours, and realized that if it did come to pass that they died she would be there to witness it.

Reason to live until spring.

By the time night came Carmen had lost all sensation in her lower body. She gave up pain by giving up feeling. And, while the first real snows of the year began tumbling through the blurs of sky and all of them, all six now, locked themselves in the winter lodge to wait, she crept deeper . . . squeezed herself into the darkest, most remote corner of her mind and went to sleep . . . .

CHAPTER 15

By mid-December they had been forced to eat the roan.

Their bodies *craved* fat. Some small game fell into the snares – mostly rabbit, far too lean a diet to sustain their needs – otherwise there was no fresh meat at all. The last of the horses that they had stolen from Jacob and Carmen,

the grey gelding, pawed the snow and shivered as if await-
ing slaughter, too; but once they ate the grey horse, a
fleshless creature anyhow, they would be looking right into
the end. So they held off.

Starvation was no longer a vague threat. Their store of
roots and tubers in two of the caches had long ago been
gnawed away, leaving only one more full and groaning in
the cold. They had never before had to dip into the reserve
cache until late February, or March. There was a bit of deer
jerky, enough for a week. Nothing else.

Nothing.

And winter, barely begun, was already in its second long
cold snap . . . worse certain to follow.

During most of their hours the brothers huddled on the
spruce boughs and rushes inside the winter hut, while
Carmen hid across the fire and watched them pass around a
pipe or dice or slap each other, or search for lice to toss into
the ever-burning fire. All of them, Carmen as well, stayed
wrapped in robes that never came off, fur against the skin.
They didn't wash. Moved little. Slept lightly much of the
day, trying to keep from losing weight.

The cold outside made for little interest in cutting wood,
though splitting logs was easier work with the weather
twenty below. The brothers were irritable and weak and
lazy.

Not Carmen.

At sunrise every day she was walking in the snow,
limping along, after the bear-trap episode lucky enough to
have both her feet. She would never again walk right,
though.

Her morning walks were never aimless. Whatever direction she first took didn't make any difference. It was all
intended to dissimulate: she always circled back to the
willow thicket where the small-game traps lay and she
didn't want the brothers to know she was there.

Carmen stopped in her tracks. Listened to the regular
monody of an axe falling in the forest.

'Elk Man', *Thomas* – she recognized his real identity from
Jacob's descriptions, recognized them all – was up and
working. As usual. Thomas was compulsive about work.

179

Disdaining the stone axe, he found a steel blade buried amongst the rubble, hafted it with lashings of spruce root and sinew, then felled some of the smaller Douglas fir. Their green and sappy wood was endless trouble to keep lit, but by burning it over the deadwood heart of the fire he cured the young logs of much of their youth . . . and the fire stayed hot.

Several yards ahead of Carmen the eyes of a porcupine, surprisingly vicious, turned up towards her advance. Still very much alive, the animal was caught in one of the sets. *Porcupine?* Carmen sat down on an ancient stump. Wary of its quills, unsure of how to approach the beast, she had no idea if there were any way to eat porcupine or how to get at the flesh even if she could find a way to kill the animal. She couldn't ask any of the brothers. They didn't talk to her, had continued to ignore her for the most part except for a grunt or whine from time to time. Nor did they give her any food from their table, willing only to turn blind eyes to the scraps she stole in order to survive. And she stole more than they knew.

But they might kill her if they realized she had been taking game from their snares.

The porcupine whistled aggressively. In most of the snares the animals were dead when she discovered them. She had killed a few but hadn't yet got used to it, wasn't sure she ever would. Nor was Carmen very hungry for the moment. For the past several days she had been sick to her stomach at some point during her morning rounds, would retch for minutes on end. All food tasted foul.

'Get farther back.'

Carmen's heart seized.

A while before Thomas's chopping had stopped and for some reason she hadn't taken it in. She looked at him blankly. He had followed her. The least menacing of the brothers, once or twice he had tried to talk to her but always stopped himself at the last moment. Not now.

'G-g-get *back*.'

He pushed her away with the axe handle.

'T-too close and you'll wind up with a n-nose full of those quills.' He set himself between her and the porcupine, kneeled down carefully. 'I'm going to teach you what to do with one of these. *N-n-n-not* so you can help us, though. It's *you* who w-won't live unless you learn.' Then he killed the beast with a quick stroke and turned it over on its side. 'You know how to build a fire out here?'

She didn't answer.

Thomas didn't ask again. In less than two minutes he had made a fire on the snow. 'If you can make a fire like that anywhere you can s-s-s-skirt a thousand d-deaths in that one trick alone.'

Carmen continued to say nothing, but she didn't walk away either.

He showed her how to singe the quills off, pushing them and the fur away with a stick as they melted. 'Get rid of every last bit until the skin's h-hairless and black. Then you bury the beast. Snow c-cools the meat.' Meanwhile he had brought a bark kettle to boiling by adding hot stones. The charred skin he easily scraped away, then tossed the carcass into his pot to cook.

To her surprise, Thomas gave her a taste. The first taste. Since they had captured her she hadn't actually shared a meal with them. He gave her more, ate himself. The meat, heavily larded with fat, tasted like strong pork.

Afterwards he buried the bones and gristle so that none of the others would know there had been an animal in their traps . . . and that he and Carmen had eaten it together.

Carmen rose, as if to go. But he had more to show her. He explained how to set the snares, where, what were the signs of which animals in the brush, the pattern of the game trails.

'Now you show me.' Thomas unstrapped the sapling that served as the snare's trigger. 'Make your set.'

She did nothing.

'Sh-sh-show me.'

'No.'

He stood up and brushed his hands on his leggings. 'If you don't catch the game yourself you won't live. *They* sure as fuck won't help, you can b-b-b-b-b-b—' Unable to push the word past his lips, Thomas stamped the snow furiously.

'I'll live.'

'*And your baby???*'

Disgust in his eyes glazed over the calm with which he had earlier been ministering to her. He said nothing more and went away.

So he knows, she thought.

It was true. Jacob's seed had taken root in her belly. Carmen herself had begun to suspect only a day or two before.

A baby. A tenacious creature. Two months of horror and privation hadn't succeeded in turning off its tiny heart, nor in muscling it from its sanctuary. The child wasn't just an idea, was small but formed, *all* the primordia formed, right down to eyelids and fingernails, and blood, brain, a grip in its small hand against the protective yolk . . . a will to be born.

It was coming, whatever they did to her wouldn't stop the child. There even seemed to be a kind of understanding with Thomas, despite the way he had sullenly marched away, that she could live and find the strength she would need to bring the baby through the gates.

A second purpose for her staying alive in the mountains was taking shape, something even stronger, perhaps, than revenge.

Starvation was on all the brothers' minds.

When Carmen returned to the winter lodge the five of them were all ranged at the top of the steps arguing. Hollering.

Thomas stood apart from the others, he the only one composed, his middle-grey eyes fixed on some ice damage to the roof of their winter home.

The others were roused to go after beaver.

'No beaver in P-Paradise anymore.' That was their name for the pool where they had stoned their father. 'All those lodges down there are old and em-empty.'

'Yeah, well we'll just go farther downstream.' Mark the raven, sorting his way through their garbage, couldn't find the caribou sounding-horn Sam had once given them, the one essential tool for hunting beaver under the ice.

'L-lots of bear denning by the big lake and I can find one.'

182

'Too far to go.'

'One bear . . . t-ten beaver.'

Thomas was right about the bear. The odds were just as good as finding beaver and one bear killed would keep them in meat and fat for several weeks.

'*Much* too far.' Everyone stopped wrangling to listen to Eric. 'It's a four- or five hour-walk to the lake even at the best of times.' They hardly ever attempted it during winter.

'You f-four g-g-get your beaver. I'll take the horse . . . bring back a bear.'

'By yourself?'

Thomas nodded but Eric had his doubts. Should anything happen to the gelding they would break the one strong stick they had to beat panic away if starvation should really set in.

'And how are you going to slog a bear carcass over the mountain, even with a horse?'

'Travois.'

'Not over the rock field, you won't.'

Nothing could move Thomas from his opinion. And Eric, as well as the others, knew Thomas normally did all that he said he could.

'Want one of us to go with you?'

'Nope.'

'All right . . . take the horse.'

That should have ended it, but Carmen saw Eric's green and hungry eyes wandering her way. The brothers had yet to leave her alone in the camp. Nobody wanted to stay behind, miss the hunt. Only Thomas knew she wouldn't escape, even if she had the chance.

He was right. Carmen had understood many things the moment Thomas had guessed her condition. It explained why Jacob's murder seemed so far away though not even three months gone. She was nesting, right amongst the vipers. She'd stay all right, because it would be a greater risk to the baby for her to struggle through thirty or forty miles of waste and snow than to stay with the brothers. In a way she was in the mountain now by her own election and not by constraint, exactly like the rest of them . . . at least until the baby was born and she'd found a gun.

183

'She'll come down to Paradise with us.'

The others looked at Eric, surprised, annoyed. But Wolf just stared them down. It wasn't that he feared her flight. For some reason he felt she ought to be with them. If they did get beaver, then at some point, though blanketed by the shadows in her corner of the cave, she would get her stolen share . . . the food that might save them would be her salvation, too. She should watch the kill.

'Just don't lose the horse down there, Tommy. That's all.'

And with that said, Thomas went his way down the mountain, his brothers theirs . . . all fallen from the highest peaks in search of meat.

At sunset Eric and his brothers, and Carmen, were miles below Paradise and still without a kill. Just as Thomas had promised, the beaver huts upstream had all been abandoned long ago.

And it had begun to snow. A half-moon above smirked through the blurred sky, the wind picking up all the time.

'One more hut and then we go.'

Mark agreed. It was he who had promised Eric they would find beaver, he who had goaded his brothers farther and farther and farther away from their camp until they were nearly out of the mountain proper, come to an immense open park, the unbroken meadow where traditionally they harvested berries, rosehips, camras root, salad leaves, everything for winter except flesh.

Everybody was exhausted. The walk back up the mountain would take hours. Bobby, *Little Bear*, who had blitzed a half-dozen empty huts already, lay panting in the snow.

'C'mon, Fats, one more try.'

'Can't do it.'

'Get up.' Eric, as tired as his brother, pointed to the drooping light. They would be able to see for ten minutes more, hardly enough time even if the lodge were better crammed with beaver than the duds they had busted up earlier in the day. The others were ready, too, even Douglas, who kept slamming his harpoon into a streamside alder, the only tree in the whole meadow. *'Up!'*

Bobby rose.

Working by reflex after rehearsing the hunt so many times already, Eric sounded the ice carefully until he located one of the tunnels that the beavers used to go from their hut to the frozen shore. He followed it to its exit hole on the bank and together with Mark laid in babiche netting while leaving several of the net's outer threads to trail along the ground where Mark would later wait, ready to pull the net closed as the beavers emerged one by one. Strands of shells were attached to the loose cords as a signal something was caught in the web.

'O.K.'

Mark gripped the net runners, Bobby levitating over the lodge itself, waiting for the go-ahead from Eric.

They waited and waited.

'What the hell are *you* doing?' Eric grabbed the short-handled harpoon from Douglas's grip. Their youngest brother, his brains gone completely soft in the mountains, had nearly blunted the bone teeth on the tree. 'Get the fuck away!'

Petulantly, Douglas sat on the bankside, right by the beaver net.

Somehow keeping his anger in check, Eric pointed towards Carmen, who was kneeling twenty yards back from the stream, shivering in the wind. 'Go stand next to her.' The brothers would snare beaver without Douglas, just as they did most things without his help.

They were finally ready, right as the sun sank.

'Jump clear to Hell, Bear. Bring us some beaver.'

And Bobby, aroused by an acute sense of animal blood shifting underneath the wood and ice, dropped his full weight onto the dome of the lodge, all the while banging with beaver-chewed sticks in either hand on the surrounding jumble of snow and spars . . . screaming like a Valkyrie.

There were beaver below. In families. Terrified. Their world plummeting down around their ears.

Animals, in panic, fled under the ice.

The nets shook moments after. The strand of shells began ringing around a beaver's ears. Mark pulled hard on the tie-strings.

Simple. Swift.

Eric, on his knees over the hole, looked down . . . looked deeper.

'Pull the fucking net up!'

Mark drew harder.

There was the face. The bleak eyes. Wet brown snout. Confusion. The beaver, startled, stuck its teeth through the net, ripped hard.

But before breaking the babiche it looked up once more to a blunt-toothed harpoon falling down out of a deceitfully vague winter sky.

'Up! *Pull it up!!!*'

Another beaver was snarled. Eric raised the spear, without stopping at the top drove it down again, and again, hacking at both animals, blasting brains everywhere, the bone teeth almost unworkable so badly dulled by Douglas . . . two bad, clumsy, nervous, graceless kills . . . *Jesus* . . . but two kills.

Meat for a while.

'*Fucko*! They're all over!'

Bobby, unable to raise himself from the ice, pointed in ten directions at once, dark rolls moving off through the rocks and snow and into the amnesty of night.

Mark and Eric emptied the net of their kills quickly, refixed the trap knowing it was probably too late for more, then ran up the bank haphazardly desperate to find a stray.

It was all furious, wasted motion. They'd lost the rest.

Downstream on the ice, Douglas, outlined against the night, was slipping and sliding, hollering, yipping, laughing an idiot's laugh.

Both brothers advanced to him.

Douglas had found a runaway. A juvenile. Seven or eight pounds of meat, at the least. Not dead. Cowering on the ice. Douglas was over it, knife in hand, playing charades.

'Kill it for Christsakes.'

'You fuckers missed one.'

'*Kill it!*'

Douglas kept teasing the infant beast.

Eric lunged for his brother just as Douglas's arm was falling. The blow knocked the knife loose. But Eric had thrown himself too far, continued sliding past his brother, unable to stop himself on the ice. He hit the bank facing backwards and watched Douglas very expertly throttle the young beaver without the knife, making a garrotte of his hands that didn't lose a single drop of infant blood on the river.

They had taken beaver after all. Even Douglas had helped.

Stunned by what she had seen, Carmen sat in the snow to watch the madness that followed.

Impatient to get at the meat, the brothers savaged the small beaver badly, cutting open the belly with stabs and slaps so that the still-working guts fell onto the ice and almost back through it before Mark caught the liver and held on. The tripe and intestines they roasted first, each of them getting one bite of the liver, all except Douglas who would never eat viscera, never, though all his brothers told him he had better do or risk getting sick. Devils lived in those organ meats, he believed, and better to lack the vitamins not to be found in the rest of the meat than to swallow a demon. Instead, Douglas sucked on the beaver's tail, almost pure fat, grease getting right up Douglas's nose as he fought the others off and kept the sweetest fat for himself.

Fat dripped from the spitted carcass and hissed into smoke on the coals. The brothers snorted and drank vast draughts of water from bark cups which Mark kept refilling. They pulled flesh off the turning roast with bare hands, ravening it down mostly unchewed, scalding lips and tongue and throat but not giving a goddamn.

Hot blood, meat juices, gristle in between their teeth. A Christ-tide blessing.

They even tossed some food into the fire, not just bones but good food, as if defying whatever scrupulous gods would have had them observe thrift and waste nothing at all. Inedible fat they threw in too, though it might have helped to light their lamps in the winter hut. Smoke from the burning fat filled the space around them on the ice, smoke so sharp on their senses they were unable to eat more, or laugh, or even gasp cleanly for the night air.

187

But they had pushed starvation's untrimmed spurs that much farther away.

The air cleared. Their voices danced in the dwindling fire.

Carmen realized that even at night, their faces sponged up by the dark, she could recognize each one of them.

Almost against her will she had learned their names. *Both* names: their given names and the animal familiars each brother had assumed, though those other, assumed names they had neglected after the bad weather and hunger set in.

To her they were no longer the indivisible crew who had painted themselves in red and black and put on masks in order to kill their father. She knew the form and figure of each brother, of every bloody hand . . . their individual quirks, habits, moods. It was a knowledge which might help her kill them one day.

In a way she had already decided on the order of her kill. It would follow the hierarchy of their guilt, in ascending order.

Thomas first. *Elk Man.* Fairest of the brothers, freckled, as perfectly proportioned as a man could be, the quietest, he always turned his eyes away from things while keeping his head erect. Carmen believed he alone had no pride in what he'd done to his father. A worker, a genius with his hands, the camp musician, he didn't belong in the mountains and yet he was there with the rest of them. Carmen didn't understand why. Jacob had once told her that Thomas was the gentlest of his sons, but she had seen Thomas lend a strong hand in his father's murder and that had cashiered all his good report. She'd kill him first. Yes.

Then the fat one. *Little Bear.* The one brother with any humour and, certainly by his own inspiration, ironically named. He was the largest man she had ever met. He steamed when he sat in the sunlight, smelled foully. Jacob had said that he was generous, but Bobby's hands, too, always reaching for something, had malice in them, especially when they couldn't find food. She'd cut his belly for him.

The youngest one of them in the mountains was called

188

Pretty Marten. She thought he must have once been exquisitely featured, even beautiful, but all that had been blasted away. Vain and sulky, Douglas was ugly now, contorted by idiocy. Carmen had no idea what had driven him into the mountains with his brothers. He did no camp work, had no discipline, complained endlessly. And yet, and yet he had some kind of fidelity, spaniel-like as it was, which might have meant something in a good cause.

The oldest two, *Raven* and *Wolf*, Mark and Eric, she had watched with special care.

Mark deserved the worst she could devise. He had planned everything . . . perhaps even the murder of their father, for all she knew. A man of stratagems and treasons. Tall and black and suspicious, he was a natural melancholic with a surfeit of intelligence, too much, maybe. He lived entirely in his head. He believed in a perfect world, for good or ill: It was the orderliness that mattered. None of the others took his Indian lore very seriously, she had learned, yet none of them would challenge it, either. The raven had his powers, uncanny powers, which she didn't understand.

She would kill Eric last. Not because he was the worst of them, though. In fact, Eric was the son most like Jacob: his hair and beard were losing their red lust and turning white in the same way as had his father's. He had Jacob's intensity, and more, everything except old Jacob's conscience.

Even the huge, green, righteous eyes.

Carmen would get him last because Eric, most loved of all the sons, the brother the others listened to, had let the pack of them go completely out of control. *He alone might have stopped the murder*. She remembered seeing that thought in his face. And he had decided not to.

If she could, Carmen would kill Eric with her own hands . . . if she could . . . .

'Eat.'

Eric was standing over her.

The others were still picking at the bones, their energy wound down, the smoke they had made dissipated.

Eric handed her a small joint of the beaver. She shook her head.

189

He put it right under her nose. 'Eat it.'

Carmen's mouth drifted . . . drifted . . . then involuntarily she stuck her canines deep into the meat and pulled away a mouthful from the shank. Soon she was eating as quickly, as barbarously as the brothers had, scraping bone with her teeth until she had sucked every scruple of nourishment from it, breaking it in half with her molars afterwards and licking out all the marrow, too.

'Eat more.'

'I can't.'

'We waste nothing.'

His eyes were larger in the dark, and still green.

Snow had begun to fall again, in larger flakes. Her jaws were stiff from eating so vigorously.

'There's nothing left.'

'Then let's go.'

The two beavers were packed on ancient Chilcotin carriers, the harpoons, nets, caribou sounding-horn, bark cups and kettle. The brothers started walking quickly, right through the blackness. Carmen went in Eric's footsteps, the route straight up the river.

'You think Tommy got a bear?' Bobby asked, his belly thinking.

'Never.' Mark didn't believe it.

Throughout the day only Eric had been thinking about their brother off chasing bear. 'Somebody should have gone with him.'

'He should have come with us.' Mark, always despondent, lamented that they had lost what might have been a much larger beaver kill.

Eric disagreed. 'We've got food for at least ten days. We did O.K.'

'Too fucking right, old man.'

Too fucking right, old man. Bobby's voice, basso and rich, expectant, had a familiarity painful to Carmen . . . for certain it was the voice of his father, a little deeper was all, with none of Jacob's civil speaking. Some few granules of Jacob, heavy with his quality, had slipped through to his sons.

'Tommy's found himself a dreaming bear, betcha,

drummed his brains out and notched his throat . . . and sliced him up like geometry. Right in his den, too. Betcha.'

Carmen knew it was true. As she and the others trudged past Paradise she began to daydream, imagining Thomas on the far side of the mountain stalking a winter bear. She could see him under the snow sky. Starting well back from the lake he worked in zigzags through the trees, looking for a bear asleep in its hole and digesting its autumn gluttony. He came up to a fallen spruce. Embroidering the up-turned hole at the tree's base was a bib of ice. Thomas paused, leaned towards the hole, looked in. A bear. Its breath had condensed on the snow as it struck the much colder air outside its den.

He picked up a stick. He started to slide the tip into the lair, stopped, pulled it out. If it were an insomniac grizzly and not a black bear, he would have the bear munching on his neck before he could sound out its hollow. Quickly, dexterously, he began plugging up the bear's exit hole. Branches, rocks, roots. A blood sculpture at the bear's door. Once the killing began the bear would never get out in time.

The hole closed, Thomas plumbed a peephole directly over where he thought the bear's heart would be. Then he sifted some grains of snow onto the bear, making a target. It was a shoulder. The fur a dark nutmeg.

He took two spears. A crazy idea, really, to be braving bears. The danger enormous, even with the animal's exit stuffed up. Bears could flick mountains off their backs. Thomas's skin was drawn in fear, his cheeks jumping. He raised one spear, took an open-legged stance, counted . . . his lips moving in the wind . . . waited for the bear to exhale so in its surprise it would suck its own blood into its lungs and drown . . . then drove the stick's lethal point right through the joint and into the viscera beneath, lungs and maybe heart.

'Die, you bastard!!' Thomas was screaming. A single momentary lapse of gentility. Then back to work.

He rived the blood-clogged middle of the bear, pushing down deeper and deeper to the centre of the beast until the spear slapped back and forth so hard it threw Thomas to the ground. He took a half-step towards a nearby tree, ready to climb. But checked his fear. Smelled the blood. Heard the fury underneath the ground tempered by the gurgle of hot fluids in the bear's throat filling up the lung cavity, snow flying everywhere as the bear whacked at the grave it had dug for itself in the hope of getting its claws into the man at the other end of the stick twisting the stick into its aorta.

Then the second spear. Thomas pushed it right through the bear's neck. A sudden and trembling stillness followed. Thomas fell to his knees, disbelieving . . . ecstatic . . . his artistry triumphant.

The bear was dead as moondust . . . .

'Fucko!'

Bobby's voice beat at Carmen's ears. She had been right next to Thomas in her fantasy, down on her knees with him over the bear hole.

'C'mon, you fuckers!'

Bobby, short of breath all day, had cursed the switch-backs each step of the way back to the valley as the brothers recovered their camp. Now he was in front, though, leading the pack down the crater side towards the winter lodge below.

By the side of the lodge there was a man standing in the falling snow, a statue, immortalized by the cold, the slouching moon behind him just visible through the haze and making a corona around his head.

Thomas. In trouble of some kind.

'. . . *winter bear*,' he kept saying, obsessively, not recognizing his brothers as they clambered over the rocks towards him. He was calling into the wind. Nothing but his mouth moved and that only with enormous difficulty, a crazy iteration about the bear fluttering on his lips as his brothers came up to him. Surrounded him.

'The horse, Tommy! *What happened to the horse???*'

'. . . some k-k-k-k-kind of rogue . . . f-f-fucking *rogue*!'

'*The horse!!!*'

Eric screamed. Nothing came back at him but snow-flakes. Not even Thomas's mouth moved any longer.

All the brothers converged on Thomas. Unsure. Eric

touched him first, tried to pick him up by his cape of ice. But his brother was limp underneath the mantle. And the crusted snow was spotted red all the way down Thomas's body, from his shoulder down.

Then Eric saw Thomas's hand. And the filigree of sinew barely holding it on.

'Jesus God!!!'

'Turn his head away!'

'. . . do it . . . oh J-J-Jesus—' Thomas, hardly conscious, though unable to talk could still plead . . . exhort.

'I said turn his goddamn head away!'

'Q-QUICKLY!!!' Could scream.

The wolf's brows curled angrily, in helpless self-reproach, blaming himself for what the bear had done to one of his brothers. If he cut Thomas's hand then all the music of their camp was gone, Thomas the only musician, the only one of them accomplished at anything.

Mark and Bobby, holding Thomas down, waited for their oldest brother to drive his knife through the last connecting tissue.

'Can't.' Eric thought only of Thomas's flute, guitar, songs.

'Got to!'

'Can't!' Eric's frame was shaking. He was losing focus. The knife had dangled loose in the confusion.

'He's almost out . . . can't see anyway . . . *just do it!!'*

The iceman in their arms was burbling, pain starting to come through as the heat of the lodge brought it on.

Blade still squirming. *'Turn his goddamn head—!!'*

'—CUT!!!!!!'

And Eric's arm drove the knife through the final braids strapping Thomas's hand to his body. Severed clean. The hand fell, frozen solid and cupped like a saint's . . . relic of an ancient life that was gone now forever.

Thomas's feet kicked spasmically, hit the hand and it flew off one of the fire logs, showering sparks everywhere.

Mark knelt down and thumbed furiously through his Chilcotin herbal, searching for a native simple to keep infection from setting in, ways to tie up the arm, anything

. . . with his other hand jotting notes so that someday he could write in perfect replication exactly what Nature dared do to them all.

'He's out.'

It was true. Thomas had gone limp in Bobby's arms. They laid him down. Turned to Mark.

'Now what do we do?'

Bobby had heard what you had to do with somebody frozen like this was to wrap them in snow. He saw Mark's withering look. 'It's in one of your idiot books, Marko.'

'The shit it is!'

Eric stamped on the rushes. '*What do we do?*'

'Get dry hides and roll him up in them until his skin gets as warm as ours.' Mark looked at the others. Then only at Bobby. '*Move*, you fat bastard! Get him the fucking hides!'

The robes and skins were gathered quickly, Thomas swaddled in them, Mark making sure they didn't put any pressure on the spots that flashed the telltale white of severe frostbite.

'Move him by the fire?'

'Never.' Mark told Eric of the dangers come from too rapid heating of frostbitten skin. 'We warm him gently . . . *we* warm him – it's our bodies' heat that does it.' And they placed the body of their brother in between Eric and Bobby, between Wolf and Little Bear, well away from the direct radiance of the flames.

They all listened to the wind rising outside the lodge . . . and the stuttering of Thomas's breath. Hearing him, the others – perhaps for the first time in the mountains – grew afraid.

Thomas's eyes trembled and then opened. He looked distracted, spoke hysterically about the bear. It had been the same size, same face as the bear that had decimated their autumn fish harvest. 'I recognized his g-g-g-g-g-g-g-goddamn eyes.'

'There are a thousand grizzlies.'

'. . . not like a bear's eyes . . . more y-y-yellow . . . a cat's eyes . . . .'

'Rest, Tommy.'

'And the goddamn thing is l-larger . . . *Christ* . . . five

194

f-f-feet b-bigger than I ever saw a bear in my wh-wh-whole fucking life!'

Mark wondered about the tremors, the speech. Thomas was fluttering, his mouth moving even when he wasn't trying to make words. 'Rest.' He took Eric's spot on the floor, steading him.

'Same fucking b-bear!!'

'Stop talking and rest.' Eric was back in control, touched his poor brother's forehead and found it still frigid. 'We're going to make a broth . . . just hold on . . . *hold on, Tommy.*' As Eric was himself now holding on. His brother wasn't going into that long, long night, not yet . . . not if there were sinew and strength and heat and light in Eric's hands to hold his brother back.

Mark whispered where the medicinal herbs were in his bag and Eric turned to get them. Stopped. He saw Douglas staring balefully at the woman.

Having been unable to watch his brothers slice off Thomas's hand, Douglas was cradling the dead limb in his arms and looking murderously at Carmen.

'Put the hand down.'

'Her hand for his.'

'Go outside and get me some aspen bark . . . and devil's bush, too, if you can find some.' Mark, better than any of them, knew how to deflect Douglas's dim wits.

'Her hand for his!'

'Do what Mark says . . . *now.*'

Douglas leaped. He was on top of Carmen as she tried shrinking away on her haunches. Something sparkled in his hand as he slashed the air. Carmen jumped back from the knife but Douglas fell on her, rolled her over so that the two of them were face against face. He got the knife on her windpipe.

And would have killed her with one short jab through her throat, but Eric was there. He caught Douglas's hand and smacked it against the floor of the lodge until it went dumb and the obsidian blade fell away. Douglas got crazier. He locked his teeth onto Carmen's neck and his hands around her temples as if he could crush her skull in from the sides, he screaming all the while like a banshee and kicking her in the belly.

Eric had to wrench his brother's arm nearly out of its socket but he got Douglas off her. Held him from behind and choked hard, trying to jam sense in or squeeze life out of the fucking fool. There were red streams running down Douglas's neck.

And in Carmen's mouth half Douglas's ear bitten off.

Wind shrieked through the marsh. Carmen's chin scraped the bark of a hemlock, her arms hugging the tree as she tried to keep the spindrift and burning wind out of her eyes.

She prayed and prayed for any kind of help, a plan, something miraculous, a way to get out their dismal valley or some easy way to kill all five of them. There was a kick in her stomach, a spasm. She gripped her middle right over where she was sure the bloody fucking bastard had kicked her baby's head, tiny head, small as a jewel.

There was a moaning. She looked up. Through the swirling snow the wolf was walking towards her.

'You'll freeze,' he complained in his strange, sad music. The wind chill was fatal. '. . . freeze in minutes now . . . freeeeze!'

Carmen nearly had already. Her own breath formed crystals around her lips. It was the coldest she had ever been in her life, colder than dreams, almost too cold for her to swing her legs even for a single step. The wind would freeze her right there, standing up.

Eric nearly walked right past her, the visibility down to a few feet, no more. He stopped.

Carmen backed away.

'You've got to come inside. You're gonna die out here.'

Her feet slipped at first but she got purchase and ran along the streambed, the ice cutting her feet. Ran towards the memorial cairn and the perch she'd had her first days in the camp. Would try to live out the night amongst the boulders, maybe dig into Jacob's grave and bury herself in the dirt . . . must be warmer than the rocks.

He was following her. She heard his voice, a child's call so buffeted by the wind they were both heading into, that it was impossible to hear his words, only the music. The snow clogged her ears. Right in front of the cairn the ground

196

swelled up and Carmen fell, sat there, wanting to sink down under the weight of those hammering flakes and disappear into a final sleep. They were going to kill the baby anyway.

'What are you doing!!!'

She sat there.

He kneeled to her, called in her ear. She couldn't hear.

So Eric put his long arms around her and picked her up, then carried her out of the rocks and back to the safety of the lodge where she belonged.

In the cave again, right in her obscure place.

But things were different somehow. They swaddled her, too, in warm robes. They were nervous. Uncertain. Dazed.

All that night there was a banging on the roof, and the brothers bucked each other up by saying it was only the wind of the rising blizzard. Yet not one of them believed that, nor would any of them mount the ladder to see what else might be clamouring up there, what intangible spirit trying to balance Nature's tables . . . or whether it might not just be that insatiable bear pounding and pounding away . . . that strange winter bear.

CHAPTER 16

After nearly two more months of extreme cold, the temperature never rising above zero, the world around them uniformly white and dead – no game birds stirring, their traps and sets empty week after week – a brief thaw did finally come. Snow shrank in the valley as land emerged in spots. Ravens were seen hobbling for food.

None of the brothers was active. Often they didn't leave the shelter for several days at a time. And all five were showing signs of illness.

They complained of sore gums and teeth rattling loose in their listless jaws, swelling and stiffness in joints, mostly in the major joints of legs and feet. Scurvy it was. During the harvest Douglas had lost a bushel of rosehips, nobody paying much mind at the time as it was thought he'd left behind just another basketful of camras root. And, with the salmon gone, the little salt they found in scraps had no iodine so there was goitre. Slight knots had developed on their necks, their eyes bulged, all were nervous. Mark said his heart trembled from time to time.

Each of them had his own ailments, too, which to some degree of effectiveness Mark treated with preparations from his herbal. He had kept Thomas's arm from infection, capping it at the wrist with a leather pouch something like the one Sam had made for himself after his encounter with a bear years before. Douglas's skin, once like baby skin, had become cankered and dry, and for some reason he seemed frightened of the long nights, wouldn't walk in the darkness – not even inside the lodge – always whining he could see nothing unless it was bright outside. Bobby's diarrhoea and prattling belly never ceased. As for Mark himself, he had walked too far and too fast in snowshoes on an expedition to find the lost gelding, which strained the tendons in his feet. At first he tried the venerable remedy of scarifying his instep, but it didn't help. He made poultices, as well. When that failed Mark wrapped his feet in pulverized cedar bark and lit the bandage until it flamed. He continued to walk with pain.

And Eric, all that happened to him was that he got thinner. And thinner. He was wasting away twice as quickly as the others, for he had thoughts burning his vigour and fuel even faster than the natural respiration of his body's cells. His was the real malady afflicting them all. Everything else was inconsequential and meant only pain. The fact was they were starving to death and were not likely to make the spring.

It was different with Carmen. And they noticed that. She seemed to grow stronger, as if thriving on their weakness, a determined parasite who didn't mind killing its host. Every day she was busy, keeping herself and her baby alive.

While the men lay on their backs dreaming of spring, Carmen was nurturing. With a needle made from marten bone and deer sinew for thread, she reseamed most of her

198

clothes where they had come unstitched. She had done the same for their robes, too. There were many small pelts around that the brothers weren't using. These she pieced together and quilted blankets for them all, herself included. She did other things to help them get through the misery of winter. Thomas, reduced to skivvying because of his injury, used her as an extra hand in preparing such food as they could find littering the camp – a spare diet of the inner bark of trees, mosses, lichens, the few herbs and tubers left in the caches or that had slopped off in the snow nearby.

And she cleaned . . . endlessly . . . trying to bring some kind of order to the pestilence they were bringing on themselves with their squalid ways. Not for them did she clean, though – all her labours came of a more subtle design. Carmen wanted a spotless crèche when her time came.

There were signs of the baby busting out everywhere on her body. But the brothers, in their despondency, in sluggish selfishness, had seen nothing . . . or said nothing.

Aside from the glowing of the ashes banked up to conserve wood, there was almost no light in their subterranean home. All the fat for their lamps had months ago been burned away. Often, in the murky light of their lodge and when Carmen was outside on her daily walk, strange passions grew amongst the brothers . . . always variations on the same argument.

'She takes from me.' Douglas's lips were blanched bitterly when he talked about her, which was more and more often.

'She takes from nobody, bimbo. There's nothing to go around.' Bobby belched.

'She's hiding food from us, she is.'

'You're out of your tiny mind.'

'I'm telling you, man, she hides food from us. And she's getting goddamn fat off it while my bones stick out . . . *stick out*, you hear!'

Bobby yawned and rolled away in his cocoon of skins. 'Somebody shut this fool up, eh?'

Mark, doing exercises on the ladder, took up his own

complaints. 'You're supposed to shit farther away from the stream than you've been doing, fat man.' This was Mark's way of protecting Douglas, jumping in on his side, as always.

'Mmmmmmmmm . . . .'

'It's not just dysentery you've got if that's what you're trying to pass on to the rest of us.' He waited for Bobby to look at him. 'Maybe you got hydatids.' Mark could see none of them knew what that was. 'If it's not hydatids it's some other kind of tapeworm . . . that's for sure.'

'Where did I pick it up?'

'You stuff anything into that fucking maw of yours.'

'Get out of here.'

'Raw fish . . . especially from small streams. That could easily have given it to you. Or eating dog shit from those fucking dogs.'

Bobby lobbed a stone at Mark just to keep him quiet. 'Shit, I wish I had some fresh fruit . . . a bunch of grapes'd do it . . . clean me right out. One dozen choking fat cherries.'

'That'd finish you off good.'

'Fruit steadies me, Marko.' Bobby kept turning over, trying to find some way of lying on his stomach that was bearable. 'Can't you find me something in that little medicine box of yours?' His brother didn't answer. 'How about bleeding me? Isn't that supposed to be Indian medicine, a good old blood cocktail? Draw me some from one of you guys . . . or maybe the lady. She's a fucking lot healthier than the rest of us.'

'Why don't we just eat her?' Douglas spoke while playing with figurines he'd been whittling for three years and still hadn't got right. He meant what he said. None of the others knew to whom he was talking but it made no difference because they didn't pay him any mind. He encumbered everything they did, was only a burden. 'We need the meat, don't we?'

Mark climbed up and down the ladder like a spider, draping his long arms and legs over the rungs. He couldn't bear to hear Douglas talk. It always sounded to him like an accusation: Not a thing had been done to mend Douglas's

200

cracks, as Mark had promised the others living in the mountain would do. Douglas's mind still held nothing. Everything of substance leached away.

And yet, and yet, as Mark's black head went above the smokehole for an instant and he saw Carmen walking in the marsh, her flanks surprisingly ample for someone who should have been starving like the rest of them, and yet, he wondered, if they had to would they eat her. . . ? If they *truly* had the need . . . ?

Thomas was listening to everything being said while he culled dried mushrooms. At least one of them looked like an *amanita*, not the death cap itself but another kind that was nearly as fatal and which grew commonly in their woods, sprouting under conifers ever more profusely the closer one went to the coast. Because of that one poisonous bud he had hidden the mushrooms throughout the winter. Since his accident with the bear, though, his attitudes towards life and death had changed. His steadiness, patience, his middle moods and application had subtly been turned inside out. He was indifferent as the weather, didn't care much what happened to himself or to the others.

Another *amanita*. Two more. Enough here to corrode his brains and those of his brothers . . . and another ten dozen brothers. The smart thing would be to toss the whole bag away, take no chances.

What the hell. If they died they died.

Those mushrooms that looked safe he dropped into the soup he was making. The rest he slung indifferently into a corner of the cave. He'd take the risk. They hadn't had anything warm in a week.

'Want some smoke?' Douglas held a pipe out. He had been dragging on wild tobacco, something Mark had said would palliate their appetites, but the more one smoked the weaker its effect. The others had long before given it up; Douglas, though, kept on puffing all winter, dreaming of better pastures, stronger dope.

Thomas, surprisingly, took some smoke, passed the pipe back, then started thickening the soup with lichens. He

201

tapped his mitt on the kettle to settle it, keep it from boiling over.

'Stop hitting your hand.' Eric's bright eyes had grown less green, more grey, dimmer. They protruded a bit, too. 'What are the white flakes? Eh?' He looked into the kettle. Those would be bones. 'How did you grind them?'

'N-n-not so h-hard, really.'

For weeks Thomas had been enlarging his range of movements by doing endless small household tasks. Not necessarily useful ones. And not out of a passion for rehabilitating the skills he'd lost. It was mere habit . . . a lifetime of doing niggling things right. But he hadn't gone outside once, not once, except to pee and shit. Eric, misunderstanding, thought it was all part of an admirable plan Thomas had not to attempt things in the world beyond his reach until he had mastered everything close at hand. There was no plan, though, just depression . . . detachment.

Thomas stirred the pot, was all.

There was a strange, strong odour in the hut. Eric sniffed the air, looked up. Mark, dropping from the ladder, stopped, too.

'What's happened?'

The two older brothers kneeled beside Bobby, snoring like the Cyclops. Mark jugged his fat brother in the stomach, distended though somewhat shrunken from its gigantic swell of his city days. 'Hey . . . .'

'Whaaaaa . . . ?' Bobby's eyes flickered. He yawned, didn't want to be wakened.

'You're sick. You've shit in your robes again.' Eric spoke without reproof.

'. . . fucko . . . .'

'Better go outside.'

Bobby strained to rise on his elbows. '. . . too tired.'

'Better go and clean up.'

'Mmmmmm . . . .'

A short time later Bobby came back into the lodge, naked from the waist down, a look of overwhelming disgust on his face. He cracked one of the struts descending, then shunted off to the deepest alcove, fully in shadow, and drew his legs up so that he couldn't be seen at all . . . went to sleep like an angry Buddha.

Another kettle was heating near the fire. Mark had started to steep roots of wild rose, a bath for their smoke-sore eyes, something which would not get better until they got out of the winter lodge and into the fresh air again.

'Your eyes look worse, too,' Eric told him.

'So do everybody's.'

Eric made his brother take the first compress. Mark had lost his glasses in the snow. Before he'd worn them only when the others weren't around; and even then only in-frequently, for he believed his eyes would get better. But they hadn't. Now he found they were tired at the beginning of every day and grew less useful with the hours.

'Why don't you come help me reset the snares on the far side of the lake? They should be catching something.' Eric took a rag from Mark now, bathed the tenderness on his lids. 'Come on.'

'I'm going fishing.'

'Again?' Eric sighed. 'There's no more fish.'

'They're in there.'

'You haven't caught one.'

The raven still sucked his black hopes. 'I'll catch fish.'

The truth of it was that Mark had been fishing in the ice once or twice a week since the freeze-over. The first two years they fished and did well, summer and winter, but Mark had grown too enthusiastic last winter with his gill net and had taken too many of the native char and whitefish. He wouldn't believe he had killed the lake. Perversely he continued to cut holes in the ice and string his net through, raising it and cleaning it and resetting it every week. But he wouldn't give up, even after falling through one of the ice holes he'd made, and without a safety line. Douglas had been close by and saved his life. Mark hadn't been wearing gloves at the time, which would have been his only chance for life if Douglas hadn't been there. There was a hint of self-immolation in all this.

Mark picked up his fishing gear. 'I can't stand it in here anymore. I'll check the traps afterwards, if you want.'

'Wait.' Eric put down the compresses. 'I'm coming.'

They went out quietly. Bobby had finally got to sleep and his guts, for the moment, were mute.

'Be careful, would you?' Eric cautioned his brother as the two of them walked separate ways in the valley. 'It's warmer, ice getting thin.'

'Not that warm.' Bloodyminded Mark, fishing in a lake without fish, with a net full of holes.

Eric stayed against the rocks and watched his obdurate brother lope down into the woods, towards the lake beyond. There was little colour, grey mostly, but the first he had seen in the valley for months. A dab here and there. Until now the only variant in the landscape had been the diminished white of shadows. Up the ridges everything was still blended into a pale and pure blank. The sky was white often, too, so that only the tracery of the soft cornices articulated the far end of the valley and broke it off from the sky.

The winter wind hadn't been unkind, had hardly come up since December, not a single day of gales. That meant less drifting of snow and easier walking, but it also made invisible the tree and bush cover which might have attracted animals for winter feed. Trees were never shaken free to show their green. Everybody had talked about clearing some willows and sedge, but in their lethargy didn't do it. Some few trees had dropped their snow garments with the thaw, but not enough to attract the wintertime herds, rare visitors that they were. Eric did what he could, beating the low branches free of snow as he trudged across the marsh.

And how will *they* live? He wondered about the other predators. How will they make it through this winter? It was barely February and two or three months before the snow really began to disappear. The earth beneath would be boggy for a month after that, perhaps longer. Yet well he knew that by summer's end he and his brothers would be cursing the sodden ground and waiting for the winter to start so that everything was frozen underfoot again.

Or so it had always gone before. But then they had never faced a winter like this one, never had been without a sure supply of food, nor endured such a cold snap.

Was he beginning to tire of the high country, he wondered, beautiful but deadly? It wasn't the rich mountain valleys of the Lauterbrunnen, that beautiful granite-pitched valley at the foot of the Jungfrau, with its glacial tarns and wildflowers and meadows at the crest of the world, that Eric had walked in travel guides and skiing brochures and *National Geographic*. His brothers and he had found something more than beauty here . . . barrenness, remoteness, loneliness . . . .

Loneliness. They had found that, all right. Nobody disturbed them. Only Sam knew just where they were. It was hard to believe their father had found his way up to them. And with a woman. Why with her? Because now they had to keep her, just another distraction from their war against the mountain, though Carmen seemed every day more and more as if she were someone made for this kind of life. *Why had their father come at all?*

In some mysterious way they had all expected him to come, almost from the first days . . . had even wanted him to come. It was only by accident that they had seen him and Carmen crossing the wash. At first they hadn't known who the two transients were, but they had had an instinct.

Eric knew that even if they'd left their father and Carmen alone there would have been some kind of violence. His father would have found them. Had Eric and his brothers hidden under the earth's rounded corners, Jacob Solomon would have stalked them and rooted them out. It was in the nature of things. So they had jumped to the conclusion by attacking first. The five of them had always wished for a time, place and fair quarrel to catch the old man once good on the hip. The bastard deserved it . . . mother-killing, child-killing bastard . . . dirty deathmaker.

Once everything started they decided not to let their father go home without suffering some kind of physical pains, but the asshole had surprised them, had got down from the mountaintop unscratched. That had infuriated them and was the reason they pelted him in the stream. Except it had all got out of hand. They were going to put the fear of God into him but once the stones started flying and they saw each other throwing hard, and to wound, the pulse of the event changed and suddenly they were furious, their father's pleas were curses, his huge mouth a whirlpool sucking them all in, and they threw and threw and threw and just . . . killed him. They had done more than watch him drown.

The funny thing was, nothing had been changed by the murder. The old man might as well be alive. But Eric felt no sorrow for what had passed. There was still the mountain to endure.

Eric came close to the ridge, craving a view of the whole valley, a chance to see the limits of his world . . . panopticon . . . like being on the castle ramparts. Somebody else might be happy bounded in a nutshell and finding there a kingdom of infinite space, but Eric needed some room. He was a big man and had to be able to open his arms.

Shining below he saw the ice-axe of his father. He went down to it, pulled it from the stones and beat the ice-cancelled ground beneath the snow, and continued to beat hard until his mind grew as blank as the sky, as clean as the driven snow itself, as pure and free from any taints of the world as the wild, white hair that was usurping the native ginger of his beard and chest, old age's colourless pennant knitting itself prematurely around his body.

Just as his father had, so he, too, would turn white, sullen, cold, pained, scared, stiff. And die. Exactly like his father had done, except in him it would come on much, much faster. Death was chasing Eric, had always been. And in that knowledge was an excellent prescription for a life, for the kind of life he and his brothers were living up here: They would keep death in constant view, not let the bastard sneak up on them unawares. And in doing so they would twist death's bony nose around, would live much longer than death expected.

It made all the difference. Every fourteen-second circuit of his blood, or however long blood took to go around, Eric could feel life's precious manufacture of food into heat, heat into power, and power into his will to outface death just a little while longer.

His brothers had to have an understanding something like this. It was, Eric thought, the reason they had all come up with Mark. They all knew for sure that in the world below the mountain there were just lots of people obscuring the view of life's simple, hard facts. They knew what they were doing, he and his brothers, and why they had to stay.

At least they had got one thing right and killed their father before he killed them.

Eric got to his knees to pray for a certain kind of death. He would fight to live through this winter, and if it were passed then the next, and the next, but when he sank finally he wished it to be on account of starvation. Not sudden but a slow and wasting death, full of thoughts, nice and gloomy, a certainty that it was happening and couldn't be escaped. That was the lesson of the world, after all, and it was best understood in their stone-crowned valley with the bunch of them banded together keeping each other upright until the last gasps . . . then dying together in a grip of love.

Since they could not run from death they would hasten pell-mell towards it and chase Mr Bones away . . . until they were trapped and made to watch his calm, complacent approach with their eyes clear.

The only fear was that at the last they would be fooled and death come in behind. With the cold. Eric wondered which it would be that would kill him, the cold or the hunger? Would it be just sinking slowly into a sleep, like that man in the Jack London tale who couldn't build a fire in Yukon? Better the purity of hunger. Nothing inside to hold Eric's spirit back from fleeing. A slight opening of the mouth, a suspiration, and the soul would just go, leaving the hulk behind, all magnificence gone with it leaving behind the brittle, stiff, empty waste of a body that had already become almost nothing at all . . . .

For some time Eric stared into the voided sky, the valley in front of him, Mark on the lake dropping his lure over and over, jigging it angrily on the bottom where there was nothing but weeds and beds of blackfly larvae dreaming of spring. Beyond the lake, on the tundra, two trees were being shaken by the wind about half-way up the slope. Then three trees. Eric's eyes stopped their movement.

Trees? Shaking? But there wasn't any wind. *Trees shaking?* What the hell was going on?

(Birnam Wood come to Dunsinane?)

Trees bending down and nibbling at the heather. Eating trees. He only saw two of them now.

He crept forwards on his knees, slowly, trying to dip below sightline and into the marsh. Down, down, down. He came to the lakeside and whispered across the hoar-frosted air to Mark, his jig-line snarled. Told Mark not to stir.

'What is it?'

'Up there . . . in the heather.' He pointed. 'Look.'

'Where?'

'*There.*' Eric almost fell over trying to whisper across the ice.

Mark looked above the willows and the thicker growth behind, seeing nothing, still fussing with the knots in his line but ever more slowly, until he stopped. And rose from the ice.

Eyes bright black. 'Caribou?'

'I think so.'

'How long—?'

'—I just saw them.'

'Two?'

'There were three a few minutes ago.'

Mark blinked. '*Impossible!*'

'Why?'

Then Mark looked at his brother and for the first time all winter his face warmed to a smile. 'Huy huy.'

Into the shelter, quickly, stealthily. Off with their plain and motley coats and on with their leggings, each brother with a dab of paint under the eyes, rehearsing the calls so there would be no confusion about who was to move which way. They chose arrowheads, quivers of fawn and fisher high-crafted, juniper bows. Excitement tensed their soft muscles after so long a slackness . . . the horde coming together, a quick chant and no more words, hand signals in the direction of the kill spot.

The five of them climbed out of the lodge. Their hair shone in the midwinter light, eyes smiling as their lips were taut in concentration. It had been a long time since they'd done this.

They put on snowshoes first, then the group split in different ways around the valley nearly at the tundra line. Eric went by himself straight through the marsh.

From her place by the cairn Carmen watched them circle the ridge. She could stand up and call, warn the caribou. The beasts would be a hundred miles over the rocks before the brothers got to them . . . the sure way to starvation for her and Jacob's sons. One shout and she settled the future. All she needed was the voice. But all she heard was the child inside her banging on the table for hot, fresh meat, fat, blood juices.

The brothers flanked the animals on both sides, a little higher up the slope, but still well over a hundred yards away from either caribou, far too far away for accurate shooting . . . and all without practice except for Eric who did it to keep alert. Thomas, in his one hand, carried a spear.

The group coming around from the left stopped. Bobby's bowels had begun rumbling and his anus itched to open. He took a false step.

Both caribou raised their furred horns into the air and looked over the snow. Ten seconds went by . . . twenty. One of them took four or five steps farther up the slope, bisecting the two groups of men who were crouched amongst the white rolls of snow and dwarfed trees. Its ears were upright and wiggling, trying to catch a sound of any kind, nose twitching for the smell of something that didn't belong. The urge to rejoin the herd over the hill kept tugging at the animal's horns. Finally its antlers' tines pointed to the cornice above and it started uphill laboriously, straight for the ridge and safety in numbers just beyond.

One gone. One left.

The other caribou had been nibbling at the frozen sedges and bell-heather shaken loose by the thaw. It took a step now, too, but without anxiety, the beast just trying to get at better shrubs . . . down the valley, deeper into the saucer, farther from the security of the ridge and surprisingly unconcerned or unaware that its partner had fled.

Eric had not reached the final copse yet, where it had

been planned the others would drive the animals. Having seen the jittery caribou he had stopped moving entirely. Nor would move until he was sure the other hadn't been alerted.

All of them waited . . . waited . . . lungs spitting and streams of vapour pouring from their noses. Bobby's bowels, which had cried out and cost them one deer, were screaming again. The bilious shit inside was bursting to come out. As tightly as he could Bobby contracted his anus, shaping his entire body like a bow around the end of his alimentary tract and pushing everything back up towards the centre. What devil wind was forcing its way out of his body . . .? and of all times, a hundred yards from salvation!

They were lost. All of them could see that. Any moment the last rare reindeer would understand how vulnerable it was and would prance away up the hill. Thomas watched the animal's infinite gestures, saw its head tuning to the tensions in the air.

The caribou let go the food from its lips. Danger. Something worse than hunger. The animal turned around quickly.

But Thomas had already better understood the caribou than the caribou the brothers, had guessed the angle of its flight and was five steps towards cutting off its escape by the time it bolted.

The beast surged right towards him. He stood up high and took a single step at the charging caribou, waving his spear and shrieking, forcing the creature to bear swiftly to its left . . . and its long body right across Mark's sights.

'Huy Huy.'

'*Huy!*'

Mark was on one knee, the whole scene playing out in an instant. His breathing stopped and he let wing a single, powerful shaft at where he thought the caribou's bucking form would pass. He heard the feathers singing along, tried to watch the arrow in the air but his eyes lost it and he thought he'd missed.

The caribou faltered, lurched forward as its front leg crumbled. Mark's shot had only been a grazing one that cut across the muscle, touching no bone. It had stunned the animal enough to drop it. But the caribou rose as quickly as it had fallen and was making steps again up the hill.

Too late, though. Thomas was already on top of the animal and drove his speartip into its right flank, this a deeper wound and one that broke bones. And Bobby was right behind, plunged an arrow – hand driven – into the spine as he batted the hooves away and threw the animal over. Douglas came around the right side and cut swiftly across the neck, not once, but three times, as he'd gone crazy watching the kill. A waste of its blood, which was sprinkling irrecoverably all over the snow.

It was done.

While the others lay in the snow exhausted, unable to believe they'd really killed the caribou, Bobby sped up the hill as quickly as he could push forwards his snowshoes. He struggled to make the ridge line in time; but, unable to, he threw off his bear coat and fell into the snow as his bowels finally burst, spilling the loose stool everywhere over the crusted snow, his insides continuing to wrench long after the first spasm was over, not eclipsing the joy he felt over the kill that he and his stomach had not, thanked be, had not quite ruined.

The hunt had been made. They had killed one of the beasts. Food. Warmth. Strength and conviviality . . . for a while longer.

During all this Carmen had seen only a part of their successful kill. Her eyes had been strung on another sight.

Just as the caribou had broken for the ridge, an unexpected movement near the marsh had pulled her attention away. There was another animal dashing laterally across the lake. It took some six or eight steps then halted, stood motionless for a long moment, then sank down on its front legs at the elbows with its hooves curved inwards. An instant later Eric emerged from the willows and stood over the beast, his bowstring still quivering. He dropped to his knees, gathered the animal's head in his arms and twisted until its neck snapped.

Eric had doubled their plenty.

He looked up at her in the rocks, called something but

211

Carmen didn't hear what he was saying. She thought it would have something to do with the thousand things that needed to be done in the coming days. Long after the meat was dressed and some of it dried, she would still be making babiche from the hide, treating the sinew from its back, working the horn with the rest of them, fixing the webbing of their snowshoes. She had learned about all this listening to their talk. And she would join in.

Joining in?

Carmen was overcome with a strange feeling, confusing in its mingled sense of power and ugliness: She was going to survive with them.

As Eric hollered to his brothers to come and see his kill, they rushing over with their own beast dragging behind, Carmen came down from the hillside bearing her own small offering: A basket of summer fruit that she had stolen to sustain her during a flight down the mountain. It was the last of her escape stash – frozen, but otherwise perfect.

She'd stay the course . . . at least until the child was born.

CHAPTER 17

Spring came. And grew to its full strength.

The sky thickened with blueblack and white clouds. And Carmen moved in riotous shafts of sunlight.

On most days she sat on a crumble of boulders high above the cairn where Jacob was buried, dreaming for hour upon hour with her eyes wide open. The men had got used to seeing her there and would expect to look up from their work – for they were working again – to find her pale yellow form pressed into the mountainside.

'Up near the ridge.' Thomas pointed to the opposite side of the valley. He rested on the handle of his axe and watched her for a few minutes. It seemed to him that

212

Carmen was traversing the whole valley, walking around it clockwise . . . resplendent in the light.

'C'mon.'

'Beautiful l-lady, that . . . even at the distance.'

Douglas, holding the wedge for Thomas's axe blows, said nothing, just scratched his wrist in a fury.

'Let me take a l-l-look.'

'Don't you fucking touch me.'

'You don't wash enough.'

'I wash all the time.' Douglas put the wedge into the weak point of the log they were splitting. 'Hit it.'

Surprised by how talkative he felt today, especially with Douglas on whom most all words were wasted, Thomas brought the hammer head of the axe crashing onto the steel, riving the pine right down to the end.

'Too yellow.' He rubbed the flat of his hand against the deepest heartwood. 'This one will take forever to d-dry out.'

'I hate cutting this stupid fucking wood.'

Thomas shrugged his shoulders and pushed his brother back as he raised high the axe – turned now to the cutting edge – and struck a thin nick in the timber, following a false cut he'd made while felling the tree from its last splintered connections to the stump. The gap widened with each stroke and in a grand final effort, lifting himself danger-ously back on his heels, Thomas quartered the tree entirely without the wedge.

'Jeezus you do wield that thing.'

And with one hand.

'C'mon, man . . . enough.' Douglas, as always, had little time for hard work. He watched his brother set the wedge in another rail, clearly intending to keep driving the axe. 'You even like the work, don't you?'

'I do.'

Douglas sat down on the stump his brother had just cleaned, chin in his palms, and watched the woman in the distance. All winter long he'd been watching her. His eyes had got smaller, meaner, and more stupid. He spit. Scratched angrily. There was no attempt to hide his bitter feelings towards Carmen.

'Why do you hate her so much? Not j-just because of thhhhhat ear of yours.'

Hidden under the long tangle of Douglas's hair the trimmed lobe couldn't be seen at all. He looked up at his brother with a face pinched from never understanding anything. And, seeing no particular sympathy for his hatred of Carmen, Douglas sprang off the log and walked away whining to himself, all the while gouging that maddening itch in his skin which seemed to run everywhere on his body right in front of his fingers. 'Go to fucking hell.'

Carmen, meanwhile, had managed to get three-quarters the way round the valley on her progress. She felt much more tired than she had in earlier days when the footing was considerably more difficult. The baby was finally beginning to restrict her. Going altogether more slowly than when she'd started, she found another resting spot not far from her perch, the circuit almost done.

The snow had been melting rapidly for some days, and intensely this morning since right after sunrise. It was almost a summer's day, the temperature somewhere in the high sixties or even warmer. Everything had gone into fast motion. Large holes were opening in the snowpack, bubbling and steaming, hissing. Sounds of the thaw.

The brothers had talked about possible flooding. Mark didn't think the lake could drain so much snow quickly enough and their entire camp might become a sinking pool. If they managed not to get sucked into the mud and kept from drowning then the insects would eat them alive in a month's time. Mosquitoes and deer flies and black sedge hadn't started but would soon. Ever since the weather changed Mark had been in a foul temper, able to think of nothing but the coming pestilence.

Sunlight reflecting off the snow bowl looked a little pink to Carmen. Everything did. She had strained her eyes during her walk, sat down in the snow and tried to rest them.

Someone was clapping hands in the valley. Raising herself part-way she saw Douglas doing a dance of some kind, an invocation to the spring. The steps weren't formal. Dance, stop, clap, sing, dance. It was his crude idea of what had once been done in the valley. Playing Indian.

'Stop that clapping!!'

Bobby, up in his shitting area – they had marked off a bare section of hillside just for him, where he was least likely to get anything into the lake – screamed at his brother whirling below.

'What's the matter with my just dancing if I want to?'

'The shitting snow is loose up here!'

Everyone in the valley heard, laughed as they watched Bobby's backside pink and luscious stuck over the hole he had dug in the snow. They all whistled, even Mark from the lake where he was clearing ice.

'CUT IT OUT, DUGGIE!'

'NOOOOOOOOOOOOOOOOOO!!!!!!!'

More hooting from all of them.

And then, astonishing Carmen as well as the rest of them, the corniced snow just above Bobby slipped and hurtled all the way to the marsh, carrying Bobby along with it. Douglas slapped his sides in a paroxysm of laughter but the rest fell silent. The avalanche could have killed.

There was no movement inside the snowball. Everyone waited. A full minute went by. Then, sure enough, came a chipping and pounding inside the huge white bollixed piece of mountain. A naked foot pushed out, a leg, arms, the whole man emerging finally, shreds of his robe hanging slatternly on him as he rose free of the ice ball and kicked the softer debris away.

'Well, now this shitice I've been cooking all winter is gonna melt down here and not up there and it's gonna trickle right into the lake. So you mothers can get ready to carry your own fucking water for everything . . . *fuckers!'*

Thomas answered by throwing his live axe as high as he could in the air and everybody ran in different directions to keep clear of its fall.

High spirits. Following a winter that would have snuffed the laughter in almost any other men.

The four brothers took off their robes and threw them in the stream to soak. It was the first time they had been out of their clothes since early winter. In a file they walked up to the waterfall and showered under its soft spray. Frolicked. With an innocence Carmen had never expected to see.

Exhausted, they found a place at a direct angle to the sun, cleared it down to the scree, and fell asleep in the daylight.

Spring.

The child in her belly had finally begun to show through. For over seven months she had held onto the false hope that they would never notice the palpable fattening of her breasts, the swelling haunches, her shortness of breath. Thomas's pale eyes had found out the child but for some reason he said nothing to his brothers. Slowly she had come to understand that all the rest knew as well. Conspiring in silence they had agreed that the baby would be born.

Just as they had conspired to say nothing about the extra food she stole. Her appetite in riot, the baby insatiable, several times Carmen had found ptarmigan in the snares, had peeled the bird's skin away with fingers numb from cold and then, beginning at the breast bone and working away from it symmetrically towards the back, she had crushed as much of the raw bird in her mouth as she could bear . . . cursing as she swallowed. She ate until she could no longer fight back the impulse to throw up, and then would eat her own vomit, twice sometimes, until it stayed down. Other horrors, too. Once Carmen had seen Bobby dash a rabbit's head open and suck out the raw brains. There had been times she'd done that herself and then slung the rest of the precious carcass away, not out of physical disgust but because it humiliated her to think that she was surviving only by living like the five of them.

The child was surviving, as well. Jacob's child. Since the very moment of conception in Paradise he had endured a lifetime of woes and was not yet born, a baby conceived against all likely odds. Carmen realized that throughout her entire term she had believed she was carrying a male child, one more Solomon son. It was crazy that she didn't try to kill the baby. The last good man in the world had been taken away. She should bring forth women children only. But then, she had done that once before . . . and not done it well. Thoughts of her first child made it easier to look down

216

at Jacob's sons and feel no anger. She might still loathe them but she knew now she was no better than they. Maybe far worse. Jacob had only been murdered by them and left to rot in unsanctified ground; but she, during the winter, had let Jacob's last screams in the river – his calls for vengeance – weaken and die. She had abandoned him, too.

Carmen stood up and took off her wet garments, laid them down in the sunlight. Parasites scurried away from the seams and into the snow. A cape and girdle of rabbit skins. Chilcotin clothes. A month or two before she had slung away the city clothes they'd once given to her in mockery, and put on native dress. For no particular reason.

And during the long cold snaps she had lain down to sleep near the fire . . . their fire. No matter how ferocious the weather was, it didn't explain why she lay *so close* to the fire. So unnecessarily close to comfort. There were times she dreamed the fire in their winter hut was scorching Jacob's spirit still unannealed in the air somewhere about the camp, above their heads . . . while warming her. The same fire.

The grave where they'd tossed their father wasn't so many yards from the lodge that she couldn't have circled a little wider on one of her walks to the marsh, dug up Jacob and given his body the few sweet remembrances and obsequies all the muted dead asked for.

Their food, too. She had helped to cook it. And had waxed fat on their leavings.

Did she do that? She had done still worse. Done it with downcast greygreen eyes. And submissiveness. Though Carmen hadn't understood until she saw the sky this morning and decided to walk all the way around the valley.

The wind was from the west. Carmen held up her hands in the ragamuffin currents. They were not only warm but wet. Rain was coming. The life in this world of theirs was shuddering out of winter's barrenness. Under a canopy of high-capped clouds and the dance of light, besieged by sweet-smelling and warm freshets out of the west – poetical wind, medieval and copious – Carmen had begun to realize that she was in some small way happy . . not happy, not happy at all, but feeling something that could be called by no other name than joy. She had endured.

Lying there and scratching her pest-bitten legs, she begged Jacob's spirit cased up in his sons' valley to forgive that she had survived in the ways she had, and that she had not avenged his murder, nor even had the rudest of plans to do so, nor even the desire. And, worst of all, that she had taken one moment of pleasure on such a high-fantastical spring day.

She asked to be forgiven the spring . . . .

'What was the noise?'

Carmen's shawl fell away. Eric stood atop the ladder leading from the winter hut, half in shadows though the sunlight struck his head. He rubbed his eyes and drew an arm roughly across his mouth. Spat. For several weeks he had fought a fever. The worst of it had broken the morning before. Eric had confessed he didn't remember a thing: three entire days were wiped clean from his memory.

'I heard a rumble and then a crash.'

'Snowslide . . . a little while ago.' Carmen's hands were covering her nakedness. With a lowered head she nodded towards the gouge in the hillside's snowy cheek. 'Not a very big one, though.'

'Anyone hurt?'

'No.'

Eric saw his brothers heaped naked and sleeping on top of each other. 'What am I missing?'

'The spring.'

He nodded, took a step out of the shelter and into the light. It was easy enough for Carmen to see how weak he was, his arms meagre as the disease had taken him down even more in weight and made now a pale shadow of what had once been a much more substantial man. His big hands seemed almost comical, undiminished giants scraggling along his depleted body. Of all the brothers Eric was the least inclined to eat; at first it had been because he wanted to see the others eating and then, when they had enough food, just not eating much. Monsters in his mind even more than microbes in his body were wasting him.

Like Carmen he had on no clothes. 'It's warm out.' He spoke tentatively, unsure of what his senses told him.

'Very.'

'I'm still cold.'

She had seen that.

'Under my arms it's worse.' He raised both arms and showed her the swollen nodes bulging. 'They're hard and hurt like hell. All I have to do is graze them and they scream.'

Conscious again that she had nothing on, Carmen's eyes swept the gravel, looking to see where her shawl had gone.

Suddenly the wolf came forwards, straight at her, and her heart stopped beating. But he slid past her and bent down to finger something in the dust-blown snow under the platform of the summer lodge. When he straightened up he held a small, white flower that had struggled up from the grit of their campsite.

'*Every* year,' he exclaimed, 'right in the same spot.'

Thinking he was holding the flower out to her Carmen reached for it. His mind was elsewhere and he didn't see her grasp. Then he crushed the flower abstractedly and threw it to the ground.

'There are things to do,' he said then, talking more to himself than to her. 'I wish I wasn't so goddamn weak.' Eric's eyes were blank, as if he were still having trouble understanding where he was. 'Where are your clothes?'

'Drying.'

'Put some on . . . a blanket . . . anything.' His eyes wouldn't pass over her body. Finally he couldn't avoid looking at her anymore. He saw her distended stomach. 'How much longer is this thing going to take?'

'I don't know.' She lied. She knew the day itself.

'And then what do we do with it?' A meanness had crept into his weakened voice. She didn't answer. '*Get a blanket, I told you!*'

Her face red and stinging, Carmen fell away from him and went to rummage for something dry, furious that she had asked him how he was or given the slightest damn when he had slipped into the higher burn of his fever.

219

Back at her perch, sitting against a flatbacked rock, Carmen sat smouldering. With the weather changed she wondered if she mightn't just stay amongst the rocks again as she had during her first weeks in their camp. She kicked the snow away, rubbed her hands in the dirt beneath, filling up again the seam she'd spent a lifetime trying to clean out. Thoughts of escape peppered her wrath, inchoate thoughts . . . plans the likes of which she had long given over. If she were going to do it, it must be soon, because her strength was diminishing rapidly with the baby beginning to drop lower in her stomach. In her head she did a quick calculus of her needs for flight . . . and a rough guess of her chances for success.

The shrillness of her anger soon levelled off. She grew calm. Escape was a complicated thing. And escape to where? She had almost forgot what life was like in the flatlands.

And then it occurred to Carmen that there was no other life for her. Despise them as she did, as she always would, nevertheless her life was with them in this mountain valley . . . here with them, nowhere else, with the five of them and, in a few weeks, with her child . . . forever.

The brothers had decided to move everything outside, from the winter shelter to the summer lodge, from underground to above. It was time to brush away the dead year's ashes.

Still naked, all five of them began to clear an immense space around the campsite, pushing the snow well back from where they lived and worked during the summer months. As they worked they sang, a common chant with no leader.

A large flock of snow geese circled around the valley several times, dinning away over the lake, then descended to the bits of open water, eclipsing the sun as they fell. The roar of their wings echoed off the mountainside. Carmen remembered seeing a flock of the same birds on their way south. It was when she and Jacob were swimming in the pool at Paradise, only moments before his sons killed him. She wondered if it were those birds now landing on the lake . . ? *The indifferent rhythms of natural life.* No doubt

220

some birds had died in the warmer waters of the Gulf of California, some on the way.

She had never eaten goose. Carmen mused on hot meals in holiday times. A bird on its back with sauced drumsticks stuck up in the air. None of the brothers were looking up from their labour but she knew they would find a way to snare a goose tonight. She would probably help them in their catch. Why not? She lived with them.

And shared the pain.

Though her eyes were still burning terribly from the glare, Carmen came down the hillside and found a piece of bark large enough to scrape with, then started at a corner of the rapidly enlarging open space and joined in their work. Imitating the men, she picked up their rhythmic sweeping of the debris and snow. Moved in closer to them. The five of them had formed a straight line and now Carmen fell into the group, squaring herself in the row as all together they filled up their shovels with the soiled snow, dumping it against the hillside and away from the camp so that when it melted water would not run back over everything but into the marsh.

Like Levin cutting the wheat with his serfs, though on a smaller scale, Carmen spent the better part of an hour bending and scraping and lifting and carrying, each person profoundly aware of his neighbours . . . the singing stopped soon enough as the hard labour began, only the rhythm of their work sensible, not a thing else in any of their minds, not one thing . . . the swing of arms filling up the whole valley . . . the world . . . while the great white birds wheeled over the lake, and more of them came, and more . . . and still more fell from the sky . . . .

Carmen's eyes suffered badly from the snow. The constancy of the glare kept turning the valley a darker shade of pink to her, pink tending more and more towards red. By the time she realized she had better stop they had finished. The camp was open. And so Carmen sat down for a few minutes to catch her breath and close her vexed eyes.

While she rested they worked on. With a space to manoeuvre now they brought out load after load from the winter hut, everything, the entire kitchen, even the rocks they used as an oven and the stones for boiling, odd pieces of fur and their bedding and woodworking tools and the polished gambling sticks, all the water vessels, even green wood that had been drying by their fire, Mark's notebooks, the root diggers and sap scrapers, baskets, hunting weapons, rushes from the floor, assorted animal teeth and hair and bone and horn and gut and hide, junk, garbage of every kind, every meagre thing in their material world.

After laying it all out on the ground they started a parade to the lake, taking the smaller items down to be washed there and bringing back kettles full of water to rub down the bulkier things.

They cleaned everything, renewed it, reconfirming that there was some order in the war for survival . . . because it wasn't only for hygiene they were labouring so hard, so efficiently, exchanging few words as they worked.

Though she could barely see, stumbling as she went, Carmen carried her own things out, then helped them with everything else. Several times during the winter she had provoked bad feeling by inadvertently touching some objects they venerated, mostly their hunting gear. But now the only thing worrying the five of them was that she not break what she handled and that she didn't kill herself staggering back and forth to the water.

Slowly she was being acknowledged. She had a right to live, even amongst them. She believed they now thought so, too.

'What do you see?'

Carmen felt a hand on her arm, holding her back. The fact was she hadn't been moving for some time.

'Do you see anything at all?' It was Eric's voice . . . his hand.

'Only pink . . . like a halo or a fog. Just the colour, no detail at all.'

'You're snowblind.'

'I know.'

'Go inside.'

'Where?'

She could hear him thinking for a moment. 'Go into the sweat house.'

That was their private place, almost holy. 'You're going to have to help me.'

Her robes were drying on the rail of the summer lodge. Carmen reached up, felt they were still wet.

'Just wear your shawl. You won't be cold.' He told her the rest of her clothes would continue to sweeten in the wind. He'd watch out for them.

'Will it rain?' she asked.

'It might.'

There were rain-swollen clouds in the sky, but he explained that for the moment they were all to the east, over the plateau.

He pulled her gently along.

'Not in there!' Mark's hoarse voice stopped their progress. 'She's *not* going in there.'

'What do you care?'

The raven spoke again. 'I said she's not going in there.'

Eric dropped her arm and moved a step backwards. 'Do you say so?' He mocked his brother.

'She's changed everything.'

'Things change.'

The others had stopped what they were doing, drew closer.

'No woman in the sweat house.'

'She's snowblind.'

'I don't give a fuck.'

'She n-n-needs to be in the dark.' Another voice began pleading for her.

'Let her dig a hole in the ground and bury herself in it for all I care.'

Once again the wolf's grip guided her forwards, very surely. He raised her hand to the wooden latch. 'You go in there . . . *go*.'

For an instant she paused, witless of what would happen and unable to see their faces. She was frightened, but she went inside. The door was closed behind her.

There was a bench of unworked wood against one wall. Carmen sat down on it, found it was long enough to stretch out on. The argument outside grew more heated. She couldn't distinguish the words but the tone and speakers she followed easily enough.

Douglas's voice was the angriest, the loudest. He screamed like a snared animal. Pretty Marten. She had always thought of him as the most dangerous. He, more than any of the others, was beyond touch, especially that of a woman. For a long time Douglas had been looking for an occasion to do something savage. It would not rest here . . . he would be after her. Maybe that night.

While the sons of Jacob Solomon laboured outside to prepare the camp for summer and the high time of life, Carmen had mathematical dreams, entirely without people. In pink she conjured up geometric shapes, grills and grids and mazes with endless sides and angles. Abstract. Regular. A faultless, peopleless world.

When she awakened with a start sometime later, she found the rose-coloured shapes of her dreams had been overcome by darkness, for she couldn't see anything at all.

Carmen raised herself up. It hadn't been dark when she went to sleep. Either she had slept through the sun's setting or the snowblindness had plunged her more deeply into a daytime night.

Voices outside were shouting and laughing crudely. She stood up and felt her way towards the door. Her eyes were heavily crusted and stuck together, as they had been weeping fluid for some hours and the fluid, unable to drain, had simply hardened. The latch was closed. She pushed sideways and let the door swing open.

Much laughter. Very coarse, too. She could hear that the brothers were having a game with the dogs. As mysteriously as they had disappeared last autumn, the dogs were back now, having got through the winter somehow without being eaten by the wolves or coyotes from which they were in large part descended.

The bitch was in heat. A couple of the others were after her. And the men had formed a pentagon around the dogs, cheering them on. Even though Carmen couldn't see what was happening, it was easy for her to imagine how lean the

224

dogs had become. They had, in fact, lost weight alarmingly. Much of their pelts had scraped off against rocks and the barks of trees, so much so that they were nearly hairless over the back half of their bodies, their skins a mass of boils and eructations feeding a hodgepodge of infection.

They growled as they limped around the bitch.

Soon Carmen had a rough idea of what the dogs were doing. She could smell it as well as hear it, the blood of the bitch dripping profusely as an old male kept mounting her and missing her, shredding her anus with his claws, snapping at her . . . but getting nowhere.

Dizzy, sick from the smell, Carmen made her way towards the men . . . groped along, her feet slipping off the rocks as she tried to find the path. She knew they had seen her because their well-breathed jeers slowed down.

She kept on coming. The dogs were still rutting and the men turned back to watch. So Carmen shrieked, in anger and revulsion.

All the sounds in front of her stopped. Carmen stopped. She couldn't see it herself but she was going to break off their spectacle, once and for all turn their noses away from barbarism.

Silence. Not even a breeze.

One of the brothers slunk towards her. He came close enough that she could feel his heat. It was Douglas. He got behind her and curled his arms around Carmen's waist, then spun her forwards like a top. But he held the bottom of her shawl. All the slack lengthened out. With one tug he pulled it right off, leaving her naked and blind.

They looked at her. It was the first time that they had seen so much of her so close.

Big with child she was, but always the golden girl. She had her legs, her thighs weren't dimpled with fat, her hips remained unstretched. Carmen had always had strong breasts; they were fuller now, the areolae darker, cinnamon. And coiling down from her head the long filaments of gold, grown to her waist.

She had lost nothing. She was still miraculous.

Douglas crawled next to her on his knees, laughing cunningly. The others were amused by his game. He rubbed

225

her belly like a totem. Carmen tried to move away but he caught her and kneaded her stomach more aggressively, then bent down to kiss the baby.

Putting her hands on Douglas's head, she tried to make out from the hair, the beard, the eyes' ridge which one of the brothers was touching her.

Suddenly he pinched her flanks. Hard. She sucked in air and groaned. She knew it had to be Douglas.

He prodded her again. Carmen gasped. She had been wrong all along. Their plan wasn't to rape her first and then kill her. They were going to let her live.

And rape her continuously after.

'Get away from her.' Eric was snarling.

'Uh uh.'

'*Get away.*'

There was a pause.

Then, without warning, Douglas clapped her tremendously, knocking her over. He swarmed on top of her, his rough skin chafing her, his hands reaching up her ribs to her breasts, while he jammed his legs in between hers trying to climb inside.

The others jumped to help Carmen, their many hands confusing her at first but all falling on Douglas and not her, caught him and pulled him off. She could hear the spittle catching in their beards as they fought to get control of Douglas.

It wasn't working. Finally, enraged, Eric beat his brother's soft mouth. Three more chops and he got him on the ground.

Nobody moved. Their breaths were heaving as they all listened to Douglas whine, the blood dripping heavily from his lips and bubbling in his nose.

A pair of hands reached around Carmen, long arms, and lean, big hands. Eric drew her upwards, pulling her all the way into the warm cup of his body while he spoke to his brother.

'Do something like that again and I'm going to kill you.'

'*Go to fucking hell!!*'

But Douglas stopped whimpering soon. He at last understood the others weren't going to stand around while he tupped and rammed Carmen – even Mark was against him, Mark who had seemed to hate her and who had once said he'd regretted they hadn't killed her before.

With the insides of his fingers Eric stroked Carmen's neck and brushed away the caked sand from her eyelids, opening a channel for her tears. She was shaking badly, her mouth and cheeks gone into spasm. Eric gripped her tighter, rocked her for some time until all the twitching stopped.

When she was all right he held her a little away from himself and studied her. It was as if he'd recognized an affinity for the first time. 'Little Blondie . . . .' He probed her stomach gently, where Douglas had savaged her worst. 'You O.K. . . . ?'

She wouldn't say.

For some time Bobby had been working on a name for her. He laughed from the bottom of his immense paunch, but wholly without malice or derision. 'C'mon, doggo, you O.K. or what? Eh, Crazy Dog?' It was his kind of welcome.

'Cr-crazy Dog.'

They all picked up the chant, finally giving her an animal familiar. She was becoming just like them. One of them.

'Sister.'

Crazy Dog was one of the pack. Brothers and sister.

'*Sister*.' There was some small triumph in Eric's voice.

'No sister.'

'*Sister!*' They were all shouting it, determined on this one point, as if it were the very axle of their understanding what they were doing in the mountains. '*Sister!*'

'*NO!!!*'

The vehemence in her throat shocked them. She was not their sister. Not now. Not ever.

'No!'

Not their sister.

Eric, confused by her denial, kissed her on the forehead. She turned away from him.

'You're with us, you are . . . whatever you think.'

She tried to get up. Couldn't.

'C'mon, doggo . . . gonna fix you a place in the summer house.'

Their shadows were over her.

'Hold off!' Eric kept Carmen in his arms. He wasn't letting her go anywhere until he knew her mind exactly. The five of them were offering to treat her like a sister but she was telling them it wasn't like that.

'What are you, then?'

The thing she would never understand afterwards was that she really might have stopped it. But Carmen believed everything that had happened was in some large measure her fault, and that her only path to judgement and salvation was the hardest one. She would tell them the truth.

She was not their sister. She was more than that. She was their dog . . . Carmen the Dog . . . *'Crazy Dog'*.

And she would render a dog's service.

Carmen kissed Eric hard.

He tried to pull back his lips but she found them again and kissed him harder.

All of the others backed away. Their breathing altered, they were frightened.

Eric still tried to push her away but she stuck to him, slipped her swanlike arms around and brought a touch to him far more delicate than his rough expectations.

She overpowered him with kindness . . . kissed his chest, legs, his fever-bent fingers, feeling her way along him by touch and smell, Carmen unable to see what she was doing. Finally she kissed his penis. It, too, was wasted, and bitten and chewed by the parasites they all lived with, foulsmelling and hair-clotted. She kissed it. She sucked it. She would not be pushed away again.

And whatever he wished to happen, nevertheless instinct aroused him, his penis thumping larger and longer with every pulse of blood.

Eric coughed as his excitement grew, his lungs shattered by the fever he'd endured. He rolled over on the dirt with her, her mouth holding on his, juddering with his lips, he almost suffocating her smaller, copper mouth he kissed her so strongly . . . down to her neck, long and sylphlike and still soft after all the winter's outrages. She held her throat up to him yieldingly. Eric bared his incisors and plunged them into her skin, he losing all semblance of control now, rolling her over again until she was on top of him, her thighs lifting up as she climbed onto his swollen prick.

She mounted him under the canopy of spring air.

The wind returned now, pushing clouds in front, rain coming for sure. His hands squeezed her breasts and she leaned forwards so that he could suck them.

Just as the light began to go from the day she pressed down on him and got him up into her – hard and dry and difficult for her to dilate but she did quickly – right up to the cervix where she could feel him hammering away at the head of her child, touching the plug of mucus between him and the baby. She held him, throttled him enough to get him pumping more rhythmically, until he got to the top of his arc. For a moment he felt nothing but a powerful blistering in all the nerves of his body radiating out from his stomach. Then he expended everything right inside her.

They stopped completely, all except for their lungs' screaming. Both were shattered. They stayed like that for a long time and might not have moved at all if the rain hadn't come suddenly and smacked on them so sharply they both screamed in relief over the thunder's roll.

The showers eased soon, and then grew more steady, melting snow on every side of the valley as Eric crawled out from underneath her and the next brother lay down on the ground under Carmen to be served in his turn . . . not one of them, not the brothers, not Carmen, able to hear the voice of Jacob Solomon rising white and frozen from its sepulchre of stones near the mountain stream . . . rising in hysterical wrath as it oathed a song of treachery and revenge on all of them – *all six* – though it went unregarded, usurped as it was by the call of children growing older and forming their own bonds of love . . . a voice forgot, like the lion of Judah himself . . . out of mind but not extirped quite . . . .

BOOK III

Sarah

CHAPTER 18

Joseph and Rosalie Solomon's second child, a boy, was born at home.

His little life still reckoned in minutes and hours, the baby took to the breast right away, blackening the nipple with his furious sucking as if he already knew the way to have what he wanted in the world. It was a good baby. Rosalie knew that from the first moments after delivery. The child would take care of himself all his life.

Seeing how Rosalie's body glistened, the midwife wanted to put fresh sheets on the bed, but Rosalie told her no. The crumpled delivery sheets had life in them, were as fertile as the veins and stalks of pale green plants in the cloth's pattern that wound about her legs. She didn't want them changed yet.

The baby fell asleep guarding the nipple. It was a sign. For seven hours the midwife had toiled and she needed a break. Joseph had kept her going with mugs of spiced tea, but now she had to get off her feet, not necessarily sleep but lie down for a while. Joseph offered her the guest room but she refused.

'I'm gonna go home,' she told him, pulling a light cape over her shoulders, pushing down the rolls of her gown's sleeves . . . a big woman, a big block of a woman who had wrapped her hands like metal squares around the baby's head and drawn him into the world. Birth was no gentle thing, not to her mind, and life afterwards no easier. A good birth that went fast and sure, as this one had, augured for a good life. 'No more need of me.' She was satisfied, pumped Joseph's hand a few times at the door. 'Healthy child that . . . healthy woman, your wife.'

Joseph paid her and then let her out into the rain, a weak June storm that had blown up from the tropics. He thought he could use some sleep, too, after a shower.

'Mr Solomon?'

The hallway was dark but a door was open at the far end where a nurse stood in silhouette, the faint yellow of a nightlight coming from the room behind her. Mrs Barlow had been with Joseph and Rosalie for several weeks already, watching over their first child. She had agreed to stay three more weeks with the new baby. An English-woman, she was deceptively into her seventies and might have been taken for a woman much younger except that her unhealthy, pasty, vein-vexed skin betrayed her.

'Your Theresa's up again.' The nurse spoke disapprovingly. She thought most American children spoke so much in order to fill up the silence of their parents, though that was not the case with Rosalie and Joseph's child. 'She says it has something to do with her teddy bear.'

'What?'

'The young lady refuses to tell me.'

'All right.' Getting the old woman to sit with Rosalie, Joseph went into his daughter's room guided by the night-light.

He found her not in bed but sitting in a small rocker glossily painted one afternoon by her and Joseph. She was absorbed, staring at the iridescent eyes of a stuffed bear that had been her mother's a generation before.

'What's the itch, Miss?'

'Sssshhhh!' Theresa was waiting for the bear to blink back at her. She would brook no interruption.

Joseph crossed the room as quietly as he could, his flat feet sliding across the carpet pile. He wore no shoes, only socks. By the chair he sat down, crossing his legs Indian style. 'It's about the middle of the night, you know.'

'I'm not sleepy.'

'When are you ever?' In the dimness Joseph could see she was perplexed, her soul straining as if she were listening to some distant music. 'You hear something?'

'Teddy.'

'What's he saying?'

233

'He's not talking now.' She spoke petulantly. Her father's entry had broken off the bear's speech. 'Teddy's gone.'

'He's right there in front of your eyes, Miss.'

'No he's not.'

His daughter had a strong inclination to speak in mystical figures. 'Gone where?'

'Buried.'

Joseph's eyebrows arched. This was the first word connected with death he had ever heard her use, 'death' a notion she could only imperfectly understand. He thought his daughter's anguish must have something to do with the vague but long-promised event they had told her about, the baby brother who'd be stealing into the household. With his knack for directness Joseph told her exactly what had happened on the far side of their house by the nursery, that the baby had finally come.

But Theresa sat sullenly, her eyes still transfixed on the little bear's.

'You want to sneak a peek at your new brother, Miss?' He watched her rock a few times, letting her feet graze the threads of the rug as if she were on a swing. 'C'mon . . . .'

'Take Teddy to see.'

'You don't want to see for yourself?'

'Tomorrow.' For Theresa 'tomorrow' was the entry-hole to oblivion, where she stuffed all her cares. 'Take Teddy away,' she sighed. '*Please*, Daddy.'

There was something plaintive in her voice, some sadness in the way she rocked her chair, some unease. Joseph wasn't going to let it pass. 'I have a feeling you're angry at Teddy . . . is that right?' She shook her head without conviction. 'Did he say something wrong?' The small head paused. 'What did Teddy say to you?'

'He said he wasn't died.'

Joseph stopped. He was hearing, he thought, his child's first flowering of grief, a kind of self-mourning. Theresa sensed the beginning of the end to her invincibility. A baby brother had arrived in the darkness at the other end of the house, and she had heard the cries of pain. She knew the baby had come bloody into the world. And Theresa, barely

234

four years old, guessed that the price to pay would be some blood and pain of her own.

He rubbed her forehead. 'Listen to me, my little bag of sugar, you're tired . . . Teddy's tired . . . can't you see how tired he is . . . ? Look at his silly eyes. He doesn't even know what he's saying. Time for sleep, for both you and Teddy . . . I'm tired, too.'

'Teddy said he wasn't *died*, Daddy!'

All he could do was to rub and rub and rub his daughter until she grew limp in his hands. It had been his one real anxiety about having the baby at home that the shadows and whispers and nightmoves would baffle her completely. They had. He picked up her totem. 'I'm going to take Teddy and let him sleep with me tonight and if he says anything about anything I'll tell you tomorrow. Deal?' He usually won with her. 'Howzabout it?'

Theresa's arms went up in the air so that her father could carry her over to the bed and slide her under the sheets. She held his neck for a long time before finally dropping onto her pillow, saying nothing, not even goodnight. Then she rolled away from Joseph and disappeared into midnight thoughts. She trusted her father, but had a mind of her own.

'What was the matter?' Rosalie took her husband's hand, kissed it.

'What do you think? She's jealous. She's got a rival.'

'A little early for that, isn't it?'

'She knows all kinds of things it ought to be impossible for kids to know anything about.' Something caught Joseph's eye. 'You think I'm wrong, Mrs Barlow?' The old woman was surprised. 'Why are you shaking your head?'

'Was I?'

'Yes.'

The nurse bit her lips, asked to be excused. The day had wearied her, too.

'Good night, Mrs Barlow.'

'Good night, then.'

Joseph rolled carefully onto the bed, snuggled his wife with the sleeping infant between them. He smelled the moisture of the sheets, a sweet smell something like the potpourri which was usually by their bedside. Now, instead, oils and emollients crammed the ledge.

'You want me to rub you down with something?' The Los Angeles air, humid as a Venusian day, had licked its way into every room and recess, through all insulation. 'I'm sweating like crazy myself even though you've been doing the work.'

'Doing's easier than watching, I've got a feeling. Anyhow, I've been on my back. Why don't you just relax?' But Rosalie could see there was something else. 'What's going on, Joe?'

His thoughts were far away.

'Work?' -

'Don't be crazy.'

'Your shoulders are leaning halfway to your office.'

'I want to check something.'

'So do it.'

'You'll be all right for a minute?'

'I'm not going anywhere.'

Joseph nodded and went down the narrow hall to his study, dragging his daughter's bear behind him.

In his filing cabinet were some old, yellowing bills of his father's which Joseph had paid long ago. He took out one of them and sat in his swivel chair, studying the bill with the teddy bear staring at him from a sofa opposite his desk. It was a stupendous bill from Eddie Bauer's. Fully itemized. His father had bought enough gear to outfit himself for a run up the Himalayas to roundelay on Annapurna's sharp flanks. There were no ladies' items marked, but Joseph knew Carmen had gone up after his father and certainly followed him into the mountains. She, too, had not returned.

With Jacob supplied as he had been, the two of them might have lasted out a Russian winter . . . with that and a little help from Joseph's brothers for food, shelter, warmth.

Except that Jacob had died. Reportedly. One of the locals in Chezacut had sent a letter to say Jacob Solomon owed him for two horses and was presumed dead in the mountains, probably pursued, attacked, and eaten by a bear, the area notorious for grizzlies. No mention had been made of Carmen. Nor of his brothers. Jacob might never even have found his sons. Maybe.

Joseph pointed accusingly at the toy bear. A worshipful creature was a bear, dear and blessed company to all children, the one doll they all remembered . . . the best of secret-sharers, the most faithful of friends. It was hard to conceive that a bear had gnawed and chewed all the flesh, sinews, blood of his father. Even the hair? The old white head of his father? The letter said it must have happened, was common enough. Bones and all? Joseph wouldn't believe it. Bones? *Bones!!*

In front of him, the bear's lifeless green eyes seemed to fill up with love for his lost father. Joseph watched until the eyes were the colour of blood, of wine . . . bright and flaming. The bear, having shared Theresa's inchoate grief about the passing of her singularity, was now helping Joseph with his own grief. The bear was quick with life.

Strange bear.

Joseph squeezed the desk's teak edge and rose out of his chair, all the hair across his back up as he himself stood . . . fixed fast on the bear but unwilling to believe what the bear was doing—

—Illusion? Projection? Hallucination . . . ?

Or just a wish?

Whatever the reason, the bear's eyes opened and its mouth moved slowly as it spoke. The room was sombrely lit, the night long, the day had sweated and made the air so thick it confused Joseph, smothered his brain. But he had enough sense left to hear and see the bear. And it spoke to him, no doubt about it, *spoke*. Just as it had to his daughter. Joseph even recognized the voice. It was his father's.

King Christ!

The old man wasn't dead . . . not completely. Not yet.

All night long Joseph strove with the bear. The animal lay at the foot of his and Rosalie's bed. They watched each other, he and the bear. Neither moved. Neither spoke. Joseph waited and waited, but there was no life in the bear's eyes now.

About half past six in the morning, just as the sprinklers hissed on, Theresa came into their room unannounced, trailing behind sleepless eyes. She saw the bear, saw her infant brother bundled over her mother's nakedness, but she looked only at her father. He saw her and knew why she'd come.

'Teddy talked to you, didn't he, Daddy?'

'Yes.'

'What'd he say to you?'

He watched her whispering eyes. Joseph had sworn to tell her all. 'Just what you said he said.'

'Did he talk to Mommy?'

'No.'

Rosalie smiled in half-sleep and curled an arm around her daughter's neck though she kept on nodding. She wasn't listening.

The baby was a dark squirm against her mother's flesh. Theresa jerked her head contemptuously towards her brother, he just a crooked thing in the middle of the bed that breathed and coughed and spit all without breaking his sleep. The sounds of the morning were calming and obscure, but Theresa had no peace, for the bear had taken it away. 'Teddy's all hurt, Daddy.'

'I know, my sugar.'

'Why?'

Joseph shrugged his shoulders. There was no answer for his child any more than there was one for him. 'I don't know yet . . . .'

His answer satisfied her and she yawned. Her eyes were quickly bolting closed. Theresa had had so little sleep during the night that she would sleep much of the day. At the foot of their bed, next to her bear, she dwindled and then slid all the way to the floor where she stretched out like a suicide on stage, not moving a hair . . . .

'What's going on, Joe? I want you to tell me this time.' The soft damp of the morning, sweet, floral, was in Rosalie's voice. She commanded in her own way.

'I want to go see my brothers.'

She looked away, towards the gauze of the curtains. The sun's first light irradiated everything on her dressing table,

238

ointments and the silver handle of her hair brush, lemons in a bowl, the inlaid rosewood. 'What a funny time for you to be thinking of them.'

'I keep wondering if my father isn't alive somewhere up there.'

'I'm sure he's dead, Joe.'

'A man doesn't just disappear.'

The baby trembled and Rosalie rocked him. 'That's just about all you can be sure a man does, I would have thought. Isn't that what death is all about?'

'No.'

'What's happened to you suddenly? You've always been such a realist about these things.'

'I just don't believe the man was eaten by a grizzly bear.'

'It's plausible.'

'Not very.'

'It's also what we were told did happen.'

Joseph sat up, his back against the headboard. 'How can you not be curious about what really went on? Suppose it were your own father?'

'I'm sure he's dead, Joe.'

'And Carmen?'

His wife shrugged.

'And the rest of them?'

'Maybe they're all dead after a winter like that. Or maybe your father got stuck up there because of the weather and had to winter it out with them . . . only he hasn't had a chance to get out yet to let us know.'

'That's what I'm thinking.' Joseph saw her frown but didn't stop. 'Somebody has to go up there and find out.'

'Not you.'

'Why not me?'

'What's to find, Joe? If anybody's alive we'll hear.'

'If they're alive I want to see them. If not, I'd better go bury them, hadn't I?' Joseph's hand was right under his infant son's nostrils, so close he could feel the moist breath streaming out and immediately being sucked back in. 'You have to bury people.'

'Oh boy.' Rosalie lifted her son from her breast and set him down in the region of Joseph's groin.

'Stay in bed. What do you want? I'll get it . . . stay in bed.'

'I want to pee.'

'There's a bedpan.'

'I'm *supposed* to get up . . . I *want* to get up.'

He listened to the household sounds, the tank refilling, the faucet turned on . . . off. There were comforts here, and a family. He'd have to give them up for a while and go to Canada. Something had happened. He was afraid to think what.

Rosalie came back in, pendulous breasts red and black and rich as a spice chest. Her toes caught the sheet and she lifted it up to her hips, lay down.

'Rosie, something of my father lives up there.'

'This is a fable. It was crazy for him to go in the first place. You said so yourself. He's dead, Joseph.'

'I'm going to find him and I won't come back until I do. Whatever it is that remains – I don't care if it's a *fingernail* or *a wisp of hair* – whatever is left I'll find and bring back and bury.'

'Let the dead bury the dead.'

'It has to be done, Rosie, it has to be. I don't know how else to say it.'

'I don't understand.'

'I'm sorry you don't.'

'And why should you think about it *now*?'

But he wouldn't try to explain. There was no way to tell her he had heard his father's voice . . . saw a stuffed bear's jaw jabbering.

The baby started moving. He was looking for the breast again. They stopped talking while the child sucked. When he seemed to have settled Rosalie asked Joseph when he thought he might be going. It was something Joseph hadn't yet had a chance to think about. 'But you mean to go soon . . . this summer?'

'Maybe after Labor Day.'

'What can I say? I wish you wouldn't do this.'

He shrugged. 'I'm going to need a break by then, anyhow.'

Rosalie wanted to warn him about his brothers – as she would have warned Jacob Solomon before he went, had

240

she had the chance – and she had another thought about Joseph's being sure to keep his head out of the bear's mouth. She left it alone, though, and instead offered to go part of the way with him, to Vancouver, or even farther if he wanted, whatever was the next city along the way.

Who knew, maybe Jacob Solomon really was alive, after all?

But the telephone rang, it just eight o'clock in the morning, Saturday morning, the eight tones on the chime clock not even struck yet, and there was the telephone yowling loud enough to wake the dead but couldn't raise Mrs Barlow who, God-a-mercy, slept through everything with the unspotted conscience of a child.

Joseph finally answered. It was the last person in the world he and Rosalie could have expected to be hearing from. There was somebody else, it seemed, wondering what had happened when Jacob Solomon went north to see his sons.

CHAPTER 19

On the Friday after Labor Day Joseph slept in a hillside home near Oakland. It was the first overnight of his trip and he had agreed to spend it visiting a woman who knew his brothers almost as well as he.

Joseph, toting a considerable amount of luggage, climbed the sixty-six redwood steps from the street through a jungle of rhododendron and ferns and iris and eucalyptus trees to the front door. The house itself, wood-framed, was small but complicated, almost fussy in its floor plan, with not a square wall in it. Most of the furniture had been built into the walls or the floor. Tiling ran the length of every room. Raffia mats, Navajo rugs. Skylights. A grand piano. Books. The house of someone who spent a great deal of time inside.

When Joseph came there was a fire roaring, the chimney having been swept twice a year by the woman who rented the house. A woman who was handy. Diligent in making small repairs. Who would have her guests soft-pedal the piano at late hours even though nobody could hear the music, not on the street nor in neighbouring houses.

Tall and sharp-featured, with splendid legs, Sarah Massey had lived in the house for over ten years, much of that time with Eric Solomon, eldest of the six Solomon brothers.

Once the wonderchild of the Berkeley psychology department, Sarah was the director of a small but prestigious and very well-funded home for autistic children in Walnut Creek. Some years before, while still a graduate student, she had read a job application from someone who wished to work at the hospital and, following some unaccountable instinct, had invited him to visit.

It had been a grand and windy day, autumn, hard gusts blowing up the sky to a pitched battle of grey and blue and fleshy pink. Sarah, walking in the wind, had seen an old Pontiac coming down the hospital driveway way too fast, slipping at the end of each of the bends and racing faster to the next, raising dust and gravel all the way.

When the dust he'd kicked up finally settled she went to meet him in front of the administrative offices. He held his ground until sure the woman walking between the avenue of poplars was in fact coming his way.

They stood a few yards from each other.

She held out her hand and Eric took it reluctantly, flaccidly, as much as to say he didn't like shaking hands with her, he clearly unhappy the director hadn't come out himself to greet him. His face had been full of cracks, steam coming out. He was angry from the beginning.

They walked. Onto a sheltered greensward where the grass had been mowed as fine as a golfing green. Several paces away a woman was tending some of the children. Eric had stopped to watch as the nurse tried to contact the most remote-seeming child.

'And what do *you* do here?' he had asked Sarah, not really looking at her, nor much interested in her answer, his eyes fixed tightly on the child.

'I'm Bernie's second-in-command.'

'I got it . . . .'

She could see he understood she was the director's pencil carrier . . . or perhaps even the boss's office fuck. Eric had never had any interest in hiding what he thought.

The nurse nearby had circled around and around the boy, who was about five. Neither made any sound. A kind of dance. Sarah had watched the same scene countless times, turned to continue the tour, but Eric couldn't pull away.

Then the nurse had struck the boy . . . once, twice, a few more times, hitting him and trying to call through the mystery which the child had wrapped around himself.

'What in fuck's name . . . ?'

'A lot of the treatment seems cruel when you first see it . . . especially if you don't know it's coming.' Sarah pulled at the big man's sleeves to get him away from the sight. She couldn't unstick him. 'You get inured to it . . . believe me.'

'Inured to it! You tell that cunt if she hits him again I'm going to slap her silly!' Eric jerked his arm away from Sarah's and was sprung halfway to the woman and child, when the scene was transformed and the nurse, holding the boy, began to mother him, protecting him from the fall of a leaf.

Eric rocked on his heels.

Then the group scurried away, other careful attendants helping, nurturing the children as they went . . . ignoring Eric as best they could.

Long after the dancers had vanished from the lawn, shadows stealing everywhere, Eric still wouldn't move from where he had fixed himself.

'I thought you knew more about autism . . . had taken some coursework.' Sarah realized she had read too much into the spaces in his letter. 'Well . . .?'

'I expect to.'

'But not already?'

'I've applied for February admission.'

'You should have said that a little more clearly in your resumé.'

'Listen,' he said, turning on her, 'I wrote about a job. Not to you but to your boss.' He snorted and spit, showed his

243

teeth for the first time . . . not nice teeth . . . large enough to chew a thighbone in two. '*He* is going to make the decision about what qualifies and what doesn't . . . *him* . . . not his fucking secretary. Okay. Now, what I want is to see him . . . your "Bernie".'

Sarah pushed the wind from her eyes. She spoke softly enough. 'I am not his secretary.'

'Fine . . . you're not his secretary . . . next you'll tell me you've even got a degree in the field—'

'—*Three*, as of June.'

'Terrific for you.'

But by then it was Sarah who had rooted herself to the spot and was prepared to grow old telling him the truth about his future. 'You're not going to work here, Eric, no matter who you ask.'

'*He* can tell me that.'

'I'm telling you. I'll say it again. You're not going to work for us here.' Sarah shook her head, regretting she had followed the zany instinct which had allowed him to visit in the first place. 'You're not being hired because you don't qualify. In a year or two, maybe, if you do those courses, do them well, somebody might have a job for you . . . though with a mean bugger like you I expect anybody with a little good sense is going to turn you down.'

His nostrils were sucking up the air and spitting it back out. His feet were clawing the ground clumsily.

'The decision not to hire you was made before you were asked to come.'

The words fell hard on him. For a moment he seemed to lose his orientation, his eyes pools of green confusion—

'—*You bitch!*' His arm was up. Speech blustered out. 'You incredible fucking bitch!!!'

Eric's fist coiled and shook in front of her nose. Neither moved. Nor spoke more.

He would not hit her. Sarah soon knew that. And she waited for the spasm to die away. His hand unclenched. 'The kids need to see anger, but not this kind. You're out of control. And, anyhow, I'm not interested in fighting with you.' She watched his arm drop all the way to his side. Wind tossed the great, red-brown buckles of his hair. 'As it

244

happens the only reason you're here at all is because of me. Bernard had thrown your application into the reject file when I fished it out.'

'. . . why did you invite me then?'

Sarah looked directly at him. For the first time she could bear the perturbation and stiffness in his jaw and neck. 'There was something in your application that interested me . . . though right now I'll tell you I'm wondering what the hell it was . . . .'

And things hung there between them, balancing perfectly.

Something passed across her face. It wasn't apology or contrition . . . but a kind of openness . . . vulnerability. He looked at her for the first time without filtering everything through his blood-angry stare. Ironically, Sarah had felt her cheeks grow hot. She and Eric had made a kind of contact. She was completely surprised . . . and delighted in the same measure.

'You don't have to be nice to me,' she continued, feeling she had to say something, 'just don't let any of the kids see your bitterness. Otherwise I won't show you around. Your choice.'

'I came to see . . . still want to.'

It had been mere divination guessing about Eric's real quality from his photograph and his roughly phrased application letter, but she had been right. Not many times in her life had Sarah trusted to the irrational. Hers was a life as intricately arranged as a piece of filigree . . . as well ordered as the next two hours while she led Eric on a progress around the entire home.

Inside her, though, all was in consternation, as if the missing voices of all the children at the home were gathered in her head singing in choir, a thousand voices amplified and singing to Eric, in perfect key, songs of welcome. When Eric looked behind the children's silence she knew he had seen their suffering, and in that suffering a little bit of his own. He was a man as out of touch as the children, and so deep within himself that somebody was going to have to find a place for him in the empty spaces of their heart. She and Eric might yet be friends.

Later, after the tour was over, she loaned him books. And still later guided him into the right programme of study.

A guarded affection quietly grew between them.

Then, months later, Sarah had asked him to give her an arm at a friend's wedding, an outdoor party at Berkeley City's well-known Rose Garden. On a sweet and sad spring day, Sarah and Eric lingered for some moments after the wedding train had ambled away, kissed under an arbour, she in a primrose-coloured smock and a posy he'd picked for her in Tilden Park, all wildflowers, he in the same grey suit he had had all his adult life, a light flannel with the texture of butter and a warm cross-thread of yellow rising out of the plain grey. He had smothered her in his arms for a long time, a kiss with his full mouth.

They had both got lost in the kiss.

And that night Eric Solomon had gone home with Sarah, stayed, the friends became lovers and lived together right until Eric fled with his brothers to Canada, nearly five years later.

During the time they lived together Sarah had always expected, certainly desired, to have a family with Eric. She had hoped they would find the way to make a traditional life of hard work, children, and the acquisition of patience.

'Even though it's a long time since he left me I still haven't given up the hope,' Sarah told Joseph, surprising herself that she would tell anybody what she felt. 'It might sound crazy but it's what I dream about.'

Moved, but unsure what to say, Joseph just nodded. There was something in him, too, that prayed for his brothers and, if not an ordinary kind of life for them nevertheless a life with other people, down and out of the mountains, way below the rocks and streams. 'We'd like to see him back home, too.'

After unpacking his smallest bag, an overnight kit, Joseph went back into the living room, found Sarah playing the piano. A calico cat sat upright listening, royal Egypt on a settee.

Joseph was surprised. The household, at least the years

246

when Eric lived there, had never been very musical. And the piano, stoutly set in the middle of the room, was something he would not have forgotten.

He lay down on cushions behind her, not breaking the spell. Debussy. A water scene. Easy to picture. A restaurant by a riverbank, a dance floor, bathers bright in old swimming clothes, yellow and sand coloured, coral and blue, a light blue, sky blue, spiritual blue . . . pennants striped, waving in the breeze . . . light twittering . . . waterlilies. Love, rare and tenuous, everywhere in the air.

Love.

Sarah suddenly stopped. Her hands drew back. Her long legs came away from the pedals, swivelled around the seat.

'That's all I know of the piece.'

'I don't remember your having a piano.'

'I didn't play when I knew you.'

She had learned after Eric left.

'Why don't you let me buy you dinner?' Joseph offered. Her head was shaking.

Joseph was sure he could insist to the point where she would give in. She looked in need of a night out . . . he thought her drawn and anaemic, though the light in the room was too weak for fine discriminations. 'You and Eric and I used to go to some fish house . . . almost to the Bay, under a freeway bridge.'

'I've got fish here, two nice fillets.'

'Freeze them and let me take you out. No . . . ?' He saw it was hopeless. It was as if Sarah were afraid of anything that savoured of celebration, of letting go . . . perhaps the night itself made her uneasy.

'Open a bottle of wine.' She pointed to a dust-encumbered cabinet. 'Then come into the kitchen. I talk while I cook.'

He watched her conjure the sauce, piquant and red, pepper and tomato. Fresh basil. He hadn't remembered Sarah as much of a cook, either. First piano. Now *grande cuisine*. Should Eric come back to her he would find a woman of countless refinements and it would be impossible for him to choose to leave ever again.

They sat down on her balcony, an open deck which went all the way around the house and gathered the compost of leaves and animal droppings that fertilized the yard's green exuberance. The table there was glass with glass legs. She had put out fine porcelain. Crystal. Silver servers. Fish knives and forks with ivory handles inlaid. Tall church tapers pushed back the nightgloom. Almost a romantic dinner.

Sarah set the halibut down. Moist still. A flatfish supremely poached in its own juices then sauced at the end. *Salade aux noix*. A plank of goat cheese. Rhubarb tart.

A royal entertainment with everything, it seemed, but joy.

The wine, Joseph soon learned, was entirely for him. She wouldn't take a drop of it. In the life Sarah had led since Eric's flight there were no pleasures taken.

She had business on her mind. 'What have you heard about your brothers?'

Joseph quickly told her the few fragments of news from Indian Sam's visit, his reconstruction of Jacob's voyage north, the single communiqué about his father's death.

'That's it?'

'That's all of it.'

A gust of wind passed over the table and the candles, nearly to their stubs, wavered in the night. Sarah's hair fell free of its wooden clasp. She leaned towards Joseph, a white hand sharply around his wrist. 'Since you've got this idea about barging in on them, wherever they are up there, whatever kind of wild life they've found, I think I ought to tell you a few things about your brothers.'

He knew she could. Sarah had knowledge of his brothers that even Joseph had never been schooled in, particularly about their lives at the close of the Sixties and in the early Seventies when Eric and she were living in the Berkeley hills together. During those years Joseph had rarely seen any of his brothers, except for Eric, with whom the bonds were always strongest. Unwittingly, just by loving Eric, Sarah had become the Solomon family historian, for Joseph's other brothers had kept in touch with Eric, too.

'They're all exiles, your brothers. *Outcasts*. At least that's how they liked to think of themselves . . . as wanderers, carrying the curse of Cain. Even Eric, for all the years he was with me, had one eye on the door while he slept.

'They used to float through here – too often for me, but I wasn't about to say anything, not on the subject of your brothers, uh uh, not to Eric. The visits were short usually. Once Thomas stayed with us a whole month. Thank God it was him. I couldn't have pretended to bear any of the others for that long a time. Eric must have been the one fixed point in their lives, because they kept coming back. They looked up to him, depended on him to fulfil some unspoken need for guidance . . . came for friendship, too, friends always being hard to come by for them . . . there were other needs, too, more obscure, unconscious urges, familial . . . something to fill up that great, black hole in each of them. You know what I'm talking about.'

'I *don't* know.'

Sarah hesitated for a moment, as if her frankness might be a mistake. 'Maybe you really don't know.'

'Go on.'

'The thing that was really strange about them was that they were all – Eric, too, *all* of them – so out of touch, completely disconnected from the things that mattered to everybody else. It might have been the 1960's but you'd never have known from them. Your brothers popped right out of some *mythical* time, I think. Not like the Amish or hermits or even characters from some crazy cult. They were living in the middle of things – L.A., San Francisco, Berkeley – and yet they moved *right through* their times like ghosts. They really were different. And when they dashed off into the wilderness it wasn't just because everybody in the Sixties was fed up with the cities and wanted to give life in the country a try. Your brothers didn't even know it was trendy. Maybe I'm a little strong on this. I don't know. Living in Berkeley always made it seem like there was a lot going on . . . especially then. What's incredible is that none of it ever touched the Solomon boys . . . not a bit.'

'We grew up on a ranch,' Joseph reminded her.

'So you did, but as what? You weren't raised as Americans. Nor as Jews. Your father must have left all that in Europe and your mother never got you six to identify with the Swedish side of your ancestry, either. A cultural void. Zero. Not even TV. Just you and the avocado groves, as Eric used to say. *Disconnectedness*. That's the word. And now they're supposed to be Indians. I like *that*. But I doubt it goes very deep . . . don't you?'

'Maybe not. I'll see when I get there.'

'I have this theory about them. Each one has a tendency to some kind of excess that isolates him from other people. So all they've got is each other. I can remember Bobby eating compulsively, growing beyond all human measure, working as a disc jockey, then managing a rock group, always looking for cash to turn it into food or drink or smoke, or silk clothes, handmade, he was too large for anything else . . . anything sensual, he'd gourmandize on anything, he'd eat the clothes if it pleased his taste. And Thomas, an innocent, temperamentally the model of an artist, who had all his life hoped for architecture but who wound up designing type for a small poetry press as if he had decided his was going to be an unimportant life and it suited him to live on the margins of other, less talented people's ambitions. And Mark up in Canada, priestly, self-righteous Mark, with a scheme for everything except how to be happy. He might even be a priest now, the mountain vicar . . . hip shaman. And then Douglas, a moral wreck as you know, as your father must have known – and for God's sake could *certainly* have done something about, too – dealing from his earliest days and ever more seriously into crime until it was the habit for a lifetime, too lucky for prison, extraordinarily handsome as I remember, almost pretty, whose brains were soft as a pudding and whose charmed life was like that of a holy fool's. We once went together to see *Bonnie and Clyde* and he nearly choked to death from pleasure, sure that it was *his* life written up on the screen, romantic and bloody and pure. Not a shred of truth to it. See what I mean?'

'What about Eric?'

Sarah unclenched. Thought for a while. The lights had gone out long before. They could barely see one another.

'He's a man who feels everything around him and yet can do nothing. No allegiances.'

'I don't get it. What might he have been?'

'A psychoanalyst.'

'What!'

Sarah's eyes were heavy but full of play. 'Seriously, he has a special quality, your brother Eric . . . seems he's able to believe in other people's dreams. Like a poet . . . and, yes, I suppose like Freud must have done. It leaves him wide open and makes for a tenderness that's rare, almost comical in a man his size . . . something that can really move a woman. It did me.' She paused. 'He can't lie, though. He never did learn how. It probably would have done him some good.'

'Or not.'

'Or not . . . .' Sarah stopped herself from remembering. 'Anyhow, it's all just a theory, a quirky idea, nothing more than that. But there's some truth in there somewhere. They were incomplete, your brothers, just tendencies . . . pieces and fragments of personalities that never quite got finished being made. Enough. *Pace*.' She got up, pulled her long frame back from the table and slid off her seat. 'It's the middle of the night, if you hadn't noticed. My eyes are gumming together. I'm pooped.'

'What kept them from getting "finished", Sarah?'

'*Each other*.' She could see he didn't quite understand. 'The group of them. They cancelled each other out. It's like a throwback to some earlier stage of man.'

'I'm not sure I buy this.'

'There are other families with six children so close in age and all of the same sex. Your family is different.'

'Why?'

'Your brothers feel they have a task to do . . . some kind of mission.' She pointed over the eucalyptus trees, north-wards. 'Up there.'

'I tell you I only half-follow what you mean.'

'That's all right. I only understand about half myself.' She was going into the darkened house, but stopped at the threshold, lingered for a moment. 'One other thing. You know there are risks in going, even for you. Personally, I'm not sure it's a good idea for you to go. But somebody has to, I guess. O.K.?'

'Good night.'

'Good night, Joe.'

In his own bed, Joseph sat up and read, unable to sleep, unsatisfied with how the conversation had gone but sure that Sarah had been unsettled by it as well. He listened to her moving around in her room and wondered how long it would take her to settle. The crickets picked up. The several chiming clocks in the house went around the hour. She was still shuffling.

Then there was another, brighter sound, slipper heels clicking along the tiles. Sarah, as live a wire as he, was right outside his door, the cat with her, too, rubbing its patch-work fur against the hinges. The door handle twisted, squeaked.

'I'm wide awake,' he whispered. 'Come on in.'

She came in stumbling, for his room's lamp had long been off. 'No, no . . . leave it off,' she implored. Sarah blew her nose, crushed the Kleenex and let the cat, who could see, chase it along the floor.

'What's the matter, Sarah?'

'Who said anything's the matter?'

'I can feel you're upset.' He could see nothing. Not a thing. They were both soaked in blackness, even though each had been lying in the dark for hours, the house that tightly muffled. He sensed Sarah, and the cat, by sound only . . . like a bat.

'What time is your plane?'

'Noon.'

'Not been much of a visit, has it, Joe? My talking your head off. I've hardly asked you about yourself.'

'Maybe that's not necessary.'

'It's very fucking necessary!'

Joseph could hear the buttons on her nightdress scratch the floor. The cat, nervous, was turning and turning around her legs, its fur sparking. Sarah picked up the cat in her arms and stroked it, while Joseph told her of the modest good fortune in his own life, of his wife and two children, their health, their house, the law business, promotions, raises, a small investment turning dividends, a little security, ambitions to be a jurist, retire a winemaker, his life taking root and drawing sweetwater.

The bells of five o'clock ended his story. Crepuscular life

252

was creeping outside, early feeders, insects. The first bird-calls. With the sunrise coming Joseph could see the outline of Sarah sitting cross-legged at the foot of his bed.

'Just an ordinary life, Sarah . . . you see?' He meant it.

'I didn't hear any of what you said as ordinary . . . not considering how you grew up.'

He was amazed she had heard at all.

The cat's eyes were on Joseph. And Sarah's skin had a dull, unearthly glow, like cerecloth. She was thinking about Eric again.

'Your brother had his moments. I want to respect that.'

'Tell me about them. Looks like this is going to be an all-nighter, anyhow.'

Holding nothing back, Sarah described the turbulent final days with Eric before he had led his brothers north. Ironically, everything had come together at the time of Joseph's marriage.

For several months before the wedding letters from brother Mark had been arriving, fat manila envelopes fatigued with stamps and sealed several times over with tape and staples, sent from Mark's outpost in British Columbia. As Eric's moods changed with the letters Sarah had started to worry.

Eric became more restless than she had ever seen him. He would charge around the house hating his hands, which he thought insufferably clumsy, swearing at them, resting his fingers limply on the peachwood shelves of an armoire which he had nearly finished. His work slowed. It was clear he might not do anything more on the piece though it was the first fine thing Eric had done with his hands in his entire life. He seemed to have lost his grasp of the wood, as if he were giving up a lifeline . . . which in a way building the armoire had been for him.

Sarah had broken into his brooding and asked him what it was all about and did it have to do with Mark's letters?

Although Eric wouldn't let her see the letters he did divulge much of what they said: Mark had read the early ethnographies of several Pacific North Coast Indian tribes. Having studied his subject, Mark threw over his books and went into the Indian country to see if there were any

253

descendants of his Indians still keeping traditional ways, observing the Stone Age life that he'd read about. He met there a Chilcotin of the Stony sept, named Sam. Pulling the white boy into the glacier's vastness, Sam had given Mark a princelike education, teaching him the mountain's sorrows directly. For nearly a year the two men had lived in the mountain's highest valley, a bitter place littered with the bones of generations. They had survived. And Mark soon after began to wonder if his brothers, giants in heart though not in fortune, could endure the mountain as well as the Indians had. So he conceived his plan, wherein all six Solomons (Joseph, too) would square off against Nature's hellhill, actually trying to *live* in the permafrost. He wrote the long letters to Eric, fierce and Orphic accounts of how such a physical ordeal might have spiritual benefits, a quest that could transform them all: Life could be bled out of the valley's stones . . . if only a man banged hard enough the bones of the dead would stand up and walk again. *It would be the Age of Heroes again.* Malicious gods lived in the valley, having strangled all nurturing life there – well, then, it was time to rise up and throw out the old gods, go after them right on their own mountaintop. What was there to lose? What kind of life were any of the brothers making for themselves in the shit world below the clouds, anyway?

A question to be asked. Or so Eric thought it was.

Hearing of Mark's plan Sarah ridiculed the whole thing. She couldn't believe Eric, or anyone, would take it seriously.

But Sarah had had no way of divining Mark's formidable powers to persuade . . . nor of understanding then how deep was the call of brother to brother.

In order to plead his case Mark had decided to come to the wedding. He swooped down the coast gathering brothers – Thomas in Portland, Bobby from the woods where he was then lumbering and brawling, Douglas from whatever dope-smoked room they'd find him in.

Forewarned of Mark's coming, Sarah convinced Eric that just the two of them, Eric and she, should make their own way to Los Angeles. There was a present of some vine cuttings to pick up in Napa Valley, something for Joseph and Rosalie from all the brothers.

They had picnicked in a vineyard. A hidden spot under some olive trees and canopied all around by sunflowers taller than a man. The valley was white with heat, clear, slight wind, all the dust settled. After eating, Eric and Sarah lay back.

Their picnic blanket sat at the foot of a chromatic and most spectacularly blooming garden. Everything pungent in the high summer light: fruits and flowers and legumes and salads . . . Nature's dance . . . a horn of plenty holding beans and sweetpeas trellised nearly to the top of their pitch, zucchini sweating under wide-handed leaves, giant marrow, eggplant, a melon patch farther along, cucumbers creeping everywhere, low bushes of peppers, waxy and yellowing already, the dark stalks of beets, dill and sage and thyme in flower, red berries and green berries, and over against a stone-sided shed the last peaches on the climbing tree, a pear at one far corner, plums small and dancing in the light breeze at the other.

'Almost hurts the eyes, doesn't it?' Eric had said, not complaining, not at all. 'What would happen to those text-book therapies of yours if all the kids at the hospital could get one good look at this tiny, mite-sized vista of the earth's crowded love for itself, eh Sarah? *Sarah . . . ?*'

She wondered if he knew he'd said her name? It was something he almost never did.

'Let's have some of that sweet wine we bought.'

'Don't you want to save it for your brothers?'

'I can waste it on you, Sarah.'

'Say it again.'

She watched him pour. She held her glass up to the sun. The wine was a deep straw-colour, thick-legged against the glass's sides. It rose effortlessly to her mouth.

'Say it again . . . *say it.*'

'. . . Sarah.'

Oh rare.

She licked the sugar remnants at her lips. They drank the whole damned bottle.

Eric had come across with tenderness. She had been worried, suspecting the pull of his brothers might take him away from her for good, and all he'd done was to serve up a rough slice of perfection. A wasp was wanting to get deeper into the neck of the wine bottle. She was laughing and crying at the same time.

Then, in the field full of olive trees, oaks and vines, seeing no bull nor farmer nor other obstacle nor any reason why not he took her down onto the swollen knob of grasses and made love to her, the first time that either of them had made love out of doors. However many others had done the same simple thing before them, both Eric and Sarah liked it even better for the commonness of the wish to do it. They were almost beyond the act, beyond the hard fact of it, unperturbed by fears of bees on naked buttocks and dirt in the balls and stinging grasses and the general lousiness of the sex – all that might have happened to them and they wouldn't have minded. For it wasn't the sex but the being there that mattered, their wish to do something so plain and fertile and unconfined that it made believers out of both of them . . . both of them knowing by the time it was done that they, like all creatures in God's bestial Glory, began in a garden and are forever trying to find the way back . . . .

He told her afterwards, in the car, the dust of mid-summer flying by, the windshield of their Saab brittle with insects, about gardening when he and his brothers were young, about his mother before she died. A garden had been at the very centre of their lives. It hadn't been left to strangers to cut and mow and prune and trim. The brothers trailed after their mother in every garden in every home of theirs right from the Montana beginnings. Eva Solomon always had a producing garden, her own vegetables on the table, something, at the very least chives or mint or another savour she'd nurtured with her own hands. Eric spoke pictures, told Sarah of the long skirts his mother had worn gardening. He had been given wooden shoes to wear; and as they were passed to each succeeding child, Eric, the oldest, got a new pair.

'Where are the shoes now?'

Eric shook his head. He hadn't a clue if there were a single thing left from his childhood. 'They had miniatures on them, tiny scenes of outdoors life. Thomas painted them on. Maybe he still has them. We'll ask in L.A.'

All the way down the Central Valley Eric had continued to talk about his school years, about the ranch where he'd grown up, the isolation, the wild animals, the sun and starlight . . . and in the middle of it all their mother's garden. Did Sarah understand? *Did she???* 'My mother believed we could learn *everything* we would ever need to know in that garden. We'd know about our bodies, she said, garden work was as good a teacher as gymnastics: which muscles did what work, balance, how bones were joined, the health of other creatures, just by our studying the colour, posture, fluids, and nervousness of plants; oh Christ we learned about patience, and the fair division of labour, and how to plan . . . and how time passed in different ways; we arranged flowers for composition, learned the natural vegetable dyes, architecture in trees, the music in a reed; and compassion for animals, courtship in birds, war and famine and pestilence and death in the insects; geometry, too, when we laid out our rows, history in the rings of a tree branch, and names, just the *names* of every goddamn thing under the sun . . . *a school* . . . it was the book of the world that garden and we had better fucking well learn it perfectly, every one of us . . . even Douglas!!'

He was frantic for her to understand.

His life, his mind and heart, were strapped to his brothers plodding through the topsoil, half-beasts, half-savants . . . they had shared a strange childhood. The imagery of it flooded him all the time, waking and dreaming, probably always would.

And then one day, unaccountably, their mother had begun to wither. *Quickly.* The brothers, hushed by the speed of her decline, just watched insensible, completely confused by what was happening to her and why. When she died something in each of them began to dry up. Their lives had been cut at the source, Joseph alone spared by his youth . . . .

All the way down to Los Angeles Sarah had listened, leaning forward, to his song of youth. She and Eric had never been so close.

That day was the very best of Eric.

As for what had happened afterwards, at the wedding,

she had little to explain to Joseph. He had been there, after all, as unhappy a witness to the events as she.

The reunion of brothers had been even more violent than Sarah had feared, an initiation into the deepest strata of Eric's mysteries. On their own they weren't bad men, swaggerers perhaps, listless, sunning dogs, without interest, unable to fix on anything. Once they got together, though, it was like a chemical mix . . . an explosion of crude energy, despotism, something of man's origins, pristine, a dim relic.

They were too large for the ordinary world.

Their vital signs changed. Nerves, skin, voice, bowels, blood in their throats, war in their hands, murder in mind. Douglas, by then completely out of control, had attacked their father and tried to kick the old man's head open. But the tents had caught fire already and Jacob was saved a bloody thrashing.

Sarah had beat Eric on the chest, hopelessly, hysterical herself, and had asked and asked and asked what was so particular about Eric's pain, and that of his brothers . . . ? as if everybody in the world didn't hurt about something . . . why couldn't he and the rest of his bloody crew just live in the world like normal people did?

Eric, great dumb beast of a man, could say nothing. Shook his head merely. There was no explaining. He didn't understand himself much of what had happened.

She had struck him hard on the chin.

And he, for his part, had touched her lips with his fingertips, as if that were the last softness he would ever know. Eric had been right. He must have known that whatever he said to Sarah about staying with her he would be leaving with his brothers.

Sarah certainly knew it.

The five brothers left for Canada very soon after. With few skills to survive, no real plans, and a fanciful idea of the world they would find up there, they went north to find the lost garden of their youth, as if the mountain was a mother and would nurture, succour and provide.

As the years passed, Sarah did not forget Eric. For Love, though blind, could imagine and imagine forever . . . .

258

Sarah was finally silent. She had unstoppered the bitterness that had been rotting inside her for so long.

Sunlight and morning were everywhere in the house. For the first time since he'd arrived the night before Joseph could see Sarah. Love, like a compulsive sculptor, had whittled her away. She had never got over his brother Eric.

Not imposing at first sight, Sarah was nevertheless a large woman, tall, but balefully thin. It had been a very different woman at Joseph's wedding. Sarah had weighed twenty pounds more then, at the least, was better fleshed out everywhere, an athletic body if not a sensual one. The weight loss had destroyed the balance in her face. A long and bony nose now dismissed her other features from regard. Against the sunlight her skin was almost translucent, bloodless.

In a person otherwise healthy, Joseph could never remember witnessing such a fall from physical grace.

Yet underneath her ill-combed hair, half of white and half of insipid black, it was obvious to anyone that Sarah was still a young woman, not yet thirty-five, who had somehow contrived to look old enough to be her own mother.

That's what had come of living with Eric Solomon and loving him beyond all bounds.

'I want to go with you into the mountains.'

'Oh Sarah . . . .'

'I mean it, Joseph. *I want to go.*' She dropped the cat unceremoniously from her arms. 'It's *five years* I've thought about him. He and I had settled into a life, you know. We were even getting to like each other.' She was almost accusing Joseph. 'There was no reason for him to leave . . . no *real* reason.'

Joseph sighed. He had hoped against hope she wouldn't ask. She had lived with his brother almost as long as Joseph had himself, her claim to kinship nearly as great as his own. 'It is *not* kind country up there, Sarah.'

'I've climbed worse mountains,' she scoffed, 'far worse.'

'What do you think you'll find if you go, anyway?'

Sarah stopped, then spoke more cautiously. 'Eric. The truth about him.'

'I think you already have most of the truth.'

259

'I want to see him.'

'You do? *Which* Eric? Which one, Sarah?'

'I want to go . . . I think I have to.'

'*You can't.*'

He knew, and she did, too, that the Eric Solomon Sarah had loved years earlier wasn't in the hills, was nowhere except in her reverie. A dead love was pulling her by the nose.

'You've mourned long enough, Sarah. Maybe too long. It doesn't suit you. It's only yourself you mourn for now . . . so let it go.'

For a while Sarah sat impassive. Threads of light reflected off the tiling and onto her hands. She looked at her own wasted fingers. Fat tears began rolling out of her eyes. She sobbed as she wept, nearly choked on her own juices, fought for her right to breathe. She had always been dry as cork. She hadn't cried once since Eric left.

'I think I've felt guilty all these years that I didn't have to suffer what he's been through in his life. There are people around whose share of suffering seems all out of line with the mere facts of their lives. He is one of them and he has suffered. No peace. Never had a moment but here and there. He's all on fire inside. *On fire.*'

'He's a Solomon.'

'I don't understand how *you* bear up?'

'I'm a Solomon in that, too.'

'You really are on a mission, your family, for good and bad.'

And she understood why she couldn't go into the mountains with Joseph. She wasn't one of them. *It was a matter of blood.*

Sarah burst into tears one last time, crying not only for her own woes and the woes of the brothers but for the world, too, as it has been given to us, for the shittiness of things.

'Do what you have to do, Joe, but be a little cautious, hmmm? The thing between your brothers is almost religious. Anything could have happened when your father went up to see them. Anything could still happen.'

'I understand.'

'I'm sorry you got no sleep.'

'A big breakfast would help.'

'You'll stop here on your way back down . . . ? And tell me what happened?'

'I will tell you everything.'

'Solomons never do.' But she kissed him in thanks as if this time a Solomon would tell everything there was to know. *'Godspeed.'*

CHAPTER 20

Joseph had planned his trip as far as Vancouver. Once there, he began to improvise.

At the airport he talked to car rental people, then sorted amongst the counters for a local air carrier who might be able to help. It didn't take him long to find a small airbus revving its propellers, ready to leave with a half-dozen people who wanted to go deeper into the province, stops scheduled as tickets were sold.

'Two hours to Chezacut,' a flame-skinned clerk told him, her speech just distinguishable from that of Americans below the border, 'seems far better than two days by car.'

Had Joseph seen the plane before agreeing he might have reconsidered the car, nor would he have flown so fearlessly had he realized the hauteur of the mountains the plane had to vault over. Yet once in the air he was unruffled, determined to enjoy the ride even when the ride got rough.

The Comanchee lurched to the left as if the plane were going to sit right on top of the white ice spires. Finally able to lift the plane out of its fall the pilot regained lost altitude and straightened the nose towards the horizon again. He turned around to his passengers. Smiled. An air jockey, he had exaggerated the drop. But some of the passengers had been worried, including a few of his regulars.

Joseph stared at a crust of glaciers, long lines of milkblue against the mountainside to their left. *Going to be fun finding them if their camp is on the ice*, he thought. 'What's the tallest peak in this chain? Anybody know?' He asked the whole compartment.

'Mount Waddington.'

'How tall?'

'Thirteen-thousand-two-sixty.'

'How high are we flying?'

A man, a rancher and certainly wealthy, got out of his seat and came across the aisle, tapped his thumb on Joseph's window. 'We're at eleven or twelve thousand. That's Waddington in front of you . . . the one we're heading right for.'

'Maybe the pilot will see the peak by the time we crash.'

'He'll know it's there.' The man had been leaning awkwardly, and when he went to sit by Joseph a dog under the seat growled menacingly.

'Handsome dog.' Joseph was at ease with animals. 'Yours?'

'A Weimeraner. They were once used to hunt bear . . . descended of a German breed if you go back far enough.' The rancher tapped his boot and the dog, circling his tail one time around, lay back down. 'They have trouble when they're confined. The bitch is at home.'

'You hunt a lot with them?' Joseph asked.

'No. It's not a sport I much fancy.'

'Not even for food?'

'I'll kill pests to protect my stock.' The rancher – who wore much silver, turquoise, too, and pieces of coral, yet who was quite obviously not a gaudy man, plain despite his ornaments – raised his eyes from under a new hat. 'It's cattle country. We have both banks of the Chilcotin for some miles.'

Joseph sucked in as much air as he could. 'Unpressurized, isn't it? Makes me feel a bit like I've been drinking.'

The rancher nodded. 'Come to fish, have you?'

'Nope.'

'Hiker?'

'Not really.'

'There's not a lot to do in the Chilcotin but fish, hunt or take to the trails.'

'I'm looking for somebody . . . actually it's my father and his young wife who went into the mountains last summer and never came out.

The lines on the rancher's face grew more profound.

'They were themselves looking for my five brothers who are up here somewhere, been living in the wilds for several years.'

The older man knew nothing about a band of brothers. There was no deceit. He was a man who didn't hear rumours.

'Is it likely people could actually live in the mountains?'

'Survive, perhaps . . . for a while. There's no kind of livelihood to be had up there.' A ridge of sweat had built up under his hatband, which the rancher rubbed away with the back of his hand. 'Even the Indians gave up . . . many years ago.'

Joseph introduced himself and asked the man his name.

'Nethercott,' he said simply, his peregrinate hat again covering the brushed metal of his hair. 'Ted, if you would.'

'Are the mountains close by Chezacut?'

'Forty miles away at the least, I'd guess . . . thirty-five or forty.'

'I got a letter from the mayor of the town. He talks about a place called "Jack Mountain". Do you know it?'

'That's a local name for Mount Downton.'

'What would be the best way up there?'

'Float plane – quickest and safest. And not so expensive as you might think.'

'How about by horse?'

'Easily hired.'

'Rough country?' Joseph's mind was racing.

'You'd have no trouble getting to the foot of the mountain. After that I couldn't tell you.' He noticed that Joseph was rubbing several days' stubble of soft, brown beard. 'First time you've grown one of those, is it?'

'First time.'

'Give it two weeks and you won't even know you've got it.'

'Then what fun will it be?'

That got the rancher laughing, and relieved him of a

certain curiosity about Joseph. A man had to have some humour to be a survivor. It was the one thing without which the mountains were likely to prove fatal.

'I'd suggest you find a man named Colin Mackie and tell him to bring you up to my ranch. The wilderness, especially where you want to go, isn't at all well mapped, and Colin's the only man – White or Indian – whom I'd trust to know what's up there.'

'And the horses?'

'I have a few I can happily let you borrow.'

'It would be better if I paid you, Ted. Money's a great equalizer.'

'Then we'll find a fair price.' The rancher could deal with Joseph on any terms, for he had an instinctive trust of Joseph and felt, rightly, the trust was returned in kind.

Then the plane fell straight through the haze of late summer. They came over the plateau, down towards the rolling lands, stock grazing on the bunch grass, forests and lakes in the higher country, and landed on all three of the plane's points with hardly a bump in it all.

Chezacut.

There was no problem finding Colin Mackie who, Joseph discovered, was the sometime resident of the only lodge in town. It was also the only saloon.

Joseph bought him drinks and, when the old drunk was well seasoned, he proposed the two of them should hazard the mountains together. Colin swallowed steadily and seriously, watching Joseph's fingers tap on the counter-top. He recognized a cash hand and an arrangement was made.

'Can you go tomorrow? In the morning?'

'I can.'

'Good.' Joseph also wanted to ask a few questions of Harry Blyde, quondam mayor of Chezacut, who had written to Joseph about his father's death. The mayor claimed an outstanding debt for hired horses unreturned. Yet he was nowhere to be found.

'No surprise there,' Colin told him. 'Your dad probably paid Harry twice over what those horses were worth before Harry ever let them out of the stable.'

264

'I still need to ask him a few things.'

'He might not want to talk to you.'

Colin then explained that the mayor had worked for two weeks under the oily brow of his lamp composing the bear story. It was all taken from folklore, of course, but apparently somebody had given Harry an old half-sovereign to write the letter and so Harry had kept hard at his feeble artistry: Jacob Solomon was supposed to have been pursued and attacked, mauled, chewed and digested by a rogue grizzly. A tall tale. Colin believed Indian Sam might have helped Harry with his invention. Sam was always chasing bears that had six arms and stood fifteen feet tall, even taller in the autumn.

'What does the mayor have to say about Carmen?' Joseph asked.

'Old Harry pretends he doesn't have a bird of an idea about any girl with your dad. But *I* saw her, talked to her, too. And so did Harry, I can promise you. She told me she thought he was one fine asshole.'

'Sounds like Carmen.'

Joseph never found Harry, though, to hear it for himself.

The following morning Colin brought a jeep around to take Joseph up to Ted Nethercott's ranch. He bounced it hard over the root-ribbed turf and dry channels of dirt, much too fast for the jeep's frame. There wasn't any hood on the car, the engine works bandaged over with rags like a wounded soldier.

Dust spit in front, behind, and straight out from the jeep's wheels, but Colin refused to slow down to where it was either safe or comfortable.

Ten miles along they came within sight of the river. Colin hooked the jeep into a small spur road which led to the water. A hand ferry was on the stream ready to take them across and an electric bell there to alert the ranch house on the other side.

Colin rang the bell and drove the jeep onto the ferry.

They floated over stillwater, a wide bight in the river. The flatbottomed raft was crotchety but sure and the ride brief. Joseph's shoulders were stiff with expectation.

With a thump they were on the far dock, a ranchhand

265

pointing them the way over burnt grasses, open skies above them singing with insects and goldfinch, the bare and sandy hills of the badlands skirted all around.

Ted Nethercott stood in the doorway, his arms crying them welcome, his hair resplendent as unmined silver.

The visitors pushed their way through the wagonwheel gate and along the path, paced the last ten steps by a Weimeraner bitch, mate to the dog that had snarled on the airplane. The dog went in front of them, prancing, matching their step and smelling their sweat for any palpable signs of treachery or deceit.

Finding nothing but true hearts, however, she let the men pass.

Inside the house Joseph opened closets and drawers, smelled the fresh lavender, marvelled at the carpentry.

'We have only simple comforts,' the rancher told him. He was mixing lemons and ice-water, sugar and a little gin. 'You might enjoy a ride around the property . . . help you get oriented.'

'Great. Room in the truck for Colin?'

'He'll have some work to do.'

Colin had already eased out of their company. In part it was a question of natural social grouping, Colin more relaxed with the sweating leathers of the ranchhands. Anyhow, he had wanted first shot at the ancient, outdoor shower in back of the kitchen. Joseph saw the old drunk pulling down one of the long-handled brushes strapped to the wall. The stiffest brush. It would take some application to rub away Colin's grime. Colin sang for a while . . . but they were songs of hard life, sombre . . . mournful even. The man did have his moods.

Outside in his Land-Rover Ted Nethercott was tuned to another key. As he drove towards some low-lying hills, the best vista-point on his property, he began to speak of the rare and particular beauties of the Chilcotin. He opened the Thermos of lemonade, drank and handed it on to Joseph.

His song, for it was that, was first of the land, its contours and colours, its geological oddities, the wildflowers and

266

ubiquitous bunch grass, the few peculiarities in its bestiary.

'Who lives here?' Joseph wondered.

'Indians. Most of what you see is Reserve land . . . at least beyond our property lines.'

As for the others, Nethercott explained, they were bred of English and Scottish, and latterly seepages of the American West, everybody so mixed with Indian blood, though, that hardly a person wasn't a confusion of some kind, a ragout of genes and habits, just like the other domestic creatures, the piebalds and painted cattle, the sheep and red barnyard fowl, spotted apples, wide-waisted plums and long pears, and the cross-pollinated grasses that grew so quickly they turned carnivorous and ate into the graves of the dead.

Under the noonday sun they stood on a hill and looked around the panorama of Nethercott's many-thousand-acre home.

'I don't tire of it, not even after sixty years of doing much the same thing every day . . . which is something, I suppose.'

'I would get lonely.'

'There's that, too.' Under the fierce sunlight Nethercott's jewellery seemed on fire. 'I was married once upon a time. We weren't together long . . . first the war years and then . . . she died rather young.' He took a long swallow from the Thermos. 'That was the only time for me. I don't think I could've taken it happening again.'

'I'm sorry.'

'It's too hot to stay out here, young man.'

'Anywhere to swim?'

The rancher took Joseph by the arm and led him back to the Land-Rover. 'The river's where we go.'

'Cold and clean, eh?'

'Oh it gets warm enough in the pools and backwaters.'

'I didn't bring a suit.'

'Don't worry. I've got some extras.' Ted Nethercott smiled. 'They're a little old, is all.'

About fifty or sixty years old, Joseph learned. It was like strapping into another time, but the two of them swam all afternoon anyhow, until they were tan from the neck up . . . and below the knees.

By evening the sunlight and exercises, and the bourbon they had been drinking, finally unstarched Joseph. The dinner bell rang. Joseph heard it but could not make the call. In fact he couldn't even make it to his bedroom without Ted Nethercott's arm.

'Sorry, Ted. We'll have to break bread when I return.'

'You'll need the sleep more than the food. Tomorrow's going to be a long day for you.' The rancher helped Joseph out of his clothes. 'I've had an alarm set for five.'

'Everything's ready . . . ? Colin and the bags and horses . . . ?' Joseph could hardly mumble more. '. . . can't believe I'm going . . . .'

But the rancher didn't even have the chance to assure him it was true. Joseph would find out soon enough. The mountain was no respecter of persons . . . nor of rest or dreams or anything on the meagre scale of men. He doubted Joseph would sleep so well again.

CHAPTER 21

Shortly after dawn Joseph strapped a blue knapsack over his shirt. Although the saddlepacks could hold everything he was taking, he wanted a few private items close at hand and out of sight.

'Give me two weeks, Ted. That should be enough time.'

Nethercott shrugged. 'You'll be able to judge once you're up there.' He cinched the saddle and Joseph got a leg over. 'The weather could hold for a month.'

For a moment Joseph seemed all right. The horse shuddered, rocking Joseph in the stirrups and making him clutch the saddlehorn.

'Think you can handle the horse?'

'I'll stay in the seat.' Joseph rode at home, though rarely.

'O.K., but this kind of horse has the spirit of contrariness. She'll run if you need her to. Spur her only once, no more.' The older man swatted the appaloosa on the rump. 'I suppose you've got some expectations of what you're going to find up there.'

'Not really.' Prepared for anything, Joseph had from the beginning decided to anticipate nothing. 'I'm hoping they're alive.'

'We'll all hope that.'

'Thanks, Ted . . . for everything.'

Nethercott's hand was outstretched and Joseph grasped it firmly. Then, following Colin's lead through the stable gates, Joseph waved one last time as the horses took the bank and headed upstream towards Mt Downton, thirty or more miles on, still ringed in last year's snow and, Joseph hoped, father and brothers arm in arm.

'Pull your horse up here next to mine.' They had been going along in single file ever since leaving Ted Nethercott's. The afternoon had turned hot, the horses lathering from their mouths.

'This horse doesn't seem to want to go any faster.'

'Give her a nudge.'

'I did already.'

'Well, boot her again.'

Joseph remembered Ted Nethercott's warning, and hesitated.

'Christ!' Colin reached behind and caught the appaloosa's bridle, pulled her even with his horse. 'So you think you'll be able to survive up there with your brothers, do you?'

'I'll make it . . . at least for ten to fifteen days.'

'Not likely.' Colin began humming an old hymn under his breath, laughing from time to time. 'Not very likely . . . .'

A little while later he asked Joseph if there were any beer left after what they'd gone through for lunch.

'Two bottles, but they're hot.'

The old prospector made him take one out anyway. 'The beer ain't hot, my friend. Hell is hot.' He ripped off the cap and drank half the bottle at a swallow, looking around as he

did. The forest was closing in on them. 'We're going all right
. . . fifteen or sixteen miles already. In a little while all this
green will disappear and you'll see the real high country.'

'Have you got a camp in mind for tonight?'

'I know just what log is gonna be my pillow.' Warm air
from meadows beyond the trees blew right into their faces,
a sweet-smelling breeze carrying an aroma like flowers
burning in a jar. 'You ever take drugs down in California?'

'Nope.'

'I've been told everybody does.'

'Not everybody.'

'Your brothers sure do.'

'Where would they get them up here?'

'Make them. The Indians knew all kinds of herbs and
potions.' He could see Joseph was sceptical. 'Oh, it's true.
Your brothers dress themselves like animals, get juiced on
some local plant and start doing Christ knows what. I came
down past their camp last spring and heard a woman
screaming her poor lungs out while the five of them were
chanting . . . hard to say whether she was screaming from
pleasure or pain.'

The two men traded sombre looks. But then Colin
smacked Joseph's thigh and threw the last bitterness of the
hot beer onto the dust. 'You are so goddamned easy to
tease . . . I don't know what they do to amuse themselves.
It's all rumour about them. They keep to themselves.
Nobody knows what goes on . . . not really.'

That night they stopped at the meadows where a year
earlier Jacob Solomon and Carmen had also camped.
Colin's humour got more unpredictable with the whiskey
he was taking. He would eat no dinner even though Joseph
cooked more than enough for two. All he would do was
drink, flasks appearing as if by sleight of hand. By the time
the moon rose he had got to the point where he couldn't
unbuckle his saddlebag to find another bottle. So he
hooked Joseph into getting the drink from his pack. He
held it up to the firelight. It was a pint flask of bourbon,
half-full.

Colin nursed the bottle for a while, then unexpectedly
pushed it into Joseph's hands. 'Have a nip.'

'No thanks.'

'Go on, you little bastard . . . *drink*.'

Joseph had a few small sucks. Colin laughed.

'More.'

He held the bottle so hard against Joseph's lips that Joseph couldn't take it away, had to drink more. The bottle started to drain.

'That's good . . . great . . . *ha ha ha*.' And he nearly broke Joseph's teeth as he forced him to gag on the last drops.

Then Colin fell back in a stupor and leaned against a tree. Half-sitting, half-lying, he stared into the fire with eyes black from dreaming of some unbearable past . . . ungraspable future. There was an old cotton bag he had, army surplus, but it stayed unrolled next to him all the night as with a sudden fall of eyes he passed out and didn't resurface until well after dawn.

Colin was even more uncommunicative the next day. He watched Joseph clean himself off in the river, disregarded Joseph's questions about how they would get up to the lake.

'You sure do drag ass for a kid, don't you?'

In silence they crossed the wash and rockfield, the only sound the horses' hooves kicking a path through the sea of black and grey rocks which Colin knew how to pilot. Fathoms below sightlines as they were, the peevish old drunk still knew every pebble.

When they were crossing Downton Creek, Colin unexpectedly jumped from his horse and plunged both hands into the water. For a minute or two he panned the grit and sand away, until nothing was left in his fingers but the cold of the stream. He rose slowly, the glacier's dust dripping down his cheeks and beard. 'You and your fucking brothers . . . bloody fucking fools, aren't you, believing everything you hear about these Indians up here!' There were no japes nor hidden smiles in his voice, not even irony – just a thin and reedy sadness that kept him whistling through his nose all the way down to the lake. For it had been the same Indians who fifty years before told a young man about gold in the mountain, and he, he had believed them.

Wind rushed over the lake. The two men crawled under-

271

neath the roots of a blown-over hemlock that lay close to the shoreline. From his plastic pouch Colin rolled a cigarette, stuck it in his mouth so that it hung loosely from his lips. Lit it.

Joseph tried to break him of his bad humour and asked about the mountain, and if there wasn't something wrong with the lake water. 'It has a strange, chemical kind of smell.'

'Now why ask me? I'm not Mother Nature.'

'How is it you keep coming up into these mountains if you get so goddamned depressed when you do?'

The old man took a final drag on his cigarette as it burned into his round, dirt-flecked fingertips, the skin having long ago lost all sensation. The trifle of burning paper that remained he flicked into the lake. He had no intention of giving Joseph an answer.

'I'll water and feed the horses,' Joseph said evenly, the wind having eased somewhat.

'You do that.'

'How about letting me fix you some dinner?'

The drunk looked up through eyes nearly shut by age, by the years of iron and adversity he'd looked on. 'I don't need your bloody fucking food.'

That was the last they spoke for the evening.

Joseph would not be roused, though it was getting harder and harder to bear Colin's moods. He tended to his tasks, ate his food alone, did the best he could not to hear the old man kicking trees and beating them with curses for the mountain and all its false hopes, and for having passed such a long and unhappy life that was all the worse for his having been made a thorough fool in the course of it.

In the middle of the night they were awakened by unfamiliar noises.

'What's the matter?'

Colin was on his feet, crouching very low to the ground. 'Shut up, you fool.'

Joseph waited until he was told what was happening.

'Something's out there.'

'Animal?'

'Uh uh.'

The moon, which had risen early, was gone from the star-tossed sky. The wind had all but died. Joseph strained but heard nothing at first. Then there was a kind of groaning amongst the branches. 'The horses don't seem spooked.'

Colin reached to his pack and drew out a rifle. 'Those aren't just forest sounds, let me tell you. Something's scratching the valley floor, thrashing dead boughs around.'

'What could it be?'

'Anything.'

'Birds?'

'Oh Jesus! At this hour?'

'. . . my brothers?'

Colin's eyes were smouldering against the night sky. 'Now *did I say that*?' He caught his anger. 'O.K. You hang fire. I'm going to take a look in that clump of trees by the deadfall.'

'Maybe I ought to go with you.'

'Don't be a jerk. I've got to pee anyhow. Go back to sleep.' And he slipped away along the shore.

To Joseph's hearing the sounds hadn't been so unlikely as Colin made them out. A manic fire was in the drunk's mind – Joseph had no idea how much more booze he'd run past his lips – and its heat had made an ordinary event in the natural world, like an animal doing its midnightly business, into something infernal. Joseph was more worried about Colin than whatever was out there rooting in the forest floor and tossing grubs. So he buttoned up his mummy bag and went back to sleep, as he'd been bid to do, much too exhausted to resist.

When Joseph awoke, he found the digits on his watch just turning over to eight o'clock. He had passed a dreamless night, as instant and empty as surgical sleep, and something of that dullness, too, which he noticed as soon as he pushed himself up to a squat.

There was no sign of Colin.

And no horses.

Joseph, still naked, got all the way up.

No Colin indeed. No Colin's shredded old bed roll nor the mangy pack the man had hugged like a child attached to

273

his first blanket. The ring of their coffee pot was impressed in the ashes but the pot itself was gone.

Joseph's first thought was that his brothers and Colin had staged a practical joke. He looked up and saw the food stash missing, stolen from the bough where they had hung it the night before. There was nothing left to their camp except Joseph's sleeping bag and the few items in his knapsack, which along with his clothes from the day before he'd balled up as a pillow. Everything was to look as if Joseph had been abandoned, left with almost nothing to survive. They would be watching him from closeby as he fretted about what in Christ's name he was going to do. Some joke.

Unless, of course, there was a darker purpose . . . and he had been abandoned for real.

He thought more. Colin couldn't have been party to any sort of ruse. The man had the marks of his burden, and knew the path up Calvary from frequent use. His testiness wasn't put on.

There was a much simpler explanation. Colin might well be looking for the passage into the mountain, so difficult to find he'd mentioned the fact three times over.

But with *both* horses?

Joseph called into the hills. Not even an echo came back. Could his brothers have done the drunk any harm?

By half past ten Joseph's hopes began to waver, by eleven to droop. At midday he got up from where he'd been sitting. It was true. Colin had really gone . . . the frantic old man had simply left him alone in the mountain.

Jesusmotherfuckingchrist.

Joseph got out of the sun, came under the shade of a mountain hemlock, his temper cool. In a way he pitied Colin. Two days in the high country and the air had leached out any anger Joseph might have felt. Anyhow, oaths and roars would do nothing.

There were few choices what to do, he realized . . . one, really.

He turned to face the mountain. Not so majestic as the Sierra, nor the red and crammed peaks of the Colorado Rockies, the small range above him had its own power nevertheless, even vanity. The central peak of the three

274

frowned its scars down on him some two thousand feet below, a mocking face, slit with pitches and dangerous scree falls, long runs of snow that would be suicidal to attempt without an ice-axe.

Joseph wondered how in the world was he going to get up there?

No way but *up* the mountain. No means but his own feet.

So he slipped the knapsack on his back and put the rolled, stuffed bag under his arm, and began to climb towards the first run of rocks. His mind was clear . . . very clear. He had been given a kind of unlooked-for happiness to be going all by himself, by his own wit and energy, into the sky. And he would take it.

Joseph had moved only a few steps when he stopped. There was a sound in the valley. Like crying.

It was a horse. Pale grey, without a rider . . . come straight from Revelation. Unaware of Joseph, the horse ate as it followed the tenderest growth into a small clearing. Joseph could see no marks from bits or bridles or saddle lashings. If it weren't a wild horse then somebody had neglected to brush it for a long time, and as it grazed closer to where Joseph crouched he noticed a number of large welts and scars that made a crazy lace of the beast's hide.

A flash at the horse's feet caught Joseph's eye. A pair of steel shoes. No wild horse, it was only one that had lost its need of men and gone feral. Something like his brothers had done.

As Joseph rested upwind, the horse chewed its way along the woods' edge unwarily, nose in the mosses and sedge, following the rocky stream to drink some and to cool its feet only a few yards from where Joseph knelt unblinking.

Finally the horse sensed him and sniffed the air. As if by instinct it backed away from the smell of a man.

Joseph held out his hands, supplicating the horse not to run. He even sang a lullaby. The horse was nervous but held ground. After several minutes he came up to the animal. The nostrils flared over Joseph's outstretched hand. He stroked the horse along the jawline. The horse sniffed deeply, reached out and nudged Joseph's knapsack.

What was this?

Again the horse nudged the pack.

'No apples in there, old buddy. No food at all. What do you want?'

The horse pushed insistently and Joseph opened the pack. Along the blue lining ran an orange track, bright and powdery. Somehow a scissors had wedged itself into the emergency rations – which Joseph had long ago forgotten about – slicing the neck off a foiled package of drink mix. Bits of orange gave the mix colour, and an artificial flavour was only vaguely like the fruit, but the rest was pure sugar. The horse had nosed it out. *King Christ.* Who would believe it?

They licked the bag together. Joseph turned out each crease of the lining to the creature's tongue. It was like feeding a baby. And while the horse searched for every granule of sugar Joseph rubbed his hands in the horse's mane and held on to the grey strands as he lifted a foot up and then over the horse.

He was soon mounted. And the horse wasn't protesting. Hardly had he settled in the shallow of the horse's back, though, when it lurched forward at a fast walk. Joseph barely did hold on.

The horse seemed to know just where it wanted to go. Instead of rising directly into the mountain, they cut across the moraine in a westerly direction, through some scrappy country densely shrubbed. Joseph noticed they were travelling a natural path well worn by game. All along they had been rising, so when Joseph turned around to look behind him he saw the distant tops of the Coast Range over which he had flown.

In front of him was the massif itself. The path appeared to stop but the horse broke right through a brace of junipers and suddenly they were in a narrow gorge, which the horse climbed steadily. They drove into the shadows.

After a while Joseph began to feel the cold coming off the canyon walls. He reached around for his sleeping bag, to make a jacket of it, but felt nothing. The spiky arms of the juniper had picked the bag from its cache under his knapsack. By reflex he tried to stop the horse. The sleeping bag was survival. Already he was cool. Once night fell his meagre clothing wouldn't keep him warm enough. Nearly everything – parka, rain gear, heavy socks, string underwear – had disappeared with Colin. Joseph had one wool jumper in his sack . . . summer weight.

He knew he had to go back down and find the bag or risk freezing to death. So he reined the horse by its mane.

Except the horse refused to stop. It was as if the creature, once going, were unable to change course. Not so very strange, Joseph realized. The canyon was so skinny the horse might have real difficulty in turning around.

Joseph had to get the poor dumb beast to try anyhow.

'Leave your bag.'

A voice?

'Let it go. Let *everything* go!'

In perfect oratory the mountain spoke, gave command. The horse's steps continued unbroken, unhurried. Only Joseph had heard . . . *but he'd heard*.

The voice had surprised him. It was just his own conscience that had spoken, of course, and of course the voice came from within himself . . . except that it goddamned well *seemed* to ring right out of the rock walls. Certainly it was nothing more than his own imagining, the unlapsed hope that his father was still alive. He'd gone through the same ruminations with his daughter's teddy bear.

The bear, now that Joseph remembered it, had first talked to Theresa. She was always having imaginary conversations, anyhow. And was it becoming his habit, as well?

What were the alternatives? Had he tuned in to spirits? phantoms? bits and immaterial tatters from the world on the other side? That would mean he was hearing disembodied gibberings of a voice simulating his father's, a voice that wandered the earth looking for a sympathetic ear, as old Hamlet's ghost had once done. Joseph, who had always scoffed at sorcery and spiritualistic ideas, wasn't much inclined to change his mind. Nevertheless, to pass the time he conjured the voice again.

'And are my brothers up here somewhere, wherever this horse is taking me?'

The voice seemed to groan something like '*They are.*'

'You'd better speak louder. What do I do when I find them?'

You kill them.

'So peremptory, old mole?'

'KILL KILL KILL KILL KILL!!!!!'

The whimsy on Joseph's lips turned to spindrift and ice . . . a cold panic rising.

Not the voice itself, not the command to murder, but the *vehemence* of the voice had finally got to him.

What the hell was happening?

For the very first time on his trip Joseph was frightened, unsure of what madness he might find on the mountaintop and what he would do if it threatened him.

The voice was a warning. No doubt about it. And he heard.

The horse stumbled on in near-darkness. Joseph had no idea how far they had gone into the canyon, but at a certain point his weight shifted and they were going downhill. The tiny cleft of blue sky above them began to widen. They were coming out of the defile, rapidly, too, and into the mountain's heart.

Within minutes they emerged into the amber light of late afternoon amongst striations of rock which the horse crossed like a causeway. Suddenly the horse stopped, its body screwed tightly around its spine.

There was a low growl coming from the boulders.

On all sides of them the earth seemed to lift up.

Dogs. Wild dogs in a pack, fangs dripping, all of them the same grey and brown and black of the rocks from which they rose.

Threatening to attack, they circled the horse. But the horse shied, its upraised height chastening the dogs backwards into a wider circle, and still wider, until they finally sat down on their ragged haunches, tongues lolling . . . waiting.

'Go ahead,' Joseph urged the horse, sure somehow that the dogs were no longer a threat, finished, *completely* finished. He dug his heels into the grey horse's ribs. Several times. Hard.

The horse stepped cautiously through the boulders and as it did so the dogs dwindled and dwindled until they finally vanished into the rocks from which they had come. Like apparitions gone.

Joseph looked up.

He and the horse were about to descend into a small valley isolated in the mountain's most obscure part, with a small lake and ever-greener girdles of trees banded around the water.

A hidden valley.

At the northern edge, directly across from Joseph, there were incontrovertible signs of human habitation: A low, round hut, another one higher and covered with a gabled roof, some smaller structures, all of them looking ramshackle even from a distance. The houses seemed to be sitting in the middle of a field of litter. To Joseph, the litter looked like bones.

He knew where he was. It was his brothers' home.

Halfway across the valley the horse crossed over a stream. Off to Joseph's left, set away from the main camp, lay a cairn of stones and spruce boughs. An ice-axe stuck up from the middle of the heap. A grave, certainly. *Yes* . . . Whose?

He wouldn't guess. (Yet tears were stitching up his eyes.) *WHOSE GRAVE?*

Joseph stared at the stones.

At the very least there was one gone . . . father or brother . . . one face crumbled to clay, one that he would not see, ever, again. *At least one—*.

—Joseph gripped himself hard. He was going at this far too fast. He might be seeing a ceremonial cairn with no bones beneath. And there was truth in bones – whether fleshed or dead. *Only bones*. That's where he'd find the truth about his father and brothers.

Give him *ocular* proof . . . nothing less!

Steadied, for the moment composed, Joseph came on towards the settlement. As he approached, the grey horse walking slowly, a figure emerged from the open shelter.

Whoever it was, and Joseph didn't recognize the person

right away, was round-shouldered, despondent. Dressed in animal skins and barefoot. Someone who wore a cap of gold tight against the head, a skull cap. But when Joseph came close enough to dismount and walk towards the figure, he saw it wasn't a hat at all, only the broken shafts of hair that had once tumbled down halfway to China.

Carmen. *Alive.* And walking along with a bag strapped around her neck like a beast of burden . . . limping on her scars.

Joseph could not – absolutely *would not* – believe the sight.

He sat down and watched her, baffled, his spirits crushed by what he saw.

Though no more than ten yards from him, Carmen wouldn't acknowledge that he was there watching her, and he didn't have the wherewithal to speak first. It seemed a sacrilege to say anything at all. There was an obvious madness in her movements and Joseph had the thought the least word from him might bring it on much worse.

For a while he watched her slaughtering things. Hares and wildfowl for the most part. One after another she drew a knife across an exposed throat, hanging the still-squirming animal to vessel the blood with the same nonchalance butchers and fishmongers anywhere have with flesh, blood, tripes, sinews and bones. The meat she jointed, then cleaned the skins of fat and started them soaking to be worked into something, clothes or blankets he thought, later on. Wet sapling sticks, resin-smelling, green, she punched through the meat he suspected was to be eaten right away. It was enough for a feast of twenty ordinary men.

She had become part of his brothers' mountain life. Completely.

After she had done, Carmen sat unmoving, hands resting in her lap. Only then did she raise her face to Joseph. He looked into her grey eyes and saw exactly the colour of the mountain. And a bottomless sorrow. She was gone somewhere he would never know, nor would she be coming back. Her soul had certainly flown.

The strangest thing of all was that he found her still beautiful, even as her light was nearly faded.

280

'Carmen . . . what's happened?' He laboured to speak, tears thick in his mouth. 'Tell me, Carmen.' But she wasn't going to speak to him. '*Sweet Carmen* . . . who's done this to you?'

He waited and waited for an answer, any kind of answer, a grunt or sigh would have done it. Nothing. She was mute to him. Ten minutes went by. Fifteen. The light turned crimson in the sunset but Carmen stayed the colour of ashes.

Then her eyes grew heavy and, without changing her position at all, her lids closed and she fell asleep right in front of Joseph as the sun sank.

He had been right not to guess what he was going to find in his brothers' camp, nor to hold too tightly to the thin and brittle line of hope.

The truth of things in the mountain was much worse.

Jacob Solomon, the old lion of Judah with whom Joseph had walked in joy many times in his life, his father, who had filled Joseph with the heat of life, was dead. There was no need to ask. Dead. Yes.

Carmen was proof enough.

Joseph fell forward to his knees. Quickly he prayed for his father's peace.

He opened his eyes again. The truth was what he'd come for. He had it now . . . some part of it, at least. But things weren't going to end there. Joseph needed to know much, much more.

He would not go back down the mountain until he knew all.

In the meantime Carmen lived, praise God, and all his brothers might well be alive, too . . . for which he would praise the Lord in equal measure . . . if it were true.

Raven's Flight

CHAPTER 22

The following day Joseph found himself unable to stop goggling at Thomas's hand.

'What can't you do with it?'

'I c-c-can do everything.'

All of the brothers, except for Eric who was off somewhere in the mountain's upper reaches, lay by the streamside spot they called Paradise. It was hot. The brothers torpid. Only Thomas, sitting on the bank assembling parts of a weir, was doing any real work. Joseph stretched out beside him.

'How did it happen?'

Joseph wanted to hear the whole story and Thomas told him.

'We were about f-five or six days short of starving. B-bitter fucking cold. No meat for weeks. They went after beaver, I wanted bear . . . got a sow the year before, we did, made nice jerky.

'The wind of the few days before had died right down and brought in a storm with three or f-four inches of fresh pack. But by d-dawn all the clouds had g-g-g-g-gone east. Cold. Clear. First thing after I got up I read the sky, knew the weather would probably stay cold for a few more days, at the least, maybe some more snow, maybe not. A good time to hunt, the world was all white.

'I took the gelding. Down the same defile you came up. He didn't seem afraid even with the canyon so n-n-narrow, walls must be eight or nine hundred feet high, air damned thin at the bottom and worst in winter it always seems. I'd rolled a kind of smoke from w-wild tobacco . . . cheroot. Kept it for after, though. I was sure I'd bag a bear. Bear come up to that lake in the fall. It was likely I'd find one sleeping. Just didn't want to run across any k-kind of r-r-r-rogue. Seemed too cold for that. There'd been a good berry crop, enough fr-fruit to

282

wrap the fat around the bears, even grizzlies, keep them from having to break hibernation and go foraging for f-food.

'Found a bear. Stuffed up his crawlhole and pushed a spear through his ribs. Cut him up and went to cache him from the r-ravens. They'll shit on meat, foul it, have to be kept completely off. Then I went looking for some spruce r-r-roots, lashings I wanted for the travois I was making to c-carry the fucking meat home, back up the defile . . . .'

Thomas stopped talking. For a moment it seemed he had finished. Then he took hold of a rope he had ravelled while telling his tale and handed it to Joseph.

'Spruce root. A l-lashing like this. I found some all right. Smoked my cheroot after. But I needed just a l-little more rope . . . just a little. One more coil.

'There were ravens around. One was eyeing the bear meat I'd dressed and s-s-so I kept a k-kind eye on him while looking for a spruce. Found one. Found one w-with half a horse sticking out of the ground nearby, the carcass rotted and clawed . . . the stink so high I turned away from it and . . . just stopped. I was looking into the tiny eyes of another bear, live bear, b-bear the size of a nation . . . t-t-t-t-ten yards away. Shit.

'I just watched him . . . waited . . . d-didn't fucking breathe . . . just watched him snorting, smelling me, his m-mean little mind wondering whether to get back to gnawing that appaloosa or whether to start in on me.'

'And . . .?'

'I remember just the smell of the thing. It was on top of me with its fetid f-fucking breath and saliva and those screaming needles in its mouth biting down somewhere around my wrist, cracking the bone right through . . . whacked me sliding across the snow and I p-played dead . . . him over me on all fours and then he just ran like crazy away along the side of the lake. He'd bolted after hearing the gelding pull himself free from the travois . . . I guess.

'Couldn't get up, no strength and no rope to bind the f-fucking artery. There was nothing holding my hand on but three ligatures of tendon and a shred of skin . . . would've fallen off in a s-slight breeze. Jammed the arm into the snow, thought ice would kill the bleeding . . . jammed it right into a package of blue cord, some hiker's, fifty feet of it just left there.

N-nylon. Electric blue. In a plastic bag. Eddie Bauer's price tag still on it. I dammed the blood, got up, and w-walked home . . . .'

'What happened to the horse?'

Thomas shrugged. 'I don't know.'

'He's the horse I found by the lake that took me up here?'

'It would seem.'

'And after you walked back up the mountain Eric cut off your hand?'

'With a d-dull knife.'

'*Jesus Christ!*'

Joseph's eyes shifted from Thomas's phantom hand to his other hand, which Thomas was using to secure baskets to the weir. Over the mountain, coming up one of the white-water rivers from the sea, was a winterful of fish to be caught with the trap and so Thomas retied the lashings over and over, working without cease. The weir would not fail again. In the moonlight the year before, he explained to Joseph, while he and his brothers were working the fish Thomas had seen a bear's shadow eclipse the moon. And just in time he had. His calls had shaken the others from their labours and together they had shinnied up to a tree perch before the bear had made his hectoring way down the mountainside. The brothers had watched helplessly as he cut into the waters, plundering their baskets rank with salmon, sucking a few of the silver and red bodies into his enormous maw and letting the rest go. When he had done with the fish he then chewed through the withes of the weir's guides.

And what the bear had begun in malice the river's current in its icy and compulsive course had finished minutes after. The dead fish had floated away and the weir itself had followed.

The winter without fish had nearly killed them all. They could not endure another one like it.

Thomas believed the rogue grizzly that had bit off his hand was the same bear that had attacked their fishing. It was likely they would have more trouble with him. So they had devised a plan for this year's salmon hunt. While their baskets filled with spawning fish the five brothers would be waiting on top of a platform they had built in a streamside cedar. The bear, seeing easy pickings again, would rush out of the night's dark fabric and rip at the salmon. Except that Thomas and his brothers would be ready, weapons to hand. With his left hand Thomas hoped to stick the bear under the moon's light, right through the neck. He had practised throwing a lance all summer and wouldn't miss . . . nor shrink from the slaver of the bear's jaws if he had to get in closer for a second shot.

'It's an old r-ruse the L-Lillooet used for catching bear . . . worked damned well, too, the Indians say.'

'Sounds pretty unlikely to me.' Joseph, already alerted to fanciful bear stories, especially those told by Indians, wondered if his brothers' fear of winter's approach might not have been translated into a trumped-up fear of the bear. 'I can't believe any bear's going to remember the chow you guys laid out for him a year ago.'

'Oh, he'll remember.'

Then Thomas, who was going to be prepared, whose every second thought was of the bear, went back to his obsessive stitching, while Joseph slipped into the green pool in order to cool off and wonder how Thomas really lived with his rage.

'C'mon over here!'

'What do you want?' Joseph, alone in the water, didn't particularly want to get out.'

'Jeee*sus*, come on!!'

His brother let out such a monstrous whine that Joseph climbed onto the rocks where Douglas was kneeling. Joseph had thought his dimwitted brother was hiding so that nobody could see him scratch his skin against the boulders. Douglas had scabies.

All of his brothers had parasites of one kind or another. There was a regular tick inspection during the season. A constant combing out of lice. But Douglas, more than any of the others, had suffered hard the loss of his shining skin and was now wound in a carapace of plugs and cankers and long scabs where he had dragged branches across the unendurable itching points. No part of him was spared. He was rotting inside and out. All the membranous tissue in his mouth, nose, throat, piss tract, even the corners and inside lids of his eyes, completely cracked and bloody. Of his brothers the least able to bear pain, Douglas was the most vilely ill, or so it seemed to Joseph at first glance.

Joseph thought, though, he would rather have Douglas's malaise than lose a hand to the bear.

When Joseph, still dripping, got to him, Douglas was chipping away at an ancient petroglyph the Indians had left behind. In cleaning off the carving Douglas was killing it.

'What do you think, man? C'mon, tell me what?'

Joseph stared at the rock sheath. The relief had been painted in black and vermilion and white. From dyes of wolf-moss and alder bark and some kind of crushed chalk or limestone for the white. Quills and bones for brushes, tipped with hair . . . moustaches of wildcat. Joseph's eyes could beat no sense from the stones, though, despite the artistry.

'Tell me what it is, Joe.'

'I see circles and squares.'

'It's a crowd of people, man . . . soldiers.'

'Oh yeah?' Joseph touched the circles of the petroglyph, concentric some of them, others intersecting . . . veins of basalt, lips black . . . swelling humps of rock for noses, concave red eyes, and white, empty brows where the soldiers had knocked heads trying to find the enemy. 'What are they doing?'

'Holding their ears.' There was a kind of wicked triumph in Douglas's voice.

'Why is that?'

'There's ghosts in this place, real weird music.' He slid his hands away from the rocks and around Joseph's ears, cupped them like shells. 'Can't you hear it?'

There was the stream sliding by *sans* effort. And Joseph could hear Bobby squealing to himself as he pulled at the legs of some crayfish he had taken from a quiet sidepool. Trout whacked their tails at wasps fallen in the water and God's balmy breath blew gently over everything. But all Joseph could hear were the fractured wits of his brother, Douglas, halting along. 'Can't hear a fucking thing.'

'It's there, man, and I'm not the only one that hears it, either. I'm not nuts.'

Joseph sighed. He could see his brother was about to get defensive. 'Tell me about living up here. You like being an Indian?'

'Sure.' Douglas's hands fell from Joseph's ears and he flayed himself savagely. 'Except for the *shitholing* bugs!'

But Joseph saw no insects for the moment . . . not a one. 'Tell me more.'

'I like the summer, kind of. Not so much work then. We pick berries and lots of honeycomb. I catch frogs sometimes.'

'Like camp, eh?'

Douglas nodded.

'But people come back from camp, you know. Can't be much fun up here during the winter. So why do you stay? Why . . .? *Hey*, Duggie! I'm asking you something.' For some reason Douglas had gone sullen. Joseph turned away for a while and let his eyes work freely over the carving. The shapes, seeming less abstract, did suggest a group of soldiers. Hurling things. Discs. White stones crashing the middle of the scene. 'It's a hunt of some kind, no?'

'Shit, I don't know . . . not really.'

'Food hunt? Or maybe it's Indian war? Can you read it?'

'How the fuck could a dummy like me read this shit, man?'

'O.K., O.K.' He didn't want to browbeat Douglas anymore. He didn't want to browbeat any of them and tell them what dismaying thoughts were gathering in his head as he watched one, then another brother's seeming indifference to the pain in their lives.

There was Bobby, too. Howling. The ground beneath him shaking. Bobby was under the trees, his gargantuan buttocks pointing towards the canyon wall and the rest of him in a squat facing the stream. The crayfish he had ravened down unchewed were now being juggled in his belly, while his gut blew out an earlier meal from his other end. The rest of his brothers were all laughing. It seemed this kind of thing was happening to Bobby nearly all the time.

Though for a long time he wouldn't believe it, Bobby had tapeworm. Early in the summer he had considered a retreat to Williams Lake or even Vancouver for treatment, but Mark had sworn to find a native remedy that would kill the thing or at least get most of it to slide out. They had tried several different purgatives, none of which worked. In the meantime, until Mark could come up with something, Bobby had enough gas to keep himself and everyone else running around night and day. His stomach was distended badly and showed itself no matter how he tried to hide the bulge under his robes. There were other pains he had to live with, too, terrible cramps that only eating relieved. During the springtime he had broken the cycle of diarrhoea by consuming no fats for a while, ate instead everybody else's meagre ration of carbohydrates. But he couldn't stick that diet long . . . and the worm waxed fatter in his guts no matter what he ate.

'You all right?'

Bobby waved a hand to Joseph, then quickly fell back to the tree trunk where he was supporting himself against the next blast from his bowels. The others found Joseph's solicitations as funny as their fat brother's pain.

Joseph turned away and lay over the rocks, dispirited. His feelings pulled many different ways. If looking on Carmen had filled him with confusion and even anger, seeing how each of them had degenerated blunted that anger utterly. So much so that Joseph was overwhelmed with pity, and even a little horror at what they were doing to themselves. And for what?

Sarah had said his brothers were just tendencies, pieces and fragments of people. Well, *Jesus*, what the fuck did she know about it! They were flesh and blood, his brothers. Poor, bare, mutilated and plagued.

Flesh and blood. Real people. Not abstractions in a theory about the group mind. Just people. Brothers. Suffering. Though what in the name of God's sweet kingdom kept his brothers in the mountain after what the mountain had done to them, Joseph didn't know.

And he hadn't even seen Eric yet . . . Eric, whom of all his brothers Joseph had most longed to see. Joseph found himself half-hoping Eric wouldn't be coming down from the mountaintop for a while. It was a sight he'd rather not witness. 'Eric goes off by himself a lot or what?'

288

'There's a dead volcano on top,' Mark explained.

'What does he do up there?'

'He says it stops him from dreaming.'

Joseph didn't see the point.

'Down here he always gets bad dreams and the only way he can get away from them is to sleep out a few nights on the mountain where he says he never dreams at all.'

None of them, Joseph was beginning to realize, had escaped the mountain's infection. Douglas's skin was corrupted everywhere, Bobby was being devoured by a worm, Thomas had lost a hand – his work hand, for him the most precious part of all – and Eric it seemed had lost his sleep. 'You mean if it's not wild enough where you guys are in your valley you have to go find someplace even more desolate?'

Mark's smile was thin and ironical. 'Guess so.'

Strange Mark. Melancholic Mark. In looking at him Joseph could swear that Mark alone of all his brothers had passed no ordeal in the wilderness. Mark, though it had been his idea to come into the mountains in the first place, Mark looked healthy enough under the geegaws and feathers and ruffs of native dress he had so meticulously copied out of books stolen from the University of Vancouver library. But Joseph could see right inside his tall and narrow brother, right through the black chinks in his disguise. Though pretending that life in the mountains was just fine, Mark, too, had the rot, except for him it was growing from the inside out, from his own native bitterness, the harshness of the inner landscape was wearing him down.

Mark told Joseph he loathed that Carmen lived with them and that she had become a permanent fixture in their camp. It was blasphemy. Mark seemed to think that in accepting Carmen all of his brothers had violated the purity of their love for each other. So he wore his Chilcotin finery and sat at the edge of things keeping his log of their life in the wilds, less and less interested in the common concerns of the camp.

Mark wrote in a stiffly bound notebook, black and white on the covers, an old composition book. He had filled five already, one for each year. There were no lines on the paper, but Mark's writing went evenly across every page, scrupulously horizontal. In pencil. But it was his last pencil from the world below, only a knuckle of it left, a few sharpenings.

'What will you do when that's gone?'

'Improvise.'

Then Mark explained how he would harden charcoal. It would be more tedious to make each day's entry but he would chip away with the native stylus anyhow. The record had to be kept, would be kept.

Joseph looked up and found himself staring right into Mark's dark brows. Uncanny the thing that had always gone on between him and Mark; they anticipated each other's thoughts... questions. Joseph could see it wouldn't work to ask Mark for a peek at his diaries. Not a chance in the world that Mark would agree. There were obviously things recorded in the little books which his brothers didn't want Joseph to see. Joseph could guess what: They held a first-hand account of what a dismal failure the camp had been ... damning evidence against the brothers, particularly Mark.

No wonder Mark detested Carmen's being with them. She, a stranger, had witnessed their fucking-up. Even though Carmen hadn't spoken to Joseph when he first arrived in camp – she had continued silent all night – there were accusations of compelling eloquence in her stoop, her clothes, her dead eyes and shredded hair.

At some point the whole story would come out. Joseph would demand to know everything that had happened. And somebody – Carmen or his brothers – would have to tell.

'*Hey!*' Douglas jerked at his baby brother's attention.

'Hey.'

Douglas laughed at the mock. 'What you thinking about, man?'

'About how mouldy the bunch of you look ... couldn't be brothers of mine.'

'It's us. Shit, I'm glad you came. I like being six again.'

'I'm not one of you.'

'What you mean?' Douglas was perplexed.

'I didn't hang around with you guys. You were all always too nutty for me.'

'*Sure* you were with us.'

'I never liked drowning cats and burning puppies.'

'*We never did shit like that!*' Douglas trembled visibly. But then he looked at Joseph's round and expressionless face, and reckoned that his brother was only pulling his leg. 'You want a little smoke I got?' He lifted a pipe from a stash in between two of the boulders that made the rock carving. The pipe itself was stone, quarried a hundred years before by a tribe that lived along the Thompson River, bartered for by the Chilcotin . . . pipestone . . . more of Sam's thievery.

'What is it?'

'Mark says it's wild tobacco.'

'What's it do?'

'Burns my tongue mostly.'

'So even up here you found a way to smoke dope. *Jesus*.' Douglas's hands shook as he made a light from some touchwood he had pulled off an aspen. 'It's got a little kick . . . dizzy more than high. We got some other stuff Mark makes for really getting loaded.'

'If I'm one of you guys what's my hunting name? Eh, Indian?' Joseph had heard all about their animal familiars.

'You don't have one yet.'

'What's yours?'

'*Pretty Marten.*'

Pretty Marten. Joseph could hardly believe Douglas had said that. His brother's soft face had been eaten away by bugs and he was a rough-skinned man now. But still called himself 'pretty'. Not even five long years in the mountains had cut down his brother's vanity.

'Now you come here. I've got a secret you ought to know.'

Joseph took his brother's hands and dragged him to the waterside, made him bend down to see his reflection in the green pool.

'Who's that?'

'Me.'

'And who are you?'

Confusion twittered around his head. 'Me . . . *Douglas* . . . .' But he knew that wasn't the looked-for answer. 'Pretty Marten.'

'Are you "pretty"? You think that . . . ? you're "*pretty*"?'

Douglas looked and looked. He saw himself in the still pool, the once-perfect teeth now jiggling loose in his gums. He liked what he saw, however. Nothing could shake loose his vanity.

Then he bent down and kissed his own image in the water. Even in the shallows he had found water enough to drown his little sense in. He smiled as he raised his face to Joseph, the ridges of his pest-scarred skin dripping water. He guffawed. He thought it must all be a joke of his baby brother's. Sure he was pretty. Looked like a million bucks.

Joseph, for his part, couldn't bear Douglas's smirk. All his brothers had mouthed great assurances that the mountain air would replenish Douglas's feeble mind. It hadn't done anything of the sort. He was a moron before, now, would be always.

There was something worse, though.

They'd not only not saved Douglas's mind, they had led him into a dark room where he'd withered. Douglas was ugly now, so fucking wretchedly ugly that Joseph couldn't bear to see him.

Joseph jammed a hard shoulder into Douglas. He dunked his head into the pool. Again and again and again, not giving a goddamn if he choked his brother to death. And Joseph might have done just that if he hadn't looked up to see the others stirring, all risen from their seats and facing upstream, away from where Joseph held Douglas's head under the water.

He gave one more shove and Douglas went completely into the pool. Then Joseph got up and looked upstream himself.

'Joseph?' It was an aged voice, older than that which had once been his father's, lacking in penetration, weary, half in love with death. It was a voice older than its time.

Some fifty yards higher in the gorge, standing upon a

rock in the middle of the flow and supporting himself with a sapling for a walking stick, stood his eldest brother.

'Is that *you* I see, Joe?'

'It is.'

'*Really* you?'

'It's me, Eric.'

'Jesus, so it is . . . *Jesus!!*'

Joseph saw the older man throw away his stick and step brightly across the stream. His long robes trailed in the current of air. Eric splashed across the riffle and onto the bank nimbly, in two immense strides. Leaping. Bounding towards Joseph.

He was thinner now than Joseph remembered him. Narrow as a cat's-tail. And – was it possible? – his hair not just foam-flecked from water kicked out of the stream but Eric's hair itself all white? Not even grey but white!

Joseph stood straight and waited to be swept up in the arms of his onrushing brother. The closer Eric came the more sinuous, until his robes blew away from his chest and Joseph, gasping at all the changes, could count his ribs. Although the big man leapt yards at a stride he seemed crooked, listing to one side.

Unable to stand still any longer Joseph inched forward. Then started to run. His brother's hands were open like talons. And when they did meet they actually snapped together like the thunder.

'*Huy huy!*'

Both men's eyes were thick and briny, their voices too flooded to speak. The others set themselves around them like a Stone Age ring, pointing the shafts of afternoon sun to the middle.

Eric and Joseph settled, and drew apart.

'I told you I'd come one day.'

'And I remember your saying it.'

'I meant it.'

'I believed you then.' Eric pushed his beard away from his mouth. 'My Christ, Joe . . . .'

Joseph, for his part equally confused, didn't know just which man he was looking at. Or what to feel. It was impossible to know if he was hearing weakness in Eric's voice or patience. Or maybe even the humility that comes of living years above the timber line in a grinding world of ice and rocks and fevers of long duration. He was caught in between pity for the way they looked and admiration for the five of them to have survived four years of such a life . . . nearly five.

The circle was stretched to take all six brothers. Up the stream the sun fell right in between the walls of the canyon, resting on an outcrop of rock several miles above them, losing its force every moment. And in the tumbling rays of light and the slackening breeze the insects came.

A true million of them.

They slapped at the sucking hordes but it didn't do much good. Eric leaned towards Mark.

'Get some oil.'

Mark reached into his bag of mysteries and brought out a bark bottle. The brothers stood up to wind their robes tightly around themselves. Then they smeared the foul-smelling tincture over every flash of skin and in their hair and beards and then on their clothing. Joseph did as they did.

'Now I'm going to smell as bad as the rest of you.'

'You learn not to smell the oil, Joe . . . but the fucking bugs you'll never forget about.' Eric reached towards a bush nearby and plucked a bud, popped it under Joseph's nose. Its thick, sweet incense hid the foulness of the oil. Eric spoke in pale tones. 'There's some sweetness here, too. It's not all as bad as it looks.'

Sweetness? Joseph, last of his father's sons, only half-believed it. He could still smell the oil . . . and hear some knave bird in the trees mocking what his brothers said. They were diseased and wasting away. Honey words and mountain spices wouldn't hide them. Joseph saw the truth all too clearly. Too many bones showed.

He heard something else, as well: a thought. Unspoken but on every lip. *His brothers wanted to get down off the mountain but not a one of them knew the way.*

Though he had tried hard not to anticipate how things would be with his brothers, in his own innocence Joseph had dreamed of finding them singing as they worked in the sunlight. Pleasure. A crude but honest prosperity. But nothing in all his experience could have prepared him for seeing them so ill and desperate. They thought they could live forever in the high country, squatting on the edge of the empyrean itself. The truth was, though, they'd be lucky to live another year. Somebody had to help them get out. Now he felt the straps of another burden, more than just recovering his father's bones: he would save his brothers, who were, after all, the living bones of his father.

A double burden.

Finding his brothers wasn't the end of his business in the mountains, as Joseph had all along thought it would be. He was just at the beginning of his voyage.

A double burden, but there was no question in Joseph's mind which end of his task he must grab hold of first. It had been the centrepiece of his father's teaching that the dead had no need of a physician and that they might be buried after many sundowns and take little offence thereby (though they did have to be buried in the end). He would join his brothers' life, and then lead them away from it.

'Let's get back.' Eric rose. 'There's a winter coming.'

'*Huy huy.*'

Each man balanced a section of the weir – Joseph, too – which they would assemble over the mountain. Then they filed up the canyon, back to their camp and their first meal together for many years, listening the whole way to Eric's news about a grizzly he'd seen crossing the volcano and heading west towards the salmon-choked rivers that emptied into the Pacific. Just where the bear should be going. And where they would be following soon . . . hard upon.

CHAPTER 23

During the following days Joseph entered into the life of the camp. There was some urgency, only thinly veiled, about the bad weather coming early and catching them unprepared. Memories of the preceding year were sharp indeed. Their hands moved almost fearfully. Joseph thought he picked up a hint of irritation at his coming, too, for in doing so he had no question slowed them down.

Together they made new caches for the fish and field harvests, redug the underground shelter, cut wood ceaselessly. The insects moved around the camp in heavy swarms, driving the men into the lake or brook many times in a day. It was chaotic but things got done.

Nothing at all was said about their father. Not a word. Carmen, a domestic, a skivvy, kept to herself and her housewifely tasks, speaking to nobody except Eric, so Joseph couldn't approach her, either. They were all avoiding hard talk. Joseph grew tense under the constraint, unsure how long he could keep his peace. There was work enough to forget other burdens, though, at least for a while.

'What we gonna call you, JoJo?' Brother Bobby thought Joseph would be the better for having a Chilcotin name.

'What's "*Little Bear*"?'

'"*Ses*".'

'Maybe I ought to be "*Very Little Bear*".'

'"*Ses ntodl*".'

Eric waved a hand at the others, breaking off the joke before it got started and became an all-day divertissement. 'You don't just pick a name, Joe. Somebody explain it to him.' He pointed at Thomas and then turned back to the weir assembly. 'C'mon! I'll be fucked if we're going into winter again without fish.'

While the others picked up their labours, Thomas led Joseph out of the camp in search of his proper animal familiar. They crossed the brook close by the sepulchre of wood and stones. Near the ice-axe Joseph hesitated for a moment, his eyes unable to let go of the apparent grave. 'What's under there?' he asked.

'A l-l-little dog.'

'So special you buried it?' Their camp was littered with uncovered bones.

Thomas didn't answer. He just drove Joseph along.

They passed out of the valley and then across the rock striations. The terrain kept changing. Soon they were in scrub country, a few trees raised above the shrubs, pygmy-sized trees, all of them gnarled and leafless. 'Good spot here.' Thomas himself had trapped the area for goat and lynx.

'Looks dead to me.'

'Sit down.'

Joseph's knees bent and he eased into a natural rock chair. 'What am I supposed to do now?'

'Sit and look and l-listen.'

'That's all?' The whole business seemed silly to Joseph.

'That's all, just daydream . . . k-keep alert, though.'

Joseph was to wait until he felt the presence of an animal.

'You'll know what I mean r-r-right away . . . if something happens.' Thomas saw Joseph's doubt. 'I don't have much faith in any of this, either, but it w-w-works . . . whether you believe it or not.'

Having said that Thomas wandered forty or so yards away, into the bush, sat down amongst spiked plants until he was part of the camouflage, and watched Joseph . . . resting so still as he watched that mice scrambled over Thomas's moccasins and never mistook him for a living man.

An hour went by. Mist began to fill the blue spaces of sky in between the rock spires. No animals called to Joseph. Except for the circles of an eagle above him, so high it was only a small fleck sewing itself in and out of the gathering grey, Joseph saw nothing.

Joseph grew nervy. He lost patience and finally called out to Thomas that he had seen an eagle a little while before.

'Where?' Thomas walked out of his cover and up to the throne where Joseph was sitting.

'What do you mean "where"? In the sky.'

'High?'

'Very high. And it didn't talk to me, either.'

'Animals don't talk, Joe.'

297

'I'll say.'

The two of them started to laugh . . . Joseph, at least, laughing in relief, joyed to find that Thomas, always the very model of reasonableness, found the whole business about animal familiars a little ridiculous, too.

Then Joseph described how Sam the Indian had called Theresa 'Little Eagle', and that he wouldn't be surprised to find out that he was himself 'Great Eagle'. 'But what was that scratching all about?' Joseph asked. 'If there were any animals around you sure did a masterful job of scaring them off.'

Thomas's steps seized. 'What scratching?'

'You were scratching. Trying to fox me into thinking I was hearing something.'

'What kind of scratching?' Thomas persisted.

'Oh come on.'

'*D-d-describe it!*'

Thomas leered like a fool. It was the wildest look Joseph had ever seen on his brother's face. And deadly serious.

'It sounded like a bird scraping the rocks with its feet.'

Thomas thought for a few minutes, then, without speaking, scrambled up a skinny gully, hardly kicking dust up from his buckskin soles.

Joseph followed his brother, trying as hard as he could to keep up. 'Like a chicken . . . clawing at the dirt. How could you not have heard it? I don't think it stopped from the time you left me sitting until I called you.'

'There was no scratching that I h-heard.'

The two of them continued through the scrubs, checking snares, neither talking. Thomas stopped Joseph in the shadow of a cliff. His clean, thin lips were set ironically. Thomas was himself again, though he had hugely confused Joseph. 'It's just p-possible, Joe, that instead of b-being "G-Great Eagle", you're r-r-really "Wild Chicken".'

Their laughter once again rang out against the cliff stones, but for Joseph it was a different release, less innocent, more suspecting. He didn't know if the cheer would last or disappear as suddenly as it had come.

'Sssshhh!' Thomas raised a hand and drew out a knife that had been sheathed in his leggings. By himself he went

298

ahead, not disturbing a single twig hanging over the game trail. He straightened up and called Joseph.

A fawn had snarled itself in the twisted babiche of a snare meant for other game. The deer, just on the edge of adulthood, had somehow been overlooked by predators while helpless in the trap. It grew quiet as Thomas talked to it. Joseph noticed that his brother didn't slip over a single syllable in talking to the fawn.

'That'll make a nice skin for you, Joe, plenty large enough for a shirt.' Thomas's fingers were but inches from the deer's nostrils. Several flies buzzed around its black tail, landing close to the anus and making the deer twitch as they chewed the soft membrane. It had gone almost tame with Thomas. 'You know how to kill it, Joe?'

Joseph refused to move.

'The animal's as good as dead already.'

'Not yet it isn't.'

Thomas frowned. 'M-might as well be.'

'Why is it better dead?'

'Gone sentimen-men-men-men-men-men-men—?'

Thomas cut himself off . . . rolled forward on his haunches and looked right into the young deer's eyes. 'You don't know where you are, Joe. No c-cosy sentiments here, just work. *W-w-work*. Constant and m-mercifully unending. From one task, f-friend, you go right on to the next. No treachery up h-here, either.' There was just he and his brothers, as Thomas put it. Work and no people disappointing you. And from time to time, when the blood sang in the cold, mountain air, when work was done, he and his brothers laid down their stony burdens and held arms over arms and loved each other about as much as men are able to love. Those few times in a long and bitter year made everything worthwhile. Hard, unchanging love.

'It doesn't mean anything to kill this fucking fawn, Joe.'

'Well I'm not going to.'

Thomas's pale eyes studied Joseph. They had always had an easy understanding, the two brothers. Many years in the mountains had changed that. But it was more than the passage of time and diverging experience that strained what they could know of each other. Thomas took the knife in his one good hand, patted the fawn with his stump, whispered to it in soft, sucking tones until the creature was beatifically calm.

'Please don't.'

'We need it, Joe. If n-nothing else it's a couple of days' feed . . . sweet meat, too.'

'Don't.'

Back and forth in the air Thomas waved the tip of his knife, balancing the life of the fawn against his own wants. One last time he stroked it on the crown of its soft head, distracting it, while with the knife he made a quick and clean cut right under the neck, straight through the babiche, freeing the animal in a single stroke. Both brothers watched as the fawn kicked away the ligature and thrashed roots from its hooves, straightened its legs and sprung into the brush. It was gone in an instant, into what hungry jaws they reckoned never to know.

'Thank you.'

'You still need a shirt . . . and a name.'

'I'll find one.'

Thomas nodded, reached into a bark wallet he carried and took out a piece of flat cake, tore it into two. It was a sliver of pemmican from the previous autumn that had, miraculously, survived the winter unnoticed. 'Always nosh a little when you're moving . . . keep a c-constant feeling your body can do what it has to. Dr-dr-drink water, too. *Often.*'

'Right.' Joseph chewed the cake, sweet but somehow not satisfying, while with careful eyes he searched his brother's face for some sign of a shared relief they had let the fawn go free. He found nothing there. The small bird of mercy that had flapped its wings over them for a moment had already flown . . . if Thomas had even heard it at all . . . .

'No luck,' Joseph told the others shortly after he and Thomas returned to camp. 'I guess the animal world has decided to ignore me.'

Eric looked askance at his little brother, seemed about to dispute him, but thought better of it. 'I've got something for you.'

'What you got?'

'I've been working on it every free minute since you came.'

'Show me.'

The big man led Joseph around the summer lodge, to a spot under the gable overhang. It was the garbage dump, scattered tools of steel and plastic which had been discarded during their first years in the camp but which they had been making more and more use of lately. From the pile Eric plucked a stick, handed it to his brother. An ordinary, unornamented curved stick. A bow. The gift he'd made.

'Juniper. Authentic Chilcotin design.'

Joseph examined the bow with more care. It had been worked patiently . . . finely . . . to a surprising smoothness. He slid the flattened bow along his arm. 'You got anything to string it with?'

He watched as the wolf slipped on a strand of caribou hide.

Eric's hands moved with assurance. 'Practise with the bow as it is now and I'll restring it for you with sinew if and when you're ready to go after an animal.'

'Where's the ammo?'

Eric lifted up a quiver made of wolverine. There were several arrows inside, all with signs of constant service. One had a triple head, thin splints of bone broader at the tip than at the base where they were attached. 'For smaller game,' Eric explained.

'What's this one?' Joseph held up a point cut from a milky rock, blue, transparent.

'Silica stone. You can see the arrow as it flies, the head reflects sunlight. That one I chipped myself, with a fucking moose molar. Stone-sharpened it, too!'

Joseph found himself clamorous with feeling. Eric had worked hard to make him the bow . . . and with traditional Indian tools, Indian craft. 'How did you guys learn to do all this? Not from books.'

'Some.'

'I'm impressed.'

Both men paused.

'Why don't we go over to the trees and I'll show you how to shoot this thing.'

They walked through the tundra to the outer apron of green. Joseph picked the thickest-trunked Douglas fir he could find to use as a target. He pulled the unloaded bow several times to feel its draw. Then he took the arrow Eric held out to him.

A steady draw. The bow tense. A breath. Release.

The arrowhead streaked brightly, flashing across the valley not high above the ground. It hit the tree but too obliquely to stick.

'You're right. I could see it all the way.'

'Get down on one knee. It may sound like movie nonsense but it happens the Chilcotin did it that way. Go on.'

Joseph kneeled, shot. The second arrow flew more crisply, and true. It chipped tree bark but held, quivering in place.

'*Well done.*'

Together they went to retrieve the two shafts.

'Mark seems to think you've all forgotten why you came here.'

'Mark would think that.'

'*Have* you forgotten?'

'We stay, don't we?' Eric's lupine mouth opened, teeth dull and scum-choked, rotten down into the gums. 'We're all dead tired, Joe . . . lived through a winter last year you wouldn't believe. It can't be anymore like it was in the beginning, when we used nothing but Indian tools. Most everything has broken, anyhow, and there's not much point in repairing it. So we use modern tools or whatever else that will keep the camp going. Mark doesn't like that. But the rest of us aren't looking for extra work. Mark won't make any concessions. The rest of us don't give a damn . . . that's not why we're here.'

'Why *are* you here?'

'What the hell kind of question is that? We *live* here. This is our blessed blasted mountain. Keep your eyes open a little and you might understand.' Then he stopped, cut himself off as if he'd already spoken more than he wanted. 'Thomas tells me you heard some scratching this afternoon. You say nothing happened.'

'Thomas is kidding you. He made those noises himself.'

'You're wrong about that.'

'I just don't believe in animal spirits, Eric.' Joseph sighed. 'What can I say . . .?'

'Let me tell *you* something – neither do I.' The wolf took Joseph's hand and set it on his forehead. 'No spirits? Well, I can't think of anything else to explain what sits up here behind my eyes and barks at the moon. *Can you?* Eh . . .?'

Grim Eric. His white beard had a tiny sparkle of ginger just at the hair ends, and knots of hard times and worry bulged from his brows . . . a soothsayer from the Ancient World.

Joseph's soft eyes padded along the ground. He didn't want to look into his brother's face. For years he had believed it was idealism – an idealism of some perverse, bastard form, maybe a search for the religious life – that had swept his brothers up the mountain. Now he had to wonder if he'd been wrong . . . or if, once in the mountain, darker instincts had sustained the five of them as soon as their better parts had burned out.

'Thanks for the bow.'

But Eric, aroused now, could not settle. '*You want to know why we're here?* It's no trial to see how tough we are. We *have* to be here. It's all we've got!' He smiled savagely and held up his hands like a deaf mute trying to signal the world outside. 'And just what the hell was I supposed to do in life with these dumb things? Eh? . . . dumb fucking hands!' He snatched the bow and dropped an arrow onto the polished wood, pulled back the drawstring, his muscles richly set on his ribs. The arrow screamed.

And a scream in the woods answered.

Eric's eyes were wide and spinning, his black tongue thick. '*Oh Jesus!!*'

Somebody had been shot. One of the others had caught the arrow. They all came running, men and dogs.

Eric's hands had wrought havoc again.

'Netsin . . . *netsin!*'

It was Bobby. Wounded, the fat man was lumbering towards the marsh, ahead of the others who followed his calls. He hid in the muskeg, fortunately holding onto a willow by reflex.

It took a while to discover where he was. They found him only by his weeping.

Even after they got him out of the bog it was difficult to restrain Bobby. His red-brown curls, brittle, splayed down the back of his neck and onto his shoulders, were stuck all with greenery – sedge grasses and aspen leaves and dark needles from the pines. He was decked like a holly bush, half-asleep from the terror of having seen his *'netsin'*, a Chilcotin's second soul, which was said to appear to a warrior when death was near.

'But what about the arrow?' Joseph was incredulous.

'Must have missed him.'

'It didn't miss him!'

Eric's shoulders were hunched over. 'Then it hit him. I can't see it so it couldn't have gone deep. Fuck, I don't know!'

'Eric . . . what in hell's name is going on?'

The big man, furious with himself, wouldn't lie. 'Fat Man's nuts.' His mouth was a fumarole. *'He's gone nuts like this before.'*

Earlier in the summer they had found Bobby in the lake, in the shallows but completely submerged and face up on the bottom mud. He had a reed stuck in his mouth for breathing, a ray of sunlight bisecting his belly. They had been lucky to find him at all.

'He sometimes sees himself – a kind of pale vapour that looks like him – detached and walking around in the trees. Then he runs away for a day or two . . . doesn't remember a thing afterwards.'

Mark rushed over.

'He's getting worse.'

Thomas and Douglas were doing all they could to keep Bobby immobile and on his backside, away from the fire. The afternoon sun was approaching the rim of the sky.

'Now it's the shadows rattling him.'

Bobby squirmed free of his brothers' grasp and maundered in close circles around the fire, muttering to himself as he lifted the largest rocks in camp and grubbed in the

304

dirt beneath for his *netsin* . . . his double . . . his ill-at-ease and peripatetic soul.

'He's going to get wilder. I can feel it coming, god-damnit!' Eric's cheeks were sucked in. 'Distract him with something!'

'Let me try tattoos.'

'What's the point of that?'

'It's either a little pain that settles him now or a whole lot after. *You choose*.' Mark was stiff with disgust. 'Who shot the fucking arrow, anyhow?'

'Me,' Eric admitted.

'Well you sure did set him off. Fucking lucky it didn't catch the femoral artery.'

'Get off it! I only grazed him.'

'Oh yeah? There's a good six-inch-long gash. If the angle had been a little different it would have gone right through his leg . . . even *his* leg.'

Eric's rage finally hit flashpoint and he broke the bow over his knee, hurling the polished splinters into the scrap.

'Let's go.'

He and Mark started running towards their distraught brother, Joseph right at their heels. But Eric stopped suddenly and caught Joseph's arm. 'You go sit down.'

'I want to help.'

'*Sit down!*'

Joseph went back to the target tree and watched as the other four swarmed around Bobby, approaching him cautiously. On the other side of the fire from all of them Carmen was peering out of her sweatbox. For several days she had been fighting a bad fever. Though he had hardly seen her since entering the camp, Joseph had come to understand that the reason the camp ran at all was because of her. And yet, in some way, though living in the camp she was not *of* it. The grey grist in her eyes caught Joseph and fixed on him huddling amongst the trees. Then the chink in her doorway went shut. Joseph could hear a wooden bar being latched across on the inside. Double latched.

Only lightly tattooed before, Bobby now pleaded for a skein of scratches to veil his face . . . a trick to keep his *netsin* from recognizing him. Mark, reluctant at first to

305

do the surgery even though he had suggested it, was pushed into it by the others and began to lance Bobby's once-bright face until the points of the bone needles had set charcoal deep beneath the skin where it would most likely never come out. Things began to get bloody.

'*Ses!*' Bobby called to his double, hoping for amity. '*SES!* Little black bear out there!'

'Stay *still* or I'm going to wind up jabbing out your eye!'

'*Netsin . . . Netsin,* old buddy . . . .'

The tattooing wasn't enough. Bobby continued to writhe in anxiety, he who was never afraid fluttering at every passing shadow, a man wrestling with flies.

He jumped away from his brothers' grasp again and headed towards the marsh, but they speeded after him and caught him and this time dragged him back by the hair, their own titanic strength finally overmastering Little Bear's.

'Spread his legs!'

Joseph could tell his brothers' movements weren't haphazard any longer. They had a plan to tether Bobby somehow.

'*Wider!*' Eric was in full cry, every utterance loud enough to wake a sleeping god. He kicked at one of the dogs, dogs everywhere underfoot, sensing something crazy going on and strutting nervously, the very picture of anguish. 'His *feet* first!'

The others bound Bobby's feet. Then his hands after.

Bobby wasn't resisting any longer yet the deadweight of his hulk made it difficult for them to pinion him standing up. But it was done. The free ends of the binding were hobbled to posts at the quarter points so that Bobby could move no way. At most he could turn or twist, fall backwards or forwards some few inches.

'Will it hold?' Eric asked the others.

Mark didn't think so. Neither did Thomas.

'Then what the fuck do we do?' None of them answered. Their shoulders were bunched together. If they were to give Bobby the one pain certain to settle him, Eric would have to decide. It was his lot. 'Well . . .?' Still they didn't speak. 'O.K. . . . O.K. You going to lay it on me? *O.K.*, I'll decide. But *you* cut him!'

306

He spoke to Mark who didn't move.

'I said cut his chest!'

Mark did.

Right into Bobby's breast muscles on both sides, cutting across nerves, sinew, meat. Veins spurted. The ruptures were clean. Before Bobby knew what was happening his brothers drew leather lashings right through him and tied them to distant stakes.

He was secured by his own body. Any motion he made, though it were the tiniest part of an inch, would pull muscle cord off his ribs.

Little Bear had found his pain.

The others dropped away, exhausted, unable to look at Bobby staked like a carnival animal. Joseph took a step closer, but Eric, seeing him, held up a fist. 'Stay away.'

'What happens to him now?' Joseph's throat was clutching. He could barely whisper.

Eric, shattered himself, his elbows raising him so that his white hair was only a little way off the valley floor, just kept shaking his head. 'It's the only thing that stops him . . . just for a couple of hours is enough . . . only thing, believe me . . . the only thing . . . .'

Joseph ran away, desperate to be alone, wandering deep into the forest. Towards the water's edge. The overcast, which had been diaphanous all afternoon, had finally given way to a clear night sky big with moon. A witching kind of night, much the coldest since he'd been in the mountains. Hints of frost pinched the air. He would need to borrow blankets in order to keep warm. Indian blankets. Maybe even dress in their native clothes.

The forest around him for the first time seemed menacing. And loneliness joined hands with the cold. His bed with Rosalie, their sun-daubed room, the lemon bowl, all felt so far away . . . the smell of his daughter, his infant son's round, direct, unblinking eyes. The heat of family love. Their modest, lowland paradise. He had left it all and now it was farther away than miles could measure. And he would have to travel more than miles to return, for he would have to get his brothers out, too, and that didn't look easy.

The crazy things in his brothers, which were coming out one by one, were cutting him off from them. It was all well and good to try to see the mountain world through their passions, their eyes, but his trip was beginning to seem like a descent into madness and Joseph wondered if that was the best way to help get his brothers out of the mountain.

Also, he was scared. He had no idea to what lengths he would go in order to defend himself against their madness.

And, worst of all, he was beginning to have flashes – lunatic, *troubling* flashes – of what might have happened when his father surprised his brothers in their camp.

The thoughts were hard, too hard, and he pushed them all away.

He approached a deadfall. In between the timbers he had hidden his knapsack when first entering the camp. Stowed inside were things not to be seen by his brothers. Joseph had his secrets, too. In looking for the pack, though, he found he had hidden it too craftily. With a branch of willow Joseph poked and prodded the grooves between the logs, careful not to push the whole assembly over and crush himself under several tons of wood. He jabbed hard but scraped only rotting bark and leaves.

Was it possible one of them had discovered the pack?

He lay down on the valley floor and rested, listening to the world. There was a midnight howling, wolves or coyotes, or maybe the dogs in camp . . . hard to tell what but much too far away to make his flesh crawl.

The time left for him to inveigle his brothers out of the mountain was fast disappearing. Joseph himself would have to go back soon or risk getting stranded in their camp for the entire winter. As for his brothers, once they ambushed the marauding bear and killed it, then trapped and split and dried the year's salmon catch, Joseph would never convince them they had to get out. He should be scrambling fast but didn't even have a plan.

And if they stay this year, he asked himself, *am I going to come back and try to get them out next year? And every year after?*

Once again he heard the baying. It had come much closer, or he was hearing it as closer. Certainly it was the dogs at the campsite, where his fat brother was trussed up like a bear at a bearbaiting. *Jesus!*

Jesus. Maybe the pain itself was keeping his brothers from going home? Pain . . . a sure encounter every single day . . . its thousand-fingered hands of cold and hunger and bugs and skin rot and loneliness always extended like a friend, out there and ready to glad-hand it. *Pain was their real familiar.*

Joseph's willow stick finally hit canvas. Two luminous buttons peeked out of the deadfall. He reached in and caught the straps, pulled his bag out and searched inside to see what was there.

Everything. The bag hadn't been meddled with, thank God.

In one of the side pockets he had secreted a weapon. Joseph opened the inconspicuous cardboard box. Inside were thirty or forty small packets of seeds: lettuce, onions, radishes, beets, beans, potatoes, carrots, squash, cucumbers. Even melons. He had no idea what would grow in the mountain soil. Anything planted right away would freeze, of course, even the few winter vegetables, the cabbages and sprouts and cauliflower. It didn't matter. He had brought the seeds for his brothers' spring. But he was no longer sure they would see another springtime. So he'd plant the seeds immediately. Plant them all. What difference did it make? He wasn't worried about producing fruit of the seed. If only the slightest growing tendrils sprouted out of the ground before the cold killed them it would be worth all labours.

For Joseph believed the idea of a garden in flower – *just the imagined, seedling image of it* – would be enough to save them.

If they could only remember how it had once been, that there were other, happier, better times, his brothers might, just might break out of the spiral that was leading them inexorably upwards, into the sky and right out of this life altogether.

Or maybe just the hope of a single seed lasting the winter out would free them.

Who knew? But he had to try. And soon.

His lucubrations were broken off by the dogs' baying which had grown loud enough to fill the entire valley. The cries focused Joseph's mind on what to do. He had learned his brothers planned a harvest of the berries and local wild tubers sometime in the coming days. He'd make them set out a garden – plumb the row lines, turn over the soil, furrow and seed. All he needed to find was a spot of earth in between the rocks . . . and a brief moment of clarity in the day.

It could be done.

CHAPTER 24

Three days later they were all in the harvest fields below Paradise and picking fast.

'"Land of many uses".' Joseph was joking but he liked what he saw. A meadow two or three miles around. In the middle a river coiled a few times, flowing slowly, before finally quitting the limits of the park. A few trees, all in small copses, gave shade. The entire field was bordered by heavier growth, deciduous, broad-canopied and wide-leafed, amber in autumn dress. 'What grows here?'

'Every brave little weed and shrub,' Bobby said.

Joseph smiled and looked at his feet. The ground was burnished black, volcanic debris everywhere, fertile, teeming with insects. *Perfect*, he thought, for he had brought his seeds without telling anyone. His brothers were going to have a garden, like it or not.

The men, each with a bark basket, were widely spread out and hurrying along. Winter, they knew, might roar in at any time. A dozen different berries grew in the field, but they were only gathering service and soapberries, the two kinds of fruit most richly massed in bushes at the field's edge. From those berries they would make a cake to last them through the cold weather.

310

Joseph followed Bobby, worked right alongside him. Unlike the others, they were digging for camras root, a potato-like vegetable that grew wild and uncultivatable in all the valleys of the plateau. It didn't take Joseph long to learn how to prod the white, oblong tubers from the land. Most of what he picked was merely lifted from the walls of boglike depressions scattered around the meadow. He crumbled the black dirt away and the roots nearly fell into his wallet. For other, more deeply-rooted tubers, he used a digger made of antler. Bobby had one of bone.

It was hot. The two brothers pounded the earth for its cache, stopping momentarily only to slap on more insect oil – the stinging bugs everywhere, pricking every exposed shred of skin. Until noon they continued. They took their clothes off, Bobby his lynx and rabbit robe, Joseph stripping down to jeans, then to nothing at all. The sun beetled right over them, drawing water out of them so quickly it seemed their lubricious skins would slide off with the slightest tug. Finally, having filled several large wallets with roots, Bobby sat down for a break. Joseph, hotter than he could ever remember feeling, his expense of work stupendous, lay down on the side of a bog and dropped his feet in the water at the bottom, sinking down past his knees.

'How you faring, JoJo?'

'Hot and wasted. I thought I was in reasonable shape.'

The fat man rolled in laughter, even though his chest was still sore and pained him if he moved too quickly or breathed deep. 'You're working the digger all right, I think. Fucking ancient little tools, they are, but they do do the work.'

'Where'd you get them?'

Bobby's eyes were merry. 'Sam.'

'Sam stole everything for you, didn't he?'

'That's right, little buddy. Every now and then he pops by, checks us out from the mountaintop. Hasn't been around since our lady's in camp, though . . . don't know why.'

'I got another question for you, Fat Man.'

'You're full of questions.'

'How did Carmen wind up in camp . . .?'

311

Joseph glanced towards the middle of the field where Carmen was lying in the shade. Her fever had raged uncontrollably for days. They had put off the harvest as long as they could, then packed her on the gelding and brought her down the mountain with them. She would have to cure spontaneously . . . and on the road.

'*How . . .?* Tell me.'

But Bobby just broadened his Oriental smile, refusing to talk about her. He held a hand over his eyes, though they were already in shadow, his cheeks so blubbery they reduced his eyes to slits merely. 'When you gonna take off, JoJo?'

'Maybe I'll stay up here. Why not? You guys do.'

'This isn't your kind of life, little buddy.' Bobby and his brothers had whispered amongst themselves about Joseph, that they might abandon him naked and alone on the volcano top, as they had done with their father, but this time for love. Joseph would live somehow, and in surviving understand why they had chosen to stay in the mountain.

'*Is it anybody's?*'

The big man shrugged. For some minutes he had been dallying with a single mushroom growing by the bog side. He bent it back and forth with finesse, testing the stalk's elasticity, careful not to pull off the delicate, pinkish cap. Now he pulled it from the ground and pointed the root end at Joseph. 'You know what this is?'

'They edible?'

'Eat and die, JoJo.' Bobby looked more carefully at the fungus, examining the faint spots on the cap, the gills, stem, the bulge in its tail. 'Looks like one of your genuine *amanita* to me . . . the old "destroying angel". Want a nip, JoJo? We share it?' He held the mushroom under his nose, smelled it all around, his eyes taking on their gourmandise phase, an animal change in him as natural as the chameleon adapting. 'Mmmmmm . . . perfumy.'

'Why don't you get rid of that, big fella?' Joseph's heart was beating hard. He thought the mushroom just might be poison.

Bobby brought the mushroom's shy hood ever so slightly closer to his lips. Then he touched it with his lips, rubbed its

312

vegetable skin against his own. With the grace of a cat, the very prince of cats, he lifted a tiny piece with his tongue and sucked it into his mouth . . . nibbled daintily . . . tasted for trouble—

'—Hey, c'mon. Spit it out. *Please*, Bobby. Enough!'

'My theory,' Bobby explained, chewing imperceptibly with his front teeth, 'is you eat just the right amount, a weeny weeny bit, and you get this nice high . . . mildly psychedelic . . . nothing too trippy . . . eat a bit more and you might keep on dreaming forever.'

He was relishing the taste. The danger. And he liked teasing his little brother. Bobby was the swami who could swallow fire. He opened his jaws wide and shoved the whole mushroom in. Held it suspended between enormous, spatulate teeth—

'—*Stop it, Fats!!*'

But he wouldn't stop it. Bobby's teeth came down mightily, his jaws crunched. He chewed and swallowed the entire mushroom – dirt and all – in a matter of seconds. It was gone.

'—*Jesusfuckingchrist!!*'

Joseph, still in the bog, flopped forward as far as he could, trying desperately to stick a hand into Bobby's mouth, make him vomit, scrape out what was left. Couldn't do it. The mud at his feet pulled him back into the sinkhole. So he hollered for his brothers. They looked up. Saw Joseph's arms signalling frantically.

But Bobby was waving, too . . . and laughing.

The others waved back and went on culling berries.

Joseph was staggered. Numb. He caught his breath only slowly. Calmed a little. Thought. His brother must have been trying to get a rise out of him. Poisonous buds? *Some fucking joke.*

'Were those *amanitas* in fact, you fat asshole? Were they?'

Bobby sat unable as a mystic.

'*Were* they or *not*?'

'I don't know, JoJo.'

The truth? Joseph fixed hard on his brother.

'I really don't know. It might've been one of those bad

angels . . . there's some around, for sure. Looked more like *phalloides*, though, which makes you sicker than shit, gets you dancing and gyrating, but you don't always die, they say . . . or maybe not . . . maybe it was just a nice, fucko little snack.'

And Joseph knew his brother was telling him straight.

Holy God.

Bobby had eaten the mushroom without certain knowledge it was safe . . . with even a fair suspicion it was one of a lethal species. He was hazarding his life. *Might die.*

'*Why* . . . why, Bobby?'

'You wanted to know why we're in the mountain and you're not. Now you know, kiddo.'

Now he knew. His brothers were genuine, but gone. To the country of the mad.

And what else had they done in their madness? What could they remember?

'Did you guys first find Carmen with my Dad . . .? My Dad *alive*? Tell me. *Give me a piece of the truth.*'

'She just wandered into camp one day, as I remember.'

That didn't sound at all like the truth. 'I don't understand. Wandered in from where?'

'I wouldn't have a clue.'

'Alone? How? *Tell me.*'

'Don't know.'

'*Oh yes you do.*'

For over a week all of Joseph's brothers had sidestepped every question that might have helped him recover his father's final tracks. Joseph had been kidding himself that it was their ignorance of what had happened blotting out the facts. He had been wrong. It was their cunning. *Conspired cunning.*

They were orchestrating the whole thing. They weren't going to tell him anything at all.

'You're hiding something from me, you guys . . . all of you.' He was sure of it, sure as stone.

Bobby hoisted himself up, belly and all. Unflappable Bobby, who might be dead by midnight. 'Mountain's getting to you, kiddo. Better make your move downhill soon. Heavy weather's on its way . . . any day, maybe.' He put out

314

a hand. 'Why don't you get out of that hole?' He kept out his hand even though Joseph wouldn't take it, pointing with his other arm at the rest of their brothers congregating in the middle of the field, near to where Carmen was stretched out, and around several large, bark kettles they had carried down from their valley home. 'C'mon, Little Joe. We had a good morning, got plenty of spuds. Now we're gonna teach you the Indian recipe for fruitcake. C'mon.'

'No.' Joseph wasn't doing anything with them anymore. He was in revolt.

'C'mon.'

'I don't want to know about your fruitcake. I want you to talk to me about something that matters.'

'Food matters,' Bobby said, pulling back his hand. Then he walked away towards the others. 'Hope you get out of that hole. It'd be the wrong spot to spend the winter.'

They began to set up their cooking gear. Joseph didn't want to watch them but he was facing their way. The bog was cool. He didn't need to move. So he watched reluctantly.

First they constructed a platform for the two kettles. That done, both pots were raised onto the sticks with conduits leading from their bottoms to smaller, flat vessels, also of spruce bark. Bright service berries were crushed first, afterwards loaded into one of the kettles. Hundreds of pounds of them. Then the soapberries, which when mashed foamed a startling rose colour. Carmen, barely able to stand up, had found the strength to make a fire, from which Thomas plucked hot stones and added them to the kettles, boiling the berries in their own juices. The heated fruit mash was pressed down continuously until all the liquid remaining ran out the conduits. Once the juice was extracted they kneaded the residue and spread it in thin layers over hurdles of willow so that they could expose the fruit to the sun and air. Finally they sprinkled the toughening cakes with juice until everything coagulated into a kind of meatless pemmican of a certain thickness.

Indian fruitcake.

And, for a final savour, the cakes were glazed with honey which Douglas had stolen from wasp nests in the woods.

They worked faster and faster as the afternoon wore on, racing the day, running before the season . . . pricked on equally by the joy of hard labour and memories of the winter they had passed.

When they had completely done, the five brothers took off their moccasins. Their bodies red with berry juice, they began frisking, wrestling at first and soon after crushing uncooked berries on each other, some of the load for the next day's bake. Douglas took one of the honeycombs and smeared its waxy liquor on himself first, then on all of them, in their hair, chests, genitals.

Tired as they were, welted all over with countless insect bites, they seemed to delight in wasting a little of their harvest, as if mocking the cold to come, a moment of unrestrained holiday in an otherwise sombre year.

Their play wore them down fast enough. They drew into a huddle. Joseph, whose thoughts had been drifting, his back bronzing under the last rays of summerlight, saw them looking his way. He stiffened.

Eric pulled a small corner off one of the cakes and walked over towards where Joseph was resting. The others marched behind. Bobby was carrying a cup of grouse fat.

'Pass me that.' Eric pointed to the cup.

Bobby did. Eric dipped the cake into the fat, the traditional way to eat the pemmican.

'It's not completely dry, Joe, but give this a taste. At least you'll get an idea of what we eat.'

'One fine bonbon, little buddy.'

All of them were looking at Joseph as if his judgement mattered.

'Go ahead and taste it. It won't hurt you.' Eric waved the cake under Joseph's nose.

'No.'

'We'd like you to.'

'I won't eat that shit.'

Their shadows loomed over him in the ditch. They were grinning in an odd way; something he didn't understand came into their eyes.

'You have to do like the rest of us. While you're here, at

316

least.' Eric tickled Joseph's moustache with the pemmican. 'You'll eat our food, you will.'

Nevermind that Joseph had done already, and for many days, without asking questions accepting most everything in their roughed-out lives. But things had changed. *'No.'*

'How you gonna get out of that muskeg, JoJo?'

Bobby's question had a razor on its back.

Without taking any care, Joseph had simply crawled into the bog and lay against its side. He hadn't made any determined effort to get out because he hadn't wanted to get out. A tickle of fear passed up and down him now. He pushed gently with his feet to raise himself from the bottom—

—there was no bottom.

Joseph's hands clutched the roots and adventitious veins inside the lip of the ditch. While his brothers watched he struggled to hoist himself up by his arms. Couldn't. All that happened was that he sank a few inches lower in the heavy water.

He breathed out a moan.

Then started to panic. Thrashed for a moment. Knew that was exactly the wrong thing to do and just in time he dug his nails into the soft, black walls of the ditch . . . held . . . held ferociously for his life.

While his brothers looked on. Indifferently. Indifferent to life or death, ready for either—

'Get me out—!!'

—They bent over the muskeg, all hands extended . . . Joseph gulping on water, splashing and sinking . . .

. . . fumbling wildly for any hand, got it, got one . . . Mark's hand, fingers like reeds, he hooped it with his own and held on as they caught his other arm, waist . . . a leg up. . . then all of him pulled clear of the water and out, high in the air and then down gently on the bunch grass of the meadow.

'Eat.'

He wouldn't.

'Eat or back in the bog!'

He bit into the cake and chewed and chewed and chewed, some of the paste dribbling down his chin but the moiety he swallowed.

317

They got down on their hands and knees to brush away the moss and leaves sticking to Joseph's nakedness. Then, without needing to speak, they carried him over to the river and threw him in to clean off the stink which had soaked into him over the hours, jumping in themselves right after. For there was the stinging crust of fruit and honey matted in their hair, all over them, and it had finally begun to irritate them.

They, too, had been hot, had laboured past exhaustion. They had a right to the bath. It was the end of a hard day.

Joseph jumped out of the water and onto the bankside.

'*We're not done!*' he yelled.

They looked up at him from where they were bathing.

'Everybody get out.'

It was the moment he had been waiting for. Perhaps the only chance he'd get.

He ran to where he had hidden a small bark pouch he'd carried down the mountain. Inside were his seeds. He pulled out a fistful of the packets and held them high. They didn't understand. So he flung one of the packets at Eric, who caught it before it floated away in the current.

'Things don't just grow by chance. *Remember?*'

Eric studied the writing. It was the first he had seen in over two years, having sworn off reading Mark's herbals, which were incomprehensible anyway. '"*Romaine lettuce*"?' He threw the seeds back at his brother. 'Growing season's over. What's the matter with you?'

'We're going to plant this stuff. All of it.'

'Joe, there's a freeze coming. No time to make a head of lettuce an inch across, if that. Save your seeds.'

'For what?'

'Spring.'

'*Spring!* And would you plant them then?'

Joseph dragged his brothers out of the water, one by one. He was frantic.

'What's this all about, Joe?'

'Would you plant these seeds if I left them?' he reiterated, even more vehemently.

'We gather and hunt. We don't plant.'

'You're going to now.' He reached into the bark wallet

318

and scooped every package out, dumped them on the Chilcotin earth. 'Celery, carrots, and a lot of winter stuff, cabbage . . . we can try the cabbage . . . broccoli, Brussels sprouts—'

'—*We don't plant.*' Mark's face was black.

'*WE ALWAYS PLANTED* . . . it was the one thing that mattered . . . it kept us alive . . . kept us together!'

Eric laid an arm on his baby brother, a soft arm, but Joseph threw it off.

'You're afraid to try, is what. *All of you.* Afraid to remember some of the good things that went down when we were kids . . . *Christ*, there were a few good things, you know!'

'All that's long gone.'

He stood up to Eric, his eyes but inches from the big man's, Joseph raised on his toes and refusing to flinch from the hard questions he was determined to ask. 'You remember our mother? Well *I do* and I was only six when she died. She toiled away her whole life trying to teach us how to help things grow . . . and that what matters is *you keep on nourishing, baby, you keep on until you die!!* That was all the light she made, but the only thing you *fuckers* can think about is figuring out ways to snuff it. *I don't.* I got kids and a wife. *I remember my mother!* How come you can't . . . ?'

'We remember, Joe.'

'*Then show me!!*' he screamed. But it was more in supplication than anger. 'Come on!' Joseph grabbed several of the root diggers and tossed them at his brothers. 'These'll do for spades. Let's lay out a plot. A couple of hundred row feet to start. There's water right here. The soil's rich as delta country . . . rich as the fucking Nile. C'mon. All of us. *Together.* We can do it.'

He waited. He could hear their muffled indecision, none of them sure what to do . . . a slack moment, everything poised to go one way or the other, like a tide that was changing, that might ebb or flood, carry them out of the mountain or drown them forever in it.

'*We can do it.*'

'G-g-gimme that!' Thomas reached for one of the diggers.

Joseph's heart was leaping. If Thomas helped, they would all help.

But Thomas didn't stoop to till the mountain soil. Instead he threw the digger end over end far away into the bunch grass, where it would be near impossible to find. His thin lips were blanched and foaming. 'A g-g-garden's wasted work . . . stupid f-fucking w-w-w-w-w-waste of time!'

'Thomas . . .!'

'NO!'

Joseph reeled in the dying heat. He wouldn't believe it. His brother Thomas, *gentle* Thomas, had been the inheritor of their mother's garden graces. He was the one they always trusted, who did the hybrids, cut the scions, replanted, healed. He had pruned, nourished, gently gathered. The rest of his brothers had moved the earth, watered . . . weeded.

'There are seeds for flowers here, too, nasturtium, daisies, pansies—'

'—We've got fucking wildflowers ev-ev-everywhere!'

And with that said, Thomas jerked away, slapped at the black fly with his mitted wrist, and went towards the fire that would roast their dinner and that he must rekindle.

The others followed silently.

They weren't going to fool with a garden. And Joseph's heart sank. It was over for them. They would never get out of the mountain.

Douglas was the last brother to go, but Joseph stopped him before he could get away.

'How about you? What've you got so important to do that you can't give me a hand?'

'I'm tired as shit, Joe.'

'So am I. *So what?*' He could see Douglas was about to start whining. 'Then how about just watching me? Too tired for that?'

'O.K. . . . I'll watch.'

'Sit down, buster.'

Joseph helped his numbskull brother to a place, on a small mound of dirt, and then, marking out an area about ten foot by ten, he began turning up the soil like a man possessed.

With his brother sitting on the molehill and gaping on, Joseph drove the dirt flying, broke the hardpan clogs, slung out the larger stones, pulled up weeds, softened the ground, sweetened it. The day crept away. An orange sundown spread over the sky. The bugs bit and bit, worst right at the sun's fall, but he paid no mind. He cut his hands, stubbed his toes, and over the course of his labours gritted away every single fingernail down to the quick, where microscopic bits of dirt had lodged themselves painfully and which would take months to work themselves out.

He continued long after the sun had set, helped by the light of the nearby fire. And the perfect moon.

A half-dozen rows. Straight. Well-furrowed. Those rocks he hadn't yet removed he would clear away in the morning. The last thing he did was to push seeds into the moist soil – the carrot and radish rows he had watered deeply before. The other rows he sprinkled once the earth was closed over the seeds. Holy water. Baptism. That particular spot of ground had never known the thaumaturgical powers of the human hand and spirit.

In the middle of the night he quit.

He had made a garden and it was not only done, it was neatly done.

With his last grain of energy Joseph looked up to see every one of his brothers asleep, Douglas, too, still sitting right over the seedplot, having not moved at all, and the ducks they had left to roast on the fire never eaten and by now entirely charred, the fire itself only embers as his brothers slept naked under the cold stars and snored, oblivious to what he'd done.

He turned again to his handiwork. It was an image of the *Good* to be counterpoised against everything wretched in his brothers' lives. Though they didn't know it, Joseph had made the garden for them. They slept.

Also he had made the garden as a kind of memorial to his parents, whom he thought of every day in the mountains with increased sharpness. His poor, benighted brothers, who had so much life, like seedlings themselves, gutsy men, once so rich in feelings, they lived on the edge of darkness now and couldn't remember anything that mattered – not·father, not mother. All they knew was to imagine themselves as wolves and marten, elk, birds and bear.

Well, he had done his best to remind them. He had tried. At least he had got something in the ground, some hope.

So, *praised be.* He left it at that.

Desperately tired and now beginning to feel it, Joseph found a natural bed in the turf, in a different quadrant of the meadow from where his brothers lay. His body was hard-lacquered with the sweat of his toil but he didn't bother washing, just covered himself as best he could and closed his eyes.

Slept heavily.

Sometime in the early hours, the moon down but before dawn, he awoke to the sounds of something – man or beast – yawping in the fields. At first he thought it was a dog scratching for bones. But the cries were unnatural, unlike anything he had ever heard.

Through the obscuring darkness Joseph saw an outline, a huge bucking form, not one of the camp dogs, as they had been left in the valley camp, but a beast five times the size of any dog, larger than a man, rising and falling rhythmically against the night sky, rooting and grubbing at the newly planted seeds in the garden. It chewed the dirt, slurped rocks and weeds, with its snout thrashed at the narrow rows Joseph had made, grunting as it worked, slavering, hissing, its movements ghostlike as it rose on its rear legs like a man, almost standing, swaying back and forth as if it were chanting or praying . . . or sexually groping its way forward to where Carmen was sleeping—

—Joseph blinked in fear.

The creature's silhouette seemed to melt indistinguishably into the night.

He blinked again.

Then opened his eyes fully. To his astonishment it was daylight. The sun well-advanced in the sky. And his brothers already off in the field culling berries, rosehips, mushrooms, more of the camras root.·

The fruitcake? Had they drugged him the day before? Tucked a little of Bobby's mushroom inside the pemmican? Or had he just dreamed the bucking dog by himself, his brain overflowing with the kind of natural terrors his brothers found all the time in the mountains?

322

There was no way to know. The turf bed under him was undisturbed. It would seem Joseph had been in the thickest of dreams all night long and hadn't shifted once, not got up, not heard the strange braying.

But he just wouldn't believe the whole thing had been his imagining.

Maybe it wasn't.

Joseph ran to the garden.

The rows were exactly as he had seen them in the nightmare, pushed over, footprints up and down each one, every row carefully turned out so that the seeds were now open to the air for birds to peck at and thieve. Not animal markings. No dog or wolf or cloven-footed beast had been there. The prints were entirely human. And much smaller than he had expected. It had been Carmen. Her fingers and hands were delicately engraved in the dirt.

Carmen had plundered the garden entirely by herself. Even with her fever. She was as mad as his brothers. And as unable to bear an image of human prosperity.

No doubt there would be a story why she had done it. And a story lying behind that one, how she came to be alone with his brothers and part of their unspeakably grim life when she should have been with her husband, Joseph's father, struggling to get out of the mountain. She, too, was concealing something terrible, Carmen just like his brothers, under the same shroud.

The beast walking at night was guilt itself, the hound of heaven.

For the very first time since deciding to come see his brothers, Joseph was beginning to suspect that the circumstances of his father's death, when plainly revealed, might cry out for a justicer. He doubted now that his father's gracious, white, lionlike head had been peaceably laid on the funeral bed. There were, indeed, perturbed spirits swirling in the mountain air.

Horrible thoughts . . . but Joseph could hide from them no longer.

Well . . .? And if it were so that his worst suspicions proved true? Why then some hand would have to swing the heavenly sword of retribution. Vengeance must come, and ferociously. It always did. *But what would happen*, he wondered, *if the only hand left to swing the sword were his own?* Would he do it? Or leave Carmen and his brothers to the mountain?

Shadows passed over the broken clumps of the garden's dark soil. Joseph looked up. A fast-moving weather front was coming in. The temperature had dropped twenty degrees from yesterday. Winter? The first snow? He almost hoped so. For he was beginning to lose a little strength . . . some of the conviction about why he'd bothered coming into the mountains in the first place. He even mused on the idea of mounting the gelding and galloping down to Ted Nethercott's without stop. Back to his own precious family. Back to the tribulations and joys of everyday life.

But an unholy cry from Carmen beat away any thoughts he had about leaving. The mountain hadn't broken him yet . . . not yet.

CHAPTER 25

'She's a lot worse.' Eric looked worried.

'So?'

'She's got to be close to delirium.'

Mark was unmoved. 'Nature has its own remedies. Besides, we don't have much time for cures. There's fish to get, remember?'

'I said she's delirious, and I fucking well want you to do something about it.'

Around noon it had hailed, in fist-sized stones, driving the brothers out of the field and under tree cover. Mark, having taken his own tree, sat over his herbal, preparing a poultice of young skunk cabbage for Douglas's ever-roughening skin. 'You don't have any confidence in this Indian medicine, so why ask me?'

'Try and think of something. Cool her down, at least.'

324

'Cold water's the best thing for that.' Mark looked up. 'You can try something yourself. Crush some needles of white pine and put them against her temples.'

'What's that supposed to do?'

It was an old Ojibway cure for a headache. 'Exactly like I said, you don't believe in my medicine.'

Carmen's gibberings could be heard from anywhere in the meadow, an anguish worse than fear. Eric straightened up. '*You find something . . . .!*' Then he stormed away smelling his hands, which had picked up a stink from just touching Carmen.

'You really do hate her, don't you?' Joseph, who'd been crouching unseen in a corner of his mutilated garden, came forward. He hadn't spoken to his brothers all morning.

'She doesn't belong here.'

'And you five do, I suppose?'

The raven pulled some spruce gum from one of his bark jars and began to chew on it. It had kept his teeth white for years. The others had given it up long before. 'I don't hate her. I don't care about her at all, one way or another, except that I'd like her to get out of here.'

'Ever since I can remember, you've hated women. Why?'

Mark didn't answer, just continued grinding his simples.

'What did women ever do to you to make you so fucking bitter? I guess you planned this whole thing up here so there would be no women around . . . just you and the boys and the Hemingway life.' Joseph crossed his legs Indian-style. 'So what do you guys do for sex, eh? Brother buggery, is it? Like monks?'

'Sure. We like manfucking.'

'Or is it animals you go after?'

Mark's eyes gloated in the broken sunshafts coming through afternoon showers. 'Who says we don't get what we want up here? Who says all of us haven't fucked her?' In triumph he nodded towards Carmen, lying under a skirt of trees and being tended to by Eric. She was sweating plenteously. 'You don't know what's gone on here . . . so don't talk about what you don't know.'

'She's my father's wife.' There was a gravelly menace in Joseph's voice.

Mark accidentally spilled part of his store of wild rose seeds, disgustedly poked in the grass for what he could salvage. 'Joseph, do us all a favour. Do *yourself* a favour. Get out of here. Get on your horse and ride right off this mountain.' He rubbed his eyes, sore again, sore all the time since he'd broken his glasses the year before. 'Perhaps women like you, Joe, they always have as I remember. You're an unusual guy, you understand? There aren't many like you. Maybe it's your good fortune, maybe your temperament. All I know is that every pain I've suffered in my life can be traced back to some goddamned bitch or other. That's the way most men live their lives . . . quiet and desperate and really wanting to take some bitch by the throat and squeeze until her windpipe snaps like a chicken's.'

'What woman drove you into the mountains?'

Flurries of hail battered the trees. 'They *all* did.'

'Well you assholes can't blame them for the pain you've made for yourselves living like this.'

'What pain? Hunger isn't pain. It's a condition of life – a *natural* condition. So is sleeping cold. So is a little gum rot.'

'Illusions, brother, that's all.'

'Shit, Joe . . . you don't know a thing, really you don't. You've been here almost two weeks and you still don't know what keeps us together.'

'I've been here only ten days.'

'O.K. . . . ten days.' Raven sighed. 'We never talk much in camp. You don't seem to have noticed that, either. You're a real disappointment. Hey, look, let's cut it off. I've got work.'

'*Making fucking herbal teas?*' Joseph hadn't been speaking rancorously, but he felt himself losing control. 'You five are going to kill yourselves. And you all know it.'

'Yeah, well then we'll die.'

'All I can see is you've piled up a lot of garbage in some mountain valley and built a couple of hovels and some kind of lean-to, leaky saunas and—'

'—You're making wind, man!' Mark crushed and crushed in his mortar. 'Some of this stuff took me months to find. Stop blowing!!'

326

'Anything that takes real craft to make that crazy old Chilcotin steals for you. What you gonna do when the Indian decides he's tired of saving your asses . . .? or Thomas gets his other hand bitten off by a bear?'

But Black Mark wasn't going to be distracted from his book. He was too busy learning how the Haida had cauterized the nerves of abscessed teeth with a sharp flint-stone. Rocking back and forth like an Oriental scholar he read his own chosen scripture.

'Most of you have scurvy.'

'A few cupfuls of rosehips cures that, doc.'

'In the meantime you're losing teeth and gums and who knows what the hell else.'

'Natural state of things . . . the body slowly dies, you know.'

'*Natural?* Like that rot creeping all over Douglas?'

'That's eczema and he'd have it anywhere . . . country or town.'

'It's *not* just eczema, goddamnit. He's got something a lot worse . . . chronic vitamin deficiency or something.'

Mark's eyes flashed. 'That's his own fucking fault. He's been told repeatedly what to eat . . . every day for years.' A mosquito, taking advantage of the calm, the brief storm passing, probed Mark's knuckles and started to suck blood. Mark saw it and drove it purple, right into the bosom of Abraham. 'What's your prescription? The junk food that nearly killed him in L.A.?'

'That's not the point.'

'*Well what the fuck is your point?*' Mark's voice, stuffed with self-righteousness, carried to the others, back again picking in the field.

'You're a moralist, Markie . . . but you're going to wind up breaking my brothers on your fine fucking moral points—!'

'—Fuck off!'

'I'm not going to fuck off. Douglas needs medical treatment that you can't give him.'

'Is that right?'

'I believe so.'

'And just what have you decided is wrong with him?'

327

'I'm not sure.'

'Well *I* am.' And Mark *was* sure.

'What?'

'He's got syphilis.'

Joseph rolled back onto his thighs, utterly stunned, knocking over Mark's bottles as he fell. 'You're just saying this—'

'—He's *got* syphilis.'

'How long have you known?'

'A while.'

'Does *he* know?'

'No. None of them do.' Mark's brows went straight for a moment. 'Thomas might have his suspicions . . . but he doesn't say anything.'

'And you . . .? You say nothing, either?' Joseph pushed away the web of disbelief forming and re-forming in front of his sad and easy eyes. '. . . and just let him stay here – *untreated* – while the thing crawls slowly up to his brain . . .?'

'*I'm a real prick, aren't I?*'

There was a long silence between the two men.

Then Mark closed his book, a reed against the binding to keep his place. 'You know there are *native* remedies for almost everything that ails us. I'm learning these preparations fucking well, I am, and once the rest of them trust completely in the efficacy of the herbs then the medicine will have a chance to work.' He paused, saw Joseph's head shaking unconsciously. 'What's the matter? Think it's all a little far out? But I'll bet you believe all that shit about microbes and viruses and allopathic medicine, don't you . . .? *You* who won't believe in animal spirits.'

If there were words to speak his feelings, Joseph didn't know them. Maybe Mark, of his five suffering brothers, needed love the most of all.

'Markie . . . are you telling me you're going to try to cure Douglas's syphilis with your herbs?'

'Not exactly cure it.'

'What . . . *exactly?*'

'I'll find a way to get rid of the secondary symptoms.'

'But they're going to go away anyhow! In the meantime you're playing around with his life!!'

'*What* life?'

'*HIS* life, Mark . . . not yours but his!'

'What life would you save your brother, Douglas, for? His mind was burnt out years ago. It was because of him that we came up here in the first place! He didn't get into trouble from things up here, you know. Given the chances he had in the city this is the best life for him – maybe the *only* life for him – *scabies and lice and ticks and mites and wind and rain and ice and blisters and sores and hunger and pain and syphilis and madness and all!!!*'

Joseph's hands crept up to his brother's face and held Mark's long chin in his fingers, smoothing the hairs of Raven's beard. 'It's you who wants to stay, Markie. I know you love Douglas, love all of us, but I don't know what to say except that it's *you, you* who needs to believe it'll kill Douglas if he comes down off this mountain and it's *you* who keeps everybody up here, finding ways to make them think you're all on some holy voyage . . . they don't leave but every last one of them is desperate to get out . . . *every last one.*'

'You don't know shit, friend.'

'Oh yes I do . . . oh *yes* I do.' Joseph dropped his hands from Mark's beard and looked right into the perpetual shadow that covered Mark's face. 'Yesterday Bobby ate mushrooms he thought could kill him. For no particular reason.'

Mark said nothing.

'That's madness, Markie. Not just fooling around . . . not play-acting . . . certifiable madness.'

'Well, we're blood mad, brother. And let me tell you something – it sharpens the mind. We're not afraid to be sick or pained or hungry or lonely . . . or crazy. We feel things and see things you'll never know. Not just because we're in the mountains, either. It's always been like that. You've been outside it so you don't know. Call it what you want but it must be a kind of love, something people in that shit world under the mists only have dim intimations of. Everything is sharper . . . fiercer. I don't want anything else in my life except that feeling. None of us do. It's the physical-ness of things that we like, the intensity. That's why we

329

wouldn't ever leave here and why you can stop trying to make us. *How come you can't see?* Everything here is so cold and hard and dead and empty and so fuckingly, *staggeringly* beautiful . . . the five of us in a useless valley, the five of us against everything else in the plenitude of things . . . all things . . . the sky and the weather and the rocks falling down on our heads and the birds we have to kill to eat and the ice and the insects that never leave us alone and that enormous fucking winter bear that's going to kill us one of these days if we can't find some way to kill him first. You've got it in your head that this is all my idea. Why don't you go ask the others? Ask them if they want to get out but that I make them stay, me and my stupid ideas. Go on! Go ask!' He waited for Joseph to bolt from their rain-cover, the hail beating only lightly. 'GO ON!!!'

But Joseph had stopped listening to his brother's words some moments before, hearing instead the beat of wings above the trees: His brother Mark's sense had flown. There was little Joseph could do but to love Mark in absence. 'I don't believe what you say . . . I just don't believe it . . . .'

An absolute stillness fell on them both.

A peace of sorts had been made.

Again Mark took up the herbal in his long hands and sat straight over his preparations. 'Someday I'm going to want you to read the log I've kept of everything that's happened to us. It's almost been written for you to read.'

'I'm your witness, am I?'

'I suppose.'

'Then witness something for me. You're all hiding the facts about Dad's death. I almost don't even *care* anymore what the truth is, I just want to know it. Give it to me straight. How did he die?'

Mark's lips closed together.

'You have to tell me, Mark.'

'Talk to Eric.'

'I'm asking you.'

'Don't.'

'I know there's something of him left. I've actually thought I heard his voice telling me so, if you can believe it –

330

starting back in Los Angeles. Maybe it's not the old man's ghost that can't sleep until these obsequies are done but just me who's got insomnia. I need to know what's what.'

'Well, you know what you know.'

'Did a bear kill my father? A simple *yes* or *no*!'

Mark's face was as empty as the mountain. 'No, a bear didn't kill your father.'

AT LAST.

'I didn't think so.'

Then Raven crushed flowers in his hand and arrayed himself in the most malignant smile Joseph had ever seen. 'No, it wasn't a bear that killed our father . . . *your* father . . . no bear.'

'What did?'

'A wolf.'

'JESUS GOD!!'

And the hail finally stopped.

CHAPTER 26

The whole sky had turned incarnadine, one single shade of flesh-red. All the brothers except Joseph sat around the fire in the evening's eeriness. Bats glided in the gory light, following currents of air that blew down from the mountain-top and feasting on the insects that swarmed over the camp.

Closest to the fire, Mark squatted over Carmen's shit, prodding it with a stick and looking for signs. He had been threshing the faeces and casting the water of each one of them. Carmen's excrement was different.

'Plague.' He whispered his diagnosis over the bat squeaks.

Breathing stopped. A florid-faced Eric leaned towards his brother. 'For sure?'

'Yes.'

'There's nothing else it could be?'

331

'It's plague and it's not plague.'

'Speak clearly, goddamn you!'

Even before Mark had sequestered Carmen all of the others had noticed her scratching a small pimple on her hand. Such things happened to them all the time. Her extreme agitation they hadn't regarded, either. Then the pimple had grown, finally turning into a much more substantial knot that quickly ulcerated. Which was when Mark separated her from the others.

Each day during the harvest she had grown paler, overcome by paroxysms of vomiting. She couldn't even hold down broth. The fever had soared beyond measurement, headache pressing in on her skull as if her head were collapsing. She was unable to move at all. And was, as Eric had seen, delirious.

For all the world they believed she had come down with the same fever that had wasted Eric so badly during the spring. It was not a mortal sickness – at least hadn't been for him. Then, during their trip back up the mountain from the harvest grounds, Mark had discovered a new symptom he hadn't seen before: Up Carmen's golden arm from the ulcer her lymph glands had tumesced into enormous balls. Worse. The balls had gone hard. And still worse. They had turned red and pustular, the colour of the evening sky. On the journey up one had broken open and begun discharging. Seeing that, Mark had asked himself if it weren't possibly . . . just possibly . . . a *bubo*.

Immediately on their return he had put her into her sweatbox.

'. . . plague or *not*? What are you saying?'

'I think it's a form of plague . . . similar kind of thing, anyhow. Called something like "*tularemia*".'

Eric's arms, big hands, waved in the air ignorantly. 'That doesn't mean anything to me.'

'It's got a pet name.'

'What's that?'

' "*Rabbit Fever*".' Mark rolled all the shit in front of him indiscriminately towards the dunghill. 'You get it from cleaning rabbits that are infected . . . in a bite or cut or any kind of open wound. Or from breathing the dust during skinning. There's a kind ticks carry, too.'

'All right, all right.' Eric smelled his hands, as he had been doing for days.

'You won't get it from her, if that's what's worrying you.'

Eric's thoughts were somewhere else, stalking other prey.

'She gonna die, Marko?'

'Probably not.' Mark's nostrils were flaring. 'She might, though.'

Bobby rolled his belly onto a log to keep pressure on his tapeworm's head . . . or so he thought. 'What you gonna do to help save our lady?'

'Nothing, fat man.'

'Shut up both of you.'

The bats returned, as if to fill up the silence. The day was nearly smothered but the colour in the sky wouldn't fade from red, though it grew a darker shade. Eric brooded.

'What's wrong with the stuff that helped me last spring?'

'It was a fake . . . placebo—'

'—just like everything up here!' Joseph, surprising them, called from a perch amongst the rocks, the same ledge from where Carmen had watched the brothers during her first weeks in their camp. For three days now he had refused all contact with his brothers, had kept apart from them and didn't eat.

'What's he doing up there?' Eric asked the others. But they, like Eric, hadn't taken any notice of Joseph's disaffection. 'Get down here.'

Joseph came far enough forward to fall inside the band's firelight. 'I'm taking her to Williams Lake.'

'Sit down here with us.'

'The horse is strong. If I start before sunrise I'll get her to Chezacut by night . . . some way.'

'You're not going anywhere. Sit *down*, I said.' The wolf was losing patience.

'She may be dying.'

'She's not dying.' Mark pointed to the chair where Joseph was going to have to sit. 'Eric had the same thing.'

Eric was sceptical. 'She's a fucking lot sicker than I ever was.'

'It's the *same* disease.'

'You sure?'

'You keep asking that, *goddamnit*!' Mark caught Joseph's shadow creeping towards Carmen's sauna. 'Would you tell that idiot little brother of ours to keep his ass away from her?'

Before Eric could nod, Bobby was already on his feet and had an arm stopping Joseph's progress. 'Better sit down, little buddy.'

'I'm going to take her down because you bastards will kill her otherwise – if not with this fever then with something else. Kill yourselves if you want to, not her.' He pushed Bobby's restraining arm violently away. '*Not her!*'

'All right you've said your bit, now sit down and shut up.'

'*NOT HER—*'!'

'*—I SAID SHUT YOUR FUCKING MOUTH!!!*' Eric's eyes were immense green pools that could have swallowed whole seas. He turned to Mark again. 'What can you do for her with your herbs?'

'*He can't do anything!*'

Raven ignored his little brother's frenzy. 'I don't know what I can do.'

'—because *he* doesn't believe in his own shitting witch-craft, either!'

The wolf's arm was rising in judgement. 'Shut him up!'

'—that goddamn herbal medicine of his is a shuck—!'

'—BIND HIM!!'

'*Everything* here is a shuck. You all know it, don't have the balls to face it—!'

But Joseph could only dribble his truths into the dirt, he spit and sputtered as Bobby rolled right over him, holding him down by the neck while Thomas tied cords tightly around both Joseph's wrists and ankles.

'Sit him up!'

The two warders did that.

'Rip his shirt off!'

That was done.

The wolf glared. 'If you want, there are more painful ways to make sure you keep down . . . now you want that? Or are you gonna shut up?'

'I don't care what you do to me.'

'Stuff his mouth!'
'You won't shut me up, you fucking bas—!!'
'—CUT HIS CHEST!!!!'

The blades came screaming out of the red sky and jabbed into Joseph. They yerked cords against his ribs, through his chest muscles, just as they had done to Bobby.

They were rising against him.

They moved him close to the fire where the heat tightened his bonds and boiled the blood oozing out of his wounds until the blood turned crisp as it dripped down his sides. Joseph had found his pain.

Real pain.

His head drooped. He was barely conscious. The pain blinded and killed.

'What that little shit said is right, you know.' Mark pointed to his prostrate brother.

The others didn't understand, grunted in confusion. Night was falling, the sky violet.

'It's what the fucking bunch of you believe yourselves . . . oh yeah . . . every single one of you shits.'

'Don't blather.'

'You still reckon like him that the real stuff is down there in Williams Lake. Oh, you'll take what I give you, from time to time. When the smoke of the fire gets a little too much for you in winter you know I've got a good native soak for your eyes. Some of my smoke gives you a nice high, so that's O.K., too. And that compound for swellings. You do it all to please me, humour me . . . right?' He spit into the fire. 'Well forget doing me such favours. Go and pretend that if we only had that one can of Cutter's bug spray the goddamn shitting insects would get back to kissing deer cunts and leave us alone. Of course you'll still use my oil, won't you? But the truth is you think the Indians were just a bunch of savages, innocents, no science, no learning, nothing worth knowing about—' Mark put a hand to his quivering lips. 'It's all just mumbo jumbo, right? *Right . . .!*'

'Then you tell us what else it is.'

The raven sneered. His brothers no longer observed the careful rules for living which the Chilcotin had scratched on the mountain stones after living more generations in their valley than the Jews had dreamed of Israel. He had cried havoc, had Mark, had warned them from the moment they'd embarked on the trip up the mountain that their world would roll away unless they braced it with the rocks of belief. Countless times he had reminded them they had to *make* their life . . . and remake it and remake it and remake it *every day*. And just when they were beginning to cast aside the old world for their new one of ice and stone and truth . . . the old man had come up from the city. With his woman. His motherfucking stupid brothers had let the woman stay, instead of slaughtering her right along with that oozing-eyed, lecherous, milk-livered father of theirs. 'Well, now she's sick. Well, well, well. Almost comatose. Well, well. Maybe it's her *karma*.'

'*You're dreaming.*'

'Yeah, you're too fucking right I am.'

The wolf pointed hard towards the sweatbox. 'The *woman* . . . what about the *woman*?'

'You guys know everything, don't you? What cures and what doesn't? Good. Go ahead and keep her from sinking into a coma – which I-shit-you-not she is very close to right now. She probably won't die, like I say . . . but she might . . . she just might after all. She sure *is* a lot worse than Eric seemed to be, and the fever's got a ways to run yet, I do believe.'

'But you can't do anything *anyhow*. You've as much as said that.' The wolf was growing vexed with his brother, too. 'In fact the little asshole was speaking the truth – even *you* don't believe in your herbs.'

'I believe. And, what's more, they work.'

'Not for anything serious.'

'For anything at all.'

'How about for "Rabbit Fever", Marko?'

The tall man tried shutting out their jeers and japes. But the others weren't going to leave him alone.

'All right, so what can you do for the lady? We keep coming back to that, don't we? *What can you do?*'

'Lots.'

'I don't believe you, Ace.' Even Bobby was getting angry.

'Try me.'

Eric suddenly jumped up, pointing towards the cedar closet where Carmen was dead asleep. 'I'm tired of the talk! *Show us!*'

All the brothers were poised. The moment had been years in coming, since the first frames of their mountain refuge had flickered in Mark's head. All the faces cluttering around Eric's were challenging for proof of Mark's mysteries.

'*REAL* proof this time!' Eric was screaming.

Either Mark could show his herbs' power and efficacy or their whole voyage to the top of the world was a weak and slippery dream . . . *one dead father later*.

'*SHOW US!!*' They were all screaming it. Over and over.

Mark waited for a pause in their chorus. He found one.

'Bring her out.'

It was hard to tell if Carmen were conscious. They set her down on a bed of boughs while Raven stripped off her tunic and wrapped her in a crazy cloak quilted of dog pelts. *Little Crazy Dog.*

As Mark kneeled down beside her he twisted painfully. A pebble had lodged itself under his heel and with his great claws he tried to crush it . . . then bit it. It was only a stone. The monster making Crazy Dog's disease could be anywhere – even in stones. One had to be cunning to find it and kill it. Raven was that.

'Let the fire die down a bit,' he said. 'Just sit here for a while and think . . . and pray.' His voice, normally clogged with melancholy, had an unaccustomed clarity, was free of all bitter impediments. It was the voice of someone who could imagine what it was like to be a bird . . . of someone who might fly. 'Breathe and pray.'

All eyes turned towards the fire, thoughts drifting away with the smoke . . . upwards into the air, the stars, the ether beyond, following the highway of the angels heavenwards.

'Keep your thoughts on your prayers for Crazy Dog to be strong again . . . strong and smooth and cool, cool like the stream that flows down our mountain . . . *tsatl* . . . *tsire nli* . . . *tho* . . . for there is nothing in this valley now but prayer

337

. . . gentle and smooth and cool prayer . . . prayer . . .
flowing over all of us . . . *tsire nli . . . tho* . . . smooth stream
flowing . . . smooth and flowing . . . smooth . . . *ntast hetl* . . .
sleeping . . . *ntast hetl* . . . .' All went still.

Into the shadows of the summer lodge the raven went to
get his potions. He stayed there some time. The fire
crackled in the occasional riff of wind while the moon came
up in crescent . . . night obscuring, shrouding the final
purple light of day. Cool. Fresh. Autumn night.

The brothers slept in prayer, all except Joseph who
despite the soul-searing pain was struggling to keep alert.
He believed Raven was going to kill the woman while the
others were benumbed in trance.

Flames of the fire had grown thin and wraithlike, fewer
and more meagre, until only a helix of smoke rose from the
bed of bright coals like serpents entwined, no flame at all
left.

Crazy Dog groaned on her bed. Lungs shallow. Joseph
had no doubt that she was dying. He hoped that at least she
would beat Mark's poison somehow, that at the end she
would take her own last breath and not let him steal it.

The sky had foretold everything. Blood evening it had
been . . . blood night it would be.

Forth from the shelter he came. *The raven.* Rattling.
Dancing. Singing. On one hand he wore a knuckle cover of
bones which he worked like castanets, while the rest of him
was hidden under ceremonial dress. He also had a stick, a
kind of bauble held in his free hand, a doll ruffed up in
raven feathers, beak and claws and tail and all, even eyes.
His bauble. His familiar. Raven pointed the bird at Carmen
as he rattled, danced, chanted to her the same several
words over and over and over with no change in the melody
or key though sometimes the song was loud and then
alternately softer.

Never too close to her, keeping his distance but slowly
approaching the bed, Raven circled around the entire
group as if ravelling them into a web, magic in the weave of
it . . . the magic of things as they are . . . *just as they are, not
understood but simply perceived in song.*

He changed the rhythm up-tempo, awakening the

sleepers. Little Bear tapped the log under him in time with Raven's feet . . . feet like bells as they were covered with tiny pods and shells from the rivers and sea inlets the other side of the mountains. The other brothers joined, too, all growing more alert, entranced still but woken to the feeling that had stitched their lives together for so many years . . . connectedness . . . bonds. Words came naturally to them, like men speaking in tongues, each man calling his familiar. Clapping now, and stamping feet, and melodious throats opened to songs of wonder and praise for all things and their sacred names –

    'Ses!'

       and *'Nesiny!'*

             and *'Tlen . . . deneita . . . tlen . . . deneita!'* descanted with zeal by the black bird coming closer to the prostrate dog . . . *dog . . . sick . . . dog . . . sick . . . tlen . . . deneita . . . tlen . . . deneita . . .*

                  . . . the raven carried forward not by his own singing but by all of them singing together, hearts open and from them a flood, a great estuarial surge of feeling . . .

                    . . . love and belief twinned together . . . .

Joseph, sodden, half of him lumped in his pain, was resisting the horde of ecstatic men. Sweat burning in his eyes. The heat of the fire, even though it had dampened, still scalded. His skin was at the ignition point, or so he felt it. His pulse had grown chaotic, breathing laboured and heavy, his brow suddenly thick with hysteria that rose out of some red corner inside him. His chest was entirely on fire. *They had cut him open.* His own brothers.

It was a fever he had, as absorbing as Carmen's. And Joseph's hand hurt, too, the same hand as hers that had pustulated, the exact same finger.

Something uncanny was going on. He seemed to be feeling Carmen's dolours – *just as she would be feeling them.*

Mustn't believe this.

Mental tricks, he kept reassuring himself, some kind of hypnosis Mark had on him . . . on all of them. Nothing more than that.

But Joseph's finger kept throbbing away, much worse, so that he forced himself in terrible pain to look down at his own hand. The index finger was as ulcerous and carbuncled as Carmen's. The sight horrified him. His own finger was pointing the way towards damnation, where all his ideas about the world were about to get jacked open—

—Pain sharper. *Her* pain . . . screwed and screwed and screwed tighter around his finger. He couldn't move any longer, not a muscle, the pain infinite and unspeakable, completely eclipsing the pain they'd given him when they had slashed his chest open . . . this an agony sufficient to make him scream while the heat rose around him, so that it felt like a river of fire rolling out of the mountain, flooded molten white and red over his head . . . forcing him to gag on words he couldn't get out of his throat . . . and yet . . . and yet and yet he now heard his brothers singing the same words, words he didn't understand, his brothers glittering in the night, molten themselves he could see, a horde of fire, the heat so choking and close that he felt some kind of attack was coming on, of epilepsy or some kind of possession that would make him swallow fire or bite off his tongue, which only the cloth stuffed in his mouth kept him from doing.

Or he might die of fright.

MUSTN'T BELIEVE THIS!!!

He was at the edge of the world and all that filled his head was Carmen's agony.

His eyes opened wider. Something had come into camp. He looked . . . looked.

And saw.

One of the dogs crept inside the peripheral ring of camp-fire rocks. Limping mongrel. Just as Carmen had limped. The bucking dog.

Rabid dog . . .

     . . . mad . . .

          . . . crazy. *Crazy.*

Oh Jesus Christ Oh Christ. Joseph knew what he was looking at. At Crazy Dog. Her double . . . *netsin.* He was looking at her soul, sick and wandering.

340

He who mocked ghosts was looking foursquare at her soul.

Shrieking, Carmen sprung up from her bed, hands whirling in front of her face as her cries carried all the way across the valley. Seeing her quicken, Raven now screamed, too, as if taking on her fever himself. '*N-shote . . . n-shote . . . n-shote!!!*'

Joseph heard the Chilcotin '*n-shote*' but understood it as 'give it to me'. He understood the Chilcotin by direct apprehension, without translation. There were voices in his head, his brothers' voices. Then he realized that it was the other way around:

He was inside their heads. Connected to them.

'*Watch me!*'

He did what the voices told him to do. He watched through Carmen's eyes. Just as they were all doing.

The black bird shuddered. The puppet in Raven's hands seemed to spread its wings and . . . yes . . . yes . . . pulling the man over the broken rocks towards Crazy Dog. Right through the air. Yes.

His brother was flying.

At Crazy Dog's side the raven dropped down to her and then lifted her finger to his lips and began to suck very hard. Healing lips. He sucked something right out of the wound . . . long and black . . . like a gigantic worm that had hidden itself in the papule. In the darkling light Raven sucked the whole worm out, winding his hands around it lest it come into him. He drew a great breath. And blew the black spirit away, expelling it into the air and catching its tail.

He held his hand high, well away from everyone, careful to keep the worm from touching any of them. Then, uncurling his fingers he dropped the worm into the fire embers where it burst into flames that rose halfway to the treetops, utterly consuming it in moments. Terrible black smoke everywhere. Raven coughed horribly. Joseph saw – he believed he saw – great gulps of bilious matter pour forth from Raven's bill and sparkle away in the renewed coals.

The sudden emanations of light dimmed. The fire was spent again. They were all silent; no drumming, no song.

And all were exhausted. Too dazed to speak they stayed

341

slumped over for some time. Finally, in a soft voice, Raven asked Crazy Dog how she felt. Not all the fear nor fever had been dispelled from her lustreless, yellow-speckled, ill eyes, but they were brighter than at any time for days.

'Better?'

'Yes.'

'Cool?'

She hesitated. 'Yes.'

He nodded. 'The fever will come and go in fits for a week or two, short fits, but you will be all right. Not like you were tonight. You understand what I said?' Her eyes blinked. She well understood. 'You will be weak but you will be all right. *Do you understand?*'

'Yes.'

'You believe me?'

'Yes.'

'*Again.*'

Crazy Dog's mouth opened. 'Yes.' She whispered. 'I believe.'

And Joseph knew – they all knew – that she spoke for all.

'Now you're tired and you are going to sleep, too tired to talk, only fit for sleep, cool and restful sleep . . . all the way until tomorrow . . . to sleep . . . .' Before the last word fled his lips her breath had changed to rich and sonorous sighing, inhaling and exhaling with the pleasure of being alive. She was dreaming of the golden fire that stirs all things. Fast asleep she was, deeply asleep.

None of the others moved for a very long time, hours it seemed to Joseph. Not till long after the fire lost its heat. They looked at him all the while, though, as if waiting for something.

In the dead of night, utterly calm now, once again Joseph heard scratching. It grew quite loud. Then it stopped and something crossed over the sky, low and not far from the campfire. A bird, flying alone towards the lake. Laughing. Or so Joseph heard it. A loon.

'*Dandzen.*'

The word just appeared in his mind.

Wolf reached up to him and very gently removed the gag

from his mouth. The others rose silently and came around him, too, anointing him with soft touches as they unstrapped all his bindings . . . Elk Man with a delicate hand, his one hand, pulling the breast ties free of the skin and not even breaking the thin crust of blood that had formed.

No pain. No pain that mattered.

'Dandzen.' Joseph even knew where the accent went . . . and why he had not seen his familiar before: *He had been looking in the daylight but it was a creature of night*. One that laughed, which saved it from loneliness, laughed especially at night when things were obscure and not easy to know. It was his bird. It was him.

Then the six of them just sat there listening to the sounds of the earth moving through its dark tunnel of night, to the creaking of the world, the splendid silence of the starhugged universe . . . an empty vastness filled with the warm ether of deliverance. They were not alone. They had each other.

He did not know if there were spirits in the world or if all had been done by hallucination. He'd never know. Nor did it matter. What was true was the sense of connectedness with his brothers, which they had got by enduring the same stupendous pain. He had not understood the movements of his brother's dance, only the fact that Carmen was better, much better, and that somehow – miraculously – they had all helped.

Before, Joseph had listened only to his brothers' snarls and grim humours, he unwilling to hear any laughter except that of his own scorn for what he thought was the ridiculous, gimcrack life of theirs. But there was a laughter much louder now . . . of a far more exalted kind than he was wont to hear. It was a spacious sound, low and unceasing, and as reachless as the utterings of the sea's deeps . . . a song of five throats that rolled all the way up the mountain steeps and blasted away at the gods themselves.

His brothers laughed at Death.

And only now could he hear it.

They had no fear. None at all.

The spirits in the mountain world were their own. And he was one of them. So he forgave his brothers – whatever they had done to their father, whatever they had done to themselves. Forgave them all . . . loved them each one. As he hoped to be loved and forgiven by them.

They would not have to abandon him on the volcano. He would be staying with them by his own choosing. *For now they were six*. Six against the mountain.

He would stay with them all the way to the end.

The Close of the Golden Age

CHAPTER 27

The evening before, buttoned up in a wool jacket and army mittens, Ted Nethercott had taken a ride on his best horse. During the westerly part of his progress, facing Mount Downton, he had seen the most unusual sky he could ever remember in his part of British Columbia. And it wasn't the northern lights. He had got off his horse to watch.

Careful not to stare directly into the sun, the rancher's eyes had danced around the fringe of the fireball, an incandescence so unlikely that it had tinted the horse, his own hands, the aspen and alder and cottonwoods, the Chilcotin waters, even the last of the summer's swifts and martins one monochromatic and cardinal red. An ominous, a prophetic sky.

Later, while taking his dinner on the ranch-house porch, he followed the sun's final decline. He had been put right off his food, and his cook had worried enough to bring out a motley of baked sweets – corn bread and doughnuts and turnovers and popovers and flans – to try to tempt the boss's capricious appetite back. Nethercott couldn't be managed, though. His thoughts were too lenten for cake: He wondered what temptations could be keeping young Joseph Solomon so long in the hills.

The same thoughts also ruffled his sleep, which was rare.

Then, the following morning, hardly had the sun come unstuck from the rim of hills eastwards on the plateau, when the rancher's telephone started ringing. It was Rosalie, young Solomon's wife, to whom he'd talked briefly a few weeks before. Their older child, agitated ever since Joseph's leaving, had grown hopelessly bewildered why her father was absent day after day.

'She's damned near shattered, Mr Nethercott, and I can't go on like this much longer myself,' Rosalie complained.

'Why is he taking so long up there, anyhow? He was supposed to be going just to see if everybody is all right.'

Trying to mask his own concern under a grey and even voice, Nethercott assured her that checking to see if everybody was all right was certainly the only thing occupying Joseph's time.

'But he told me he would be back in Los Angeles no later than the end of the month. It's past that already and he's still somewhere in the wilds. *What is going on???*'

'It's not time to start worrying, I don't think.' The rancher looked through the curtain's gauze at the prospect of the day. Wind was rising in a dark sky. Blown leaves scratched the windowpane. Signs of a storm. 'It's early days yet.'

'Suppose he isn't down in three days . . .? or *five*? Suppose it's a *week*—!'

'—Let's wait until the week is out. If Joseph hasn't returned by then I'll climb into the hills and take him out myself.'

'I think maybe somebody ought to go after him right now,' Rosalie came back. 'Children need their fathers around.'

'He'll be down in a couple of days, Mrs Solomon, all by himself. I'm sure of it.' Probings of light pierced the morning cloud cover outside, crept across the floorboards and onto the rancher's hands. He looked carefully at his fingers, callouses separating his rings. He was a man whose habit was to avouch only what he knew to be true, nothing more; yet; to Rosalie Solomon he was garnishing his speech and giving smooth assurances he did not quite believe. So he reconsidered what he'd said. 'Why don't I gather some few things, get myself ready . . . contact the rangers, maybe? They've got planes available. Just in case. All right?'

'Thank you.'

Now things were square.

'You call me at the end of the week,' the rancher suggested, 'Saturday. If Joseph is back before, he'll ring you straight away.'

Finally they hung up. Ted Nethercott hoped Rosalie had made the waiting a little easier for herself by giving him a

346

call. As for him, she had only focused his fears more sharply. He pulled the curtains back, looked up towards the mountains, which were enamelled in sunlight. Nobody belonged in the Itcha Mountains. Nobody. The Indians had said so for years. People who went into their wilds never seemed to come back out. Even people as sane and steady as Joseph Solomon. The rancher might just have to go up there himself and find out why.

For Joseph, on the top of Mount Downton, there was a more restricted view down. The brothers' camp had been wrapped in clouds for three days, a constant rain pizzling down. Joseph, sane and steady Joseph Solomon, who had seen the miraculous, who had watched a brother fly and who in part believed it, couldn't even see the trees that circled the marsh.

It wasn't the mist any longer that obscured his sight, though. The rain cover had lifted.

Joseph was confused.

It had all promised to be so simple: He'd come up to the mountains and find his father alive or dead, his brothers alive or dead, Carmen, too. Then he'd bring them out or at the very least recover their bones. It hadn't gone like that. And Joseph was no longer in control of things. Already with his brothers for more than three weeks, he was caught up in their lives completely, in their rush into winter, and had to see it through all the way. Had to stick by his brothers, now more than ever. If that went, then everything went. But he was confused . . . disorientated. He had lost his way, forgot why he had come to the mountains in the first place.

His brothers were moving agitatedly around the camp. When Joseph asked what they were doing he was told only that he must stay with Carmen for a while. Minister to her.

'She's still feeble as hell,' Eric reminded him.

'Why does it have to be me?'

'We already know how to set the traps.' The wolf's eyes bulged. '*Yes*, it has to be you who stays.'

The morning light had come up like a flower unfolding, some few clouds trellised above the horizon in the south, small likelihood of the rain continuing. Over the volcano the rivers would be in full flood, roiled but not so badly the salmon would stop moving upstream, turbid enough to slow them down maybe. His brothers had wakened and gone about gathering the trap sections without speaking. The time had come to make final provisions against winter. And none too soon. Amongst them all was the unspoken sense that the year was decaying fast now, winter and the dark about to close over them.

With Thomas on the horse and leading, the others filed in a single line behind. They clambered to the cirque above their valley. Joseph accompanied them almost to the top.

'We'll be back tomorrow with the first fish . . . by dusk.'

'And then?'

Eric pulled a stone from his moccasin. 'One of us will stay and you'll help with the second day.'

'What about the bear?' Joseph stopped walking.

'The fish *first* . . . and if it happens that he comes after us, *then* the bear.'

'I want to be there.'

Eric, already at the ridge and descending the other side, didn't turn around again, his voice falling away. 'You'll be there . . . .' Then he slipped into the rocks as the others had done, and was lost.

Silence.

Joseph had not heard the valley so still before. He sat down in the scrabble near the falls and watched as the autumn sun grew steadier in the sky, more aureate but colder somehow, as if plodding towards noonday with no vigour.

The perfection of his brothers' valley home he well understood now. They had chosen the loneliest place on God's multitudinous earth. Even in summer, in the middle of the year's foison, the valley had the colour of metal. In winter, as he tried to imagine it, it must be as blank and indeterminate as Death itself. Which was as it should be. And Joseph looked forward to seeing the winter in all its harsh and pristine glory.

Death would be right at home with them, sitting down with them at their fire, cracking seeds and nuts with them, sharing their food . . . laughing with them.

LeanMan Death.

348

And nobody would be afraid.

Looking down the hillside a way, Joseph saw his father's ice-axe. It rested there, neglected, day after day . . . a cold mote in Joseph's eye, glistening despite its tarnishes. Though reconciled to his brothers, one of them now, Joseph still felt curiosity chewing at the strings of his conscience: Something was under the ground beneath the axe and Joseph knew he must absolutely see what.

Carmen was dozing feverishly, and far away, out of sight. He was as alone as he was ever like to be.

In a trice he stole down the cliff to the memorial.

He stood over it, his heart ratcheting. Got down on a single knee. Lower. Further down until his beard was rubbing the spruce boughs and cold, funeral stones. Not more than a few inches from his father, he thought.

Up so close to the axe, Joseph could see it had been torqued out of shape. No brother could have done that. The mountain had. Black scoring ran down the pick end of the axe. Had his father died in fire? Or died in ice and then, once dead, been burnt away with his axe in his arms like a medieval knight grasping his sword in effigy, prepared to beat his way into heaven if prayer wouldn't suffice? Or was it *stones* that had done the old man in? Had rocks and scree and the strewings of the glacier fallen on his father, crushing his bones out of all recognition and then burying them irrecoverably, the axe marking the spot? It must have been something like that.

Joseph knew his brothers had told him all they were ever going to: A *wolf* had killed his father.

Of course, that had been Mark talking and therefore there was a double meaning to it. Joseph doubted that Eric alone was responsible.

His brothers had certainly had some hand in their father's death. Not that they had actually killed him . . . but they must have let the old man die, probably could have saved him if they'd wanted to . . . but didn't. The woman had played some part, too, even if it were no more than to watch.

Well . . . So he wouldn't know exactly how his father died. *So what?*

349

His thoughts kept coming back to the gravesite.

Nobody around but him. *Just you and the stones, bub.* He looked to see if Carmen were stirring from her bed. Not that he could see. Not yet. He laid both his hands gently on the boughs and stacked gravestones.

Dare I?

Again he looked for Carmen. She was still down.

And what would happen if she weren't asleep? What did it matter to him?

He began pulling stones away. Slowly at first, and neatly. It didn't take long to level the entire memorial. All the debris he kept carefully to one side, piled in an inverted simulacrum of the original cairn, as if symmetry would hide his gravetheft.

The ground was soon flat. There was nothing to show that a grave had been dug below. He wondered what to do, debated with himself again. Another choice. More ambivalence . . . confusion. In order to dig the ground he'd wake Carmen for sure. *So what?* It was beginning to irritate him that all of a sudden he couldn't make a decision about anything. He'd always known what to do. He believed in simplicity.

So his hands cut into the mountain itself. The ice-axe wasn't an ideal tool for digging, but it served. He worked quickly. Faster. *Furiously,* as he yerked the dirt over his shoulder, like salt to keep the Devil away. He threw rocks this way and that, banging away with the axe as it sparked against the mountain. He kept rooting, widening the hole and looking for loose soil or anything else that would follow the line his brothers had dug in burying their father. The packed dirt and rocks became more obdurate as he bored deeper, getting to the grave's bottom a task almost beyond his strength. He was beginning to think the stones hadn't been moved since the earth last yawned open and the volcano flowed—

Clang!

Something.

He hit the chink again. *Clang!*

With redoubled force Joseph slammed the pick down, using all the puissance in his shoulders and arms. He struck it again. Hardpan? He could see something encased in the rock.

Trying to work around the solid shelf, he chipped away more rock. It wasn't hardpan but flawless basalt. *The mountain itself,* for Christ's sake. He banged it over and over. Hot splinters fired out of the hole at him, narrowly missing his eyes. If his father were down below then a rib of the mountain lay over him.

One final doughty stroke and the axe broke through the stone. Joseph's hands stopped. He peered as far as he could into the grave.

Something.

It was grey, too deep in the hole for him to see it well at all. Seemed like it might be wet . . . dewy . . . impossible to think the rain had soaked through. And it stank horribly.

(. . . *better not look . . . .*)

Joseph was trembling. His arm crept towards the bottom, got halfway down. The thing looked grey because the upper part was wrapped in bandages, mummified. His fingers reached slowly for a loose end of the tape—

—and he touched it.

(. . . *really shouldn't be doing this, uh uh . . . .*)

Pushed the bandages back.

Looked. Took a long look . . .

. . . and stopped cold.

Stopped . . . staggered . . . dead heart . . . not beating—

(. . . *if death had a colour, this was what it looked like . . . .*)

Joseph drew back. All the way back from the lip of the grave. In horror.

His body started to jerk but he squeezed panic back into its jar and screwed shut the cap. Breathed in, breathed out . . . hysterically reaching for something, anything, had to fix his heart somehow—

More deep breathing. His hands were flying out of control . . . pushing, stuffing all the dirt back into the hole . . . throwing the cairn stones roughly over the site, covering the secrets he had ripped from the earth below and then he—

—ran. Just ran. Down the hillside, slinking close to the

ground as he went. Into the marsh. Once there he ripped off his clothes, everything, and plunged into the lake, scrubbed arms and hands, chest, face. He had the feeling he would never get the dirt off. Scoured his skin with reeds until he was sore all over, reopening one of the wounds on his chest where his brothers had cut into him.

At last he lay down on the forest floor and drifted into sleep . . . slept all the morning and the afternoon, too. He would have been happy to sleep his life away. What he'd seen had shattered him almost beyond repair.

The mountain, it seemed, had plenty of surprises left, all bad.

It had no bones of his father, but there were plenty of dead children . . . oh yes . . . corpses of the newborn. He had only dug one hole and got a baby on his first try.

(. . . *a dead child* . . . .)

'—Get away!'

Joseph bolted up from a deep trance.

'*GET!!*'

Two of the dogs had been sniffing Joseph's deathstill face and Carmen was beating them away with a leather thong.

She had got dressed. Wore the traditional rabbit and lynx robe Joseph had seen her in before her fever. The bag that she was used to carrying, like a drudge's mark, she had strapped once again around her neck. Carmen was no longer marching in rank with the dead. She wanted to talk.

Spoke without feeling.

'Go away,' she told him. 'Get off this mountain.'

Joseph said nothing. He rubbed sleep from his eyes.

'What do you stay around for?'

'I don't want to go.'

'Wait much longer and you won't have a chance to. Haven't you figured that out yet?'

All the while Carmen had been leaning awkwardly over Joseph's prostrate form. Now, as he sat up, she seemed to sink a little, dizzy. Joseph caught her.

'Maybe you shouldn't be on your feet yet.'

She pushed his hand away. 'You told them you want bones, is that it? Why . . .? What kind of a fool leaves his family and friends to search for the bones of a dead man?'

'To bury them.'

'And that's the whole reason you're here?' Carmen pulled at the sprouting hairs on Joseph's chin. 'We use bones here, we don't waste them hiding them underground.'

'What are you trying to tell me, Carmen?'

'I've told you already. Get out of this camp.'

'There's something else. What?'

Her hands were still holding his beard. 'There's nothing else.'

'I think there is.'

'What will it take to get you out of here?'

'Why do you want so bad for me to go when I don't want to?'

'*What will it take?*' She yanked his chin harder, her hands holding all her little strength. 'I've got your father's bones, if that's what you want. Will that do it? I've got his bones.'

'Show me, Carmen.'

'Only if you tell me you'll go afterwards . . . right after . . . *today*.'

'Show me.'

'Will you leave?'

'*Show me!*' He had no patience. She had touched a nerve.

'Help me up.'

Carmen had already gathered the essentials for his flight: Dried meat and berry cakes, a stone knife, a sleeping shawl that she said had once saved her life, and a small, bone carving, a Chilcotin fishing lure.

'Don't eat mushrooms,' she cautioned, 'or blue or black berries in clusters.'

'I know the general rules, Carmen, I do know.'

'Go north. Follow the stream beyond Paradise. They won't search for you past the pond, and if they do you can hide easily.'

'Why should they search for me at all?'

Carmen's face broke into an empty smirk. 'They will.'

353

'I chose to come up here. And if I choose to leave I'll do that, too.'

'That's the whole trick. Everybody thinks they're here by choice.'

She was speaking absently, he thought, her mind in flight. But he, for his part, would keep her on line as best he could until she produced the bones. His thoughts, confused about everything else, hadn't changed about staying until he could get his brothers out. When they went home, he'd go home. Not before.

(Only why had she mentioned those goddamned bones . . .?)

Joseph told her he didn't need her survival pack. 'I've got a knapsack hidden in the woods. It'll get me down.'

'Nothing will get you down except what I give you.'

And he was sure she believed that to be true.

There were other things for the pouch. She began to stuff them in . . . insect oil, a bark cup, sinew for thread or a fishing line. She was doing everything except telling him where to find the bones of his father.

'The bones, Carmen,' he reminded her.

'Only if you go today.'

'It's too late to go today.' He pointed to the sun just passing between two spires of the mountain. 'Almost dusk.'

'Not for two hours yet.'

Fever tears filled her eyes. Fever and an overwhelming anguish that her stone-coloured eyes were unable to hide. But Joseph, instead of feeling the pity for her wretchedness that should have naturally come to him, found his hands anxiously beating on the blunt adze end of his father's ice-axe which, unconsciously, he had carried around with him the whole day. *Was she fobbing him,* he was beginning to wonder? Having teased him with the promise of getting him some piece of his father, she wasn't coming across with it. *Why was that?* She had started the whole fucking *bones* business all by herself.

Joseph looked up. Carmen was staring at the axe in his hands.

Oh Jesus.

His face burned with shame. He remembered the child

354

he'd uncovered. There would be no way to colour over how he happened to have the axe. Anyhow, she must have seen him digging into the grave . . . *must* have.

She was looking carefully up towards the memorial. Even from the distance it was obvious somebody had torn the shrine apart.

Well, there were no secrets now.

'It was your father's child.'

Joseph swallowed in mortification. 'How did it die? The cold?'

'It was stillborn.'

Something in him didn't want to believe her, now wanted to believe only the worst. 'You're not protecting somebody by saying that, are you?'

'I said it was stillborn.' Carmen's eyes were swirling, sighted on the long and grievous year she had passed through.

'The *bones*, Carmen. What about the bones?' He was almost pleading with her to keep her mind on the one thing that mattered.

Carmen pointed towards the hillside grave. 'Dig and you'll find bones.'

'Only a baby's bones, Carmen.'

'My baby!'

Joseph was silent.

'Your father was buried there but in the spring they dug him up and put my baby in the ground instead . . . as if there's only one hole in the ground to hold the bunch of you.'

'What did they do with my father's remains?'

'They gave them to me.' She pulled the bark wallet from her neck, flapped it at him. 'A widow in this tribe carries her husband's bones. Ask your brother, Mark. He's read all about it.'

'But it's empty . . . the wallet is *empty*.'

'I know.'

'What did you do with them, Carmen? *Tell me!*' He had unconsciously cocked the steel axe behind his ear and was waving it back and forth. And begging, supplicating with all his heart. 'Please stop fucking me around . . . *PLEASE*, Carmen!'

355

She looked at the axe but it made no fear in her. She had drunk from the bottom of horror's well too many times—

'—*THE BONES, GODDAMNIT!!!*'

'I don't have them. I ground them up.'

Joseph pulled back in confusion. What was she doing all this for? 'I don't understand. Why grind them?'

'Because that's the way we thicken soup around here.'

'*Why* are you saying these things . . . why are you—?'

Joseph just stopped. Looked at her. And finally knew.

For her face was in shadows, though the evening sun fell right on her. Carmen wasn't ever going to get out of the shadows: *She had stayed with his brothers.* That was her part in his father's death. She had become even more insensible and unfeeling than they, had outdone them in rapping her head against the mountain's immovable sides. All the civilizing virtues that should pass through a woman's hand to her children she had let slip . . . no memory of the dead, no compassion for those left behind to draw the Sisyphean stone back uphill.

She had given up the war against the warriors.

She was all silence . . . and hurt. She had given up.

Just as Joseph himself was starting to do.

Inside him, a tiny fistula suddenly swelled and burst. He hated her. It was only for an instant but that was long enough.

Joseph felt a little jerk in his arm and watched as the steel shaft spun from his hands towards her head. It turned over and over. The pick end would cleave her skull into two neat pieces like a surgical cut.

The axe flew true.

And struck rock . . . missing her clean.

(*Saved by instinct* . . . he had for sure never aimed to kill.)

The dogs cried out.

The mountain itself screamed, he would swear.

(*What was going on?? What in the name of sweet holy creation was happening to him, unprotected, so many miles from Rosalie's pale green sheets? from Theresa? from his newborn son's cradle under the grape arbour . . .? his memory of them nearly obliterated, blank as snow??? What kind of mountain madness—!!*)

356

'—*Kill him . . . gonna kill him!!!*'

Somebody was hollering on the ridge above the valley . . . or else it was that voice Joseph had heard on his way up to the mountaintop exhorting him to take vengeance—

'GONNA KILL THAT FUCKER . . . GONNA . . . GONNA . . .!!'

Now there were several voices, his brothers in high choler slipping helplessly down the rocks, calling to nobody in particular . . . a general threat, them against the nation, against all nations.

They were coming back early. Something was wrong. Not all his brothers were returning.

Blood had been spilled.

The fat man, Bobby, faster than the others down the hillside, could hardly breathe after the strain of running the best part of ten miles home. His gigantic chest wheezed in and out so heavily that he kept losing rhythm. He coughed . . . moaned. 'No more playing . . . around . . . gotta kill . . . him . . . gotta carve his carcass, JoJo . . . boy . . . blood for blood.'

'What happened—?'

'—*Douglas.*'

'Hurt?'

Unable to talk any longer, Bobby just nodded, looked down, tried to find his breathing rhythm. '. . . fucko bear . . . .'

Two other shapes rose amongst the boulders, fumbling along over one another. Joseph ran to them.

'*What the hell happened???*'

Not even trying to speak, Thomas just lifted a thumb over his shoulder. Grunted.

'How bad is he? Where's Mark?'

Eric took both Thomas and Joseph, shoved all three of them along, down towards the squalor of their camp. 'In the goddamn tree . . . Mark stayed behind to keep the scavengers away from him.'

'Is he *dead*?'

'Get water, Joe . . . my throat's closing up.'

'Is he dead or what? *Tell me!*'

'I don't know. Wasn't when we left. Get us water . . . *WATER!*'

Joseph rushed to the stream, brought back a large kettle of water. His brothers were sprawling on completely spent muscles. Bobby ripped the basket from Joseph's hands and threw it over his sweat-smoked body, a little on the others, too. 'More, JoJo.'

'*Much* more.'

Joseph ran and ran. Until they were cool enough to speak slowly and with sense.

Then, in clipped sentences, Eric described how they had set up the salmon machine and were just finishing erecting the platform – they had forgotten about the bear, their minds on their labour – when, without warning, and not even the gelding drinking a little ways downstream had caught wind of the bear, the beast had jumped out of the forest and savaged Douglas. '. . . hit him only once . . . shoved his goddamn hand right across Duggie's chest . . . one wound . . . *one* . . . but the thing starts at his neck and goes right down past his hip . . . .'

Joseph sat down next to his brothers.

'. . . all five claw marks showing just perfect . . . .' Eric hunched over. His body like stone. Beyond sensation. 'A perfect print.'

'Markie's never gonna stop that bleeding, either . . . uh uh . . . he's got cottonwood down on it now, trying to staunch it somehow . . . but he's gonna have to sew it up . . . needs his needle and thread, he does.'

'*Mark's bag.*' Eric was talking as much to himself as to the others. He started looking wildly around the camp. Saw Carmen sitting by the fire, building it up again with small boughs.

'I know where the bag is.' Joseph had helped Mark prepare poultices during the rain.

'Get it!'

Joseph went right to the spot under the trees where lay Mark's sack of herbs and charms and homeopathic medicines. He handed it to the wolf, who had by now risen to his haunches.

'Somebody get the dogs.'

'Huy huy.' Thomas had one by the throat already.

'Get everything . . . *every* fucking thing.'

358

They had not really expected the bear . . . had thought the chance of it attacking again was mostly Thomas's fancy. So they hadn't taken much to defend themselves with. Now Bobby ran riotously around the camp gathering spears, more arrows, even a war mace for himself to drop on the bear's head if they were able to catch it again.

The three brothers were all up and moving. Thomas collected the dogs. Eric searched the medicine bag for something . . . not finding it he looked angrily around. 'There's supposed to be sinew in here.'

Joseph had seen threads, too, and brought them to Eric. Their hands touched in the exchange.

'I'm coming with you.'

'You're staying here.'

'Never. Not with one of my brothers half-dead.'

'You're gonna get yourself killed, JoJo.'

'AM I OR AM I *NOT* ONE OF YOU? *Make up your minds.*'

There was a long pause. The fire sparked of dry branches. Finally Eric nodded.

'Get a bow, some food . . . hunting clothes.'

'These are warm enough.'

'You want to hunt, you get *real* clothes.'

Joseph understood that. His brother was right. In the growing frost he stripped himself of all his clothes . . . everything that kept him tied fast to the world below – wind shell and jeans and chamois shirt and boots . . . boots. *Better to touch the ground with my feet,* he thought, *better to feel the hard edges.* Off with his clothes, every last vestige of machine stitching . . . lendings, all.

He jettisoned everything else, too, he wholly caught up in the event. In his knapsack's first-aid kit was a bottle of tetracycline and topical antibiotics and bandages and God knows what else that might help keep his brother Douglas's life from tumbling through the gashes in his skin. He didn't give his pack a thought.

And the confusion that had corseted his will and purpose he unlaced as well. There was no place for any of that now.

Then they dressed him in a robe like one of theirs. And

on his head Wolf placed a bonnet with the wings and tail-feathers of a loon.

In moments they had transformed him. They painted his face. And lightly with a bone needle they marked his skin. Rolled buckskin slippers onto his feet.

The hunt was on. Not a sport, this. No foray for black meat of bear. They were after a rogue grizzly that had gone after them before, and might just keep drawing their blood if they didn't take up the chase themselves.

In silence, following each other singly, they slipped out of the camp carrying their weapons and headed west towards the sea, under a full and perfect harvest moon.

Blood harvest began.

CHAPTER 28

They crossed the volcano. Joseph cracked his feet against the stones but never once faltered or fell behind. His feet grew more careful.

Soon the four of them dropped down a moraine and then below the tree line, following ever-larger runnels of water that flowed off the ice-capped mountaintop and into rich valleys shelving down in steps towards the fiords and the Pacific beyond. Plenteous valleys, rough-hewn and sided by black cliffs . . . valleys copious with cedar and balsam and Sitka spruce thicker and much taller than the trees of their own home. And in the trees hid a thousand sundry night creatures . . . the brothers themselves moving like creatures of the night, as difficult to see.

On. On down the tumbling, rapturous river. The moon lit up the water and surrounding peaks all traced with glaciers. Midnight. Charms and spells controlling the forest. A hunting owl broke free of the cedars, his claws plucking a rat or a mouse. He sailed across the stream into caverns and shadows to eat the still-pulsing flesh of his kill.

360

One of the dogs gave chase as far as the waterside. Howled. Took the trail again.

They pressed on faster, right down the canyon as it widened and soft skirts of meadow grew bright under their feet. There were pools off the main flood, breeding ponds for the salmon. Some few fish they could already see . . . males . . . slapping the shallow water. Barrel-bodied things. They had by now lost all their sleekness, no longer silver but ox-blood red, fighting colours in their crust of skin. Strange beasts. At the same time lunatic and alarmingly heroic. Three thousand miles of struggle back from the Aleutians and the Arctic's farthest seas just to riot amongst each other for a cubic foot of gravestones . . . something like the sons of Jacob Solomon, as brave, as mad, who had gone upriver, too, all the way to the mountain's crown, to the very last rib of stone, only to lose their beauty there, ever trying to find their beginnings in their ends.

They slowed.

A groan.

Wolf drew out his knife. He stopped. The others jumped into the thicket and hugged trees, unbuckled weapons.

'Help me . . . .' The voice was broken. Whining. *'I can't see.'*

A black shadow was standing in the river.

The wolf clicked his tongue against his teeth. From the black shadow a low whistle returned, though to Joseph's ear it was only the wind complaining.

Mark's sure-clawed steps lifted high over the current. In his arms he carried a skin which he had filled with the mountain's clearest water to give to Douglas, mauled by the bear and alone, and crying over all their heads from the tree.

Douglas called again. Sad as it was, the sound relieved the others. They had all believed Douglas would be dead by now.

Raven had nursed his brother. Cleaned the wound and clotted the deepest punctures as best he could though knowing full well should Douglas be moved, and they would have to move him sometime, all his blood not yet lost would burst out of him. His own robe he had thrown over

Douglas and was himself naked under the moon. And also, Mark had wept. He had laid his head over Douglas's blood-matted hair and wept sorely. By such succours had Mark somehow managed to keep his brother alive . . . barely.

'*I can't see . . . !*'

'What's the matter with his eyes?'

'He's night blind.'

'*Why?*'

'He's been that way for months . . . just wouldn't say so.' By the light of the night sky Mark culled medicaments from his bag, a bone needle . . . sinew for thread. His hands moved quickly. Douglas had to be closed up – he was still venting blood.

'Can he live . . . ?'

'Help me build a fire.'

While the others started hoisting their weapons onto the platform, Wolf gathered dead boughs for a fire, Raven found touchwood. Together the two oldest brothers struck fire. The flames grew quickly, drawing the dogs into a circle where they lay tensed . . . ears cocked to the black woods all around them.

Fish were thrashing in the weir. The trap was working, but at what cost

'They're coming,' Eric said. His eyes were like moon-stones.

'They started like this a few hours ago.'

'Many?'

'Not yet, but they're the biggest I've seen in the river.' Mark sliced roots and seeds hurriedly, began boiling them in the kettle Eric had brought him. He scorched the needle's tip in the fire.

Eric dumbly watched his brother's apothecary skills. Both men raised their eyes.

'You think he's got a chance?'

'He's lost a lot of blood . . . .'

'What will you do?'

'Keep him still and clean.'

'That all?'

Raven stirred the pot. 'I'll sew him up.'

'And if he's lost too much blood already?'

'Then we'll lose a little of our own.' Mark drew a knife across his wrist and let the blood of his own body seep into the ground.

The wolf held out his arm, too. 'Cut deep.'

Though they all dreamed, not a one of them slept. All kept the night vigil, sure of the bear's imminent return. Weapons were ready . . . and nerves as tight as the caribou gut that strung their bows.

Interminable waiting. But the night was in no rush to end. Nor the bear to come.

A night of high solemnity. The brothers crouched next to each other under the moon and pointed at it until it set, then watched the star-soaked sky for signs of meteors or comets or any kind of fiery exhalation that would tell them there was something watching them, that there was, after all, mind and sense in Nature, and the lights were on in heaven.

'I'm getting colder . . . .'

Pretty Marten had been weaving in and out of consciousness all night. When awake he would call for more coverings. And for more. Without once moving, Raven sat by him, holding his younger brother in his arms, nursing him, putting a compress to the wound very gently after he had sewn parts of it together in crude and painful stitches.

'Try to drink.'

'*I'm cold all over.*'

The others touched Douglas. His body was in shock and they couldn't get him warm no matter how many blankets they put around him. There was no heat left in his blood . . . nor enough blood to carry what heat his body made.

'Drink some more.'

'I can't.' Douglas's voice was a squeal.

'It'll help you to get warmer.'

'*I caaaannnnnn't!*'

The wind, stronger on the windward side of the mountains, fell into an irregular hum. It made listening for the bear that much more difficult. The men were exhausted just straining to hear what was behind the branches.

Slowly the sky brightened, extinguishing the stars one by

one until only the great luminants were left . . . half a dozen stars . . . then three . . . then one only. *Day blue.*

And still the bear hadn't returned.

At the far end of the platform Bobby started to nod off, his nerves simply played out by the waiting. The spear slipped from his prodigious lap and Thomas just did stop it from rolling over the edge and onto the forest floor. The fat man babbled as he slept, licking his lips from time to time. Most of what he said was unintelligible, but then he would utter something about the images filling his head . . . dreams of green fields and lowland meadows and sucking nectar straight from flowers and living free. He had Paradise in his head . . . but not one that the brothers had ever found.

The others brooded nervously as the daylight grew to shining. Thomas hummed a tune. Joseph, the loon, not tired, feeling clear-headed, kept his eyes carefully on the ferns and lower growth in the forest that the wind kept in nearly continuous movement. He wanted to be the first to see the bear, the first to run an arrow through him. The forest, jumping about, played tricks with Joseph's eyes.

'A different arrow.' The wolf pulled another shaft from Joseph's quiver, one tipped with the tine of a caribou's rack sharpened to an awl shape and some six inches long. 'That's the one.'

'Shoot where?'

'Crunch bone, not flesh . . . if he's charging, in the heart, if you can.'

Together they watched the motes in a sunbeam. Unobstructed rays had just broken through the canyon. Rising sun. The white disc singing as it pulled itself above the mountain spires. A solemn morning indeed. The cliffs around them made a natural basilica. The morning sounds like hymns mounting up the fan of rocks, a vaulting above the choir. A waiting congregation . . . every man to his own thoughts—

Something.

All the dogs stood up.

Snouts pointed upstream as the dogs tried to pick out the false scents from the real smell of danger. From up in their

364

tree Wolf and his brothers watched the dogs stiffen, their rear legs retreat a step or two. Something was out there.

The men gripped their war spears, readied bowstrings. Waited for the rush.

No birds called all of a sudden. A full minute went by, an unnerving calm. Over the stream there was a rainbow in the spray. Things too peaceful now—

— a sound they could all hear, men and dogs.

Then, a few dozen yards upstream the gelding walked unconcernedly through the foliage. The day before, when the bear attacked, the big grey horse had torn his tether and run into the forest. Now he had come back, eating his way into camp, following the softest streamside shoots of vine maple, dragging behind him the traces that he'd broken in running away.

False alarm.

The dogs grew less rigid. The men above them unclenched. Blood-blanched fists opened. One at a time they slumped back down to their rest. Joseph had trouble winding down. He wondered if it weren't better they set out after the bear instead of waiting and losing all their edge and concentration.

'No.'

'I'm about to start seeing crazy things . . . hear voices.'

'He'll come when he comes,' was all Eric would say.

The others passed Joseph a stick of dried meat which he ate greedily. Then they gave him the water cup.

'Sleep a little if you can.' The wolf laid hands on his brother's head. 'We'll watch.'

'No.'

'In a little while we'll stalk him. Sleep now. It'll calm you . . . refresh you.'

'*You* haven't slept.'

'Oh a little . . . a little.' But the truth was Eric hadn't slept well for years. He had long ago murdered sleep.

Sweet music.

All the others were singing softly. A plain melody it was, of three bars. Thomas had brought a kind of penny whistle, which he could manipulate with his one good hand. It was all that was left of his music.

There had been other times for singing. Even Joseph could remember how in the avocado groves they had once made bonfires in defiance of every local ordinance and common sense, had cooked their suppers, then fried bananas and other fruit in a pan over the open fire. They had taken off their clothes and gathered in a tight group, squealing in pleasure, and had sung songs, stretched their necks right up to the starlight. Every one of them had learned to sing his piece, and on key. But then there had been no brother in the midst of them bleeding to death. These songs were more sombre.

Sang for a while . . . right to the rim of sleep . . . growing heavy-lidded all of them. Maybe the bear was sleeping, too.

Everything was slowing down. It was an autumn morning – a Sunday, but they would not know that, not even Joseph who had long before lost care of the orderly progression of days. A crispness stuck to the air, all creatures huddling together for warmth against the frost. Arms tangled in arms. The dogs, too, packed close. Even the gelding lay down with ticks and termites in the ruins of a fallen tree.

Quiet. Earth abiding.

One set of eyes still searched the forest. The wolf was *all* eyes. Green lanterns. An inner vision was lighting up. An idea had come to him.

He laid down his bow and carefully descended to the stream.

Cold, compulsive river. Deep enough. All he had to do was just to step into it . . . advance half a dozen feet into the foam beyond the rocks and he'd never pull himself back to shore. *Never.* Great Caesar himself couldn't breast the middle of this flood.

Only a few steps and then the river would carry him all the way to the sea. It wasn't despondency, though Eric's humour had *always* tended that way. It was, rather, that he fancied his disappearance, and death, might somehow save his brothers. The bear would leave them alone. Everybody would leave them alone. Douglas would get better. The others would all heal, their precious bodies naturally, spontaneously, regenerate.

Do it.

Wolf got one foot into the stream's icy flow. Then the other. The water rose just above his moccasins. He hesitated a few feet out of the main current, in the protection of several large rocks. A pebble tumbled down the cliff facing him.

The earth's movement never stops, he thought.

And suddenly he heard it behind him. The sound was like an immense rockfall.

The wolf wheeled around.

Forest boiling with a thousand thousand creatures running. Bushes spinning, boughs shaking, the horse struggling up on all four feet at once, tripping himself in panic.

The bear.

'GET UP!! Dagold Hin!!!'

His brothers fell over each other, knocking two bows to the ground, Raven's medicines . . . the whole tree juddering . . . the earth beneath them opening up.

The bear came crashing through the undergrowth, pushing over saplings and small trees as he rampaged down the mountain directly towards where the wolf was standing in the water.

There was no time to react. The dogs yelped, turned on their own tails in fear and confusion. An arrow from Joseph's bow split the air towards the ubiquitous foliage. The brown flash of the creature broke through at a far different place from where Joseph had shot, right into the middle of their makeshift camp, on all fours and yet his shoulders as high as a man's.

The bear.

Brown death.

'Jump!! JUMMMMPPPPPP!!!'

Eric ran for the tree, endless hands reaching down from the platform trying to grab him. He could already feel the bear's breath right over his neck . . . waited for the claws to smack him halfway across the valley . . . his arms flailing away at his brothers' desperate hands, Eric trying to hold just one—

'—Help me!!!'

One dog. It got tangled in the bear's running feet. The bear rolled over, crushing the dog and losing the real prey . . .

    . . . an arm caught Eric . . .

        . . . four men jerked him up just as the dripping jaws slashed at his robe. They pulled him with all their might and right out . . .

        . . . of the bear's mouth.

JESUS.
      OH JESUS
OH THANK JESUS GOD—

'—Not *yet*, you fucking bastard!!!' Eric screamed his defiance at the bear below him while the bear raged and banged the tree bole, banged and banged it trying to dislodge the men perched there.

It seemed that he would, for the tree and all its straining roots did groan and slip.

The dogs recovered and circled around the bear trying to nip the tendons at the back of his feet. One came too close and the bear scooped him up with a paw and bit his back, paralysing the animal, then fell on him with his mouth spraying blood everywhere, all the way up to the men above still grabbing the wrong weapons and frantically trying to piece together a resistance of bows, arrows, spears.

A stone war club at his side, Bobby threw the first blow back at the bear. It grazed off the beast's neck but diverted his attention once more to the men above. Again he slammed his bulk into the tree trunk, this time with too much force so that he rolled over the roots at the base of the tree, exposing his underside.

The only brother steady, Thomas plunged a spear deeply into the bear, missing the heart but striking him in the right foreleg. He twisted his spear as it went in, searching out the bear's inner strengths just as the bear had once tested Thomas's.

Twisted hard.

In pain for the first time, the beast screamed at the sky and pulled at the shaft sticking through his leg . . . whacked it against the ground foolishly thereby ripping more bands of his muscles. But finally he broke the spear right at the lashings, lodging the flint head inside him with no way to pull it out.

It was enough.

Limping severely the bear spun back into the green cover from where he'd emerged only a minute before and headed upstream. Suddenly he was gone. The forest quiet again, renewed.

One dog dead. Another, with his whole skeleton crushed to half its natural size, lungs trapped by his bones, lay on the grass taking quick, shallow breaths, trying to live somehow.

The men listened for a while. Then, sure that the bear had really retreated, they fell to talking, and soon after to squabbling about how to kill the bear before he killed them. It wasn't only Thomas, now, who believed the bear would be coming back. Strong beyond the wit of man to imagine, utterly fearless, the grizzly must have seen man's society before, had probably been wounded in the encounter . . . might have savaged men himself, or even eaten them.

There was no choice. Sooner or later they would front the bear. Better to do it when they were ready and he wounded. The time was now.

They cut the dying dog's throat, rounded up the remaining dogs. Found the gelding.

Douglas was no worse. The bear's violent shaking of the platform hadn't opened up his wounds again. He was awake, crying quietly. He seemed to understand they were leaving him for a while. They laid out drink, deer jerky to eat if he had the strength . . . then went quickly, heading upriver.

'Look here.' Thomas kneeled over two carefully etched tracks. 'The left step is much l-longer.' He walked a few yards farther along. 'S-same thing here.' Much cunning the bear might have, but by keeping to the open trail right next to the stream he had left a clear record of his passage. Fresh stool they found a few minutes later. And blood in the dust nearby. Confidence buoyed everyone. The bear was on the run. They were the hunters again and not the hunted.

369

When the tracks led away from the trail and into the undergrowth, however, a grimness came over the group. Easy as it was to follow – broken ferns and bracken, wildflowers in disarray – the path of the bear's making had numberless spots where the bear might pause and from which he could ambush them as they stole through the forest after him.

Water. Slop from the stream that had spilled over during the heavy rains. Joseph stepped into a hole hidden and filled with water. Disappeared down to his waist. They dragged him out, cleaned as much of the mud off as they could.

Had to move. Must not let the bear get too far away.

The air still cold, the sun sweated away plenty of their energy nevertheless. They came to a place where the growth was so dense they would have to crash through. The dogs were sent first. *No bear.* Spear tips pointing straight ahead, one at a time they followed. Safely. Nothing but bright forest on the other side. It was becoming much more open, the trees wide apart. So much so that the dogs were soon too far ahead of the men and didn't return to their whistles. Thomas started to go after them but halted suddenly. Something strange ahead.

The dogs were barking. The brothers listened. A few moments before the peal of dogs' voices had sounded remote. Now their music had gone up a pitch, got more frantic. And the cries were coming closer, returning to where the brothers waited.

Jesus.

'They've got him . . . !'

Everyone looked for cover but there were few trees to provide it. This was not the meeting ground they had wanted.

'Keep close!' Eric spoke sharply.

They stood their ground on both sides of the freshly cut trail as the beast pounded towards them through the greenery ahead. The dogs cried louder . . . their snapping easy to distinguish in the chase. A gleam of the brown body appeared for an instant in between high shrubs. *Closer.* All eyes on the spot where the bear would break out of the

370

green. Bowstrings taut. There was a blur and suddenly he charged right towards them, zigzagging across the trail. Head up.

Antlers up.

Elk. A fine rack on his head. The dogs had raised a buck from the autumn rut. Unable to hold his fire, Joseph sent an arrow streaming towards the beast, feathers twirling in the sunlight. It passed over the elk's rack and into the brush. The buck swerved into the forest and was gone. The dogs blasting behind would have followed, except that Bobby threw the blunt end of his spear in their path, stopping them well enough.

'Dumb fuckers . . .!' The fat man picked his shaft and prodded the nearest of the mongrel dogs.

'Stop it!!'

Mark and Thomas caught the overwrought dogs, all of them, rubbed their noses again in the bear dropping Thomas had found earlier, setting the scent one more time.

'The *bear,* you fucko dogs!' Bobby was in a high rage, as if it was his bear only to kill.

'LEAVE OFF!!!'

They moved higher into the mountain, towards the timber-line and far away from the river, and at nearly full run. Joseph fell behind. The pace was killing. They had run uphill for some miles already. The day was hotter and the forest had started to stink. And with the smell of decay came insects. So bad were they that Joseph had to roll in the wood chips around a fallen tree to stop their mad sucking. He heard his brothers calling him. Called back.

Caught up. They were angry with him for drifting off. The bear would chew their necks one at a time if they got separated.

'Huy huy.' Thomas stopped them all.

They had risen out of the rain forest at last and were come to open meadows. In between two bunches of shrubs, not more than a quarter-mile above them, the bear could be seen moving uphill past a patch of red, the last berries before the tundra began.

'Good.' The wolf sat down on a rock to catch his breath.

371

'Hold the dogs before they see him.' Thomas did. 'Sit down
. . . all of us sit down and take a breather.'

'Are you *crazy*! What are we doing . . . giving up?' Mark
wanted to press on.

'Sit down, I said.'

'We're going to lose him, goddamn you!' There was a
knife in Raven's voice, the cutting edge outwards.

'The bear won't get away.'

'Why not??? What's going to keep him from just continuing on up the canyon and away? *Eh?*'

The others, confused, caught in between their two older
brothers, swayed in the heat, unsure whether to sit or
stand.

'This is the spot we've been looking for.' The wolf's
great, sad head shook slowly. 'He can't escape. That's a box
canyon. We tried to climb out of it yesterday. There's no
way unless the bear's got a rope and pitons. I tell you he's
trapped.' Eric watched his black brother walk a few feet
away, stamp the ground. Mark's shiny hair was swarming
with black sedge flies, which he kept trying to curse away.
'This is the only way out.'

'What do we do?'

'We'll wait for him. He'll come down.'

'I don't want to wait. What's the point?'

'Because we're tired. And I don't want us to be tired
when that motherfucking beast comes claws-out at us. I'm
sore and I'm thirsty. Now sit down with us, Markie. Get
your strength back.'

'For how long do we wait?' Joseph wanted to know.

'We'll see. It depends mostly on him, doesn't it . . .? Until
he decides he's ready to paw us around a little.'

They sat.

The afternoon came on quickly as the five of them sat in
cold sunlight and ate cakes of dried berries. Found a spring
for water. Joseph marked the passage of the sun's shadow
in a line of rocks. Thomas, forever at work, watched the
dogs carefully for any hint of nervousness.

And the afternoon went. They all shivered in the wind that
had started blowing down from the mountain's ice pack.
Each brother in his private thoughts wondered if Douglas

372

were still alive . . . and which of them would be alive if they really had an encounter with the bear again.

'If we're going to do it, g-g-gotta do it before dark.'

They all agreed.

The bear wasn't coming out and so they must, themselves or the dogs, go into the canyon and get him.

They rose and gathered the dogs, advanced to the berry patch at the base of the gorge and released them. While the pack went rushing after the bear, all five brothers arranged themselves in a semi-circle right at the canyon's mouth – bows and arrows on the outer rim and the two men with spears, Thomas and Bobby, inside. And in the middle of the crescent, leaning over his bow, stood the wolf.

A cold mist was coming in from the ocean, thin at first but coming. The sun staggered amongst a regiment of clouds forming to the west, burnishing the sky with gold and red like a royal pennant. A royal sky. A fight for sovereignty: It was *their* home, the mountain, or it was the bear's.

Soon they heard the dog pack crying high in the canyon. Everyone tensed at the sound. Checked weapons. The dogs were coming down now. Quickly, too. That would mean the bear was hotfooting it down the mountain in front of them. The brothers glanced nervously at one another, in part to see which of them were nervous. *They all were.* Seeing this they smiled.

Hands went out, one atop the other – that bond reaffirmed which had kept their hearts together all their lives. There was goodbye on every lip, but not a one of them said anything.

'He'll have to make for *one* of us.' Eric spoke rapidly. 'We collapse around him . . . kill him any way we can. Don't hold back for the perfect shot. *Kill quickly.*'

'Here comes fucko.' Bobby pointed. His lips bubbling with a joy that ran deep in him. Whispered to himself. 'Come at me, fucko bear . . . at me . . . .' It was an incantation, Bobby putting himself into a trance, taking a step into the unknown inside him . . . into supernature.

At the end of the alpine meadow the bear bounded along well in front of the dogs, taking huge strides and moving faster than any of the brothers believed a beast of his size could.

'*Dagold-Hin!*'

The wolf called first.

Then they all screamed. '*Dagold-Hin!!*' The bear turned towards the half-moon of men, as if provoking them to call again. Chilcotin they were speaking . . . calling the bear 'old man'.

'*DAGOLD-HIN!!!*'

The bear had stopped so suddenly that the lead dog ran right into him, and was caught. It seemed the dog might tumble safely away, but the bear hit him at the last moment with a stupendous shot that sent the dog high in the air, his guts flying like a burst of shrapnel.

While the rest of the dogs circled cautiously, keeping their distance, the bear finally looked towards the brothers arranged against him. *No exit.* His mean eyes blinked. For the first time he seemed to comprehend, however dimly, that he was in a trap of some kind. There was no way out for him except through the men.

He took a few steps forward . . . feebly studying the brothers. Another step, this one towards Joseph, who raised his bow and drew back the string. The bear's eyes seemed not so narrow and stupid as a bear's eyes should be.

Joseph. The loon. It was as if the bear were choosing him as the weak strand in the holding net. The bear was looking *only* at him.

Joseph's arrow jiggled against the bow as he strained towards full draw . . . the shaft bouncing irritably back and forth. The animal skin he wore suddenly felt wrong on his shoulders, outsized, desperately hot, encumbering, making it impossible for him to steady himself and hold the tension or to perfect his aim.

'*Dagold-Hin!!*' he heard himself cry, amazed at the power in his voice, the hatred in him for the bear that was, step by step, making towards him—

Why didn't the others shoot? Why him . . . *why him?*

The arrow steadied. He screamed the oath one last time, stiffening his nerves with the rod of holy anger . . . all his senses stripped and his knowledge of everything in the world falling away . . . aware only of the bear's eyes straddling the point of his arrow sighted to kill.

374

Eyes.

Eyes.

Green, almost yellow, large and round and bright. The eyes of suffering. Like Eric's eyes. Like his father's had been. These were not the bear's eyes but those of another spirit inhabiting its body.

The eyes of Judah. *The lion of Judah.*

Joseph paused. And dropped his aim. He could not shoot the bear. It were like casting an arrow at the eyes of his father. And his father's father.

Somebody had to stop the killing.

Lowered his bow . . . .

Which was when the bear broke for him, bellowing as it came on, murder in its arms . . . and its gigantic jaws open and snapping, sweat and saliva and the blood of the dogs spewing out, teeth rotting, abscesses in the gums, which had been driving it for years—

—It was just a bear. A maddened, mindless, rogue grizzly, nothing more. *Just a bear.* And in several more steps would be clawing Joseph to death.

He let his arrow fly.

Somewhat lowly shot, nevertheless the arrow struck the bear's foot. Not enough to break the beast's stride, though. Two other shafts from his brothers spun for the bear, both hitting him, one in the shoulder and grazing off into the meadow, but the other entered the brown fur just where it was spotted with the red of his own blood, the same spot where they had rived the bear's foreleg in the morning.

And that stopped him. Pained him.

Joseph thrashed the dirt at his feet desperately for his second arrow. All his brothers were whooping curses, jumping in towards the bear. They had him. The beast was sinking.

Thomas came in first. But too quickly. Too close to the sweeping arms. The bear couldn't quite claw him but in avoiding the flashing nails Thomas banged his leg with the butt of his own spear and tripped—

Oh my God . . .

Thomas teetering . . . the bear leaned towards him and caught his stumped wrist in its mouth and

375

snapped down viciously, biting Thomas's arm halfway to the elbow . . .

. . . not done with him, the bear reached out with those huge hands . . .

Jesus, no—!

—Thomas down on the spongy grass trying to hold his arm up in the air and keep the blood from draining all his life away . . . scrambling on his knees but the bear scrambling just that much faster until . . .

. . . arrow comes, right from the raven's bow . . . slight wound and not enough to distract the bear from Thomas—

'—*FUCKO!!!!*'

An immense scream. Almost laughter. Bobby. Little Bear.

'*FUCKO!!!!*'

Bobby was mocking the grizzly. With a maniacal look on his face, his jaws open, Bobby rushed towards the bear, dropping his spear, went after the beast with his hands only, as if his enormous will alone would let him break the bear apart. He crashed into the bear, his own jaws ripping, arms flailing in ridicule, Bobby locking his teeth onto the bear's neck just as it stuck its fingers in Bobby's groin and ripped open his stomach, pulling out the innards of the man – all the way out – in a single stroke. Sweet, glistening viscera lay coiled on the ground. Bobby gurgled blood. Death's shadow passed across his eyes and left them black. It had happened before any of the others could grasp it. Dead. A brother gone.

Dead. Gone right out of the narrow world. Laughing done.

The bear was not down. Not at all. It broke through their ranks. And then it fled.

Thomas, enraged, still holding up his gushing arm, gripped his spear with his left hand and hobbled after the disappearing brown body while the others watched, too stunned to shoot, none of them believing what they had seen. Able to run only a fraction as fast as the bear, even the bear wounded, Thomas angled across the field and came within a few yards of the fleeting feet, flung his spear as hard as he could. But it was fecklessly thrown, not straight nor with enough lust, for he was off-balance and growing weak. The spear's nib did touch the bear, on his back, but not with the force needed to stick. The shaft fell away from the bear, hitting the soles of his feet and kicked by them some forty or fifty feet behind, finally coming to rest not far from where Eric, Mark and Joseph lay close to the hulk of their dead brother.

'*Down you bastard!!!!*' Thomas screamed shrilly, no stutters now, his mouth rimmed with his own blood. He dropped to his knees, his life on a fine point as his arm bled furiously. He crawled forward towards Bobby's body, all of them gathering around.

The fat man on the ground.

The great heap of him, the bulk that they had teased in life, was now as precious as rubies, garnet, carbuncle. Bobby was afloat in his body's fluids, sluiced as he was, everything draining out of him. There was something on his lips and cheeks, too, a darker blood, the bear's, for Bobby had cut through the bear's coat and skin and gristle, got himself a grisly last supper, a single, sacred cup of his familiar.

'Close him up.' Eric was whispering hoarsely.

Mark fluttered distractedly, cracking his brains for a way to tie up his brother's bowels before the night fell . . . stuff the man together again and seam the belly. 'Got to find a spruce . . . get me roots . . . get—'

'—*Close him up!!*'

All of the others yelled at Mark now. Thomas pointed with his stump, pointed right at the guts of their brother.

At *it*.

It was wiggling, it was. *IT* was still alive. Bobby was not, but the worm that had been driving him crazy for nearly a year was still living. Wriggling along out of his intestine, slithering out, unrolling itself . . . yard after yard after yard of it.

Eric fell on it and slapped the earth with his bow, dashing hundreds of segments of the worm, splashing himself with his brother's abdominal blood . . . roaring himself.

Three brothers tending three others dead or dying. Three dogs left. A bitter symmetry. And a bear whose lives were infinite and will singular, who was mincing away all the Solomons in a kind of mathematical trick . . . doing it by halves.

Stupefaction.

In the late sky, the final shadows of the day, the three healthy brothers wandered. Stunned to the marrow. A brother was dead. It had really happened.

Ashes seemed to fall from the sky. A sullen and grey mist.

Mark had braided the stalks of wildflowers into tourniquets and stopped the flow from Thomas's arm. That done, there was no movement other than the brothers' hot and rheumy tears.

Eric, the wolf, sat by himself and surveyed the carnage. His hoar-frosted head stooped all the way to his stomach. In a single afternoon he had grown into an old man . . . debilitated . . . beyond grief. He saw Joseph sitting on a mound nearby. For a moment Eric had trouble recognizing his baby brother. His gritted snout fell open.

'What are you doing here?'

Joseph knew no answer.

'Go away,' the big man whispered. 'Time to go.'

'We're *all* going out . . . together.'

'Bear's going to get hungry . . . be back. We'll try to get him then.'

The bear? Joseph couldn't understand why his brother was worrying about the bear. He no longer believed they would kill it, not this one. The bear had been schooled.

'He's always back,' Eric said, his voice without tone.

'Not anymore.'

'Oh yes.'

'It's *over* . . . can't you see that?' Joseph's whole family was being torn into chunks of flesh to feed scavengers. Up to this point, he now realized, he had understood nothing at all. His brothers had been hunting a very different kind of animal from the one he had seen tear open his brother, Bobby. 'What do you mean the bear's *always* back. You've seen this bear before?'

378

'We're always hunting the bear.'

'Even though you think you can't kill him?'

Lids closed over the wolf's sad, bulging eyes.

'But why?'

'It keeps us together.'

'Is that what we've been doing? *Is that what this whole goddamn thing is about!* There's no other way for us to stay together than to risk getting killed together . . .?'

'We've been hunting the bear.' It was a sleepy reiteration, but all that Eric had to say.

Joseph's face was flaming, his eyes a plea that his all-too-well-loved brother tell him once and for all what dark power had so corrupted their lives that they had invented ways to self-murder? 'What the fuck do you mean you've been hunting the bear? What does that *mean?* Tell me *exactly! What????*'

'It means,' said Wolf, in the merest voice, 'finding a fit way to die.'

'BULLSHIT!! That's just a bear! *A bear!!* Not a spirit or one of your *netsin.* Not your father. *Not anything* but a dumb and mean-tempered old fucking rogue male whose teeth have gone crazy with infection or something like that and whose brain is turned by the pain. That's all. *A bear!!!*'

Joseph hollered but only the hills had ears. For he knew at last that whatever the bear was to him, to his brothers, who had lived unprotected and out of society for many years, who had insensibly watched their father gasp his life away, that for them the bear had become the embodiment of their own murderous feelings walking the world.

There was a crashing in the forest, then, and all of them jumped in fear towards the edge of the meadow, expecting to see the bear descending, they resistless now.

It wasn't the bear. It was a horse and rider. A pale horse and a slumping, near-dead rider. Douglas came forward, leaning halfway off the horse, his eyes closed.

The three of them still whole enough in body left all other thoughts and quickly rigged up a travois behind the horse to carry Bobby's corpse and on the horse itself they put the others, Thomas in front, *sans* hand, and Douglas behind, still in shock and fevered now as infection spread rapidly within him. Then they led the hearse back over the volcano, all except Joseph wondering if the bear might finally leave them alone or if its depredations on them were not yet done.

Only Joseph's mind was free. For he believed that they would never master the bear's spirit even if they managed to kill the body of the beast . . . its spirit was within them, within each of them, crying out for a death . . . and the death it called for was their own.

CHAPTER 29

In mid-afternoon Ted Nethercott took a short break. Already twenty-five miles northwest of his ranch, he sat amidst two coils of the river which flushed through the mountain's wash. The glacier was just above his perch, several miles up the fan of rocks. He ate his packed lunch and tried to correlate the evidence of his eyes with what his maps of the area were telling him he should be seeing. Three times now he had retaken the declination, laid his map out at true north and then looked up at the glacier. The map was wrong . . . or the mountain had moved. There seemed to be no way into the mountain except from the north, at least a day's hard ride from where he sat, maybe two. He had a recollection of Colin Mackie's saying that the two of them – he and young Joseph Solomon – would walk right through the mountain from the southwest. Perhaps they had. But Ted Nethercott couldn't see how.

One last time the rancher raised his field glasses towards the rockfall. Back and forth he passed his glasses over the field, looking for a secret entry. Ran his eyes from the scree's bottom to the tip of the ice. Devilwork. Nothing but piled rock. It would take till the end of time to quarry so many stones, they stretched so far. Madness to live up there.

Somebody apparently did, though. For not halfway up the rocks, near the centre of the wash, Ted Nethercott saw a figure moving. One of the demons escaped, no doubt, coming out to greet the rancher and inveigle him into the mountain. Not just a solitary figure . . . two or three of them. Nethercott stepped up the focus ring. It looked like a man with two horses. For several minutes he followed the three silhouettes. They seemed to be tracking the same plot of rock over and over again, prospecting maybe.

Better go see who or what that is, he told himself.

Then Ted Nethercott bushwhacked his way to the foot of the mountain and up through the boulders, preparing himself to question with whatever vapours they were percolating out of the depths and whether they had any News of Nowhere.

The two horses were real enough. Nethercott recognized them both. They belonged to him. But the man was of an altogether more questionable shape. He had obviously seen the rancher approaching and tried to hide amongst the rocks – the ruse not availing, though. Ted Nethercott called the man to come back.

Colin sat on a stone and scratched the backs of his hands with a small lump of some metal blackened by fire.

'Looked like you were going around in circles, Colin.'

The drunk wouldn't answer. A droplet of blood clung to his hand. Colin had more than an itch. He was gouging the skin on the back of his hand. He looked completely beat, unclean. Ted Nethercott had never seen him look quite so bad.

'You're pretty scruffy, Colin. Looks like you might have lost some weight?'

Colin scratched the bloody spot on his hand more roughly.

'I've got some rye, if you want.'

'Don't like rye.'

Nethercott got out the booze nevertheless, handed it to Colin. The old drunk's eyes fastened onto the neck of the flask, then he grasped it in between the iron rings of his fingers, pulled it up to his nose. Smelled the fumes.

'Go on. I think you need this one.'

He took a drink. A second swallow.

'Have another . . . slowly.'

'Aye.' Trembling, Colin drank again. Some of the whiskey dribbled down the fluting of his cheeks and onto his hands . . . burning its way into the gashes he'd made. Then he put the cork back in the bottle, tightened the screw cap. He had done.

'Where's the boy, Colin?'

No answer.

'You're going to have to tell me, you know . . . .'

'I haven't done anything to the little idiot!'

The rancher nodded. 'You've got both horses, Colin . . . and from what I can see all the gear, too.'

'Yeah, well he ran off and left me holding the booty, he did.'

'Ran where?'

'Now why don't you ask him about that?'

Ted Nethercott reached out and stopped the drunk from bloodying his hands any more, confiscated the tiny weapon. He looked at the small, many-faced piece. Scorched. Few enough spots where the metal was manifest. But Nethercott knew what it was. Even in the dread and bilious afternoon light the life of the stone shone forth. Gold. The old prospector had found his motherlode.

'Where did you pick this up?'

Colin jerked a thumb over the shoulder of his shredded buckskin coat.

Gold, all right. Ted Nethercott doubted, however, that Colin would be staking a claim. What he had found was a gold inlay from someone's tooth. One of Colin's own, that had someway worked its way loose? Perhaps the old drunk had been chewing on stones.

'There's a way into this mountain, is there not?'

'If you can fly.'

'I think we had better go have ourselves a look at the top of the mountain, Colin . . . see if we can find young Solomon. What do you say?'

'You won't get me up there . . . uh uh.'

Colin backed away and vehemently shook his head,

repeating many times that nothing nor nobody in the world could drag him up that barren pile of stones.

'I'm going to need you up there.'

'. . . not going.'

He relented soon, though. The drunk dropped to his knees and begged Nethercott for food, that if there were anything to eat it be given him because the fact was he hadn't eaten a thing for some days.

'There's lots,' Ted Nethercott told him. 'If you want, I'll cook something hot for both of us right away.'

Then Colin wondered if after they ate might he not be able to sleep for some few hours before they went in search of Joseph and his elusive brothers. He'd not had much peace the past nights, had been hearing animals in the forest, even up in the rockfall where he had taken refuge . . . coyotes it was, or maybe wolves . . . all of them clawing and ripping and, as best he could tell, eating each other up.

'We'll eat first and then you'll sleep.' The rancher had been riding since four o'clock in the morning. It was now almost dusk. A yellow mist was settling over them. He would eat with Colin and sleep some himself, too.

But there would be no hoodwinking him afterwards. If Colin thought he could sneak away from a sleeping Ted Nethercott . . . well, that wouldn't happen. The man had been running away from the truth of things for the better part of sixty years. No more of that. No more. He was going up the mountain with Ted Nethercott. That was a certainty.

Nethercott told his friend so. And Colin knew the rancher would prevail.

CHAPTER 30

In the glaucous morning light the cortège arrived bearing Bobby's body home. Carmen was sitting on the ground over a pile of dry wood she had gathered, as if it had been foreknown to her that one of the brothers would have to be burned that day. Like an Indian widow she had cut her hair again to the very roots – as she had done for Jacob's child – and she had flayed herself as befitted a widow, as well, done it with the bark of a hemlock.

A beaver robe had been laid out. This the brothers used to dress the corpse and the dead man's weapons. All was ready. The pyre lacked but a mere body. A brother. A son. Which one of them should it be? They chose Little Bear, since he was already dead. They loaded the fire machine.

And with trembling fingers lit it. A piece of punk at each of the four corners. They were fastidious with the death rites. Observant. Scrupulous in burning him right.

It was about midday when they began.

Carmen played the widow's part exactly as she had been instructed. While the flames shrivelled sinews and muscles and tendons and blood vessels, pulling the hulk a thousand ways, Carmen braved the fire and kept it straight. Bobby's knee joints and hips bent in the heat, his elbows crooked, as if he were going to rise and stride the earth again. But Carmen levelled him. She had to, no matter how it scorched her. Bobby had to pass into the land of shades without stooping or changing in any way his posture while he lived.

When all the softer parts of the body had vanished, Carmen went to prepare a ghost supper. The others waited out the whole burn. Even Douglas, somehow not dead yet, whom they had strapped to the travois and raised up so that he, too, could watch Bobby melt into the general grey mist.

By the middle of the afternoon Bobby's ashes were already cool to the touch.

Autumnal winds had scattered some of the cinders but the larger flakes jiggled against each other like windchimes, the only sound in the valley. Low sky. Grey and hopeless. Snow somewhere above them.

Everything that had belonged to Bobby was then burned, too . . . right down to the quills he had used to pick his teeth. Every last notion of the man razed from the book of life. They even rolled stones over his crapper on the hill, having first poured flaming fat into the hole to seal it.

Thomas continued to feed the fire. He had, God knows, little enough strength, his arm in a crude sling he had tied for himself, yet he found a way to keep on his feet and gather more combustibles. Whirling through the junk heap he took his tools – not Bobby's but his own – and burned those. His axe went first. Woodworking tools. Frames for stretching skins. Coiled baskets he had made – he the only brother ever to master a design recognizably Chilcotin. His whistles and crude harp, too . . . their music long stopped.

He couldn't gather things fast enough . . . came and went to the burning bush and fed it everything he had gathered over the years. He was through, he was.

Through.

Then he went after chattel that belonged to the rest of them. He didn't work indiscriminately. He burned first what they would miss most. More than anything else, though, Thomas wanted to get ahold of Mark's scribble books, all those fine chronicles telling what they had done with their time in the mountain, legends of fathers murdered and brothers swallowed by bears, all the foolery that not even credulous children might believe. He kicked over every rotting bone in their camp but couldn't unearth Mark's books.

So he kicked over every bone twice.

Evening came. Sightless air. A heavy, yellow fog pressed its belly down the mountain spires. All of the brothers sat somewhere close to the fire, a ring of stones. Though they could not see them, they heard the chatterings of ducks in the marsh, a few geese, the birds' eyes of no use, either, in the frozen fog.

Carmen had made a kettle of soup for they were bitter hungry. No meat in the pot. A thick broth, light in colour, assembled of every weed she could gather from the wilderness. The pods of waterlilies she'd used and the young leaves and stalks of cow parsnip, pigweed that looked like spinach, wild carrot, the roots of vetch and bracken. Lemon lichens. And many heaps of dried mushrooms which she had dug out from the bowels of the winter lodge.

The mixture had been too copious for a single bark, so she had used two. Everything was served from the smaller kettle, passed around and drunk. The other she kept at a boil by continually dropping in hot stones.

'Feed him.' Eric hadn't been able to hear Douglas breathing for some minutes.

But Mark hadn't even been able to get Douglas to drink water.

'I think he's cold.'

'It's the blood loss . . . the shock.'

Eric's hands were dumbly kneading each other. A second brother, it looked like, was dying too. Oh Jesus. 'Bring him over here.'

So they brought Douglas's carrier still closer to the fire, threw more rugs and skins over him. He had turned the colour of sea water. Not yet dead . . . but in the suburbs of that great city. Infection had by this time spread throughout his entire body. The wound itself was caked in pus and lumps of dried blood, smelled unholy.

Mark scrubbed incessantly around the claw marks . . . uselessly, too, as if there weren't infection enough already to kill his brother twenty times over. None of his disinfecting ointments worked, but Mark had grown frantic and was now bathing the wound with his own urine. This he knew to be sterile and he had an idea there would be an antiseptic action in it. Not that Mark had read this was so. His herbal had no remedy for a wound so grave. The Indians had betrayed him in the end.

Nor could he dance Douglas back to health. No.

'*Make* him eat something,' Eric insisted.

'I'm telling you he won't eat.'

Farthest from the fire and feeling none of its heat, Thomas kept to the shadows. He was watching the dogs . . . those that were left alive. Three of them were growling over the small kettle where the slops of broth had been left uneaten. Wild things . . . ungovernable . . . would fight over almost any bone. Thomas threw a rock at them, which missed, though it did knock over the bowl.

At first the dogs ran quickly away. At the rim of the rocks, though, they slowed down. Stopped. It was as if they paused to consider how little authority the men had left, their quondam gods, the Solomon brothers whose little brief authority had seemed to vanish. The men were just men now.

So the dogs walked back towards the fallen food pot without fear of men. They ate the food, nobody threatening their boldness. Then the chief dog of the three pushed over the soup pot that was still bubbling near the fire. Hot as the soup was they ate that, too, scalding tongues but doing their will.

Riot and revolution.

Mark climbed up to the shadows and tried to minister to Thomas's arm. But Thomas wouldn't let his brother get close, knew his brother now for no physician but only the sorcerer's lean apprentice.

'Don't be a fool! Let me look at it.'

Thomas had his stump out of the sling and behind his back, his one good hand clenched and ready if Mark were to take another step towards him. What did Mark need to tell him? That his arm was turning gangrenous?

He had seen it already himself.

'Y-y-y-y-y-y-y—!' And the most temperate of all the brothers threw gravel in Mark's eyes, then ran off into the mists.

Joseph left the others to their wrangling. There was no time. Medication was in his bag. Antibiotics. It might keep Thomas and Douglas sound enough until help came.

And they would have to let help come, not go and find it. Thomas probably wouldn't last out the trip down the mountain. Douglas certainly not. Joseph would descend alone. Ride throughout the night. Get a medical rescue team flown up to the valley and then all would fly out tomorrow night by air ambulance. Bobby was dead. And the words of previous guides in these matters unperplexed Joseph: *Let the dead bury the dead.* All obsequies were done. Now he would worry only about the living.

Not one other brother of his was going to die in the wilderness.

NOT ONE.

The mountain had too many already. And Joseph had had too much of the mountain.

He ran to the marsh. He was racing with the bear for his brothers' lives. For two nights he'd had no sleep, no food for as long. It was difficult for him to put one leg in front of the other, yet he was running. Death – the fear that somehow he would lose all his brothers, his whole family – kept Joseph's feet shuffling in double time.

So remote from the firelight, the fog and forest darkening his steps, Joseph had trouble finding the deadfall where he'd hidden his pack. He circled over and over the same set of trees absolutely sure his pack was buried somewhere nearby. But no deadfall.

Fucking hell.

No deadfall, but he did see eyes, small green and unblinking dots. The buttons on his pack. He blinked himself and suddenly *there* it was, his pack lying on the forest floor. It had been picked out of its woody cache. *Been fiddled with?* he wondered. He didn't really care. He unzippered the side flap and all the medication fell out. No thief.

A thought seized him. It was possible his brothers would try to stop him from going for help. Just possible. Their minds and sense were unhoused by Bobby's death. He might need protection from his brothers, for their own sakes.

So Joseph reached for the gun in his knapsack.

It didn't come at first, seemed to be caught in the stitching. Joseph tore the bag inside out to get the gun in his hand. It was caught, all right, somewhere in the past, in the same web of madness that had inveigled his brothers into the mountain in the first place. They had taken his gun. Left the extra ammunition but the gun was gone. With six silver shells alive and spinning in the .38's revolving chamber. Just enough to kill six.

First things first. Joseph would face the adversary in his own proper colours. He took off his cloak of credulity. Not a bird any longer, here in the loneliest part of the valley Joseph set down the animal skins he had worn to hunt the bear, unlaced his mask. Not *Loon*, but Joseph. Joseph Solomon. A family man with two shining children.

With scissors and a single-edge razor blade from his first-aid kit, Joseph did what he could to hew away the weeks of beard that had browned over his face and disguised it. He wanted to be seen again for just what he was.

He brushed his hair.

He washed his hands in the stream, with camping soap. He put on a clean undershirt. He put on his true livery. *His* clothes. Every last tuck and roll of them.

Then he walked back to the firelight arrayed finer than the lilies of the field.

Thomas still hid in the darkling fog, well away from the rest of his brothers. Joseph could hear him out in the winter lodge, stump and hand pushing away debris that cluttered up the entry. Thomas was crashing around in the lightless cave. He wanted to find something very badly. He would tell nobody what he was after, though.

The dogs were acting strangely. Approaching the fire, Joseph tripped over one of them. It snapped at him and then glided back into the fog. The others chased it into the nimbus of light coming from the fire. All three dogs snapped wildly in the air. One stepped into the fire and out again without even seeming to notice. They howled. Then choked. Rubbed their snouts against the gravel. Wanted to copulate, all three together. Strange, unsettling behaviour, that much more spookish because of the fog.

Something was wrong.

Mark had found some berry wine made after the past year's harvest. On his hands and knees, he was over Douglas and trying to decant some of the wine down Douglas's throat. Most of it trickled off Douglas's teeth, but Mark did get one swallow into his gullet. Douglas, inert still, neither chewed nor spit the wine out.

As Joseph came up, Mark was pushing the chalice his way. He stopped, though. Looked at Joseph's clothes, clipped nails, propriety. 'What the fuck's with you?'

Eric looked up, too. 'Leave him alone.'

'You want some of this wine?'

Joseph shook his head. He would take no medicine of Mark's hand.

'Why not? It's restorative . . . berry wine. *Drink,*' Mark insisted.

'Leave him alone.' Eric was on his haunches.

Only Carmen sat unperturbed, alone, watching them, wrapped in silence.

Kneeling by the fire, Joseph tried to read the directions on the pharmacy label. He was shielding the vial with his body, but mark moved closer to him, always cautious, now aroused.

'What is it?'

'Tetracycline.'

A long pause. 'What's that doing in our camp?'

'I brought it for an emergency.'

'We don't want it.'

'Douglas does.'

'You try to give that shit to him and I'll kill you . . . you hear that?'

'What you got?' Eric, pensive and remote since the brothers had returned, stood all the way up. It was the first he noticed that Joseph wore different clothes. He put his fingers on the wool shirt, traced the checks. Saw the medicine jar full of spansules.

'What could that stuff do for him?'

'Maybe slow down the infection—'

'—*Fuck all,* that's what it can do.'

But Eric ignored Mark and his melancholy as he shoved his way in between his two brothers. 'Let me see that stuff.' He laid hands on the bottle. Opened the cap and removed one of the capsules. He touched the parti-coloured plastic. The pill was of another world but dimly remembered. 'Just an antibiotic . . . nothing else?'

'Like what?'

'Sleeping pills . . . pain killer?'

'It's just what it says it is.'

Eric mused on the world of down below. 'But he's fucking *crawling* with infection. What can little doses do?'

'We might give him a day or two or even three—'

'—Let him die without that shit, goddamn you!'

'We might even save him.' Joseph, speaking only to Eric now, paused. He needed the perfect words. 'Just one thing matters: That every one of the rest of us lives and gets well. I'm going down on the horse. I should make Chezacut by late afternoon. An airplane will be here before the sun sets. The pills might keep Douglas going until then. Thomas, too.'

'No fucking planes come up here!' Bile had surfeited on Mark's tongue, a bitterness powerful enough to wear away even love between brothers who had nothing else. But it was mostly himself he really loathed. He blamed himself for his brother's death. And two more dying. He couldn't bear that.

These weren't the times he had wanted to chronicle.

A strange sound interrupted them. It was the meekest of whispers, repeating every few seconds . . . a bubble on Douglas's lips. He had been listening to what the others were saying. There was every chance to expect he would die. If there was a *thin* chance he might live, Douglas begged for it. For life. Tears rolled across the sores at the base of his nose. He asked that they might let him have his best chance.

Eric leaned over him. 'You want to take the medicine?'

'I'm on fire.'

'Antibiotics, Duggie . . . *might* help.' Eric untangled the strands of Douglas's blood-matted beard, clumps of candied ginger it seemed. He soothed the skin of his cheeks. His brother was hot. *Jesus* . . . was he. 'You too close to fire now? Want us to move you back?'

' . . . fire inside . . . .'

Douglas was crying softly. Eric held him close and would not let his brother see the LeanMan behind. 'Take the medicine, Duggie . . . you're not going to die because I'm not about to let you. Joe's going to get an ambulance. You're going to live . . . *believe me.*'

' . . . fire . . . !' Fear and fear mingled in his voice.

The end was coming for Douglas. The wound spoke too well. It was streaked yellow and purple like a pansy, the rest of him colourless as every last bit of blood had been pressed into battle against the swarming infection, legions of bugs, billions of tiny mouths eating up his strength in order to spawn more of their own kind . . . bacteria digesting their parents. Blind mouths.

'Give him the drugs. Crush them up and put them into water so he can swallow the stuff.'

'Don't touch him, you bastards!'

'Make him take four or five of the fucking things . . . don't worry about the recommended dosage . . . kill those fucking bugs that are killing him.' Eric half-believed in the efficacy of the pills. Maybe there really were miracles in the world below. Enough, maybe, to buy Douglas a day. 'In the meantime give me the ointment. We'll try it all.'

'I said *don't* touch him!'

Mark's knife was out.

Eric watched the knife. But he heard the mountain snorting in pleasure. 'It's not the bear . . . not the mountain anymore, either. It's *you* who wants to kill him, Markie . . . *voluntarily*. You.' Words were pleas merely. The big man still tried. 'Your brother's going to die unless you and the rest of us get off this killing ground. It's over for us up here, Markie . . . it's over. Finished. I don't know how you can't see it . . . .' He stretched out his hand towards his brother. And the words finally came out. *'WE'RE GOING HOME!!'*

'Not on your life, man—'

'—*HOME!!!*' Eric screamed. And would have screamed the word a hundred times, could his brother only have seen the light that word made when struck hard. 'It's over. Joe's going down to Chezacut . . . they'll call Williams Lake.'

'Nobody's going anywhere.'

'Joe needs help getting down. Go with him, Markie. The horse can carry you both.'

'. . . not ever getting out of here.'

'Oh yes.'

'We're going to die here first, we are.'

Eric's big head shook only slowly. His hair was brittle and yellow in the foglight. He had seen everything. All at once. The mountain wasn't home for them. Nobody lived in the mountain. People died in the mountain, of loneliness if nothing else. And he was lonely . . . even with his brothers.

'Joseph will go down that trail tonight if he has to ride the Devil's back. What did Bobby want with a stomach full of worms . . .? Eh? What did he care about the Indian ghosts who once walked the hills up here?'

'He wanted to stay as much as the rest of us.'

'Only because we were here and he wanted to be with us. No other reason. He hated this fucking place . . . *all* of us hate it. *Even you,* Markie.' Eric sighed for his fat brother, once the doughtiest spirit in the mountain, now a skull on a crooked pole and ashes in the crotchety winds of October. 'You see only what you want to see, Mark . . . I'm telling you to put the knife away. Joe is going and we're giving Douglas this medicine.'

'*Over my dead body.*'

Pause.

What does one do with a beast born blind that believes it can see?

'If what you want is to stay . . . then stay. I love you. I want you with us. But not here. Down there. HOME.'

'This is the only home you've got or ever will have. I never made you come up here.'

'It's over, Mark. Thomas is going to get himself a new arm . . . and you and Duggie and I are going to have a new life. I got a woman down there somewhere.'

'She won't remember your name.'

'She remembers his name,' Joseph jumped in, 'only too well.'

'Does she now?'

'Somebody might remember you, as well, Markie.'

Mark's lips were curled back, his gums the colour of ashes. He turned the knife point towards Joseph. Daring Joseph to speak another word more.

'We're wasting time.' And Eric turned his back on Mark. He couldn't go on looking into such blankness. *It is done,* he thought.

He crouched down by Douglas, kept his tears away from Douglas's wound, then ripped the top off the tube and started squirting the ointment into the thickest pockets of pus on his brother's chest.

Time for healing.

Joseph made his quick way to the water jug, believing they would save Douglas. And would save Thomas after. And then maybe one day resolve Mark's chafed soul. All events were running Joseph's way now. The fog of his brothers' five years' folly lifting at last . . . the Age of Gold coming back. Effortlessly, too. With a few pills and a nightride.

Too effortlessly. Things never went like that.

Mark grabbed the bottle. He pried off the top with his claws and tumbled all of the pills, every last goddamn one of them, into the fire rip-roaring away, and thereby snuffing Douglas's last hopes . . . Douglas, the witless one, whom Mark had always loved most of all. He had killed him for certain.

Joseph jumped forward. He knocked Mark back into the rocks and then stuck his naked hands into the fire to flick out the few capsules he could see. Got nothing. A twig nearby. He snapped it, jabbed the prongs into the fire, acrid, eye-burning fumes, and managed to salvage four capsules scorched only . . . something . . . something . . . near faint, blood rilling down his face, drops of it hot from the fire and scalding his arm . . . Joseph burned by his own blood.

While the other two brothers fought.

Eric had caught Mark from the back, by the neck and tail, Mark's arms and legs flailing like an insect. With his knees slashing Eric's side, Mark had got free. And the animus between the two of them finally emerged.

Huge creatures. Their shadows flickered on the boulders behind them many times taller than they were in life, a spectacle, buskinned men, Greek legendary heroes on the stage levitating the rocky seats. Both of them hammered away, kicked and tore, ribs, ears, thighs, anything they could, no rules now, savage, street-fighting without chains and tyre irons. Mark, trying to push Eric into the fire, got his own foot in and withered away from the coals, his moccasin smoking, the flesh scored black underneath. He was no match for his older brother close in . . . astounded to find Eric still had such strength. But he revenged himself right away. Landed a rock right on Eric's collarbone as Eric was charging him, the blow so clean and frugal that there was only the sound of fracture, a pure one. It knocked Eric back, and down, and unable to continue the fight.

In struggling to get up Eric found his feet slipping on the loose stones. Nor could he control his breath. His whole chest had been shifted – two pieces of his collar lay atop each other like piled pipes. No way to get up. He fell again, like a puppet.

Mark, seeing this, put his hand out to the knife. Found its crude, bone handle. *Time to finish things he had started.* Knife up—

Joseph rose in silence. Clasped his meagre hands together high over his head and then with all his strength cracked the neck of his brother right at the base. Mark fell instantly. Sprawled on the cinder-strewn ground at the edge of the shadows. Gone right out.

'. . . help . . . *help* . . . .' Again and again. It was Douglas calling out, still night-blind but he heard the scuffle, was now raising the alarm. He buzzed on hardly able to control his voice, his cry only reflex, a spasm. Yet he meant something. Feeble-minded he had always been, but there was a life inside him, and enough of a mind to make distinctions between love and hate. He was not crying out for himself. He would rather have lived on the streets and died there. Yes, he hated their mountain life but never told his brothers so. *For he would not have hurt them . . . not for the world.* He had idolized them, each and every one. Feeble wits, oh yes, yet with a fidelity as obdurate as the ice of winter. Now he heard them fighting over him and it made him cry help.

Joseph, unsure of which brother to rally, went to Eric, who still couldn't stand up. Both men could see where the rock had spliced Eric's collar. Eric was wheezing badly. Joseph made him lie down as he tried to jam the collar straight. It snapped but not into place. It looked worse. *Jesus.*

'Don't fuck with it . . . .' Eric was gasping, his only way to talk. He pointed to the water bottle. Joseph fetched it quickly. Eric shook his head. '. . . not me . . . Duggie . . . .' The big man was growing dizzy . . . hadn't been feeling right in the head for an hour or more and the fast breathing was only making everything heavy, hard to see—

—he pointed at the few blackened pills, then at Douglas. Joseph picked them up.

'. . . give him the tetra . . . cycline . . . give it to him.'

'He can't swallow. Not even water.'

'*Try.*'

Joseph tried pouring water down Douglas but couldn't.

'. . . get a reed . . . tube . . . cat's-tail . . . blow it gently down his throat . . . gently . . . .'

Stumbling his way through the yellow mist, tapping the rocks to keep his path, Joseph managed to get down to the marsh and the rushes. He pulled up a cat's-tail, came back the same path, cleaning the hollow tube of all impediments. No time to stumble. No time for anything in the world but to keep his brothers from jumping off.

Back. He scraped the capsules of their powder and put it in his own mouth, gulped some water and swirled it around to dissolve the powder, smoothed the sides of the reed so he could get it some ways down Douglas's pipe. He had turned away for an instant but that was too long. Joseph had forgot he hadn't tied up Mark. Mark was up now.

Moving.

Joseph saw it all.

His brother had awakened. Had listened. Had decided. And now was over Douglas, threading the knife in his long fingers until he had it firm and could in one simple cut slit Douglas's windpipe. Blood, the little left in him, rushed into Douglas's throat. *That* Douglas swallowed. Choked.

The endless whining stopped. Douglas was dead. Just like that.

OH JESUS JESUS JESUS JESUS JESUS.

Now it was brother murder. And not entirely finished yet, either.

'*He* won't die down there, he won't . . . none of us will. We stay, *all of us.*' Exhausted, twirling, Mark swaggered with the knife. He was over Eric suddenly. The dagger hanging. 'You say *"yes, we stay"*, or I'll kill you, just as easily!—'

A FLASH OF FIRE.

It cut right through the freezing air. The gods were talking. And the sound shattered stones.

The first shot.

Mark flinched and dropped his dagger.

A second report and he jerked backwards.

On the third shot he was dead, the bullet entering his right eye and exiting behind his ear, dragging much brains along with it.

Then he fell straight backwards, his head into the centre of the fire, sparks billowing around his black hair, hundreds of little embers scattered everywhere and lighting up the valley floor.

Instinct ran deep and Joseph reached forwards to pull Mark out of the fire.

'*Don't!*' Carmen levelled the gun at him, moved the barrel rapidly towards Eric, then back and forth from one to the other. 'Don't touch him!!' She stopped the pistol at Joseph's chest. 'Just sit there and don't move. You just let him burn.' The golden girl sat unmoved, her arms gold, neck gold . . . the breasts that had fallen out of her opened shawl . . . gold. But a darker gold. 'We wait . . . we don't move.'

Hot coals were burning everywhere. Smoke. Carmen's shawl was glowing and Eric pointed to it, tried to tell her, but she threatened him with the gun and her wild eyes. She knew all that she wanted to know. She felt the heat on her clothes and brushed away the sparking wood, rubbed her leg where the cinder had burned through. Never moving the gun, though.

On Douglas's corpse a large coal had landed, too. On his neck, where it embedded itself into his cooling flesh. The others could all hear it.

The world was ending in fire.

'We wait . . . .'

They understood her soon.

Thomas, away all this while, came squealing. The dogs right behind him, circling around each other, biting each other. Thomas had a score of marks in his fair skin from the dogs. He had given as good as he had got. He was suffering like the dogs, except his hallucinations had a special tie to truth. He saw his father struggling in a red stream.

Just before the spasms had eclipsed his sense, gentle Thomas had found what he was looking for. Some time during the winter he had put a skin bag aside. Now he carried the bag, which was empty. He sniffed deeply, his head in the bag. Mushrooms had been in the bag once. Until very recently. Their smell was still pungent.

Thomas pulled his head out of the bag, trying to figure out why he'd wanted to find the pouch in the first place.

It was more than an hour that Thomas had been jerking hard. The jerks were now giving way to paralysis. He had it in his broken mind that there was something he ought to tell his brothers. He sat down near them, grinning, but couldn't control voice or tongue or mouth. Teeth chattering.

Why was that funny? he wondered.

Dead brothers were stacked in masses around him, the dogs dying, too . . . .

Joseph was just beginning to understand, started to crawl towards Thomas but the girl with the gun tightened a finger on the trigger.

Eric had grown alert to his brother's strangeness, as well. 'What, Thomas . . .?' He tried to sit up. *'What?'*

'Don't move and don't talk to him.'

But Eric didn't care about guns. He called again to Thomas.

Ever deeper in trance, Thomas fell near his brothers. His feet were splayed out under him. Naked, he was. He had taken off all his clothes. His skin was still fair . . . the colour of mother's milk.

The fire attracted him and he looked stupidly at it. Close enough to stretch an arm to his brother in the fire, he set a hand gently on Mark. But his hand rested in the embers, Thomas seemingly insensible to pain.

'Thomas!!!'

Gun or no gun in the woman's hand, both Eric and Joseph squirmed to get the water bag, throw it over the fire, the fuckingfuckingfuckingfucking fire . . . save Thomas's one good limb. Joseph got his hands on the bark sides and . . .

. . . stopped.

He was too late again.

Thomas sat motionless, his tongue to one side. There was a movement in the fire, Mark's body shifting, gravity turning his skull as the fire cleaned it. Thomas's arm had fallen free. The whole man had. Both Eric and Joseph heard a kind of music.

Their brother Thomas's heartstrings were burning. Burning. The cords being seared in two. They snapped and Thomas went rigid. His mouth opened slightly and a few acrid puffs of smoke floated out.

Done.

He was gone, too.

And Joseph suddenly knew why. *'You dirty fucking cunt!!!'*

Eric's legs kicked violently, unintentionally, hitting the water jug in Joseph's hands and dousing the entire firesite with water. Carmen fired once. The bullet split the narrow space between Joseph and Eric, his one brother still alive. So close did it pass to his head that Joseph heard the separated air snap back to fill the pocket vacuum the bullet's passing had made.

And that frightened him.

Water over everything. Some on the spitting fire, some running down Thomas's arm, hissing diabolically. Eric's leggings and robe were soaked.

The next time Eric jerked, he screamed. Thinking he saw a bat over his head, a bat as big as himself with the face of his father, he held his eyes closed. The rabid mouth was open, its fangs virulent and dropping straight for his throat—

'—*HELP ME!!!*'

He blinked and pulled his useless hands away. There was no bat. Only Carmen . . . smiling it seemed.

Joseph put a hand to his brother's brow. Fever? Yes. The woman told him to get away from Eric but Joseph's mind was whirling too fast to hear. He shook his brother. 'Did you eat the soup . . .?'

'Eh?' He didn't seem to comprehend.

'Did you eat the soup that bitch made you????'

Eric's jaws snapped and bit deeply into his tongue.

'Put your fingers down your throat . . . vomit . . . get up everything you can.' Eric couldn't understand. 'Hurry up . . . *vomitttttt!'*

There was no way Eric could help himself. Seeing this, Joseph tried to do it for him, stuck a finger into Eric's mouth and made him gag a few times, but without being able to get the poison in his stomach to retch up.

'*You're gonna die if you don't vomit!!*' No answer. '*SHE'S POISONED YOU!!!*'

Quite feebly, Eric put his hands around his baby brother's wrists. Holding on. The once stately mansion of his body had all but dissolved away, had become so desolate and wasted that there was now nothing left but eyes, immense sea green eyes, haunted and haunting, which popped out of his wolf's mask . . . eyes filled with the unspeakable sadness of the brothers' empty mountain lake, the glacial floes, their valley, their little city in the wilderness.

'I know what she's done,' he said.

It was as much as to say Eric knew he'd eaten more than enough to kill him.

Then he asked that Joseph raise him up so that he could see Carmen better. Joseph did.

'Did you do this?'

'I did.'

'Who'd you do it for, Carmen? Eh . . .?' But he raised no more answers from her. Eric could feel Joseph wanting to lunge at the woman. He held tightly onto his brother's soft hands to make sure he didn't jump. 'The dogs are dead?'

'I think so.'

'All of them?'

Joseph looked around. Nodded.

It seemed as if Eric were trying to look for something behind the yellow slime that rolled down the ridges of the valley, but he couldn't make out anything more than ten yards away.

'What's out there?' Joseph asked him.

'Rain. Cold rain.'

Hardly had Eric spoken when the rain began in soft, occasional drops. Eric had smelled it. The rain picked up steadily. And got colder. Nearly frozen.

'Going to rain for a while. And then snow. This whole place is going to disappear under it. Get out of here, Joe.'

'I'm taking you.'

'Don't be an asshole. Just go! And take her when you go, goddamnit. Do you hear me? You *take* her!'

'That filthy fucking cunt killed Thomas, and Mark, maybe you—'

'—STOP IT!' Eric gripped his little brother as best he could. 'Leave her alone. Just leave her fucking well alone. And get her down off this mountain!' He never looked at the woman, though. 'I killed my father.'

'I know.'

'You *don't* know. You say you know but you don't know.'

'Tell me.'

'That bastard ran and that bastard ran and that bastard ran away all his mean fucking life, he did.'

'And so you killed him for that . . . ?' Joseph shuffled off the coils of a year of mourning, breathed deeply. This had *had* to happen between his brothers and their father. It had been many years coming. Maybe even generations. It could only have been avoided if his brothers had found places for themselves in the world, a place for each. 'You poor, blind, ignorant bastards.'

'What do you know about it? Just what do you think *my* portion was, eh? What the fuck did he ever give me? Do you know? *Do you?*' He coughed horribly for a long minute, his lungs shrieking for some air. Throat whistling. He tried to speak again, holding Joseph hard, asking ten thousand things. 'And then I had to raise the rest of you . . . I . . . like I was your goddamn father . . . father for all of you . . . *goddamn* you all—'

'—No, you weren't.'

'Somebody had to be . . . .'

His voice broke off. He just couldn't talk anymore, the fits seizing his throat as well as his lungs.

But Joseph understood. Better, he thought, than his brothers ever could have. They had defied their father in order to deify him. They had never forgiven the old man for the way he had diminished in their eyes when they grew up. They had killed him and made him a god again. Crazy. But it happened in every generation. It was every child's experience of life to learn his parents are mortal . . . and what this means for him. There is anger. Always. But it does not often govern lives – though for some it does. There are some who are angry all their dark days, angry at the world as it was given them . . . imperfect, finite, and lonely to contemplate. The world must be joined nevertheless. His brothers hadn't done that. They had gone to live in the darkness beyond the city walls . . . in the nightmare itself.

The horrible thing was that *somebody* had to live out there and send reports back. His brothers had followed a hard destiny but they had followed it. Courage in that . . . much, much courage.

Once again Eric twinged furiously, the bat inside his head now beating against his brains. He had sight of crazy things, strange and vertiginous visions that ringed streaks of red and fire around his luminous eyes. Eric screamed about what he saw, an idiot's tale of bits and pieces and scraps of bodies . . . places under the earth, he swore he could see . . . the smells, the *smells* of it . . . the whole fucking material world burning—

Squeaks and gibberings.

For an instant he seemed to forget who Joseph was, reached down and started fondling his little brother's ankle, calf, thigh, grabbed his cock and started slurring wild things, sexual and grotesque . . . his mind unhinged by the shaking fever.

Repulsive to see in any man . . . but worse in a great one.

Joseph looked down the chamber of Carmen's gun – once his gun, for she had stolen it. Two rounds were left. 'Shoot him.'

Without speaking she moved her lips to say 'no'.

'You going to let him sink into this kind of death, are you?' Joseph saw that she was going to do exactly that. 'You filthy fucking cunt!—'

'—*LEAVE HER ALONE!!!*' Eric was wheezing into the grave, death rattling his ribs, and yet he was going to go out making sure that Joseph would get Carmen down the mountain. She had got caught there by chance . . . and he would have peace with his father now. .

Joseph Solomon looked at his brother's eyes. They were

spinning into the next world already. Familiar eyes. For they had been the green eyes of his father, as well.

The eyes of their patriarch. The eyes of the lion of Judah.

Bear . . . lion . . . wolf . . . man . . . Jew . . . Chilcotin Nation . . . the whole race of Man. All the multitudinous heroes of the earth. All the dispossessed heroes rising, savage and angry, unhappy with mortality.

And unworthy of it.

His brothers were . . . had been great of heart. Great men, in their way. They had searched endlessly for the world of Love the gods themselves never made. *Who had ever done more?*

Eric's lungs were moaning. It was almost music. He was howling at the stars.

'I hear you, Wolf . . . I hear you singing.'

His body was pouring water like a spring. It was horrible to watch.

Suddenly Eric stopped shaking. Stopped completely.

Both Joseph and Carmen were stunned. There was an instant of beatific peace in the man, and in the world around, too, as the gently falling rain touched their heads, not hissing on the fire any longer . . . stillness. The world nearly perfect.

Then Eric started to revolve on his knees in circles growing ever wider, slowly descending until at last he lay with his back almost touching the ground. Thereafter he stopped moving altogether, grew limp, fell into a coma, and died. Joseph didn't know exactly when. A life ended. A life full of love, perhaps too much love, but not wisely given.

Joseph waited. He and Carmen sat in the middle of the ring of corpses, the fire thankfully out, having eaten up its last fuel in burning away all the tissue from poor Mark's head.

'You've got two bullets in there.'

'That's enough.'

'You going to shoot me?'

The gun was pointed at his head.

Carmen had borne this thing out to the edge of doom, and then a little farther still, over the edge. She was tired, but she was not done, not quite.

'You wanted to know everything that happened, didn't you?' With her free hand she loosened a bark wallet which she had been carrying under her shawl. 'The book of the dead.' She threw the wallet at him. 'Open it.'

Joseph did. Inside were all of Mark's diaries. He thumbed rapidly through one of them. Stopped at a page. It was winter. The detail rich. The brothers' life immediately apprehensible. They had just eaten a cake made from the edible pulp underbark of trees. It was Douglas's birthday, by Mark's reckoning. They were happy. They had let Douglas smoke some kind of local plant that was mildly psychedelic. He was happy. While he was loaded they had cleaned him of some of his vermin. They were happy. It sounded crazy to Joseph but though they were freezing and near starvation they were nevertheless living the life they wanted.

He closed the book. Would read it, read every page, every fine, calligraphic letter of his brother's careful, cursive script.

The first sense of dawn was beginning to break rapidly through the curtain of mist that had hovered over them all night. As it got brighter, the sun melted the fog, appearing first as a broad, yellow patch over the marsh, not yet an object, the sun growing to something clear and material. The sky had lifted enough to see the mountainside. An azure sky. No snow. A beautiful day. Perhaps autumn's last.

'You didn't poison me.' Joseph needed to speak.

'Maybe I should have.'

What she must have seen, he thought to himself . . . *what she must have seen.*

'Why do you keep pointing that goddamn thing at me and not shoot?'

'Why not?'

'My brother wanted me to take you out. Are we going or what?'

'Go.'

'And you?'

'I know my place.'

He believed she did.

'It wasn't revenge for my father, was it?' Joseph asked. But it was a stupid question, he knew, one that Carmen wouldn't bother to answer: The brothers belonged in the mountain, alive or dead, and she had seen to it that they would stay. She had killed to be kind. For though she had found a way to live with Jacob's murder, the death of her child had broken her completely. It didn't matter that the baby's death had been a natural one. A dead child breaks the order of things, calls everything into question. In the end Carmen had come to believe in the mountain more than any of them. It was her place, too.

She, not Joseph, was the sixth creature of the camp.

His thoughts broke off as a rifle shot rang out over the ridge to the southwest. Two more in rapid succession. Joseph looked towards the rocks, sharply glaring in the sunlight now. He had to shade his eyes, strained to see. Nothing.

Then turned his eyes back to Carmen. And his jaw fell. The barrel of the pistol was in her mouth and her hand was about to squeeze the trigger. He lunged for her. The gun went off just as he touched her arm. Her head exploded, he so close to the concussion it knocked him on his back.

The sun beat on his face. He couldn't get up. He wouldn't if he could. The gunburst in his ears had split his senses and for a time he didn't know where he was or whether he'd been wounded.

Voices were calling across the carrion field, to see if anyone was yet living. Whoever it was, they had guns and shot them. They might kill Joseph for lack of any other moving target. So he didn't stir.

'Young Solomon?'

He heard that voice very clearly. A good man's voice.

'Joseph!'

As if rising from the dead, Joseph got to his feet and turned to the two men on horseback. Ted Nethercott it was, and the old drunk who had abandoned Joseph to the mountain. They were coming at him slowly, a rifle in the rancher's hands pointed ahead . . . but quickly raised on seeing it was indeed Joseph who waited to be met.

Some twenty or thirty yards before they reached the spent campfire, both riders stopped. They saw the dead. The horses themselves refused to come closer.

Nethercott got off his palomino in some solemnity. Held the reins. He beckoned to Joseph to walk towards him slowly. No need to say anything . . . just to come to him. And Joseph did, gripping the wallet Carmen had given him stuffed with Mark's books.

While Joseph washed himself in the brook, the two older men tended to the bodies, making rough graves for them until a float plane could be sent up to collect them, graves secure enough to keep the predators away. Meantime, Joseph washed over and over.

Not far from Joseph's feet, in the day's clear light, something was sparkling. He walked to the spot, which was not far from the cairn where his father had once been buried. Joseph bent down. A ring. A simple ring studded with tiny garnets and white opals. He hadn't seen it in the camp before, but Joseph knew right away what the jewel was. His grandmother – his father's mother – had first worn it. It had been her engagement ring. She had given it to Jacob Solomon when he fled for Poland. Later, it had also been on Joseph's mother's finger, until her death day. And Jacob Solomon had made Carmen a present of it when they got married.

In his dimmest recollection, Joseph had the idea that opals such as the ring's were bad luck. So many who had worn the ring had died young. He decided to bury his brothers in Los Angeles, but the ring would be the mountain's, for it had promised falsely. In time he knew the mountain would claim back the stones, wear them down . . . retrieve the gold, too. All the work in the ring would disappear and it would become, in the end, merely material. Idealess. He laid the ring down where he'd found it, rendering to the mountain what was the mountain's. For his part, he was going to take home bones – just material objects, like the ring, but the idea of a man could never be beaten out of their true grit. Never. There was a distinction here he was sure his father would have understood (would even have made himself): Civilization was first of all *exalted* memory . . . and Joseph would remember his brothers better if their bones were nearby. The reach of civilized life was weak enough. Sometimes the touch of something physical helped.

Just as his hands were already reaching for his own children. He could feel their skin against his.

Then the men found the grey gelding not far away, eating juvenile shoots of willow, a horse with a fine stomach. They put Joseph on the horse. And took him down the mountain asking no questions of him as to what had happened to leave so many dead.

At least they didn't talk much until the three of them were well below the barren land and Joseph saw the river, fish jumping, some yellow bird for which he had no name . . . life shuffling forth. Joseph wondered then about the shots he'd heard when Nethercott and Colin had approached the valley camp. It hadn't been them firing, they told him.

'Sam most likely,' the rancher believed.

They had seen a man shooting at a bear and Sam was always finding some poor sonofabitch bear to take potshots at first and then tell tall stories about afterwards.

'A grizzly?'

'For sure.' Colin had seen the bear better than the hunter.

'Sam kill it?'

'No . . . gave it a few crackling shots but didn't drop it, not that I saw.'

The rancher confirmed what Colin had said.

'I think the bear's gone off to live a while yet.'

For some reason Joseph was relieved to hear it. He hoped the bear would create as much havoc as it could before taking its rightful place amongst the stars.

Ursus major.

Bears in the high country were savage and lonely, but they did have remarkable courage. Great staying power. Such had been the heart of the beast that had warred with his brothers . . . and such the heart of his brothers who had lived only to hunt it.

Well, they had died to live their particular lives. The amazing thing was that they had endured so long.

Fontana Paperbacks

Fontana is a leading paperback publisher of fiction and non-fiction, with authors ranging from Alistair MacLean, Agatha Christie and Desmond Bagley to Solzhenitsyn and Pasternak, from Gerald Durrell and Joy Adamson to the famous Modern Masters series.

In addition to a wide-ranging collection of internationally popular writers of fiction, Fontana also has an outstanding reputation for history, natural history, military history, psychology, psychiatry, politics, economics, religion and the social sciences.

All Fontana books are available at your bookshop or newsagent; or can be ordered direct. Just fill in the form and list the titles you want.

FONTANA BOOKS, Cash Sales Department, G.P.O. Box 29, Douglas, Isle of Man, British Isles. Please send purchase price, plus 8p per book. Customers outside the U.K. send purchase price, plus 10p per book. Cheque, postal or money order. No currency.

NAME (Block letters)

ADDRESS